A DUKE IN THE ROUGH

A Regency Era Romance

LONDON LADIES' LEAGUE
BOOK I

TRISHA MESSMER

DEDICATION

To Jane
Thank you for giving me Wentworth.

CONTENTS

ACKNOWLEDGMENTS

I wanted to start with something witty here, but it seemed inappropriate for a section where I'm thanking people, so I'll try to be serious.

First and always foremost, to my family. I can't imagine a more supportive group of people—especially considering that three of my four children are male and I write romance! They don't laugh at me, and they always give the appearance of being interested when I talk about my books (or they're good fakers—which, as a mom, makes me worry). My daughter even reads my books (although she admits she has to throw up a mental barrier when she reads the love scenes). Anyway, I'm very grateful for them all.

To my critique partners at Critique Circle. We started out as strangers, but I truly consider these folks to be friends. I only worry they might be too easy on me. So thanks to Brad, Ellie, Izzy, Jess, and Lisa for helping me make each story the best it can be.

To Lisa Messegee, at the Write Designer for the gorgeous cover. I can't stop looking at it and going "Ah!"

To my editor, Peter Senftleben at PES Editorial. You helped me take a good book and make it so much better.

To my eagle-eyed proofreader, Jess Kelly, at Gray Cat Publishing and Designs. Any errors remaining in the manuscript are all mine.

To my readers who helped select the name for the sharped-tongue Aunt Kitty! Jeri made the most excellent suggestion of Kitty, and Jane Willard suggested Griffin (which I changed just a little to honor my favorite magical boy, Harry Potter). My critique partner, proofreader extraordinaire, and all-around wonderful friend Jess Kelly suggested Dickens to honor good old Charles (and she made the suggestion to work in a reference to him). So Aunt Kitty Dickens, the Countess Gryffin, stormed in my heart. All my critique partners (and my editor) absolutely adored her. And even though she will never read this book, I want to thank the incomparable Dame Maggie Smith for helping me envision this feisty woman.

And last, but certainly not least, to you, dear reader. I wouldn't even be writing this acknowledgment page were it not for you. Thank you for allowing me to do what I love.

CHAPTER 1

LONDON, LATE MAY 1829

"He's here! He's here!"

Lady Honoria Bell's gaze jerked away from the agenda as Anne Weatherby rushed all aflutter into the room. The meeting had already begun, but Anne was late—as usual.

"Goodness, Anne. Calm yourself. And who precisely is *here?*" Honoria gestured around the small group comprising only women.

Anne plunked into the chair. Her bonnet sat askew, strands of red hair fell loosely around her face, and pink colored her cheeks. "Well, not here, here, of course. But here in England!"

Honoria exchanged glances with the other ladies. Operating under the guise of a charitable organization, the small group called themselves the London Ladies' League to couch their true purpose. Her gaze drifted to a copy of *The Muckraker* in Anne's hands—the subject of which precisely *was* the reason they had gathered.

"I just called the meeting to order. If your news is in relation to that scandal sheet, then discussing the latest gossip is first on my list."

Still breathless, Anne huffed. "But you don't have the latest. A boy is handing out this copy on the streets right now!"

Contrary to what many would imagine occurred when women discussed rumors, the London Ladies' League did not delight in the sordid stories presented in *The Muckraker,* but were on a mission to unmask and stop the perpetrator who spread the ruinous bits of calumny.

Although she was the unanimously elected leader of the group, Honoria still believed in giving everyone a voice. "Anyone in favor of starting with Anne's news, please raise your hand."

Anne, of course, raised her hand. The sister of Andrew Weatherby, she had received her fair share of attention from the despicable paper which called her a brainless flirt and voted her most likely to face the parson with a white swelling.

Lady Miranda Townsend, daughter of the Earl of Easton, also raised her hand. Not only had her brother, Laurence, the notoriously straitlaced Viscount Montgomery, been caught in a compromising position with Beatrix Marbry four years prior, but Miranda had confided in Honoria that she had her own motive for wishing to stop the horrendous paper, although she refrained from providing those reasons.

Lady Charlotte Talbot, sister of the Marquess of Edgerton, lifted her hand. Her second eldest brother, Lord Nash Talbot, had been the prior year's target of *The Muckraker* when he was accused of murder and then—to society's even greater disdain—married an American.

But of all of them, Honoria received both the most attention and the most vicious attacks. For the last eight years, she'd been the target of gossip, starting when she was but seventeen-years-old. Whispers of her *ruination* by a servant had been so damaging her parents delayed her come-out until her nineteenth birthday in an attempt to quell the wagging tongues. Subsequent scandals followed, all associated with suitors. However, little did the gossip sheet know that when Dr. Timothy Marbry ended his courtship with Honoria to marry Priscilla Pratt, Honoria was the one who encouraged the action.

Most recently, her feigned attachment with the aforementioned Lord Nash Talbot had sealed her fate as unmarriageable.

Raising her own hand, Honoria said, "Everyone is in agreement, Anne. You may proceed with your news."

Anne cleared her throat and straightened her shoulders, adopting an air of seriousness contrary to her bubbly, youthful personality. "The Duke of Burwood has finally arrived in England. Rather than coming to London, as one would expect, he's taken up residence at his ducal seat in Dorset."

"It *is* late in the Season for him to appear before Parliament," Charlotte said. "Edgerton says the session will soon close."

"And he seems in no rush to assume his duties," Miranda said. "It's been nigh on two years since old Burwood passed on."

Honoria nodded. She'd heard the same from her father. "Which means since this may be our last meeting before we return to our country homes, perhaps we should concentrate our efforts on more pressing matters than a newly minted duke."

The corners of Anne's mouth tipped down, but just as suddenly, her face brightened. "We can hold more meetings during the new duke's house party."

All heads turned toward Anne.

But Miranda, being the most vocal among them, was not one to mince words. "What house party?"

As much as Honoria liked Anne, she wanted to shake the girl— only a little, mind you—as she held up the horrid scandal sheet dramatically. "*The Muckraker* says he will be hosting a house party next month at his estate to introduce himself to society. Invitations will be forthcoming."

Honoria blinked. "How in heaven's name does he find out these things?"

Miranda, astute as ever, picked up on Honoria's reference. "If the perpetrator of *The Muckraker is* a man. It could be a woman."

"It pains me to think a woman is responsible for such tripe," Charlotte said.

Honoria couldn't agree more.

"But this isn't tripe." Anne waved *The Muckraker*. "Oh, very well, the scandal sheet is tripe, but the bit about Burwood is exciting. Just think. A house party where all of society will be invited." A dreamy expression crossed Anne's face. "There will probably be a ball, and games, and"—she waggled her eyebrows—"lots of eligible men."

All things considered, Honoria expected no such invitation. Or, at the very least, the new duke might invite her parents with a *suggestion* that the *esteemed* Lady Honoria remain at home. Phrased in the politest of ways, certainly, but the meaning would ring clearly. *You are not welcome.* The new duke would want his introduction into society to be scandal-free.

Not that Honoria herself caused scandals, but they followed her without invitation.

Charlotte sent their younger companion a chastising glance. "If you're planning on becoming the new duchess, Anne, you might want to reconsider. *New* Burwood is probably as ancient as *old* Burwood."

"Actually . . ." Honoria grimaced, her gaze bouncing between her friends. No doubt her information would encourage Anne's dreams of marrying a titled man. "Father heard he's quite young."

The gleam in Anne's eyes became lethal.

Miranda snickered. "Now you've done it, Honoria. She's planning the wedding already."

Anne crossed her arms over her bosom. "I am not!"

She truly was. Honoria tightened her lips to hold in the laugh, remembering how she was also once full of hope.

Charlotte placed her cup daintily on the saucer. "What's taken him so long to claim the title?"

Anne held up the wretched rag. "It says he was in India. Imagine the exciting stories he'll have to tell. Andrew and Alice were there and loved it. Well, Alice loved it. I think Andrew was simply glad to have found her and brought her home. The way she describes everything is so engaging. The colors, the scents, the sounds. It's like you're there." Anne sighed.

"That settles it," Charlotte said. "We simply must all attend. If for nothing else, to keep an eye on Anne. The poor duke doesn't stand a chance."

"And we can find time to hold a meeting or two," Miranda said.

"Hmm." Honoria nodded, more out of reflex that actual assent. Her mind had frozen on the words *'It says he was in India.'* The last she'd heard of Drake Merrick, his regiment had been stationed in Bombay. But that had been almost eight long years ago.

She pushed it from her mind, the earlier memory turning bittersweet. "Then we shall do our best to make the most of it."

◌◌◌

HANDS ON HIS HIPS, DRAKE MERRICK GAZED ACROSS THE EXPANSE of Hartridge House's gardens. The ducal seat, located west of Dorchester and north of Lyme, boasted gently sloping lands and small rolling hills. Air ruffled through his hair, the strong coastal winds reaching inland and gentling to a caressing breeze.

Peaceful.

Idyllic.

Mine.

Simon stepped beside him. "Magnificent, isn't it?"

Drake nodded, too overcome to form the words.

As his best friend often did, Simon slapped him good-naturedly on the shoulder, bringing Drake out of his pensive musings. "Plan to gawk all day? We have work to do."

"Are you certain this is a good idea?" Drake envisioned throngs of people trampling the pristine gardens, a cacophony of voices invading the tranquil solitude. Hordes of blood-thirsty debutantes eager to marry a duke. Perhaps blood-thirsty was too harsh a word.

But perhaps not.

He shivered.

"A necessary evil more than a good idea." Simon delivered a tight-lipped smile. "You'll need a bride to produce a legitimate heir. What better place to find one than at a house party filled with aristocrats and their marriage-minded daughters?"

Drake groaned. "Pompous lot, all of them."

Simon raised a dark brow. "Would that include the Duke of Burwood?"

"Him especially." Drake forced his lips into what—he hoped—was the semblance of a smile. "I wish Mother were still here. She would have things in hand. Even Juliana would be a welcome face. One month was not nearly enough time with them after so many years apart."

"And how would that look to the guests? A man of business's family invited among the *ton?*" Simon shook his head. "No. To pull off this ruse, your mother and sister must remain in Dorchester for the time being. Stop your worrying. The servants will handle everything. Invitations were sent out this morning."

The knot that formed in Drake's stomach the moment he—again —set foot on English shores tightened. "Was *she* . . . invited?"

A name wasn't necessary. Simon knew full well who Drake meant. He nodded. "And her parents and brother. Should I have left them off the list?"

"No. Yes . . . I don't know." He threaded a hand through his hair. "No. It would be seen as a slight to exclude them. After all, her father is a marquess."

"You'll be fine, Drake. Now, come. The dancing master awaits."

As Drake followed his friend inside the palatial home, he doubted Simon's words. How would he ever be fine once he laid eyes on Honoria again?

CHAPTER 2

THREE WEEKS LATER . . .

The journey from Honoria's father's seat in Somerset to the Duke of Burwood's in Dorset had been fraught with difficulty.

Not long after they had set out, their carriage had become mired in mud from a sudden downpour. She and her parents huddled under umbrellas as the driver and footmen worked to free it, cracking a wheel in the process.

Two hours later, with the wheel repaired and their clothes damp from the rain, they piled back into the carriage and proceeded onward.

The storm eased, the persistent splashing of rain against the carriage roof and windows slowing to a *plop, plop, plop,* and the sun broke through the clouds.

They'd left at ten that morning, but heat from the midday sun— although drying the puddles on the ground outside—turned the inside into a damp oven reminiscent of the waters of Bath.

Air, thick and sticky, saturated the cramped space of the carriage. Perspiration dotted Honoria's upper lip and brow, and she dabbed it with a handkerchief.

In vain, her mother waved the fan to generate a breeze, only to stir the hot air. "It's stifling in here."

Honoria's father barked a laugh. "Given his time in India, no doubt it will be as a cool breeze to Burwood."

Mention of India made Honoria's mind wander to . . . Drake.

Memories of him had risen from the recesses of her mind more often than she cared to admit over the past eight years.

Memories which had prevented her from opening her heart to another.

When her father had released her dowry, she'd hoped her days of fending off suitors had finally passed. None would ever compare to Drake, and she grew weary of finding excuses to reject perfectly nice gentlemen.

But with her father's enthusiasm over the new duke's unmarried status, it would seem she would be put to the test once again. Her stomach churned at the prospect.

She stared out the carriage window.

India. Drake. Memories pushed themselves front and center.

Her father pulled out his watch. "With the time we've lost, we'll have to stop in Chard for the night." He banged his cane on the carriage ceiling, then gave instructions to the driver.

At the inn at Chard, they discovered only two available rooms remained. As if her father could change the situation by demanding it, he said to the innkeeper, "But I have servants in need of lodging as well."

The innkeeper's smile reversed direction. "If I had more rooms, I would gladly offer them. What would you have me do, my lord? Turn the current occupants out?"

Honoria held her breath, hoping her father wouldn't make a scene and suggest exactly that. From the expression on his face, he no doubt considered it.

"Perhaps the ostler will allow them to sleep in the stables," the innkeeper suggested.

Honoria caught the horrified look on her maid's face. "Father, Susan may stay in my room."

Her father pursed his lips. "What about your mother's lady's maid?"

Watson was another matter entirely. The woman's sour expression spoke of her constant disapproval over just about everything.

Honoria worried her bottom lip with her teeth. It was only one night, after all. "Of course, Watson as well. We shall make a nice cozy night of it." She forced a weak smile.

"I suppose the men can sleep in the stables." Her father tossed coins down in front of the innkeeper. "Very well. The two rooms will have to be sufficient."

After the footmen brought in their trunks, Watson left to assist Honoria's mother.

Susan helped Honoria out of her damp gown. "That was very thoughtful of you, my lady."

Honoria patted Susan's hand. "I couldn't have allowed you to sleep in a stable with the men. It would be neither proper nor safe."

A sly grin spread across her maid's face. "I meant about Watson. She snores, my lady. You will be regretting your kindness in the morning."

The anxiety she'd felt all day eased, and a laugh traveled up her throat and found release the same moment Watson entered the room.

The woman raised a wiry gray eyebrow, and her lips pressed in such a tight line only a sliver of pink remained.

Both Honoria and Susan turned away to keep their amusement from Watson's critical gaze. Susan let out a little snort sounding very much like a snore.

Defenses down and weary to the bone from travel, Honoria struggled not to devolve into fits of laughter, something she had rarely done in the past eight years and sorely missed. Her shoulders began to shake as she tried desperately to hold it in.

"Susan," Watson barked from behind them. "I suggest you lay out some dry clothes for Lady Honoria and cease your childish behavior. If you ever wish to become a lady's maid for a first lady of the house, you must maintain the proper decorum."

"Yes, Watson." Susan removed a muslin gown from the trunk, laying it out on the bed. The moment of shared merriment vanished.

Later that night, Honoria lay in the bed while Susan and Watson slept on pallets made from extra pillows and blankets the innkeeper provided. No doubt at her father's insistence.

True to Susan's prediction, Watson snored loudly, the sound coming in fits and starts.

The maid rolled her eyes, let out several rather loud pretend snores, then covered her head with a pillow and turned over.

Alone in the dark, Honoria released the laughter she'd withheld earlier, laughing so hard tears came to her eyes.

She hadn't laughed that hard and long since . . . since Drake. Like a phantom, the memory resurrected itself.

Near the river on her father's estate.

She'd gone riding, and, as groom, Drake had accompanied her.

Bright, midday sun lightened his hair at the crown, giving the appearance of a halo. Whenever he cast a glance her way, her heart increased its pace, and her stomach became all tingly. His little lopsided smile made her think he held a secret.

She could gaze at him forever and never tire of the sight. Unwittingly, she exhaled a sigh.

"You're tired. We should stop and rest," he said.

He dismounted, then assisted her down—the action performed numerous times in the past suddenly more intimate as his hands lingered at her waist longer than was appropriate. His gaze locked with hers.

Her heart increased its tempo, and her cheeks heated. When he grinned at her, her stomach performed an odd flip.

"Wait here." He turned and stooped near the river's edge where the water forget-me-nots grew. Buttercup, her gentle mare, nudged him from behind with her muzzle, pushing him into the water.

Her rapidly beating heart rose to her throat, lodging there like an unmovable boulder. "Oh, no!" she gasped, her hand covering her mouth.

Poor Drake. How mortifying.

He sat up, his cheeks reddened. Then he laughed, clutching the flowers in his hand. "I suppose Buttercup thought the flowers needed a drink of water."

She laughed along with him and the tension eased, as if she had come home from a long, arduous journey and found a kindred spirit waiting. Someone with whom she could be herself.

Warmth flooded her as she gazed at him. Love. Pure and simple. She was *in love* with Drake Merrick, the feeling so overpowering it occupied every inch of her.

Even eight long years later, the feeling had never left, preventing her from even considering another suitor.

New tears formed, not from laughter, but from a deep longing and regret. And in the dark, amid Watson's snores, she let them fall silently into the night.

ॐ

"ARE YOU CERTAIN YOU WANT TO DO THINGS THIS WAY?" SIMON asked. "It's not too late to change your mind."

Safe in the confines of the study, Drake stared at his friend. Should he? Frampton, the butler, informed him the guests had begun to arrive. He couldn't delay any longer. "Since we've already advised the staff of the deception, it would be difficult to change our plans now."

Simon studied him, head cocked to the side and eyes narrowed. "One word to Frampton and he would put all to rights. The man is incredible."

Drake tugged on the sleeves of his bespoke coat. "I have no doubt. You would only hire the best. But . . ."

"It's about her."

Drat. Simon always saw right through him. "Not just her. All of them. Itching to snare a duke for a husband. I don't want someone who only wishes to marry a title. I want someone to want me for *me.*"

"Don't we all. But regardless of what you say, these plans are still tied to your past. Don't deny it."

"I'll admit to nothing. As is my right as a peer of the realm." Drake softened his words with a grin.

Yet, he couldn't deny it if he tried. Not to Simon. He'd bared his soul to his friend, and now man of business, one night in India. And although he'd been deep in his cups, he recalled the words clearly.

"She wouldn't choose me. I'm not good enough," he'd said, his speech slurred from drink.

"Good God, man. She was barely seventeen. What did you expect?"

He'd had no answer then, and to that day, he still didn't know for certain what he'd expected Honoria to do. Faced with the choice of marrying a green boy of twenty who had no prospects and a comfortable life as a marquess's daughter, she hardly had a choice at all.

And yet, the rejection still stung.

If he had to find a wife, he would damn well make sure his bride wanted to marry *him*, even if he purported to be the man of business for a duke.

"Very well," Simon slapped him on the back. "Let's greet your—ahem—my guests."

Drake snorted a laugh. "As you wish, Your Grace."

Simon ignored the sarcasm lacing Drake's words. "I like the sound of that. Perhaps when we're finished with this scheme of yours, I shall petition the King for a title."

Muted conversation punctuated with the soft clink of china and ring of crystal drifted upward to the second floor. Due to the number of those attending, Frampton had directed guests to the ballroom, waiting to meet their host.

Blood pulsed in Drake's head as he descended the staircase. Frampton stood at attention near the ballroom entrance, his gaze lifting to Drake and Simon. The unspoken question floated in his eyes, and Drake discreetly pointed a finger at Simon.

Giving an almost imperceptible nod, Frampton turned to face the ballroom. "His Grace, Pierce Henry Quincy Pendrake, the sixth Duke of Burwood and his man of business, Mr. Drake Merrick."

With that, Drake sucked in a deep breath and stepped into the lion's den, scanning the room for a lovely redhead with serious green eyes.

CHAPTER 3

S he wasn't there. Drake's gaze landed on several redheads, none of whom were Honoria. He didn't know whether to be relieved or disappointed.

No one paid any attention to him, instead focusing on Simon—err —the Duke of Burwood, giving Drake time to scan the crowd again— just to be sure. As they made their way around the room, going through endless introductions, he didn't know how they would ever explain the duplicity they were perpetrating.

But in all honesty, he didn't care. Let them blackball him, exclude him from social gatherings. Lord, even give him the cut direct, the highest of all insults among the *ton*. For Drake, it would be a blessing instead of a curse.

He didn't want any part of their pretentious world. Perhaps he'd show them all and marry a scullery maid. The thought made him laugh out loud.

Simon raised an eyebrow. "Something amusing, Merrick? Surely you didn't find Lady Miranda's comment about her niece falling into a pile of horse manure humorous?"

Drake darted a glance at the attractive brunette in front of them.

Her lips twitched. "Actually, I do find some humor in it, Your

Grace. Lizzie is extremely fastidious. My brother is the same way. He insisted they scrub the poor girl several times."

"Hence their delayed arrival?" Simon asked.

"Indeed." Lady Miranda answered.

"Speaking of horses, Merrick here is an expert horseman. I expect he will outride us all during the fox hunt. Now if you will excuse us." Simon nodded in the direction of the myriad of other guests anxiously awaiting them.

Damn, but Simon was good at playing the duke.

"I shall look forward to it, Your Grace." Lady Miranda's warm brown eyes assessed Drake. "Mr. Merrick. It's a pleasure to meet you."

As they moved to another group of vultures—err—guests, Simon leaned in. "Charming, that one. Keep her in mind. She obviously has a sense of humor."

Drake's eyes landed on the bubbly redhead in the next group. He'd noticed her immediately as they entered the room. She vibrated with energy.

Too young to be the lady's father, the man with red hair standing by her side still bore an uncanny resemblance. He bowed. "Andrew Weatherby, Your Grace. May I present my wife, Alice, and my sister, Miss Anne Weatherby."

Simon bent over the blonde's hand. "Mrs. Weatherby. A pleasure." He placed a kiss on the sister's hand. "Miss Weatherby. Charmed."

The young lady giggled.

Drake refrained from shuddering.

"May I present my man of business and best friend, Mr. Drake Merrick? I don't know what I would have done without Merrick when the news arrived of my grandfather's death."

Drake shook Mr. Weatherby's hand and bowed over the ladies' extended gloved fingers.

Miss Weatherby giggled again. "Will there be a ball, Your Grace?" She batted her eyelashes.

Lord, help them all.

"Anne." Her brother's censorious tone had no effect on her.

"But of course, Miss Weatherby. What would a proper English

house party be without a ball? Perhaps you might reserve a dance for both me and Mr. Merrick?"

Drake thought the girl would swoon into Simon's arms on the spot. Luckily, she remained upright.

"Now, if you would excuse us while we greet my other guests."

Moving along, Simon whispered, "Stay by my side at all times around that one. I may find myself headed to the altar, whether I want to or not. And what a disappointment for her when she finds out *I'm* the man of business."

Two men waited in the next group. Thank goodness.

As Simon chatted cordially with Lord Cartwright and his son, Mr. Victor Pratt, the hairs on the back of Drake's neck tingled. In slow motion, he turned toward the entrance of the ballroom.

His stomach tumbled. Standing in the doorway next to her parents, Honoria waited, as pretty as ever. No. Not merely pretty. A serene maturity replaced the youthful features, her figure filling out in all the right places. She had bloomed into an incredibly stunning woman. Her smile, although lovely, had a sadness about it as she scanned the room. Until she skewered him with her gaze.

Then the smile vanished.

⚘

THE AIR GREW THICK—REMINISCENT OF THE STIFLING CARRIAGE— holding her in place. She blinked, trying to clear her vision. It couldn't be.

Yet her heart said otherwise.

How?

When?

Why?

Foreboding squeezed her chest as Drake locked eyes with her.

The room tilted, sending her back in time to the day joy seeped from her life.

Drake had stared, open-mouthed at her pronouncement. "But you promised. You said you loved me."

What could she say? She did love him. But her mother's counsel made her doubt that love was enough to overcome the many obstacles they would face. "I'm sorry, Drake. But I cannot marry you. I know this is difficult, but I believe it is for the best."

His face hardened, his jaw pulsing as he flung his accusation at her. "Best for whom? You? Because I have nothing to offer? No fancy title? I'm not good enough. That's it, isn't it? Your father certainly thinks so."

Her face heated, and he obviously interpreted her blush as a *yes*.

The pain in his eyes sliced through her.

"Best for both of us." Even as she spoke the words, doubt of their veracity poked at her conscience. Before she could open her mouth to rescind them, Drake huffed and stomped from the room. Two days later, he was gone, enlisting in the military.

She had regretted her decision every day since.

As he stared at her across the new duke's crowded ballroom, his accusation rang in her ears. *I'm not good enough*. She fought to pull in a breath.

"Honoria?" She darted a glance toward her mother's concerned face. Her limbs grew cold. What would her father do when he saw him?

No longer in a uniform or the rough worsted shirt and trousers he'd worn as the groom on her father's estate, on the outside Drake looked every inch the gentleman she remembered him to be on the inside. Clearly bespoke, a gorgeous bottle-green superfine coat accentuated his frame and molded to his body like a glove. Hessians polished to a mirror shine replaced worn boots covered in muck from the stables. He seemed taller than she remembered, his build stockier than the lean boy she knew.

Perhaps her father wouldn't recognize him.

Yet, other than the sun-kissed bronze darkening his skin, his face was unmistakable. Waves of warm brown hair she longed to run her fingers through still rebelled against a comb, an errant lock breaking free and dipping against his forehead. Amber eyes searched her face, and she tried to decipher their meaning.

He didn't smile, but darted a glance toward her mother, then her father, whereupon his distaste grew evident.

Her mother apparently followed Honoria's line of sight, for she gave the tiniest of gasps, attracting her father's attention.

"That must be Burwood," her father said *sotto voce*.

What?

"The dark-haired fellow speaking with Cartwright. But who is the fellow with him? He looks vaguely familiar."

Honoria held her tongue, and her mother gave a tiny shake to her head, then grasped Honoria's elbow for support.

The butler, Frampton, appeared beside them. "Forgive me, my lord. My ladies. An urgent matter pulled me away. Allow me to announce you."

Honoria's desire to shrink to nothingness was in direct contrast to Frampton's booming voice. "The Marquess and Marchioness of Stratford. Their daughter, Lady Honoria."

The dark-haired gentleman turned, glanced at Drake, then, smiling broadly, strode their way.

Her heart rammed against her sternum in great heavy *thuds* when Drake paused, then followed the dark-haired gentleman. His gaze never left hers. She waited for recognition to dawn in her father's mind, but he appeared focused on—what had to be—the duke.

Confirming her assumption, the dark-haired man stopped before them and said, "Pierce Pendrake, Duke of Burwood, at your disposal, Lord Stratford. It saddened me to receive your son's regrets. I hope his wife, the viscountess, recovers fully from her illness. I look forward to meeting them both soon."

Honoria searched Drake's face for any sign of recognition at the mention of her brother. Oh, if only he'd been able to attend. He would shield her from this untenable situation. Honoria chided herself for her selfishness. Colin's place was at Margery's side.

Burwood flashed a smile toward Honoria's mother and then her. "Ladies. A pleasure." He took her mother's offered hand and bent low over it.

When he extended his hand to Honoria, she froze, her gaze darting to Drake, then back to Burwood. Her hand trembled as she slid it into the duke's. He bowed and brushed a kiss against her gloved fingers. "Lady Honoria."

When he turned toward Drake, she held her breath.

"May I introduce my man of business, Mr. Drake Merrick."

Under other circumstances, the shock on her father's face would have been comical. His mouth moved soundlessly as his gaze raked up and down Drake's finely dressed body.

"Actually, Your Grace, I'm already acquainted with Lord Stratford and his family," Drake said, the confidence and calmness in his voice doing nothing to soothe Honoria's nerves.

Acquainted. As if what they had shared was a trifle. The word lashed her heart.

Her father speared Drake with a glare. "Merrick used to be our stable boy."

Honoria finally found her voice. "Groom, Father. Not stable boy." She tried to smile, but she worried it appeared more like a grimace. "How nice to see you again, Mr. Merrick."

Oh, how she wanted to run. To hide from his searching amber eyes. The condemnation shining in them pressed upon her like a heavy weight.

"Lady Honoria. You're looking well." Drake peered over her shoulder. "Didn't your husband accompany you?"

An aching hollowness assaulted her stomach.

Before she could form a response, her father ignored Drake and addressed the duke. "My daughter is unmarried, Your Grace."

"Splendid!"

Although Burwood's enthusiastic reply rang in her ears, Drake was all she could focus on, watching, hoping for some sign of joy or relief.

He remained stone-faced.

Burwood extended an arm. "Please, come join my other guests. Merrick and I have yet to greet everyone."

"Does your man of business often accompany you during social events, Burwood?" Her father's question was bold, if not precisely rude.

Even her mother's eyes widened in horror.

Yet Burwood seemed to take no offense. "As I am unaccustomed to and still learning the workings of society, it comforts me to have a close friend at hand for moral support."

"I should be *fascinated* to learn how you two met." Her father's narrowed eyes said he was anything but.

"And I will be more than happy to relay it to you later, sir. But if you will excuse me."

Honoria and her mother curtsied, and although Burwood smiled congenially, Drake's cold stare chilled her through.

Her father shook his head. "Of all people to be associated with the new duke. It's unfathomable."

"But, Stratford, didn't you hear that Burwood was raised by a commoner after his mother remarried?" her mother asked.

"You did say it was why they had such difficulty finding him, Father. It's not unimaginable that he and Drake, I mean, Mr. Merrick may have crossed paths."

"Hmph. Don't remind me of his upbringing. However, did you notice how his eyes lit up when I told him you were unmarried? You may find a suitable husband yet."

"Wouldn't it be wonderful, Honoria?" Hope radiated on her mother's face. "A duke! And he's very handsome."

"Bah! Handsome fades." Her father waved a hand. "He's titled and rich. And he needs a wife who can teach him the social graces." The gleam in her father's eyes frightened her. "You'll be perfect for him. That is if we can keep that nasty piece of gossip quiet. Avoid speaking or associating with *that man* as much as you can so people don't make the connection. We must pray he didn't say anything to Burwood."

"Drake would never. And it's clear he's forgotten about it," she muttered the last more to herself.

Her father raised a gray brow. "Let us hope so."

Honoria allowed her gaze to drift across the room where Drake and the duke conversed pleasantly with Lydia Whyte. For a moment, Drake's eyes caught hers, then he laughed at something Lydia said.

And her heart broke all over again.

BITTERNESS BURNED THE EDGES OF DRAKE'S HEART, REMINDING HIM it still beat in his chest. Knowing that Honoria watched him, he purposely flirted with Miss Whyte. A direct contrast to Honoria, Miss Whyte was all frivolity, making his poor attempt at showing interest much easier.

She tapped her fan on his arm. "Mr. Merrick. It should be a crime to have two such handsome *eligible* men enter society at the same time."

He cast a surreptitious glance toward Honoria, then laughed—perhaps a bit too loudly. "You flatter me, Miss Whyte."

"Nonsense." She turned her attention to Simon. "But perhaps that is your strategy, Your Grace. Another exceptionally handsome man to pull some attention away from yourself?" She lightly tapped Simon with the fan. "Are you shy, Your Grace?"

At that, Drake gave a genuine laugh. "Si—" *Good grief.* "Shy? Burwood's never been shy his entire life." He watched Miss Whyte's face, relieved when his slip didn't register.

"Not that you've known me my whole life, Merrick." Simon shot him a warning glance. "You've found me out, Miss Whyte. In fact, I was quite shy as a lad, especially around beautiful women."

Drake refrained from rolling his eyes. It would totally ruin his pretense of showing interest. Miss Whyte was attractive, no doubt. Her blond hair and blue eyes met the much acclaimed features of young women—at least according to the man he hired to tutor both him and Simon in the ways of the *ton*. According to Mr. Burbridge, those of *good society* considered red hair and freckles *inferior*.

Nothing about Honoria seemed inferior to him. As Miss Whyte droned on about some nonsense, Drake's mind reeled back to the past. Although he and Honoria had practically grown up together, he recalled the day he knew he loved her as clearly as though it had happened moments ago.

He'd been so nervous around her at first. The daughter of a marquess had no business with the son of her father's steward. Yet Honoria loved to ride, and her father encouraged the pastime.

"My father says if nothing else, it gets my nose out of a book," she'd told Drake as he prepared her horse.

Drake laughed at that. "I love to read as well, but I can never get my hands on enough books."

"Allow me to bring you some from our library."

"That would be wonderful. Will you bring your favorites? Then we can discuss them." Feeling emboldened, he winked. "As we ride, of course."

A pretty blush covered her cheeks, but she nodded. As they rode along in the sunshine, an errant thought crossed his mind that he wanted to kiss each one of the freckles dotting the bridge of her nose, and his own blush scalded his face.

She glanced his way. "Oh, dear. You should have worn a hat. Your face is becoming red from the sun."

His face heated even more.

"Perhaps we should turn back—"

"I'm fine," he mumbled, turning away.

She was so kind. So considerate. Not only with him, but others as well. When they stopped by the river to water the horses, he noticed some forget-me-nots on the bank, so he dismounted to pick them for her, only to be pushed into the river by her horse.

Breeches soaked, flowers drooping, he looked up at her—mortified. So much for his gallant gesture for the fair Honoria.

Yet her kind expression told him she was mortified *for* him rather than *at* his clumsiness. He held up the flowers and said something ridiculous about the flowers needing a drink.

And she had laughed. Again, not *at* him. *With* him. Until tears formed in her eyes. She joined him in the water, splashing water on both of them. They laughed like the children they were.

She took the flowers from him and placed a kiss on his cheek. So sweet. So tender.

Then they stretched out in the warm sun to dry off, talking of books and music and all the things they both loved. Like one mind, they understood each other to the point that words weren't necessary.

His heart left him that day. But wonder of wonders, she gave him hers.

Only to rip it away when she rejected him.

But as he feigned interest in Miss Lydia Whyte, he glanced over once more and knew for certain. Lady Honoria Bell still held his heart.

CHAPTER 4

The ballroom became suffocating as Honoria tried desperately not to watch Drake fawning over every other unmarried woman in the room. A possessive jealousy seared her veins.

But he wasn't hers.

Not any longer.

She'd given up any claim to his heart eight years ago when she told him she wouldn't marry him, and clearly he hadn't forgiven her.

Mercifully, when she followed her parents to join Lord and Lady Easton, Miranda came to her rescue.

She threaded her arm through Honoria's. "Let's take a turn out on the terrace and leave our parents to plan our future with the new duke. Maybe they'll work something out and we can both have him. Like one of those harems in Arabia."

Lord Easton's eyebrows shot up. "That is not humorous, Miranda. Please restrain yourself." He turned toward Honoria's father. "That girl will be the death of me if I don't get her married off soon."

Miranda tugged Honoria along, leaving their parents behind in a trail of laughter.

On the terrace, Miranda's face grew serious as she studied her.

"Good heavens, Honoria. What is it? You didn't even chuckle at my joke."

Before Honoria could answer, Charlotte slipped through the terrace doorway. "I saw you two sneak out. Are we having a meeting already?"

The more serious one of their small group—even more so than Honoria—it was no wonder Charlotte's mind immediately went to something related to their "club."

However, when she glanced at Honoria, she rushed forward. "What happened? You're positively white."

"That's what I'm trying to find out," Miranda said.

The terrace door opened again as Anne burst out. "Isn't he divine! So handsome and elegant." She twirled around the terrace, most likely imagining herself dancing with the duke—or possibly Drake.

The thought chilled Honoria even further.

"Anne. Do stop. We're trying to discuss something serious here," Charlotte admonished.

Anne appeared affronted. "What's more serious than a handsome duke and his even handsomer man of business? Just think! We have two men to choose from."

"I'm sure the other unmarried men will either be hurt you haven't included them in your attractiveness assessment or thrilled to be off your hunting list." Miranda shook her head. "Our concern at the moment is Honoria."

Anne's smile vanished. "What's wrong?"

Both Miranda and Charlotte veritably shouted, "That's what we're trying to find out."

"Well, you don't have to yell." Anne directed her attention toward Honoria. "You do look peaked, Honny."

Charlotte groaned. "Will you not use that ridiculous nickname?"

Honoria finally found her voice—or at least an opening to speak for herself. "Everyone, please. I'm fine. Simply tired. I didn't sleep well last night, and the carriage was stifling on yesterday's journey."

Charlotte flicked a hand at Anne. "Go fetch Honoria some lemonade."

"Why me?"

Anne's eyes widened when all three of them responded, "Go!"

Miranda grasped her arm again. "Come sit down. There's a bench over here."

Two pairs of brown eyes studied her.

"Are you certain that's all it is?" Charlotte asked.

"Yes," Honoria choked out the lie.

They all looked up as the terrace door opened once again. Anne beamed as she appeared—without lemonade. "The duke is bringing you some himself!"

Moments later, the duke emerged, holding a glass of lemonade. "I understand someone is parched." His smile, so kind, conveyed an understanding that unnerved her.

He handed her the glass, then crouched before her so they were eye level. "Should I fetch a physician? Dr. Marbry perhaps? He seems a congenial fellow."

Good heavens! Unable to speak, she shook her head. Her hand trembled as she lifted the glass to her lips.

Burwood turned toward the little group hovering around them. "Ladies, would you be so kind as to give Lady Honoria and me a moment? Perhaps step back out of earshot?"

They all exchanged curious glances, but nodded.

Burwood took a seat next to her. Keeping his voice low, he said, "You needn't pretend with me."

She almost choked on the lemonade. "I have no idea what you're referring to, Your Grace."

Although his lips pressed together in a tight line, they curved upward enough to let her know he didn't believe her lie. "Very well. If you wish to play it that way. But know you have an ally in me. In the meantime, you'll sit next to me at supper this evening."

"Oh, I couldn't."

His dark eyebrows lifted, drawing her attention to his strikingly beautiful blue eyes. "You would refuse a duke? My, such cheek. I insist, so there's no use fighting it. What good is having this type of power if I can't use it to secure a beautiful supper companion?" He said the last loud enough to elicit a little shriek from—what had to be—Anne.

He rose. "Now, drink your lemonade, and if need be, retire to your room to rest. I'll alert Frampton to show you the way. Until this evening." He bowed and then left them.

A collective sigh rose from her friends.

But all Honoria focused on were his words. *You have an ally in me.*

LATER THAT DAY AFTER EVERYONE DISPERSED TO FRESHEN themselves before supper, Drake paced the floor of his bedroom, trying to avoid Simon's chastisement.

His friend frosted him with a glare. "Almost using my real name! What in the devil were you thinking? You're fortunate Miss Whyte didn't question your slip. Part of me suspects you did it on purpose."

"You're mad." Drake turned away and stared out the window to the terrace below.

Simon's tone softened. "She's unmarried, Drake."

As usual, when it came to Honoria, there was no need to ask to whom Simon referred.

Unmarried. Why did that knowledge give him both hope and trepidation?

Questions assaulted him.

Was she a young and exceptionally beautiful widow? If so, what type of man had been her husband? Old and feeble, dying of a geriatric malady or simply old age? Or young and virile, succumbing to something tragic and unexpected?

Had the scandal of their association years ago tainted her so severely no man wished to associate with her? Unthinkable! Yet, he was all too familiar with the judgmental minds of the *ton*.

Or had she chosen to remain unmarried? Unable to sentence herself to a loveless union because she still loved him even though she rejected him?

He held on to the last option—although self-serving—like a lifeline, because the alternative, that she had put him and their love in the past, was unacceptable.

"We can still end this charade." Simon snapped him back to the present. "Oh, there will be some reparation needed, but that will be the case regardless. It would further your cause to win back Lady Honoria."

"I'm not trying to win her back."

A soft chuckle echoed behind him. "Is that why you had me rushing over to see what was going on when she and the other ladies couldn't get out of the ballroom fast enough?"

"She looked ill. I had no more concern for her than I would for any of my guests."

"You both are deluding yourselves."

Drake spun around. "Both? What did she say?"

"See?" Simon pointed a finger at him. "I knew it. Why can't you admit you still love her?"

Drake jerked his gaze away, mumbling, "Because it hurts too damn much."

"What's that? Something about hurt?"

"Damn it. Stop!"

Simon placed a hand on his shoulder. "I'd love to stop this whole thing. To see you happy. I'd say *again*, but ever since I've known you, I don't think I've ever seen you truly happy. Not really."

"Just leave me." Every muscle in Drake's body felt numb and heavy, leaving little strength to argue with Simon. "You'll need to be back downstairs for drinks before supper soon anyway."

"You'll join me, won't you? I wasn't bamming Stratford when I said having you by my side gives me solace. If you don't select a bride soon, I'll suffocate in lilac and rose water. Those predatory women are merciless."

Although the mention of Stratford soured his stomach, Drake couldn't help but chuckle. "I've never heard you complain about female attention before."

"That was different. These women have one thing on their minds— something I wish to avoid for reasons you well know. This is your new life, not mine. And it's damn tiring to be this popular."

Drake nodded. "Go. I'll join you soon. I just need some time alone."

At the *click* of the door latch, Drake's shoulders eased. He trudged back to the window and gazed out at the expanse of his estate.

His estate.

Not Simon's.

His.

The weight of the dukedom pressed down on him, and he recalled the moment he learned the truth.

Heat from the Bombay sun had baked him. Entering the small apartments he occupied as a first lieutenant in the military, he'd swiped the sweat from his forehead. One of the servants raced forward and handed him the life-changing missive.

He'd barely believed it when he read the correspondence from a solicitor informing him of his true identity and heritage. Anger roiled at the man who'd raised him. Francis Merrick, who'd given him his name, had lied to him.

His mother had lied to him.

He strode to the desk, pulling out the dog-eared letter.

My Lord Duke,

    I realize this salutation must come as a shock. It has taken us years to locate you. Your true father was Henry Crispin Pendrake, the youngest son of the Fifth Duke of Burwood. Upon your parents' marriage, your grandfather, Percival Eustace Pendrake, disavowed your father and sent him away. With three older sons, he gave little consideration to the possibility of your father inheriting.

A large liquor stain smeared the words that followed. He'd wanted to crumple up the damn letter and toss it in the fire, giving it the same regard his grandfather had shown for his father.

His father. A man he'd never known. After receiving the letter, he'd written to his mother, hoping she would deny the allegations.

She not only confirmed them, she also told him why. They'd fallen in love, but Henry—his father—was promised to an earl's daughter. Taking matters into their own hands, she and his father eloped. Henry believed his father would forgive him once the die was cast. Instead, they were thrown out and told never to return.

A year after his parents' marriage, he was born. They named him Pierce Henry Pendrake. Although his parents struggled, they were happy and in love. But Henry succumbed to influenza when Pierce— Drake—was two, leaving his mother a young widow with a child and little in the way of prospects.

She did what she could to feed and clothe them both, working as a seamstress in Somerset until she met Francis Merrick, a bright young man with ambitions to become the steward of a grand estate. When he learned about her story, Francis offered to marry her and raise four-year-old Pierce as his own. To shield Pierce from the shame of rejection by his own family, they called him Drake in homage to his true surname.

Drake knew the rest. How his father—that is Merrick—accepted a position as steward for the Marquess of Stratford at his seat in Somerset. Merrick had come highly recommended by Baron Harcourt, for whom he'd worked apprenticing. Stratford no doubt knew a bargain because Drake's *father* had told the marquess that his son, a strapping young lad of thirteen, was excellent with horses and could work as a groom.

He glanced down at the letter again and read the final words.

As your grandfather's three elder sons predeceased him with no legitimate progeny, you are the last of the direct line, Your Grace. I implore you to return to England posthaste and assume your rightful place as the Sixth Duke of Burwood.

But Drake didn't return posthaste. He'd spent days agonizing over the news, the deceit of his mother and the man he'd called father, the heartless act of a grandfather he'd never known, and the grief over the father he didn't remember.

Like trying to force a puzzle piece into the wrong spot, throughout his whole life, he'd never felt he quite belonged. Memories of his mother telling him he was born for great things, but what great things could a groom do? Knowing in his heart he belonged with Honoria, but judged not good enough for her. The letter made everything snap into place.

And it chafed.

It had been Simon who pulled him from the bottle and convinced him to return. "Show them all," he'd said. "And find your Lady Honoria."

And now that he *had* found her, what did he do? He lied. Pretended to be someone he was not.

It had been a way of life for him, even if he hadn't been aware of it. But he needed her to want him for him, not because of a title.

When Lady Miranda led Honoria out of the ballroom, the distress on her lovely face was a gut punch. He'd put that look there as surely as if he'd humiliated her in front of the whole assembly.

War raged inside him. He'd wanted to gauge her reaction as he flirted with the other ladies. But the reality of how his actions affected her slammed hard into his chest. Guilt, visceral and raw, gnawed at him.

Back at the window, movement drew his attention to the terrace below. Wind brushed against the gown of seafoam-green that matched her eyes, molding it to her legs. A lock of her auburn hair blew loose, and she tucked it behind her ear, a habit he remembered her doing absentmindedly.

What was she thinking as she stood so still, gazing out at his estate?

Unable to tear his eyes from her, he whispered, "Look up. Look up at me."

Yet, she did not.

Although Honoria tried to rest, as Burwood suggested, thoughts of Drake invaded her mind, preventing sleep. She redressed, made a feeble attempt to mimic Susan's carefully crafted coiffure, and crept downstairs.

Earlier on the terrace, she'd admired the luscious gardens of the ducal estate, wishing she could spend more time admiring them— alone. With the crowds dispersed, she stole into the empty ballroom and slipped through the terrace doors.

Soft breezes caressed her skin like a gentle kiss.

She startled at the thought. Why did her mind travel to kisses and caresses? A lock of hair blew free and fluttered against her face. She tucked it behind her ear.

Even looking out at the serene gardens, she felt Drake's presence as if he were just over her shoulder, waiting for her to turn and run into his arms.

Ninnyhammer.

She resisted the siren call to glance back. It was simply what she had said to Miranda. Exhausted from a poor night's sleep and tiring journey, she needed rest. And yet thoughts of Drake prevented that as well.

How long would the vicious cycle last until she could break free?

Sweet birdsong serenaded her, easing the ache in her chest. She sat upon the bench, closed her eyes, and listened.

Memories crashed through, demanding to be acknowledged.

Another terrace. Another time.

She'd been looking out her window as dusk fell. Silver light from a full moon gave the gardens a fairytale appearance. In the corner, a shadow moved, catching her attention. As the shadow took shape, she cupped her hands around her eyes to shield them from the candlelight in her bedroom.

Her heart raced as Drake raised a hand in a wave, then motioned for her to come down.

Naughtiness trickled down her spine, swinging around to settle low in her belly. She pressed her lips together, debating her course of action.

Drake motioned to her again.

After grabbing the candle at her bedside, she cracked open her door and listened. Even at that early hour, silence filled the halls. Her parents were attending a soiree at Baron Harcourt's and wouldn't return until morning. Honoria had expressed disappointment at not being included, but at sixteen she had not yet had her come out.

However, as she tiptoed into the hall and down the staircase, she said a prayer of thanks for her parents' absence.

Seated on the bench of the terrace, she and Drake talked for hours under the moonlight until gooseflesh covered her arms, and he insisted she go back inside to warm herself.

He rose and held out his hand. "Allow me to assist you up, my lady."

When her fingers touched his, the gooseflesh flared to life even more. Their eyes locked, and as his gaze drifted toward her mouth, her knees grew weak.

He licked his lips.

A yearning low inside urged her to say something she shouldn't. "Will you kiss me?"

His head jerked back as if she'd struck him.

Heat flooded her cheeks. Thank goodness the darkness covered her embarrassment. "Forgive me. I shouldn't have said that."

A grin broke across his face. "Did you mean it, though?"

Nodding, she choked out a response. "Yes. But only if you want to."

"Oh, I want to. I want to very much. But I shouldn't."

She lived her life to please her parents, abiding by their rules and expectations. But when it came to Drake Merrick, a part of her she didn't know existed took control. "Do you suppose that two shouldn'ts cancel each other and make a should?"

Joy bubbled in her veins at the mirth dancing in his eyes.

"Why, Lady Honoria, I believe you're flirting with me."

She grinned at him. "Is it working?"

Rather than answer her with words, he lowered his head and pressed his lips to hers in the gentlest of kisses.

Her heart soared, her whole body coming to life—

"My lady?"

A woman's voice shook her from the memory, and she turned to find Susan studying her with concern. "I've been looking for you. I went to your room to dress you for supper, but—"

Honoria rose from the bench, leaving the precious memory behind.

"Is it time already? It's so beautiful here, I'm afraid I became lost in thought."

Susan tilted her head. "Are you certain you're not unwell?"

Honoria nodded. As she walk toward the house, she peered up toward the windows.

And although there was no one there, she touched her fingertips to her lips, remembering that first tender kiss.

CHAPTER 5

S usan chattered excitedly as she put the finishing touches on Honoria's elegant coiffure for the evening. "Not to tell tales out of school, my lady, but Watson said your mother is all aflutter with hopes for a match with the new duke."

Oh, dear. Honoria braced herself for what, no doubt, would be a flurry of questions when her mother discovered Burwood had insisted Honoria sit by him at supper.

"Cecily, Lady Miranda's maid, says he's very handsome." Susan sighed as she draped and fastened the string of seed pearls around Honoria's neck.

Honoria laughed as she met Susan's gaze in the mirror. "I suspect any duke who's eligible appears handsome to most unmarried ladies." She rose from the dressing table. "But, in this case, Cecily has the right of it."

And he wasn't the only handsome one. In fact, in Honoria's opinion, Drake surpassed Burwood easily.

"Oh, my lady, your pink cheeks give you such a glow. You look so beautiful. His Grace won't be able to take his eyes off you."

"Pish-tosh." Honoria dismissed Susan's compliment, but she had to admit her new gown was lovely. Delicate ecru lace trimmed the pale-blue satin, and the new style with a lower, more defined waistline showed off her figure to perfection.

However . . . she gazed down at her exposed bosom. "You don't think this bodice is cut too low, do you?"

Susan grinned, her eyes bright with mischief. "I doubt the gentlemen will think so."

Heat rushed to Honoria's cheeks. "Susan!"

Her maid giggled and waltzed from the room moments before a knock sounded.

The door cracked open, and Miranda poked her head around it. "I saw your maid leave." She slipped in and closed the door behind her. "Hopefully, this time neither Charlotte nor Anne will interrupt us. I still want to know what distressed you earlier. I don't believe it was only exhaustion."

Miranda was a dear friend, and although her curiosity promised to be extraordinarily helpful in unmasking the perpetrator of *The Muckraker,* it proved most annoying when it focused on her friends. "You would believe me if you had tried to sleep while someone snored like a bullfrog the entire night."

Miranda's brown eyes widened, and her lips tipped up. "Oh, you *are* keeping something from us. Who was snoring?"

Amused, Honoria shook her head. "Nothing like that. My mother's lady's maid, Watson. The inn was full, and she and Susan stayed in my room."

In a blink, Miranda's smile turned into a pout. "Well, that *does* sound like you, allowing servants to share your room. For a moment, I became hopeful you had done something scandalous."

Honoria snickered at the idea. "What? And give *The Muckraker* even more ammunition."

"Speaking of. Do you think the guilty party may be in attendance?"

"If they're truly part of society, it's possible—even likely. I suppose we'll find out if anything that happens here is reported in the next issue." She linked her arm with Miranda's. "In the meantime, why don't we go down before supper?"

Downstairs, one of the servants directed them to an enormous library where guests clustered in small groups, conversing quietly. One glance at Honoria, and Miranda rolled her eyes. "I shall join my parents and leave you to admire your first love." Soft laughter echoed behind her.

Books lined the walls from floor to ceiling in the expansive room. Her heart picked up its pace, imagining the hours she could spend within its confines. Honoria had never seen anything so magnificent.

Until her gaze landed on Drake. Miranda's innocent comment took on new meaning. Dressed in evening black with a silver waistcoat, he was—in one word—gorgeous. She'd never thought of a man as gorgeous before. Handsome, striking, imposing, yes. But those words, although fitting, didn't do Drake justice. One would think *he* was lord of the manor instead of Burwood.

"Do you like what you see, my lady?" Although soothing, the masculine voice shook her from her reverie, and she turned toward Burwood.

"It's wonderful, Your Grace. Do you enjoy reading?"

He scrunched his face. "Not especially." With a glass of amber liquid in his hand, he motioned toward the glorious books. "Perhaps I should donate all these to charity?"

Her heart nearly stopped. "You can't!" When she caught the gleam in his eyes, her face grew impossibly hot. "You're bamming me. Shame, Your Grace. Shame."

He chortled, a pleasant sound. "True. About donating them, but not about reading. But I suppose if my bride should enjoy reading, I could busy myself outdoors fishing when she finds herself so preoccupied."

"Would that be acceptable? Having a wife who liked to read, that is?"

"As long as that's not all she likes." He gave her a devilish wink.

Oh! My, he was a rascal. "You, sir, are incorrigible."

"So I've been told." He sipped his drink. "Merrick loves to read. I'm sure he'll be holed up here often enough. As my man of business, he'll be living here with me."

She hadn't thought of that.

He studied her. "Would that be acceptable? To my bride, I mean?"

"I suppose that's a question you will have to pose to your intended when the time comes."

"But I'm asking you now."

Blink. Blink, blink, blink. What on earth did he mean? "For my opinion? As a woman in general?"

He grinned. "If that is how you wish to interpret it. But I want to know if you in particular would find it acceptable?"

Her mouth moved soundlessly, struggling to form an answer that neither condemned her nor embarrassed her further. She willed herself not to peek over her shoulder at Drake.

Frampton appeared at the entrance. "Ladies and gentlemen. Supper is served."

She wilted with relief at the reprieve.

"Ah, from your expression, it's clear Frampton's interruption is most welcome. As a gentleman, I shall not press for an answer. Yet." Burwood held out his arm. "Now, may I escort you in, my lady? You did promise to sit next to me."

"If memory serves, you gave me little choice."

As she slid her hand over his arm, he patted it and gave her a devilish wink. "I gave you *no* choice."

Laughter, light and genuine, bubbled up at his admission. As he led her into the massive dining hall, she peered up at him, realizing that she liked him—very much.

He glanced over. "Forgive my manners. I should have mentioned how lovely you are this evening. That gown is most becoming. It's a good thing I insisted on having you by my side. Otherwise, I wouldn't stand a chance."

At first, she attributed his comments to casual flirting—a general attentiveness he would probably pay to any of his female guests. But at that moment, she wondered if he seriously considered her for his duchess.

Oddly, the prospect wasn't unappealing. Except for one *not so* minor detail—the proximity of Drake in the duke's home.

When they arrived at the dining table, Burwood shooed the footman aside and pulled out her chair himself, settling her to his right. Name cards rested beside the plates in the other spots.

She glanced over surreptitiously to where Drake settled next to Lydia Whyte on one side and Lady Miranda on the other. Anne Weatherby sat across from him. Even in her place of honor, Honoria envied her friends.

The Duke of Ashton sat on Burwood's left, with the duchess next to her husband. Some would have considered it a slight not to seat the other duke in the place of honor Honoria occupied. But she knew Ashton enough to know he didn't consider it an affront. In fact, he smiled across the table at Honoria. "I understand you experienced some discomfort earlier, Lady Honoria. Have you recovered?"

"Yes, Your Grace. It was nothing. Simple exhaustion from the journey."

Ashton nodded. "Good. I heard your brother's wife is ill, and I grew concerned you might have something similar."

Goodness, she hoped not. Consumption was a horrible disease. "It's been difficult, but Colin has insisted we stay away for our own protection."

"That's wise, and I'm relieved to hear it. However, if you have need of me, say the word."

"I find your choice to continue practicing medicine most intriguing, Ashton," Burwood said. "Perhaps you can give me counsel on how to adapt to the rigors of society. Word has it you inherited the title most unexpectedly as well."

"True," Ashton said. "However, my father was a duke, so at least I had the advantage"—tilting his head, he smiled—"or disadvantage, depending on how one views it, of being raised in the aristocracy. From what I understand, your upbringing differed greatly from mine."

No heat radiated in Ashton's words. In fact, Honoria sensed a camaraderie between the dukes.

"Indeed, much different. Who would have thought a boy raised by a stepfather would find himself the grandson of a duke? Certainly not I."

Compassion shone in the Duchess of Ashton's eyes. "I knew your grandfather. When I approached him for a donation for Harry's clinic, he was quite bereft over the passing of your Uncle Gyles. If it helps ease the sting, he expressed regret over what happened with your father."

Burwood's smile vanished. "Do you mean how he disowned his own son for marrying a commoner? It would be more palatable had he expressed the same regret *before* realizing his youngest son was his only remaining heir. Imagine his chagrin upon discovering he, too, had predeceased him, leaving only a common-raised grandson to inherit."

The duchess blanched, and Ashton placed his hand over hers, giving it a squeeze, the small gesture of comfort pinging Honoria's heart.

"Forgive me, duchess." Sincere contrition laced Burwood's voice. "I didn't mean to snap. Old wounds, you understand."

"Of course," she said. "I don't blame you in the least."

"For what it's worth, Burwood," Ashton said. "Although elitism still reigns, there are those of us in the aristocracy who are striving for change. I, for one, am glad to have you in our ranks. It will be good to have a like mind in Lords."

Burwood grinned, something Honoria realized she was growing fond of. "Shall we take them down, one noble at a time?"

"Something like that." Ashton raised his glass in toast, his gaze shifting between Honoria and Burwood. "But perhaps we should discuss something less serious. We wouldn't want to bore the ladies."

Honoria had been following the conversation with great interest, especially the idea of reformation. "On the contrary, Your Grace, I find the subject of change fascinating. I've been trying desperately to convince my father that the changes proposed to the Poor Laws are not actually beneficial to the less fortunate."

Burwood lifted a dark eyebrow. "My, you are a serious one, my lady. No nonsense and giggling for her, Ashton." He pointed down the table with his fork. "Much like my friend. Merrick is exceptionally serious. However, at the moment, he seems to be enjoying himself immensely with Lady Honoria's friends."

Sure enough, Honoria turned to find Drake the center of attention among his female supper companions. Anne Weatherby lifted a hand to cover a laugh, Lydia Whyte brushed his arm and leaned in as he whispered in her ear, and even Miranda seemed in on the fun.

Honoria's stomach dropped, and suddenly the fish course in front of her didn't look as appetizing as it had moments before.

"Is something wrong, Lady Honoria?" Burwood's voice was gentle. "Is the fish not to your liking? From what I understand, that particular variety is one of your favorites."

How did he know? She met his gaze, unnerved by the understanding in their blue depths. "It is, and it's delicious." She glanced back at Drake and her friends. Perhaps she should be more like them. She smiled at Burwood. "It's simply the excitement of meeting you has left me breathless, Your Grace."

Burwood winked. "Ho, ho! I think she likes me! Ashton, you and the duchess are my witnesses."

Oh, dear. Had she gone too far? She scrambled for a different topic. "Your Grace, I understand you were in India prior to coming home."

"Ah, she's not only serious, but well informed. I was indeed. Stationed there in the service of king and country." He directed his attention to Mr. Weatherby seated on Honoria's right. "I understand you are also familiar with India, sir."

"Only marginally. My wife is more acquainted with the country than I am. I merely traveled there to beg her to marry me."

Honoria couldn't help but sigh. "How romantic."

Mrs. Weatherby glanced lovingly at her husband. "It was. And a little dangerous."

Burwood cocked his head. "Malaria?"

Mrs. Weatherby shook her head. "No. A duel. But my father knows of several people who succumbed to that horrible illness."

The conversation fascinated Honoria. She had so many questions, both for Burwood and the Weatherbys. "Is that how you came by your bronzed complexion, Your Grace?"

He jerked back. "From malaria?"

Oh! She wanted to crawl under her chair. "Forgive me. No. From the Indian sun."

"Ah, of course. My mistake, my lady. I should have made the connection. Yes. The sun is intense. Much different from our cloudy English skies. I fared better than poor Merrick. It took him time to adjust, as his skin is naturally fairer than my own."

Honoria darted another glance toward Drake.

With a captive audience and his face alight with excitement, he gestured animatedly, something he did when narrating a tale—especially one in which he elaborated shamelessly. The Drake she remembered wasn't as serious as Burwood implied, and she relished that he'd shared that small part of himself with her.

He glanced toward her. For an instant, their gazes tangled, and his smile vanished like a phantom fog. Just as quickly, he turned away, his smile and attention toward his companions returning in full measure.

A dull ache pinged in Honoria's chest.

"He seems a fine fellow," Ashton said.

"He is. Wouldn't you agree, Lady Honoria?" Burwood signaled for the remove. "Lady Honoria and Merrick are acquainted. It would appear our world is smaller than imagined."

As footmen replaced the dishes on the table with the next course, all eyes within the vicinity turned toward Honoria in question. She barely choked out the response. "His father was my father's steward, and Mr. Merrick served as a groom."

Ashton and the duchess exchanged a glance. Had they made the connection to the scurrilous lies that Drake had taken her innocence eight years prior?

Honoria felt more exposed than if she'd been standing on the table, serving as an epergne.

Thank heavens neither of them enquired further.

Rather, as if sensing her discomfort, Ashton redirected the conversation. "Speaking of malaria, Mr. Merrick asked if I knew of any cures."

Burwood's attention jerked back to Ashton. "Do you?"

"Nothing beyond what is currently prescribed for treatment, which is to mitigate the symptoms when an attack occurs."

Why would Drake ask about malaria?

Burwood abruptly became tight-lipped, simply nodding and staring at the new course before them.

Chatter replaced the tense silence as guests served themselves portions of roasted meats and savory vegetables. Although each dish presented was a favorite of Honoria's, every bite was tasteless.

Conversation around her became as indistinct as buzzing of insects. When she sensed Burwood or Mr. Weatherby directing a comment toward her, she merely nodded and smiled, all the while sneaking glances at Drake and his entourage of admirers.

Mercifully, supper ended, topped off with pieces of chocolate-covered marzipan. She frowned at the confection she normally would have devoured with alacrity.

"I must have been misinformed," Burwood whispered, confusion painting his face.

"Pardon?"

"I understood you had a great affinity for the confection. Perhaps your tastes have changed?"

All the evening's food selections took on new meaning. Had he tailored the menu to please her? For what purpose? And from whom did he glean such information? Since her parents hadn't mentioned any such enquiries, she could only think of one other person. Why would he go to such lengths? A small bubble of hope rose to the surface, only to pop when she peeked at Drake and witnessed his display of familiarity with her friends. Turning back to Burwood, she forced a smile. "It *is* my favorite, Your Grace. As are all the other dishes served tonight. I apologize if I appeared ungrateful. My appetite seems to have vanished."

"Are you certain you're not unwell?" Ashton asked.

She nodded. "Quite certain, Your Grace."

At least not physically. Yet the duke had no elixir in his medical bag to treat what ailed her. There was no cure for a broken heart.

THE LIBRARY HAD CALLED TO HONORIA ALL DURING SUPPER. WHILE the women waited in the drawing room for the men to rejoin them, Honoria waited for an opportunity to escape. Her sanity depended upon it. If she had to listen to Lydia Whyte expound on Mr. Merrick's enchanting golden eyes any longer, Honoria would surely scream. She inched away from the crowd as surreptitiously as possible.

Charlotte tugged her arm, pulling her to the perimeter of the room. "Is it me or does that girl only have one thing on her mind? You would think she's never seen a man before. I think she even surpasses Anne in giddiness."

Honoria stifled a snicker. "I'm not sure if Anne would consider that an insult or a challenge."

A rare smile twitched Charlotte's lips. "Regardless, Mr. Merrick should be on his guard. Both Lydia and Anne seem to have set their caps for him." She glanced over at the group of women. "The poor man doesn't stand a chance."

Truth be told, that was precisely what Honoria feared.

A dark brow hitched as her friend turned her attention back to Honoria. "You seem to have garnered favor with the new duke. How did you find him at supper?"

"Attentive. Eager to please."

Charlotte laughed. It truly was a momentous day. "You sound like you're listing the attributes of a new bloodhound rather than a prospective husband. Do you at least find him attractive?"

Although a sharp contrast to Drake's, Burwood's dark hair and deep-blue eyes were indeed appealing. Yet, she said the only thing that came to mind. "He doesn't like to read."

Charlotte studied her as if trying to determine if she'd said her words in jest. "You're serious?"

"He told me so himself. And to waste all those glorious books in his library." Honoria exhaled a wistful sigh.

"Is that where you were sneaking off to before I stopped you?"

Honoria cast her a chagrined smile.

"Go then. If anyone asks, I shall tell them you went back to your room with a headache."

At long last, with purposeful steps, Honoria slipped out of the drawing room and headed to the magnificent library. Once inside, she partially closed the doors, hoping to conceal herself yet not arouse suspicion.

Walking along the expansive shelves, she trailed a finger across the bindings of the books, quickly reading the titles and authors. Old Burwood, or others who had occupied the ducal manor, must have loved to read, for when she plucked a few random books from the shelves, the pages fell open easily. None were dog-eared—thank goodness—but they had the look and feel of a book well-read and well-loved.

The organization was perplexing. Comedies such as Shakespeare's *As You Like It* and *A Midsummer Night's Dream,* sat beside Miss Austen's *Emma,* grouped together by theme rather than by author. Odd. She kept *Emma* in mind but moved on. She loved Miss Austen's work, but *Emma* wasn't her favorite.

A small section in the far corner held romances. Those particular books showed less wear than the comedies or the tragedies such as *Antigone* and *Julius Caesar*. She plucked *Persuasion*—her favorite Austen —from the shelf and settled in one of the large wingbacks.

AT LAST, THE INTERMINABLY LONG SUPPER ENDED, AND THE LADIES dispersed to the drawing room for tea. Drake's face hurt from the forced smile he'd worn for his supper companions—or should he say, Honoria.

She had picked at the food—which he knew well to be her favorites. He'd given specific instructions to the housekeeper, insisting she convey to the cook precisely how to prepare each. Disappointed he hadn't pleased her, he wrapped two pieces of the chocolate-covered marzipan in his handkerchief, then tucked it into his pocket, hoping they wouldn't melt.

The men joined Simon in the billiards room for drinks and cheroots, and Drake was no exception. Hopeful fathers hovered around his friend, Stratford among them. Drake almost laughed at Simon's wild-eyed expression as he parried off each man's suit extolling the virtues of his daughter.

Viscount Whyte jockeyed for position. And although Miss Whyte had paid Drake an enormous amount of attention during supper, her father no doubt wanted better for his daughter than a lowly man of business. Drake let out a chuff of laughter. If he only knew.

Yet that was the point of the whole charade. He didn't dislike Miss Whyte. If nothing else, she played a key part in gauging Honoria's interest—or lack thereof. Which hadn't brought him the satisfaction he'd expected. Each time she had caught him flirting with Miss Whyte, Lady Miranda, and Miss Weatherby, a look of such sadness had crossed her lovely face it nearly broke his own heart.

He was a cad.

The room suddenly became stifling. The smoke swirling in the air, the *clink* of billiard balls smacking against each other, the *plop* as they dropped into the pocket, the raucous shouts as one man won a bet and another lost proved too much. He slipped from the room to find peace and solace elsewhere.

Strange, but removing himself from the thick of it only freed his mind for other torturous thoughts. Such as Simon flirting shamelessly with Honoria. What was the man playing at? Drake's hands curled into fists, vowing to have words with Simon later.

Feminine chatter drifted from the drawing room, and Drake hurried past. He neither wished to see nor be seen by any of the ladies within. After he walked a good ten feet past the entrance without anyone calling his name, he relaxed.

The library doors were partially closed. Odd, as he expected them to be left wide open after everyone had departed for supper. Without bothering to open them more fully, he squeezed through the gap and stepped inside. He loved this room more than any other in the vast mansion, and he breathed in the comforting, familiar scent of the books.

Alone in the safety of the room, he remembered the joy and awe lighting Honoria's face when she'd entered before supper. She would love it here, curled in a chair for hours on end. A warm, cozy fire blazing in the hearth. A kitten curled on her lap, a dog at her feet. He pushed the image aside and strode forward to peruse the shelves for something less idyllic. Perhaps a tragedy to fit his mood.

He perused the selection, his fingers tracing the bindings. *Oedipus Rex? Hamlet? Romeo and Juliet?* He snorted a laugh at the absurd appropriateness of the last.

"Oh!"

He spun around at the tiny gasp sounding behind him, only to find Honoria huddled in a wingback chair.

CHAPTER 6

S o immersed in the book, Honoria startled at a masculine snort of laughter alerting her she was no longer alone. Her heart raced at the sight of Drake's broad back, one hand on his hip as he faced one of the shelves of books.

Unbidden, a tiny gasp escaped.

He turned, his eyes widening when his gaze locked with hers. "Honoria."

The sweet sound of her name on his lips froze her in place.

Awkward moments stretched between them as they stared at each other for what seemed an eternity.

In unison, they shattered the silence.

"I didn't hear anyone come in."

"I didn't know anyone was in here."

Before the urge to disappear into the supple leather of the chair overcame her, Drake laughed, and the tightness in her chest eased.

He took one step closer. "Why aren't you in the drawing room with the other ladies?"

A smile tugged at her lips. "I could ask you a similar question. But I know the answer." As he should with her. The thought that he had to ask was somehow bittersweet. "This library is too glorious to sit empty. I thought I would keep it company. As did you." She nodded to the book he held. "What did you choose?"

He stared down at the book, frowning as if it had appeared in his hands magically. "I . . . I don't think I chose this. My hand was on it when I heard you. I must have pulled it loose." He jerked his chin toward her. "You?"

"Well, unlike you, I deliberately chose mine. But I asked you first."

His loopy grin plucked at her heart and opened the floodgates to memories. "Going to play that game, are you?"

"But of course. If I remember anything about you, it's that you're a gentleman." Truth be told, she remembered so much more.

Color flushed his sun-bronzed skin, and she reminded herself to ask him about India.

"Do I have to tell you the title? It's . . . embarrassing."

Oh? Perhaps old Burwood had a section for erotic literature. Tendrils of heat crept up her neck.

Drake chuckled softly. "Not that kind of embarrassing. I don't think there's anything like that here. Although I haven't searched the top shelves yet." He gazed down at his feet, looking very much like the boy who fell into the river. "It's *Romeo and Juliet.*"

Oooh. Oh!

His gaze darted back to hers. "I was looking for a tragedy."

She couldn't restrain her smile. "Well, it is that."

He laughed again, his gaze darting away. "True enough." He pointed to the doors. "I should leave. I didn't mean to interrupt."

She didn't want him to leave. "You have more right to be here than I."

His gaze snapped to hers, his brows bunching over his narrowed eyes.

"As Burwood's man of business, that is. He told me you would be living here as well."

He visibly relaxed. Strange. What had she said that made him wary?

"I'm a guest. I should be the one to leave." She started to rise.

"Wait!"

Drake couldn't let her leave. If only for a few moments, he wanted her to himself. To remember how things had been. Before everything went horribly wrong. "On second thought, it's a big room. The door is cracked for propriety. May I join you?" He pointed to the wingback opposite her.

The smile reflected in her eyes battered his heart, and she nodded.

He settled in the chair. If nothing else, he wanted to gaze upon her away from prying eyes. To feast upon her beauty—which reminded him. "You didn't eat much at supper. Was it not to your liking?"

She tilted her head, drawing his attention to her long, slender neck, and especially the spot near her shoulder he knew to be sensitive to touch.

"Burwood asked the same thing. I assured him no selection could have been more pleasing. I simply had little appetite."

Remembering the marzipan in his pocket, he removed it and set it on the circular table between them. "Perhaps this will tempt you. If memory serves, it's one of your favorites." He carefully unwrapped it from his handkerchief, relieved it had not melted entirely.

"Oh. I couldn't." She stared at the sugary treat. The tip of her tongue peeked out, subtly licking her bottom lip and contradicting her words.

His mind took an inappropriate detour, and he shifted in his chair.

She continued to eye the confection. "Didn't you save that for yourself?"

"I'm happy to share. I can always ask the cook to prepare more."

Her lips quirked. "So Burwood permits you to submit requests to the cook?"

"He prefers it, actually." He inclined his head toward the temptation. "One for you and one for me."

Her dainty hand reached forward, and he admired her long, graceful fingers as she plucked a piece from his handkerchief.

He popped the remaining square into his mouth. Sweet, but not as sweet as her kiss.

Mid-chew, he stopped to stare at her.

Eyes closed, she sighed. A smile ghosted her lips as sheer rapture painted her face. Then, after glancing down at her chocolate-coated fingers, she licked them, one-by-one.

He choked on the half-chewed candy. *Good Lord.*

She bolted from her seat and rushed forward. Grabbing his coat sleeve, she pulled him away from the back of the chair and pounded his back.

Between a residual cough and laughter, he twisted enough to grasp her wrist. "Stop. Stop. I'm fine. No need to beat me to death."

Pink like the first blush of sunrise bloomed on her cheeks as she backed away and retook her seat. "Forgive me. I would hate to witness your demise by a piece of marzipan."

He peered at the book which had slipped into the crevice of the chair. "Perhaps if the good friar had provided Juliet with chocolate-covered marzipan rather than a draught of sleeping death, Romeo would have seen through the ruse from the chocolate coating her lips, changing it from a tragedy to a comedy."

"And it would have been much more enticing to kiss off than poison."

"True enough." Oh, how he'd missed those moments with her as they shared alternate endings and twists to the books they had read. His heart soared in her presence.

A new silence rose between them, not as uncomfortable as the first. Perhaps she also was reminiscing. Confirming his suspicion, she sighed, the sound wistful.

Words came from his mouth, unbidden, as if they grew tired of waiting and refused to be contained any longer. "You look beautiful, Honoria. The same—but different. I've been trying all day to figure out why."

She jerked her gaze away. "It's been eight years, Drake. I'm not that girl any longer."

"No," he agreed. Sadness hovered around her, giving her a tragic air. He glanced again at the book in the crevice. Like Juliet, had Honoria drugged herself with a sleeping draught, waiting for love to return and revive her, only to wake and find her love dead beside her? He almost laughed at the accuracy of the analogy. "I'm not the same naïve boy, either."

"There is a hard edge to you, Drake."

"Battle does that to a man." It was an easy enough answer and, although true, wasn't the primary reason for his alteration.

A shadow of discomfort flitted across her face. "Is that how you met Burwood? In the military?"

He nodded. "He saved my life." Drake kept the particulars to himself. "I owe him a great debt."

"How heroic. If the ladies present learn of it, he shall be even more popular."

Drake barked a laugh. How could she still turn his sour mood around? "Is that even possible? Don't all you aristocratic women yearn to marry a duke? Heroic or not?"

Her gaze shifted to her lap. "Not all."

Something that died the day she told him she wouldn't marry him, stirred to life. And as before, a bittersweet ache rose in his chest. "Why haven't you married?"

"Why haven't you?" She pulled in an audible breath. "Or have you? Is there a wife who's not present?" Her voice trembled at the word *wife*.

Anyone else would have missed it. But even after eight years, he was still in tune with her. The beast stirring inside yawned and stretched, threatening his sanity all over again. "I asked you first."

She gave the tiniest nod. "It's clear you've been abroad, otherwise you wouldn't have to ask at all. Have you heard of *The Muckraker*?"

"The gossip rag?"

"The very one. I have been featured in it frequently the last few years. Enough to scatter most eligible gentlemen to the four winds."

What? His Honoria? "I find that hard to believe. Whatever could you have done to be in a scandal sheet?"

"One doesn't have to *do* anything to be in that horrible publication. Yet, it doesn't stop whoever is behind it from spreading vicious gossip. If you must know, the first reports were lies about us."

49

Heat flared in his chest on her behalf. "What did they say about us?"

Color bloomed on her cheeks, and she cast her gaze away. "They were lies. Does it matter?"

"It matters to me. Please, tell me."

Her gaze shot to his. "You had already left for the military, but rumors circulated that I had been despoiled by a servant."

Oh, God. Lies, indeed! And she had faced it alone. Is that why she hadn't married? "What else?"

The enigmatic curve of her lips reminded him of the Mona Lisa, except—no offense to Da Vinci—Honoria was much more beautiful.

"*The Muckraker* took great joy in reporting how two separate men courted me but chose to marry other women."

"The cads! Give me their names!"

To his amazement, she laughed. "One of them is a guest. Dr. Marbry. And it was I who told him to marry Priscilla. It was clear he loved her, though he refused to admit it. They are very happy, and I am happy for them."

"And the other man?"

"An even more innocuous situation. Lady Charlotte's brother, Lord Nash Talbot. Both our families insisted upon the match, but neither of us wanted it. We agreed to a pretense to buy some time—for him to secure funds for an investment, and for me to reach twenty-five when my father promised to release my dowry. In the interim, he fell in love with a lovely American woman." Mirth lit her green eyes. "I quite enjoyed arranging secret rendezvous for them."

He stared at her aghast. "You . . . helped them? To your own detriment?"

"Not to my detriment at all. As I said, Lord Nash and I both agreed we were not suited to one another. Do not misunderstand. I like him very much and felt society treated him most unfairly. But he wasn't—" Her mouth clamped shut with such force, he worried she would crack a tooth.

He straightened in his chair. "Wasn't what?"

Her gaze darting around the room—landing anywhere but on him

—she twisted her hands in her lap. "Um . . . he wasn't . . . in love with me."

Something about her answer, or perhaps the way she answered, niggled at his mind. Although not untruthful, he suspected it wasn't what she had initially intended to say. "I didn't think love was a requirement among aristocrats. Indeed, had it been, we would—" He stopped short, finishing the sentence in his mind—*easily have met it.*

Unlike him, she didn't ask him to finish. Apparently, he was more transparent.

Instead she asked, "And you? Surely, judging by the attention you've received from the ladies here, you've had ample opportunity to choose a wife."

Aye. But none were you. As if clouds parted and the emerging sun illuminated everything around him, her earlier words became clear. Did she still love him? He eased into his deception, finding comfort in the lie. If she did indeed still hold affection for him, would she accept him as a mere man of business, refusing to bend to her family's persuasion to avoid such a *lowly* match?

In answer to her question, he planted the seed. "I will admit it's time for me to settle down." He forced the smile to his lips and hoped it appeared genuine. "Perhaps one of the fine ladies here might prefer a simple life over the glamorous one as a duchess." The question remained; would the seed sprout and grow, or would it lay dormant and wither if not watered by her family's approval?

Color drained from her face. Was it from the thought of him marrying another? Or did his blow land a direct hit, reminding her of their past?

Oily guilt slithered in his chest. Accepting he had done enough damage for the evening, he rose. "I should leave you before we are discovered."

Torn between his desire to flee and to stay, the door both beckoned him and mocked him as he strode toward it.

"Drake." Her voice was soft yet steady.

He closed his eyes, relishing the sound of his name on her tongue. "Yes?"

"*Persuasion.*"

The word stopped him dead, and he spun around. "What?"

"You asked what I was reading."

He placed the copy of *Romeo and Juliet* on a side table. "The staff will re-shelve this." Then he hurried from the room, too afraid of what he would say if he stayed.

CHAPTER 7

Around half past ten the next morning, Honoria made her way down to breakfast, finding a modicum of her appetite had returned. The room was deserted, save for two footmen. Both relieved and disappointed that Drake was not present, she helped herself to some tea, toast, and a slice of plum cake at the sideboard. Once again, her favorites—an assortment of morning cakes—were among the choices, giving her pause. Although, in truth, breakfast items offered at house parties were often the same.

She'd barely taken a bite when Anne burst into the room. Honoria lifted her cup of tea to hide her grin. One certainly couldn't accuse the girl of being a wallflower.

Anne tossed a piece of toast and a blob of jam onto her plate. "I can't believe I slept so late." She plopped into a chair next to Honoria. "Did I miss anything exciting?"

"Well, the breakfast is quite delicious."

Anne's feeble attempt to appear aggrieved at Honoria's comment failed miserably as a snort of laughter escaped her tightly pressed lips. "You know what I mean."

Honoria delivered an insouciant glance. "I'm serious. Try the raspberry jam."

Anne slumped back in her chair, pouting like a recalcitrant child. "Oh, Honny. Why must you be *so* serious?"

"Honny?" Drake's voice had both Honoria's and Anne's heads turning toward the entrance of the room.

"Mr. Merrick!" Anne's posture snapped back.

Yet, Drake's attention remained on Honoria, his brow still quirking with his unanswered question.

Not to be dismissed, Anne left her chair and tugged on Drake's coat sleeve. "Come sit with us, Mr. Merrick."

As if finally realizing Anne was there, Drake sent her an apologetic smile. "Thank you, Miss Weatherby, but I've already eaten. I heard voices and came in to remind you the games are commencing."

Games? She glanced at Anne in question.

"Oh, that's right, Honny. You went to bed with a headache. Burwood announced we would be participating in a variety of outdoor games today—weather permitting."

"Which at the moment is favorable. The sun is shining down upon us," Drake said.

Anne flashed him a blinding smile so bright Honoria swore the aforementioned sun sparkled off the girl's teeth. "Will you be my partner?"

Did she bat her eyes?

Drake slid a glance over to Honoria, then back to Anne. "I would be honored—if we indeed partner. I believe the first game Burwood has planned is blind man's buff." He held out his arm. "Now shall we proceed?"

Slipping her hand over his arm, Anne apparently forgot her breakfast.

"Anne, your toast," Honoria said.

With a swish of her hand, Anne brushed the reminder aside. "Since you're so fond of the raspberry jam, you can have it."

Air stilled around Honoria as Drake's gaze glided toward her. She pulled what little there was into her lungs, waiting for him to invite her to join them.

"You like the jam?" He smiled. "Burwood will be pleased." Then he turned, leading Anne out of the room, his voice trailing off as he said,

"Now, Miss Weatherby, you must tell me about the strange name you called Lady Honoria."

Staring at the practically untouched toast and cake, Honoria sighed, the remainder of her scant appetite vanishing. Yet, she forced down a few more bites, washing it down with tepid tea. It would not do for her to grow lightheaded from lack of sustenance, especially during vigorous games such as blind man's buff.

Her mother appeared at the entrance. "There you are. Thank goodness. Your father is beside himself, wondering why you're not out with the others participating in the activities."

She blinked, unsure she'd heard her mother correctly. "Father wishes me to play the games?"

In a swish of lavender, her mother breezed into the room, arriving close enough to whisper. She waved a hand as if batting away a pesky fly. "Of course he doesn't care about those silly games. He finds them ridiculously plebeian. However, he and I both noticed the attention Burwood lavished on you last evening at supper. You should capitalize on the duke's favor and continue to position yourself near him lest his attention stray to another."

It would appear her father had already formed an attachment in his mind between her and Burwood. Out of spite, and a bit of childish recalcitrance, she took another bite of the plum cake and chewed slowly, hoping it didn't reemerge later.

Honestly, she hated vexing her mother, who had no doubt been pressed into duty by her father to retrieve her. If Honoria waited any longer, the man himself would most likely come to fetch her, dragging her out by any means necessary and shoving her in front of Burwood.

After swallowing the last masticated bite of cake, she dabbed at the corners of her mouth with the serviette. "Very well. But I caution you and father not to make assumptions regarding the duke's interest in me. I believe he's only being a gracious and attentive host."

"Bah!" her mother said most uncharacteristically. "A mother has eyes. He likes you exceedingly well."

Honoria refrained from rolling her eyes at her mother and instead followed her out of the house to the expansive gardens.

Occasional squeals of laughter punctuated more subdued chatter burbling across the stone terrace. Parents, guardians, and chaperones sat in comfortable chairs in what had been a quiet place of respite the day before. Some sipped tea or lemonade as they watched the younger members of the assembly scatter across the expanse of the lawn in merriment.

Lydia Whyte emitted a high-pitched *eep* as a blindfolded Victor Pratt reached for her and grasped air.

"Lady Honoria!" Burwood called. Several women clung to his arms, perhaps using him as a shield to hide from Mr. Pratt. "Come join us."

As everyone stopped to look her way, Victor Pratt managed to catch Lydia, who didn't seem the least bit disappointed to be captured.

"Go on, then," her father said from his seat by the terrace wall. "Join that ridiculous game."

Before she could descend the steps to the lawn, her father muttered, "And allow Burwood to catch you."

With her back to her parents, she strolled toward the group and released the eyeroll. Had her parents become so desperate to see her married as to orchestrate some type of compromising situation between her and Burwood?

Perhaps not simply *married* but married to a duke.

Poor Burwood. He deserved better than to be trapped. Delicately brushing off the clinging women, he motioned for her. "Where have you been, you slugabed? We've been waiting for you."

Me?

Victor Pratt removed the blindfold.

"Here, Pratt, hand me that," Burwood called. "I think as punishment for being so tardy to our little game, Lady Honoria should be the blind man—or blind woman, as it were." He laughed at his own joke.

The delicious plum cake sat heavy in her stomach, and her limbs seemed to be firmly fixed to the ground. If Colin were there, he would come to her rescue immediately. "Oh, no. I couldn't . . ."

"Of course you can." Burwood snatched the blindfold from Victor's hand. "It's my party. What's the point in being a duke if I can't choose who assumes the most important role in the game? Now, turn around." He made a circular motion with his finger.

Drake turned from where Anne had tethered herself to his arm. "Burwood, I don't think that's a good idea."

He remembers. Oh, thank you, Drake.

Unfortunately, the duke ignored him. As he tied the blindfold around her head, he leaned in and whispered, "Remember what I said. You have an ally in me." Giving the cloth a sound tug, he asked, "Now, Lady Honoria, can you see anything?"

She shook her head. And that was precisely the problem. Panic crept in with the darkness.

Once as a child, she'd hid in the root cellar on her family's estate to escape her governess's lessons, only to become trapped inside. She'd called out for what seemed like hours in the pitch-black, chilly space until her brother had found her and pried open the stuck door. To that day, she hated not being able to see.

"Very well," Burwood continued. "The rules of the game are thus: I shall spin you around three times. Then you try to catch one of us. If you do, and you can identify who you've captured, that person becomes the new blind man. Do you understand?"

"Yes." She hoped the dread seeping in didn't reach her voice. She took a deep breath in an effort to calm her nerves.

Someone—presumably Burwood—spun her around. If it was three times, she would have to take his word for it. The action alone disoriented her.

"Over here, my lady." A masculine voice called from behind. Mr. Pratt, perhaps?

Hands outstretched, she turned around and took a tentative step forward. Her stomach lurched. What if she tripped and fell? Giggles sounded from her left. Anne or perhaps Lydia?

"Over here," someone else called from her right. On and on it went, voices calling out, urging her forward in their direction. Her hands clutched nothing but air. As soon as she moved in the direction of one voice, it would shift positions.

"Be fearless, Lady Honoria! You must be quicker." Burwood?

I'm trying!

She concentrated, trying to gauge the distance and positions of the participants, reminding herself she was not trapped. Why didn't she hear Drake? Where was he?

"Straight ahead!" Burwood again?

Something in his voice made her believe he understood her pain and frustration. Would he hold still and allow her to catch him and end this torture? She barreled forward, determined not to let fear of humiliation win.

People yelled all around her, disorientating her again. As she raced forward, she hoped—nay prayed—she would grasp onto someone.

A man shouted something unintelligible. *Drake?*

Suddenly, her breath was wrenched from her lungs as someone ran into her, knocking her to the ground and landing on top of her.

DRAKE'S INSIDES ROILED. HONORIA HAD CONFIDED IN HIM ABOUT an experience she had as a child. Not being able to see terrified her. He stood perfectly still as she stumbled his way, waiting, hoping she would reach him, but she veered off to the side.

Hands pressed against his back, and before he could say a word, he was propelled forward, straight into Honoria's path. He stumbled into her with such force she rocked back, and he wrapped his arms around her to steady her. But it was too late. She toppled backward, taking him with her.

"Oof!" Air whooshed from his lungs as he landed on top of her.

Simon jeered behind him. "I say. I don't believe you are supposed to run into her."

Drake scrambled off Honoria, and peered up at Simon's laughing face, suspecting exactly whose hands had pushed him.

Like the good sport she was, Honoria kept the blindfold on, her hands pushing against the ground in an attempt to right herself.

"Allow me." He grasped her hand and pulled her to her feet.

"Guess who it is, Honny."

Drake jerked his head toward Anne Weatherby and her ridiculous name for Honoria.

"Go ahead, my lady. Touch his face and tell us." Simon's tone and the smirk on his face confirmed Drake's suspicions.

After giving his *friend* a look that said, *We will have words about this later*, Drake faced Honoria and held his breath. Would she touch him?

As she lifted her hand, he grasped her fingers, bringing them to his face. Even after eight years, her touch still sent a thrill through him. So light and tender, she traced her delicate fingers across his face, the tips trembling against his skin—lingering.

He closed his eyes, savoring the moment, yet keenly aware all eyes were upon them. *Say it's me. Say it's me. Say it's me.*

"I'm not sure," she said, her voice as tremulous as the fingers upon his cheek. "Is it . . . Burwood?"

For a brief moment, his heart soared that she had recognized him, forgetting she was unaware of his ruse. The subsequent descending trajectory was so sharp it made him nauseous.

Unlike Drake, Miss Weatherby seemed elated Honoria had guessed incorrectly—at least to her knowledge. "No. Guess again."

Drake's heart couldn't bear hearing her speak another man's name while she touched him. "Let's not torture Lady Honoria further. Remove the blindfold, my lady."

When Honoria pulled away the cloth and exposed her seafoam-green eyes, their gazes snagged and held. Bright splashes of color blossomed on her cheeks, yet no hint of surprise shone on her face.

Pain lanced at his heart—her rejection served fresh.

Gently lifting the blindfold from her fingers, he tore his attention away from her. "Who shall be next?"

Simon veritably glared at him. It would seem Drake wasn't the only one wishing to exchange words. "Since you upset the rules, I declare it should be you."

It was a price Drake was more than willing to pay to save Honoria from more embarrassment. "Very well."

Dark shadows passed over the ground as Honoria joined the other players. Overhead, ominous clouds loomed, casting a pall that mimicked the despair infesting his mood.

He tied the blindfold on, thrusting himself into further darkness.

"Let me test it. I don't trust you." *Simon*. His friend leaned in and whispered. "How can I help you when you don't cooperate?"

Help? Help? The man was mad. Through gritted teeth, he whispered back, "Do *not* push either me or Honoria into each other again."

None too gently, Simon spun him around.

They would definitely have *words* later.

A DELUGE OF MEMORIES BATTERED HONORIA WHEN SHE TOUCHED Drake's face, the contours as familiar as her own. Of course, she knew who had stood before her.

Pride froze his name on her tongue, so she spoke the next best option. She couldn't let him know how she still ached for him. Not when he clearly was no longer interested.

Yet, when she'd met his eyes, pain flashed in their amber depths. Had she truly wounded him?

Grateful to be free from the constraining darkness, she folded herself into the crowd.

Shouts rose from the others as a blindfolded Drake moved forward, hands outstretched.

"Over here, Mr. Merrick," Anne called, placing herself directly in his path.

"No here, Mr. Merrick," Lydia countered, moving to the side in an obvious attempt to draw him away from Anne.

Drake stopped. His mouth pressed together in a tight line, and although the corners tipped upward, Honoria had no doubt his eyes beneath the blindfold held no amusement. He was as enamored with the game as she.

Fat drops of rain plopped on her arms, a few at first, but they steadily increased in both number and rapidity of descent.

"Inside!" someone called from the terrace.

Men scrambled from the lawn first. Only upon making it to the terrace did they seemingly realize they had abandoned many of the ladies.

Strands of hair stuck to Honoria's neck and cheeks. Her white muslin gown darkened and grew transparent as the contents of the looming clouds poured down.

Charlotte grasped her arm, giving it a tug toward the terrace. "Come, Honoria. You're soaked to the skin."

Drake!

She shook her head. "Go. I'll follow anon." As Charlotte raced off toward the shelter of the terrace, Honoria swiveled back, searching for Drake.

Still blindfolded, he turned in a circle, hands outstretched, no doubt desperate to catch someone and put an end to the game so he could get out of the rain.

She took a step forward, ready to rescue him and tell him almost everyone had given up and raced up to the house.

But before she could reach him, Anne Weatherby grasped his arm. "Mr. Merrick, everyone has left."

"Miss Weatherby?" Drake asked.

Bands tightened around Honoria's chest at the confidence in Drake's tone as he guessed Anne's identity. Nausea roiled in her stomach when he ripped the blindfold from his face and smiled endearingly at Anne.

"Thank you for rescuing me. Who knows how long I would have remained out here in the rain like a fool were it not for your kindness." His gaze moved from Anne to lock with Honoria's.

She opened her mouth, wanting to tell him she was on her way to him, but he turned back to Anne and smiled. A chill raced up her spine. Yet the rain was warm.

Someone slipped a coat around her shoulders, and she tore her gaze from Drake's to find Burwood next to her. "Let's get you out of the rain, my lady."

Grateful for the duke's care, she followed him inside, Anne's laughter echoing behind her.

CHAPTER 8

The moment Honoria escaped the rain and entered the house, her mother ushered her to her room. "Your gown, Honoria."

A quick glance downward told Honoria why the duke had placed his coat over her shoulders. Rain had soaked through her gown to her cotton chemise. The only thing keeping her remotely decent was her corset, and that was questionable.

Once inside her room, she slipped the coat from her shoulders and tugged on the bell pull. "I'll have Susan return this to Burwood's valet."

Her mother's face radiated hope. "That was quite gallant of him. Your father is optimistic."

"The duke was merely being kind. As for Father, given his opinion of common folk, I'm surprised he's willing to consider a match with the duke."

"A duke is hardly a commoner."

"But he was raised as one. It's clear Father still holds disdain for Mr. Merrick."

Her mother sighed, gracefully lowering herself to a chair by the bed. "Are you still fixated on that man?"

Fixated?

Of course that's how her mother viewed it. She'd said as much eight years prior when she counseled Honoria against marrying Drake. "You would both be shunned by the *ton*. How do you think that would make him feel to have deprived you of those valuable connections? You would struggle, living hand to mouth. When he realizes he cannot provide for you in the manner you are accustomed, he will grow bitter and resentful. Men have such pride in these matters. Allow him to be free to make something of himself. Give him that gift and release him from this impetuous, childish infatuation that has obsessed you both."

And Honoria had believed her mother's exhortations and allowed herself to be persuaded.

But Drake *had* done well. The friendship he formed with Burwood in the military led to an admirable and lucrative career, putting her and their past behind him.

"My feelings are of no consequence." The moment she uttered the words, the truth of them slammed into her—at least where her parents were concerned. She was a chess piece, bred to make an advantageous match, a pawn to be sacrificed to win the game—a game she learned to play on the board and in life.

She moved her knight into position. "However, considering Burwood seems quite fond of Mr. Merrick, it would be prudent for Father to treat him with more respect. That is, if Father expects to gain Burwood's approval."

Her mother's eyebrow lifted infinitesimally. "Will you consider a match with him?"

Would she?

He was considerate, amiable, and he truly seemed to like her. Although she'd accepted impending spinsterhood, she always wanted children—a family of her own. And he would need an heir.

Yet, even if he grew to love her, could she love him in return? Or would the constant presence of Drake thwart any chance of love for Burwood to take root in her heart?

She answered as truthfully as she was able, "I don't know. Perhaps."

Her mother's face brightened. Mercifully, before any further interrogation was possible, Susan entered the room.

As Susan selected a dry gown, Honoria's mother rose.

"I shall leave you to contemplate our discussion. Once you're redressed, do not delay in rejoining the company. I understand the duke planned indoor games in case of just such inclement weather."

More games. Honoria withheld the sigh. What other humiliation lay in store? She shuddered at the possibilities.

Changed into a lovely pale-blue gown, she sat before the mirror as Susan towel-dried her hair and refashioned it into a presentable arrangement.

Why was Burwood so attentive? It couldn't be her appearance. She'd never considered herself beautiful, as least compared to the other eligible ladies present. True, she was passably tolerable, and many people commented on her engaging smile and lovely eyes. But enough to capture a duke's eye?

The image of Drake and Anne taunted her. Drake's easy smile and Anne's vivaciousness—when taken separately—lightened Honoria's mood. But together and directed toward each other? Painful tightness squeezed her chest.

As much as she loved Anne, the idea of her married to Drake was unbearable—especially if they lived in Burwood's household together. Being the Duchess of Burwood would not ease the sting of seeing them so happy and in love when she decidedly—was not.

She couldn't marry Burwood. Even if that meant giving up a family of her own. If she couldn't have Drake Merrick, if she ever married, it would have to be someone completely unassociated with him.

As guests departed to their rooms and changed from their wet clothing, Drake bounded up the stairs to his own bedchamber.

"Merrick!" Simon called from several stairs behind.

Initially planning to ignore him, Drake pressed forward until, from the corner of his eye, he caught Lord Stratford peering up from the gallery below.

It would have to be *him.*

Drake spun around toward Simon. "Pardon, Your Grace." It took every ounce of willpower to keep the sarcasm at bay. "I didn't see you there." A lie, of course.

The image of his *friend's* arms around Honoria stabbed him like a bayonet to the chest. *Et tu, Brute?*

From the expression on Simon's face, he recognized the insincerity in Drake's address. "A word, if you please?"

Upstairs, they slipped into the ducal bedchamber, and Drake closed the door.

"How could you?!"

"Are you mad?!"

Shouted in unison, their words mingled together, but the sentiment was undeniably clear.

With all the sarcasm he'd held back and now could muster, Drake said, "Please proceed, *Your Grace.*"

"Blast it, man. We're alone. Drop the pretense." Simon paced before him, his usual sunny disposition changing as quickly as the weather outside. "I practically delivered her in your lap, and what did you do?" He waited. Did he truly expect an answer?

Drake lifted a brow, hoping it conveyed his irritation.

Unfortunately, Simon was well versed in Drake's mannerisms and equally adept at ignoring his displeasure.

"Nothing! That's what you did. Absolutely, nothing!"

"You pushed me into her! What would you have had me do? Propose on the spot?"

Simon had the gall to grin. "That would have been nice."

"And you call me mad?" Drake ran a hand through his wet hair. "Her parents were in plain sight. They hate me, Simon. Turned her against me. How do you think they felt seeing me falling on top of her?" He summoned his most menacing glare. "You're not helping my cause."

Simon's brows hitched. "Your cause? So you've finally come to your senses and admit you still love her? Plan to win her back?"

Drake's mouth moved, but no sound emerged. *Damnation!* How quickly his *friend* took advantage of the crack in his armor. Finally gathering his wits, he said, "I didn't say that. But my cause is to find a bride, and Lord Stratford is a powerful man. He could sway other fathers or brothers against me."

Simon studied his perfectly manicured nails. "Not more powerful than a duke."

"*They* don't know that. To them, I'm a simple man of business."

Anger flared in Simon's eyes. "Watch who you're calling simple. And need I remind you, this was your brilliant idea." He raised his voice to an annoying falsetto, the opposite of Drake's baritone. "'I want a woman who wants me for me. I don't want them blinded by a title,' you said."

Those *were* his words. Drat the man and his unwavering memory. Drake called forth the lie that he no longer cared for Honoria, but it froze on his tongue. Instead, he threw what Simon said back at him. "Exactly. Which history has shown is not the Lady Honoria. Under the pressure from her family, she rejected me because I wasn't good enough. Said it was *for the best*." He snorted a *harrumph*. "Best for *her*."

"What could a girl of ten-and-seven have done? She hadn't reached her majority, and her father refused his permission. Did you really think she would go with you all the way to Gretna Green? From Somerset? Her father's men would have found you within two days at the most."

Drake clenched his fists, wishing he could pound on something. Simon's face tempted him. "She's not a girl any longer, and yet she still rejects me. She *knew* it was me, Simon. I could see it in her eyes when she removed the blindfold. Yet she refused to admit it."

"She may have had her reasons."

"Whose side are you on?"

"The side of love."

Drake snorted a laugh and turned his back on his friend. "What do you know of love?" he mumbled.

"Enough to know two people who should be together are apart because of pride and stubbornness." He stomped to the door, throwing it open, startling Frampton.

"Your Grace, a letter." The butler held out the silver salver, his eyes darting between Simon and Drake.

"It's all yours," Simon said and slid around Frampton to make his escape.

Drake frowned at the sender's name above the seal. *Who?*

My Lord Duke,

Imagine my surprise when, only last week, I received word of your arrival at Hartridge House. Then, to my greater astonishment, I had to read in The Muckraker, of all places, you were hosting a house party. Did your solicitor not inform you of my existence?

My invitation must have been misplaced, for surely you would not be so remiss as to exclude one of your few remaining relatives on your father's side.

But allowances must be made as you, no doubt, are still becoming accustomed to proper etiquette among the ton. I am sending this letter ahead as a courtesy. Expect me to follow shortly.

Katherine Dickens, the Countess Gryffin (your great aunt).

Great aunt?

Drake searched his memory. The solicitor's letter announcing his inheritance had been brief. And although his mother's explanation of the events preceding his birth and life as Drake Merrick had filled in some gaps, there were still enormous holes in the knowledge of his paternal line.

Had the solicitor mentioned a great aunt? Drake had been in a state of numbed shock during his meeting with the man, stunned into silence at the outrageous wealth left at his disposal.

Wait. There was *something*. Or should he say *someone*? An Aunt Kitty. Mentioned in passing, her name became lost in the jumble of details about the estate. But Drake recalled descriptors such as sharp-witted, eccentric, and tenacious associated with *dear Aunt Kitty*.

He would have to prepare Simon with the little knowledge he did possess. Hopefully, given her age, Aunt Kitty's mind wasn't so sharp as to see through their ruse.

UNEASE TICKLED ITS WAY UP HONORIA'S SPINE AS SHE DESCENDED the stairway toward the large downstairs parlor. The excited chatter she'd encountered earlier upon joining the gathering outside was now subdued, no doubt dampened by the rain like her clothing.

Taking a deep breath, she entered the parlor and scanned the crowd. Although not everyone had rejoined, enough people had assembled to allow her to become inconspicuous. Her timing couldn't have been better, for Drake was not yet present, giving her time to find a safe place to hide among the other guests.

However, her mother had other plans. Next to Honoria's father, she gave Honoria an encouraging nod, her gaze flickering toward Burwood.

He stood in front of a large piano, two women draped on his arms. His face broke into a large smile as his gaze snagged hers. "Lady Honoria! Just in time."

Not again. Her gaze darted toward the piano. Surely he would not ask her to play? She played tolerably well, but being on display always made her so nervous she would no doubt make a horrible mistake and embarrass herself and her parents.

As carefully as she could, she inched toward Miranda. "What am I just in time for?" she asked.

"I'm not certain. Burwood said he was waiting for you and Mr. Merrick."

Drake? Painful knots formed her in stomach, reminding her—thanks to that horrible game—she had little to eat for breakfast.

"And here is our other party," Burwood announced.

Everyone's head, including Honoria's, turned toward the entrance where Drake stood. He squinted his eyes at Burwood.

What was Burwood up to? And did Drake know?

"Merrick, come here. You, too, Lady Honoria."

Honoria's stomach tightened further, and she cast a quick glance toward Drake, who looked as dubious as she felt.

Both complied. One did not ignore a duke.

Waving them forward, Burwood's eyes sparkled with mischief. "Your father tells me you are an accomplished singer, Lady Honoria. And I know for a fact, Drake has a tolerable baritone. Together you should provide a wonderful duet to entertain us."

Honoria was quite certain singing a duet with Drake was not what her father had in mind when he expounded on her singing prowess to Burwood. The scowl on her father's face confirmed it.

She did love to sing—in private, where no one could hear her. Each time she tried to perform in public, her throat would constrict, making any notes she produced sound choppy and strained. She'd almost prefer another rousing game of blind man's buff.

Why had they even come to this dreadful house party?

Her panic must have been evident, for sympathy shone in Drake's eyes as he approached her. He was one of the few people she could sing for and not become paralyzed with fear.

"Pretend it's only the two of us. Don't think about them," he whispered as they walked side-by-side toward the piano.

"I can't do this," she whispered back, her voice already trembling.

"You can, and you will. I'll sing especially loud and drown you out." He grinned at her, and the tension in her throat eased—somewhat. "Everyone will focus on my off-key howling. They won't even hear you."

"Promise?"

He grew serious. "On my honor."

Her skills felt too mediocre for the beautiful grand piano, so she turned and scanned the crowd. *Thank heaven!* "Lady Montgomery, would you mind accompanying us?"

Beatrix Townsend smiled, said something to her husband, and they both approached. "I'll have Laurence turn the pages for me. What would you like to sing?"

Burwood chose for them. "You both should know *William and Mary*. I've laid the music out already."

"Oooh, lovely." Lord Montgomery gazed adoringly at his wife. "Although no page turning is necessary for that one." Still, he remained by her side.

True, it was a beautiful song about true love, but singing it with Drake seemed too on point. How much had Drake really told Burwood?

Burwood's words reverberated in her mind. *You have an ally in me.*

Was he playing matchmaker?

Memories of assisted liaisons between her friends surfaced.

However, it was one thing to be the one matchmaking and quite another to be on the receiving end—especially if one party was not a willing participant.

Drake's scowl, which at the moment closely resembled her father's, confirmed it. Although it did appear he directed his displeasure toward Burwood.

When Drake refocused his attention back on her, gentleness shone in his eyes once more. "Remember, it's only the two of us. Look only at me."

After the short two measure introduction, she forced out the first few notes. True to his word, Drake's baritone drowned out her whispered soprano. She concentrated on the lyrics and, remembering Drake's words, pretended to sing only to him.

Her voice grew smoother, more confident, and soon she found it blending with Drake's, who reduced his volume and changed from melody to a harmony that complemented her voice to perfection.

Like re-reading a well-loved story, she knew how the ballad ended. Tears formed in her eyes as she pictured little Mary's beloved William dressed in rags before her to test the endurance of her love.

Her throat clogged again toward the end, this time not from fear, but from heartfelt emotion. Vision blurring, she gazed at Drake, willing him to see the truth in her eyes.

CHAPTER 9

Drake clenched his fists as they finished the last verse of the blasted song. What was Simon playing at? He would have more than words with his *friend* later. Perhaps he'd suggest a wrestling match as one of *the duke's* games.

Not a moment too soon, they finished the song to rousing applause and shouts of "Another! Another!"

Tears glistened in Honoria's eyes, and one slipped down her cheek.

His hand twitched with the urge to catch it on his fingertip. To *throw the patch from his eye* as William had and confess all to her.

Yet he did not. Not with her father scowling at them, murder written on his face.

On second thought, he might take great satisfaction in setting the old man off. But it would be at Honoria's expense, and she was already suffering from Simon's meddling.

Before he could act upon his impulse, she hastily brushed the tear away. As stalwart as ever, she remained, at all times, a proper English lady.

"You did it," he whispered. And she did; her angelic voice, clear and pure, had melded with his so naturally one would presume they had sung together for ages.

The tremulous smile she gave him set his heart lurching. "Shall we give them another? Something less melodramatic?" He grinned at her, announcing loudly. "A bawdy sea shanty, perhaps?"

She rewarded his attempt to cheer her by emitting a little laugh, then wiped her face again.

"Ah, my bad joke has brought Lady Honoria to tears. It might be best for someone else to take the reins."

More applause met them as they parted. Honoria mouthed a quiet *thank you* then returned to her group of friends. Drake sought refuge away from Simon, who was currently surrounded by a gaggle of women. Still at the piano, Lady Montgomery selected a more complicated piece, one for which she truly needed her husband to turn the pages, and the crowd seemed appeased.

"That was most gallant of you, Mr. Merrick," a feminine voice whispered.

Drake turned, finding the Duke and Duchess of Ashton next to him. He'd had little interaction with the unconventional duke and duchess so far, but Simon imparted that Drake would find staunch supporters in them—once he revealed his true identity. From the gentle kindness shining in the duchess's eyes, Drake believed it to be true.

"Gallant, Your Grace? For singing a song? Off-key at that."

The duchess's tight-lipped smile was much like one his mother delivered when she'd caught him in an untruth. "I suspect you know very well of which I speak. Although I promise your secret is safe with me. However, my curiosity is piqued that you would know Lady Honoria so well to understand her reluctance to perform in public."

Had the duchess heard the salacious rumors about them Honoria had mentioned? Or perhaps less despicable and more accurate, had his feelings been that transparent? And if so, and a veritable stranger such as the duchess noticed it, no doubt Honoria had as well, not to mention her parents. "I have a talent for sensing another's moods, Your Grace. Lady Honoria appeared distraught over the prospect of singing."

"Hmm," the duchess said, obviously unconvinced.

"Forgive my wife, Mr. Merrick," Ashton said. "She's a known

matchmaker—although other than our own happy marriage and that of her dear friend Camilla, she hasn't had much success as of late."

"Success for what?" Simon's annoying voice came from behind.

Drake turned to glare at him—thankfully with his back to the duke and duchess. "Your Grace, I didn't see you there."

"I wanted to compliment you on your magnificent rendition. Such a touching song, wouldn't you say, Ashton? Duchess? It was as if Merrick and Lady Honoria meant every word."

Drake narrowed his eyes at Simon, willing him to read his thoughts and go to the devil.

Simon, per usual, ignored him. "You were saying something about success, Ashton."

Worried he appeared rude, Drake turned back to the duke and duchess, the latter who continued to study him intently.

"I was telling Merrick that my wife enjoys dabbling in matchmaking, but without the greatest success."

"Oh?" Simon said, shooting Drake an irritatingly superior glance. "Any prospects here that might result in a more favorable outcome?"

The duchess's gaze flicked toward him. Then she turned her attention to Simon. "Word has it, sir, that you are seeking a bride yourself. At least that's what the gossip rags say."

Simon leaned in, grinning wickedly. "Have you selected someone for me, madam?"

"You seemed rather taken with Lady Honoria at supper last evening," she said.

Drake's insides burned. "Yes. You did, Your Grace." Hopefully, only Simon detected the sarcasm imbuing the last two words.

"She *is* lovely and has a voice of an angel. Once Merrick didn't drown her out, that is."

Drake wanted to plant his friend a facer. "She was nervous, Your Grace. I merely attempted to sing loudly enough to put her at ease. Perhaps you might think twice before volunteering people to sing for your enjoyment."

Drat. The shock on the duchess's face told him he had overstepped —at least as far as she was concerned, given the fact she thought Simon truly was the new duke. "Forgive me, Your Graces. I apologize for my abruptness and ill manners. It's simply that Simon and I have been on more equal footing until recently, and I sometimes forget my place."

Ashton's blond eyebrow quirked. "Simon?" He turned toward Simon. "I thought your Christian name was Pierce?"

Damnation! Drake shifted uncomfortably, darting a glance toward the door and a promise of escape before everything crumbled around his ears.

His fury at Simon eased as *his friend* hurried to salvage Drake's faux pas. "It is, Ashton. However, I was raised with the name Simon. My mother and stepfather thought to shield me from my grandfather's rejection."

Neither Ashton nor his wife appeared completely convinced. "Of course," the duchess said. "It all must be difficult for you, becoming accustomed to a new name and a whole different life."

Which reminded Drake about Aunt Kitty's imminent arrival. He needed to speak with Simon and develop a strategy. But at the moment, he needed quiet more. "As I've put my foot in it enough for one afternoon, allow me to excuse myself to attend to some of the duke's business." He turned toward Simon. "When you have a free moment, Your Grace, there is a matter of importance we need to discuss. But it can wait while you attend to your guests."

Ashton and the duchess murmured their assent. Drake didn't wait for Simon's permission, but hurried from the room. He'd barely made it through the doors when a male voice stopped him.

"Mr. Merrick, a word, if you please."

Drake spun on his heel, ready to tell whoever it was he bloody well didn't have time. He reeled in his anger at the sight of Ashton.

"Of course, Your Grace. Again, I apologize for my egregious behavior toward the duke. I spoke out of turn."

Ashton waved it aside. "Not to worry. From my perspective, you had the right of it. Perhaps my wife is correct in her observations, and you are more familiar with Lady Honoria than one would imagine. She mentioned your father was the steward on Stratford's estate in Somerset."

"Stepfather." Why did Drake feel the need to clarify that?

Ashton's brows hitched. "But that's not why I stopped you. I thought it best not to mention this within earshot of others, but I've written to Dr. Somersby about possible treatments for malaria." He cocked his head. "Burwood mentioned it last night at supper. It's none of my affair, but as a physician, I feel I must ask. Does one of you suffer from the ailment?"

Unrest twisted in Drake's gut like a nest of vipers. Simon needed help, and he'd heard the duke ascribed to less barbaric and more scientific methods of treatment. Added to the fact that he'd established a free medical clinic for the poor of London, Drake believed him to be trustworthy. And if Simon spoke to him about it . . .

"I appreciate your discretion. We haven't been back in England long, but I understand the scandal sheets would delight in such information."

"Indeed. It's the type of tasty morsel *The Muckraker* would love to chew on." Ashton cocked his head. "So my suspicions are correct? One of you suffers?"

"My friend tries to put on a brave front, but I've seen him in the throes of the illness. Doctors have disagreed about its severity and ultimate outcome. But he has episodes of fever and weakness lasting for days. Then all appears to return to normal."

"Hmm." The duke rubbed his chin with his forefinger. "When was his last episode?"

"Before returning to England. About four months ago. They had been occurring about three months apart."

"Interesting. Alice Weatherby's father spent large periods of time in India for his business. I shall write to him as well to see if he has any additional information which might prove useful."

"We would be most grateful, Your Grace."

Ashton appeared to contemplate something.

"Anything else, Your Grace?"

He shook his head. "I should let you get back to your business."

Drake nodded and hurried toward the staircase. Grateful to finally be away from the crowds, but hopeful that the unconventional duke would provide a remedy for his friend.

As much as she disliked large crowds, for once Honoria was grateful for the cover it provided. Wedged between Miranda and Charlotte, she ignored her father's disapproving stare.

Anne squeezed herself between Charlotte and Honoria. "Oh, Honny, that was the most beautiful song. I didn't know you could sing like that."

Charlotte's scowl mirrored Honoria's father's. "Would you please stop referring to Honoria with that ridiculous name, Anne?"

"Careful, Charlotte, or she'll come up with one for you." Mischief glinted in Miranda's eyes.

Anne grinned. "What about Charlie?"

"And I suppose I would be Randy or some such nonsense. Seriously, Anne, Charlotte's right. How do you expect a man to take you seriously?"

"Mr. Merrick doesn't seem to have a problem with my exuberance, as he described it." Anne exhaled a heavy sigh. "He sings divinely. It's as if he were singing only to me."

Honoria jerked back. Drake had held her gaze throughout the song. Hadn't he? Of course, she *had* closed her eyes a few times to concentrate.

"Now you're imagining things as well as being foolish," Charlotte said. "Mr. Merrick's concentration remained solely on Honoria."

Miranda studied her closely. "Yes, it did. It was almost as if he knew about your fear of singing publicly."

Honoria scrambled for a viable explanation. "He more than likely sensed my trepidation. I worry I may have been trembling horribly."

Miranda found Honoria's hand and squeezed. "Only a little at first. Once you began singing, no one would have known. I'm so proud of you."

"As am I," Charlotte said. "Still, someone should have a few words with Burwood for volunteering you like that. That was most insensitive." She stared in the direction of the new duke and frowned. "He needs to understand how things are done in polite society." A determination Honoria was well acquainted with shone in Charlotte's eyes.

"Charlotte, don't do anything rash," Honoria said.

Charlotte's gaze softened when she turned it back toward Honoria. "I'm concerned about you, Honoria. The duke seems quite interested in you. If he's planning on making you his duchess, then he needs to understand he can't embarrass you like that again."

Before Honoria could stop her, Charlotte marched off in the direction of Burwood.

"Oh, dear," Honoria muttered. "When Charlotte's ire is up, she becomes like a storm at sea."

Thank heavens Drake had left the small group comprising Burwood and the Duke and Duchess of Ashton. Then Ashton excused himself, leaving Burwood and Her Grace alone.

Honoria held her breath as Burwood's grin vanished upon Charlotte's appearance before him. She could imagine the conversation as she watched it play out before her.

Unlike Burwood, Charlotte had been carefully schooled in proper etiquette, and Honoria would venture to say, among all their friends, Charlotte held to the *rules* more closely than the lot of them. After nodding to the duchess, she tapped Burwood on the arm with her fan and led him to the side—no doubt to deliver her set down, all done so skillfully as to not even hint of an actual insult. Often people were unaware Charlotte had insulted them until days later.

Burwood glanced toward Honoria, then back to Charlotte. He held his hand to his chest and affected a countenance most aggrieved.

Oh, dear. Perhaps, in this case, Charlotte had been more direct.

When Charlotte turned to leave him, Honoria caught the slight tweak of his lips and shake of his head.

Charlotte huffed as she rejoined them. "Duke or not, that man is most disagreeable. I would caution you, Honoria, if you are considering him as a husband."

"As long as she's not considering Mr. Merrick," Anne said, then sighed dreamily.

"Did I hear that odious man's name mentioned?"

Honoria jumped at her father's tenor. "Father, Mr. Merrick isn't odious."

"He really isn't, Lord Stratford," Anne said, the dreamy look swimming in her eyes again. "I find him wonderful."

"Hmph. Then may I suggest you bring him up to scratch and keep him away from my daughter?"

Miranda and Charlotte exchanged a glance, indicating they would have questions later.

Questions Honoria truly didn't want to answer.

"Father, did you want something?" The question snapped out more forcefully than she intended.

He cast his gaze toward her companions, then, perhaps reconsidering chastising her in front of them, shook his head. "Only to suggest your time will be better served in the company of Burwood and not his man of business."

"It was at Burwood's request Dra—Mr. Merrick and I sing the duet. I could hardly refuse him."

Her father grunted again. "Nevertheless, take care not to be drawn into bad company." With that, he turned and left them.

Anne stared at his retreating back, her eyes wide. "Whatever on earth does your father have against Mr. Merrick?"

Miranda met Honoria's gaze directly. "Anne, would you please go tell my brother to stop making a display of himself in front of everyone?"

Everyone in their little group, including Honoria, turned their attention to Lord Montgomery as he toyed with a lock of Lady Montgomery's hair, his fingers trailing along her neck.

"Why should I do that? He's your brother."

"Because he won't listen to me," Miranda said with enough assurance that, after blinking twice, Anne strolled over to the piano where Lady Montgomery continued to play. She frowned as she cast a glance back at them over her shoulder.

"Now," Miranda said. "What is this about Mr. Merrick?"

CHAPTER 10

Drake slammed the door of his bedchamber, then stomped to his bed. After making several circular passes next to it, he allowed his body to fall onto the soft mattress.

"Simon, you cur!"

His hands curled into fists, and he punched the pillow next to him. Feathers flew out and floated down, one landing on his nose.

"Achoo!" No doubt to taunt him, the feather flew upward only to land again on his nose. With his forefinger and thumb, he picked it off, only to be fascinated with its softness. He rolled the delicate fluff through his fingers, remembering something even softer.

Unable to resist, he rose from the bed and strode to his dressing table. Retrieving the locket, he opened it. For eight long years, a piece of auburn hair had rested inside. Coarse string tied the precious keepsake together at one end, the rough texture's contrast only enhancing the silkiness of what it held. He pulled the soft red strands through his fingers.

With no effort, the memory rose as clearly as if he were experiencing it that very moment, and a dull ache gripped his chest.

They'd been riding as usual, stopping under a shady group of tall oaks. She'd been singing softly as they rode, her voice so sweet, he thought he'd never heard anything quite so beautiful.

Her cheeks grew rosy when she caught him staring at her.

When he helped her down from her mount, he'd held her waist a little too long. "You sing like an angel."

"Oh, no." She shook her head, the color on her face deepening further. "I didn't realize you could hear me."

He said something stupid then. What was it? Oh, yes. "I have the ears of a fox."

She laughed, the sound almost as sweet as her singing. "I like your ears."

And then she touched him, his ears, his face, his lips, her delicate fingers sending a shock of pleasure through him.

"My lady." His words, choked with emotion, tumbled out. "I must tell you something."

"What is it? You're not leaving Overton House?" Her browed furrowed, and he yearned to smooth it with a kiss.

"I have no intention of leaving you—ever—if I can help it. I have grown so very fond of you."

Her lovely green eyes, wide and innocent, searched his. A tiny smile tilted her lips. "As I have you." She blushed again and turned away. "I look forward to our rides and our discussions of books. In fact"—she toyed with Buttercup's reins—"it is my favorite part of the day. I wish . . ."

He stepped closer, daring to hope she felt what he did. "Wish what? You can speak freely to me. No one else can hear but the birds and woodland creatures."

"I wish my entire day could be spent in your presence."

He'd lain awake the entire night before, practicing the words he longed to say, longing to make them eloquent, as was befitting a lady of her station. She deserved poetry and music, and . . . all the things he could not give her. But what he could give her, he offered wholeheartedly.

Gently, he grasped her arm and turned her toward him. Then, cupping her face with a callused palm, and forgetting his rehearsed words, he poured out his heart. "I love you, Lady Honoria. With my whole being. I don't have anything to offer you but myself, but if you could consider being my wi—"

She propelled herself into his arms, pressing her face against his chest. "I love you so much, Drake."

His heart soared at her words, and, using his forefinger, he tilted her chin up. Tentatively at first, he brushed his lips against hers, but when she didn't pull away, he kissed her more earnestly. "I will speak with your father. I promise I will do what I must to provide for you."

"I don't care where we live, as long as we're together." Removing the locket around her neck, she handed it to him, allowing him to cut a piece of her hair as her own promise.

Two loud knocks at the door shook him from the bittersweet memory. Quickly, he placed the lock of Honoria's hair back into its resting place, closing the locket with a *click*, the sound reminiscent of his heart shattering when—days after he professed his love—she broke her promise and rejected him.

"Come," he called, not really willing to speak to anyone.

Least of all Simon, who strode in as if all was right in the world—when everything most definitely was . . . not.

"What do you want?" Bitterness drenched Drake's question.

Simon raised a dark eyebrow. "You said you needed to speak with me. Some matter of importance."

Oh, yes. Aunt Kitty. But first, he would express his displeasure in volunteering Honoria to sing. "Did you forget that I told you Honoria has a fear of singing in front of people? What is wrong with you?"

Simon had the gall to look affronted. "I thought you exaggerated. I hoped to bring her out of her shell. She is rather shy."

"Shy? Shy?! She's terrified when put on display like that. No doubt from her father's lofty and unrealistic expectations." He tightened his grip on the locket.

"It all worked out. You both sounded marvelous. Well, she did. You, on the other hand, sounded like a howling—"

Drake grabbed Simon by the cravat. "If you ever do anything like that to her again, I'll strangle you with my bare hands."

Simon batted Drake's hand away. "You'll have to wait in line. Lady

Charlotte threatened me first. If she wasn't so beautiful, I'd swear she was the devil's spawn."

"Lady Charlotte Talbot?" Simon's description of the lady triggered a hint of something useful in Drake's mind.

"Is there another Lady Charlotte present? That obnoxious man, Lord Middlebury, seems quite fond of her, or at least her brother. Personally, I find her cold and peevish."

Momentarily forgetting his own anger with Simon, Drake barely resisted the chuckle. "Do you now?"

"Well, yes. Perhaps her corset is laced too tightly, or—" Simon's gaze snapped to Drake's. "How did we end up talking about that ice queen? Not that I want to be chastised by you. I apologize if I upset Honoria. I'm only trying to help."

"Help? I neither want nor need the type of help you provide."

"Open your eyes, man. The woman still loves you. It was written on her face. Imbued in every word she sang. I dare say if you just tell her the truth, she could be in your arms by nightfall."

Drake ground his teeth so hard he feared he would crack a molar. How would Simon ever understand? "And I *told* you. I want a woman to want me for *me*."

Simon rolled his eyes. "She does, man. She doesn't know you're actually Burwood."

"And did you forget about her father? Flames practically shot from the man's eyes upon seeing me singing with his precious daughter. She's a bargaining tool for him. A way to continue to exert his power."

"Are you still allowing him to come between you?"

"Allow? Have you forgotten? Honoria made her choice eight years ago. I doubt that's changed. Her father still holds sway over her."

"You don't know that! And who are you trying to woo? Honoria or her father!"

When had their voices escalated to shouting? Drake ran a shaking hand down his face. The memory resurrected the insecure, rejected boy standing before the man who told him he wasn't good enough. That he would ruin his daughter's life. It would crush him to go through that again. "Can we please cease discussing Honoria? I have something else of importance to share with you, and we may not have much time."

"Time for what?"

"Aunt Kitty."

Simon's confused expression was almost comical. "Your aunt or mine?"

"You have an Aunt Kitty?"

After an insouciant shrug, he said, "Not that I'm aware of."

The man was insufferable. "Simon, I need you to be serious for once in your ridiculous life. Apparently I have an Aunt Kitty. Great aunt, to be exact. I'm not sure how she is related since her surname is Dickens. I received a letter from her before you finagled me into singing with Honoria."

"I told you, I was trying to—"

"Help. Yes, yes. Let's not start that again. What's important is she's coming here to meet me—you—Burwood." Drake strode to the dressing table, retrieved the letter, then thrust it at Simon. "Read it."

While Simon read the letter, Drake paced in front of him.

Finished, Simon peered up. "I don't see a problem."

"She's familiar with the family. What if she starts questioning you?"

He gave another careless shrug. "I'll answer her questions. So far, no one has caused a problem—except you. What's the meaning of calling me Simon in front of Ashton?"

"It was a slip. But that's precisely why I'm worried about Aunt Kitty—whoever the hell she is. What if she knows more about my background—like my mother's name and, more importantly, that she married Francis Merrick after my father's death?"

"How can she know that?"

"They tracked me down, didn't they? I honestly didn't think there were any living relatives left but me." He fell lifelessly into a wingback by the window, and he stared at the rain streaming down the panes of glass.

"Let's not panic quite yet. Perhaps we should tell Frampton to isolate dear Aunt Kitty in a parlor as soon as she arrives."

Drake straightened in his chair, returning his attention to Simon. "We can't keep her there the entire time."

"No. But we can speak to her. Determine how much she knows. Then, depending on what we learn, we can panic." He studied Drake. "Or you can come clean now and save us all more trouble. As much as I enjoy playing the all powerful duke, it's starting to tire me. And"—he grinned—"although women have been most attentive, I've yet to receive one indecent proposal. You made it sound like women would be throwing themselves at me."

Drake stared in disbelief. "Why must everything be about you?"

"Wasn't that the whole point of this farce? To see which woman would be worthy to marry you? Which would not be swayed by a title and power and would care for the man within?" His usually ebullient demeanor vanished, and he grew serious. "I think you have your answer to that, although you refuse to admit it. But perhaps if you don't want her, I might—"

With more energy than he'd felt in days, Drake bolted from the chair. "Don't you even think about pursuing Honoria in earnest. She deserves better than a rake like you."

"And you said you don't care what she thinks." Simon had the audacity to smirk. "If there's nothing else you wish to discuss, I'll leave you to ponder that for a while."

Without another word, Simon left, closing the door behind him.

The locket still in Drake's hand heated, as if it, too, accused him of denying his feelings.

WITH ANNE PREOCCUPIED WITH LORD AND LADY MONTGOMERY, Charlotte and Miranda ushered Honoria from the room and into the hallway.

Surprised at both the strength and urgency her friends exhibited, Honoria was too taken off guard to resist.

"How didn't I see it before?" Miranda shook her head. Several locks of her chestnut hair broke free from their pins and fell loosely against her neck.

"To be fair, she's spent little time in his presence for us to notice. But now . . ." Charlotte turned her probing brown eyes on Honoria.

"Honoria, either tell us the truth or we will join Anne in calling you Honny."

Honoria did hate that ridiculous sobriquet. However, before assuming the worst and confessing, she opted for bewilderment. "Truth about what? You both already know I have an aversion to performing publicly."

Miranda made a *pfft* sound. "You know perfectly well we're referring to Mr. Merrick. At supper last evening, he mentioned his father served as steward at your father's estate. And you almost slipped and called him by his Christian name in front of your father. He's the man in the gossip reports. The one who broke your heart."

Strange that Miranda should phrase it like that rather than focusing on the scandal insinuating Drake had taken her innocence.

"It has to be," Charlotte added. "The way you looked at him when you were both singing. It's obvious you still have feelings for him."

"My feelings don't signify."

Her friends exchanged an ominous look.

Charlotte, being the less subtle of the two, took the helm in the interrogation. "Of course they signify. You must tell Anne so she will cease her nonsense. In her mind, she's already dragged the poor man to the altar and produced several children."

Miranda softened the attack. "What my dear friend is trying to say is don't allow Anne to get her hopes up for an attachment with Mr. Merrick if his heart lies elsewhere. As your friend, she would want to know you hope to rekindle your relationship with him."

Did she hope to rekindle things? Of course she did. But did Drake? Wouldn't he say something if he still loved her? "I have no idea where Mr. Merrick's heart lies. Perhaps he does seek an attachment with Anne." The thought alone pressed on her like a crushing weight.

The soft *pfft* came from Miranda again.

Charlotte raised a dark brow. "What *my* dear friend is not saying is that is hogwash. And if my brother Nash were here, he'd use a much stronger term." She glanced over her shoulder, no doubt confirming Anne would not appear at an inopportune moment. "For all her faults, I like Anne. But Mr. Merrick is much too serious for her. Why, at supper last evening, he only talked about books. I would say that he is the perfect man for you."

That much was true. No one since had measured up, much to her parents' dismay. Even if they hadn't been enamored with other women, as kind and agreeable as Dr. Marbry and Lord Nash had been, they simply weren't Drake.

Honoria sighed. The need to confide in her friends overwhelmed her. "Very well. Yes. Mr. Merrick—Drake—was the groom at my father's estate, and we pledged ourselves to each other. But my mother convinced me it would be a mistake to marry him, and the next thing I knew, Drake had signed up for the military and was gone. I never expected to see him here, of all places."

The hopeful expressions on her friends' faces broke her heart. Even Charlotte emitted an uncharacteristic sigh.

"Then you absolutely must tell him you still care," Miranda said.

Charlotte agreed. "Let us help arrange a meeting between the two of you. Somewhere quiet where you can talk alone and uninterrupted."

Honoria blinked at her friend's suggestion. "You of all people, Charlotte? Do I even know you?"

A sly grin crossed Charlotte's lips. "Perhaps not."

"It would be for naught. I've already spoken to Drake alone. Last evening I encountered him when I slipped into the library for a moment's peace. He also came in seeking refuge."

Miranda stepped closer. "And?"

"Mine wasn't the only heart broken. I fear he still hasn't forgiven me for rejecting him. He made it clear that he's put the past behind him."

"But you haven't," Miranda said.

"No," Honoria admitted. "But I should. If he has a chance at happiness with someone else, whether it be Anne or another, who am I to stand in his way?"

Once more, her friends exchanged a glance, and Honoria feared they did not believe her.

But to be honest, she didn't believe herself.

CHAPTER 11

Mercifully, Simon refrained from any more attempts to throw Drake and Honoria together. At supper that evening, Drake found himself seated across from Ashton and the duchess. Mrs. Weatherby sat on Drake's left, and Lady Miranda Townsend on his right.

Seated to Victor Pratt's right, Honoria appeared to converse with him comfortably. With each smile or tiny laugh she graced the amiable young man with, jealousy—visceral and sour—ripped through Drake. Across from her, Honoria's father seemed to pay more attention to his daughter than the delicious food in front of him. What Drake couldn't discern was if Stratford approved or disapproved of Lord Cartwright's son and heir.

He needed to focus on something other than Honoria. "I understand you've also spent time in India, Mrs. Weatherby. Might you know of a place to purchase the spices that make many of their dishes so wonderfully delicious?"

"Oh, ho! Now you've won favor in my wife's eyes, sir," Mr. Weatherby said.

Drake blinked. One would think enquiring about spices was a mundane topic of conversation.

"What my husband means, sir, is my father and my husband are in the business of supplying items from India to interested parties. We offer the finest quality of silks and spices. However, my father's shop is some distance away in Kent."

"Does he provide transportation for purchases?"

"I'm sure that could be arranged. However, if Burwood is amenable, we would welcome you both into our home should you prefer to travel and see the inventory for yourselves."

"Kent is lovely this time of year, Mr. Merrick," the duchess said. "My husband's seat is there. You would also be welcome to stay with us."

"Indeed, Merrick," Ashton said. "Although I will admit we're not there as often as one would expect from a duke. I find myself in London most of the year."

"At your clinic?"

Ashton nodded and took a sip of his wine. "But should you decide to travel when we're in London, I will leave word with the staff remaining there to provide you the warmest of welcomes."

Drake wasn't entirely sure what to expect from the members of the *ton* when he arrived back in England. Well, that wasn't precisely true. He expected an icy reception for a man raised as a commoner, but if the house party was any indication, things weren't as bad as he feared.

Oh, there were still some who obviously fawned over Simon disingenuously—Lord Middlebury being one of them. Stratford barely contained his own disdain, except when it came to his opinion of Drake. That clearly had not changed.

And therein lay the problem.

Even if Honoria professed her love for him as Drake Merrick, man of business, would her father's objection persuade her to reject him as it had eight years prior?

"You appear far away, Mr. Merrick." Lady Miranda gazed at him with concern. "I do hope wherever it is, it's somewhere pleasant." She turned slightly and looked in Honoria's direction.

How much did she suspect?

The tiny smile flitting across her lips answered his question.

Throughout the remainder of the meal, Drake used all his

willpower to *not* gaze in Honoria's direction. Instead, he decided the best course of action was to become better acquainted with the other ladies present. Perhaps one would capture his interest and drive Honoria from his mind.

After supper, while everyone gathered in the largest drawing room, Drake did his best to circulate and speak with the eligible ladies. The mental list dwindled as he crossed several off. Lydia Whyte was too much of a flirt. He worried he wouldn't be able to trust her. Even at that moment, she was gazing at Victor Pratt with the same ardor she'd exhibited toward Drake the evening before. The same could be true for Anne Weatherby.

As for Lady Miranda, as Simon noted upon their introduction, she was agreeable and certainly pretty. Yet even at supper, he sensed she had no attraction to him. And more importantly, she had apparently seen through his thinly veiled interest in Honoria.

Lady Charlotte was a possibility. But he had his doubts she would be interested in a man who wasn't titled.

Who was he fooling? No matter the lady, he would find some reason to cross her off his list of possible brides. The sheer fact she wasn't Honoria would be sufficient.

However, perhaps he could glean some information regarding Stratford's hold on Honoria from her friends.

Scanning the room, he saw Lady Charlotte speaking with the toady Middlebury.

Perhaps she might actually appreciate a rescue. To quote Willie Shakespeare, *We must take the current when it serves, or lose our ventures.*

As he strode over to Lady Charlotte, Lord Middlebury glanced up from licking crumbs from his fingers, then reached for a glass of sherry on a tray a footman held. The frown on the man's face chilled the air.

On the other hand, Lady Charlotte seemed genuinely happy to see him. "Mr. Merrick!" She glanced askance at Middlebury. "I'm so happy you decided to join us."

He could only imagine. "I'm trying to circulate and make sure all of Burwood's guests are enjoying themselves. I trust you both are."

If it were possible for Middlebury to look down his nose at Drake, even though the man was a good seven or eight inches shorter, the expression he bore was the equivalent. "Merrick." He nodded, then turned his complete attention toward Lady Charlotte as if Drake weren't even there.

"Everything is perfect, Mr. Merrick. I must compliment you. I understand you handle most of the arrangements for the duke."

"I do my best. Did you enjoy the lamb this evening?" he asked.

"I did," she said. "The seasoning was quite unique."

"It's my mother's recipe. She developed it after I sent her spices from India where I served in the military. I was pleased to find that the Weatherbys have access to the spices, as my supply is nearly gone."

Middlebury wrinkled his nose. "A bit too spicy for my taste. I shall be up all night with indigestion."

"Nonsense, Lord Middlebury," Charlotte said. "You cleaned your plate well enough."

Oh, ho! The lady has wit. Whatever was Simon's problem?

She turned a pretty smile toward Drake. "I would love if you could provide me the recipe. That's if your mother doesn't wish it to remain a secret?"

"She would be honored such a fine lady has requested it." He seized the opportunity before the tides changed. "Perhaps we can discuss it now. Would you take a turn about the room with me?"

Gratitude shone in her dark brown eyes. "I would be delighted. Would you excuse us, Lord Middlebury?"

Without waiting for Middlebury's answer, Drake motioned for Charlotte to precede him.

A grunted *hmph* sounded behind them as they walked away.

"Did you truly want my mother's recipe, or was that your way of escaping Lord Middlebury?"

She laughed, an action he was quite certain she didn't perform lightly. "You have seen through me. But I do truly want the recipe. That's if I can convince my brother's cook to use it. My brother is more like Middlebury, bland food and all."

"I noticed your brother is not in attendance. He's well, I hope."

Her gaze flitted to his, then sheered away. "I have two brothers. My brother Nash now lives in America with his wife, so it would be difficult for him to attend. But he is quite well. And happy."

"And the other? He's the marquess, is he not?"

"He is, sir." She pursed her lips, still not meeting his gaze.

"You can speak freely with me."

She stopped walking and gave him her full attention. "Yes. I believe I can. I like you, Mr. Merrick. You carry yourself well. If I may be so bold, you have the makings of a duke more than Burwood. It's a pity your roles are not reversed."

Drake froze. Had she ferreted out their scheme? No, it wasn't possible. Was it? "At times, I believe Simon would agree with you."

"Simon? I thought his Christian name was Pierce?"

Drat! He'd done it again. What had Simon said to Ashton and the duchess? *Ah, yes.* "It is. But his stepfather called him Simon to shield him from the sting of his grandfather's rejection."

Lady Charlotte looked less convinced than the duke and duchess had. "Odd." She shrugged. "Still, it is of no consequence to me. I intend to avoid him as much as possible." She turned a brilliant smile on Drake, making him suspicious. "You, on the other hand, are most delightful company."

"And your brother? The marquess? You didn't answer my question. I hope his absence isn't due to illness."

"Another reason I like you, Mr. Merrick. You don't tiptoe around things like most people of my acquaintance. Direct and to the point. I admire that. Since we're speaking freely, no, he isn't indisposed. But he is, shall we say, less welcoming to newly minted members of the peerage—regardless of their bloodline."

"So he's giving Burwood the cut?"

She shrugged again. "In a matter of speaking."

"And yet, you're here."

She pursed her lips. "He's my brother, but that doesn't mean I agree with him. However, I suspect that's why Middlebury has been hovering like a pesky insect. Not only to keep an eye on me, but to report back to my brother. So once again, I thank you for your intervention."

Perhaps Lady Charlotte could be an ally, countering Stratford's objections and persuading Honoria to stand her ground. A genuine smile tugged at his lips, and the words he delivered were heartfelt. "My pleasure."

They'd almost made the full circuit around the room, nearing the place where Middlebury stood alone.

She slowed her steps, and Drake reduced his long stride to match hers. "If we're being completely honest with each other, Mr. Merrick, might I enquire as to your intentions toward Lady Honoria?"

At that, he stopped completely. "My intentions?"

She faced him fully. "Let me be clear. Lady Honoria is my dear friend. I don't want to see her hurt. She's admitted to me and Lady Miranda about your previous . . . *friendship*."

He tamped down his anger at the suggestion he would hurt Honoria, when he risked his own heart. "Friendship?" He choked on the word. "Is that what she called it?" Was that all it had become to her?

"I'm trying to be delicate, Mr. Merrick."

He wiped a hand down his face. "Honoria—forgive me—*Lady* Honoria made it clear eight years ago severing our relationship was— in her words—*for the best*."

"That was eight years ago. Her parents no doubt objected because—"

"Because I wasn't good enough for her. And still would, I surmise. Have no fear for your friend, Lady Charlotte. Lady Honoria's heart is safe from me."

His idea to gauge Honoria's interest misfired on him with unexpected force. As rude as it was, he started walking again, anxious to return her to Lord Middlebury and remove himself from the interrogation about Honoria.

But as luck would have it, moments after he reached his destination, Stratford slithered like a snake toward him.

"Merrick. I demand a word." Foregoing any semblance of courtesy or politeness, Stratford forced his way in front of Drake, the look in his eyes deadly. His icy tone alone sent a shiver of unease down Drake's spine.

Drake stared at the man, who, years ago, he hoped would be his father-in-law. Back then, he'd liked Stratford. He'd been a fair and generous employer to Drake and his stepfather, treating them with respect.

At least until Drake had asked for Honoria's hand. Then everything had changed in the man's eyes. Instead of a loyal, trustworthy, and dependable groom, Drake became a fortune-seeking scoundrel, only intent on soiling the marquess's daughter's reputation for the sake of money.

The man couldn't have been more wrong. Other than a few kisses —albeit wonderful, exciting kisses—Drake had never laid a hand on Honoria. He loved and respected her too much. Even eight years later, he still hadn't sullied his love for her by being with another woman.

A fact Simon never failed to tease him about at every opportunity.

And as far as Honoria's dowry, he hadn't given a fig about it other than it would provide her with some of the comforts to which she was accustomed. And in direct opposition to the law, he would have insisted she retain complete control over it. He wanted none of it.

Stratford had called him a liar, going so far as to dangle a commission in the cavalry in front of him. "To better yourself without destroying my daughter," the man had said. Drake had refused, at least until Honoria had rejected him. Then he accepted, if only to get as far away from her and his heartbreak as possible.

But nothing had changed. Stratford's current haughty demand confirmed it. The man still despised him.

The feeling was mutual.

"What is it, Stratford?" Drake hoped his delivery had been equally cold.

The man arched a brow. "As Burwood's man of business, I would suggest you address members of the peerage appropriately."

"Very well. What do you want, *Lord* Stratford?"

"If you care at all about my daughter's reputation, stay away from her. I'll not have that nasty gossip dredged up again." Delivered with the same coolness, his demand was clear as the fine crystal currently holding the glasses of sherry.

"Would you have me refuse Burwood? It was at his request I sang with Lady Honoria."

"Hmph. I have no objection to you following orders. It was the way you were looking at her I have issue with."

"And just *how* was I supposed to look at her? It was a love song."

"You didn't have to look like you meant it."

Drake threw his hands in the air, uncomfortably aware of Lord and Lady Montgomery observing the spectacle unfolding before them. "Was I supposed to glare at her? As her father, you must have known she was terrified. I was trying to put her at ease."

At this, the marquess's expression softened. His gaze momentarily jerked away.

If Drake were any other man, he might have even received an apology from Stratford.

Instead, the man mumbled, "I'd forgotten."

He'd forgotten?! His own daughter's paralyzing fear? "You should be proud of her. She fought through it like a good soldier, slaying her demons and performing beautifully."

Stratford's gaze darted away, unfocused and dreamy. "She did, didn't she?"

A father's love shone in the man's eyes. Drake couldn't deny it, much as he wished to. It was easier to hate the man if Drake believed Stratford truly didn't care about his own flesh and blood's happiness.

But he did—at least his perception of what would make Honoria happy, misguided as that might be.

Drake's anger abated. "Put your mind to rest, Lord Stratford. I am not pursuing Lady Honoria. As you so accurately point out, I am simply Burwood's man of business, here to ensure the duke's transition into society runs smoothly."

Stratford gave a jerk to his head that Drake supposed was a nod.

Before he could remove himself from the uncomfortable situation, Honoria appeared at her father's side. "Mother is asking for you."

Drake's gaze tangled with hers, catching the slightest twitch of her lips. She'd always been a horrible liar.

Had she come to rescue him from her father's wrath? He did his best to hide the love bursting in his heart—especially after his pronouncement to her father.

Luckily, the man's attention was on Honoria, for Drake failed miserably.

As she led her father away, Drake mouthed the words *thank you.*

Her tremulous smile made the confrontation with Lord Stratford worth it.

"What was that all about?" Simon shook him from his stupor.

"Nothing. Just Stratford delivering his usual warning to leave Honoria alone."

Surprisingly, Simon didn't pursue it with his usual dare to defy the man. "Frampton just alerted me that Aunt Kitty has arrived. She's waiting in the rose parlor. Not very patiently from the way Frampton described it."

Drake pulled down on the front of his coat. "Then let us charge into the fray."

On their way, they discussed their strategy, and Drake reminded Simon of the family particulars.

"I know. I know," Simon said. "It's you who will have to remember to call me Pierce if necessary."

"No." Drake shook his head. "It's you who don't remember. As your man of business, I should only be calling you Your Grace or Burwood. Aunt Kitty would surely pick up on the slight."

"Right." Simon grinned. "I think I like that part."

Unsure what to expect when they entered the parlor, Drake prepared himself for a frail octogenarian.

Aunt Kitty was anything but. Although she leaned upon a walking stick—a gnarled, arthritic hand clutching the polished mahogany handle—her eyes were as sharp as a hawk's. Lined with age, her face seemed to crack into a million pieces when she smiled as they entered. Wisps of silver hair had pulled free from their pins and floated about her head like a halo, the effect a bit unnerving.

"My boy!" She hobbled toward them as fast as Drake presumed her diminutive stature could manage. After stopping a moment, she pulled Drake into her arms, then, pushing him away, proceeded to swat him on the arm—hard.

"I should use my cane on you, boy! Not to invite your father's

favorite aunt to your party. Henry"—she peered up at the ceiling—
"God rest his soul, would be appalled at your manners."

Drake swallowed hard, exchanging a terrified look with Simon.
"Forgive me, Countess, but this is the Duke of Burwood." He pointed
to Simon.

Aunt Kitty blinked rapidly, her head jerking back so forcefully,
Drake worried she would fall over. "Nonsense. I know a Pendrake
when I see one. Why, those eyes are an obvious giveaway. The color of
honey, I always said."

Aunt Kitty's eyes, a light blue, squinted, studying him. "And that
nose. That's a Granger nose if I've ever seen one." She pointed to her
own, which Drake had to admit, was a perfect replica of his own
aquiline nose. "And I've seen it every day for these past eight-and-
seventy years."

She turned toward Simon. "If you're the Duke of Burwood, I'm
Queen Charlotte."

"Um, madam," Drake said. "Queen Charlotte is no longer with us."

"Makes my point, wouldn't you say?" Her gaze raked over Simon
from the top of his well-groomed head to the bottom of his well-
polished hessians. "Just who are you, young man, and why are you
impersonating my great-nephew?"

"I like her. We should tell her, Drake," Simon said.

"Drake?" The old woman cocked her head. A wide grin split her
face again, stacking the lines at her mouth. "As in *Pen*drake?"

Drake squirmed in place under the old woman's scrutiny.

"Tell her." Simon's words grew more insistent.

Aunt Kitty lifted her cane, and for a moment, Drake feared she
would strike either him or Simon with it. Perhaps she would even
strike them both. He released the breath he held when she pointed it
at Simon. "You tell me, since you're so keen on the idea. If you're truly
the duke, this young whippersnapper isn't going to stop you now, is
he?" She gazed at Drake askance, no doubt watching for his reaction.

The old woman was shrewd. Drake would give her that much. And
like Simon, instinct told him he would not only like Aunt Kitty, he
could trust her.

"No. I'll tell you everything. But first, allow me to provide you with some refreshment. You've had a long journey." He rang for Frampton and ordered tea and sandwiches to be brought into the parlor. Aunt Kitty requested sherry, which she insisted was for medicinal purposes only.

Simon barked a laugh and received a censorious glare from both Drake and Aunt Kitty.

Then Drake settled Aunt Kitty on the settee and began his tale.

CHAPTER 12

"Really, Father." Honoria held her ground. "You're imagining things. Mr. Merrick was simply being kind. He has done nothing to deserve your disapprobation, much less your verbal censure."

Her father's eyes narrowed, no doubt sussing out a lie. Luckily, he found none. Honoria spoke the truth. Much to her dismay, Drake had made no advances, impolite or otherwise. If it wouldn't add fuel to her father's argument against Drake, she would tell him that Drake practically said as much during their meeting in the library the other evening. However, disclosing that bit of information to her father was not wise, to say the least.

"I just wish to God he wasn't Burwood's man of business. Constantly hovering around, popping up at the most inopportune times."

Her mother placed a hand on his arm, calming him. "Now, Stratford. Mr. Merrick has been the perfect gentleman, and if Honoria stands a chance with the duke, perhaps Mr. Merrick will encourage his employer."

Her father's eyes widened. "Are you mad, woman? Why would he do that? To what end?" His brow furrowed. "Unless it's to keep Honoria close at hand for his *own* purposes."

"Bertram!" Her mother blanched. "Remember yourself!"

Eager to salvage the deteriorating situation, Honoria said, "I believe what Mother is saying is Mr. Merrick would vouch for my character." She met her father's gaze directly. "Knowing full well nothing happened between us, he could reassure Burwood that the reports of my—disgrace are false."

Her father's eyes widened. "So you *are* considering Burwood?"

Did she say that? "In my estimation, the likelihood of a match between Burwood and me is negligible."

Unable to let the matter lie, her father said, "He's paid you an inordinate amount of attention. Seeking you out for his ridiculous games and seating you by his side at supper."

"One evening, Father. Since you sat directly across from me, you will recall my position next to Mr. Pratt tonight."

"Yes. That was unfortunate. I have nothing against him personally, but scandal follows that family wherever they go, especially that sister of his." He huffed and turned in the direction where Priscilla chatted with her brother. "You could have been Mrs. Marbry and, in the future, Viscountess Saxton. A step down, to be certain, but—"

"Father. When will you desist with that complaint? It's in the past, and even if it weren't, I've told you I refused Mr. Marbry's suit."

"Exactly my point. He offered for you, and you turned him down. You need to accept the next man who offers for you. No exceptions."

"Even if he isn't titled or to inherit?"

He didn't need to say a word. The *No* was in his eyes.

Honoria loved her father. Truly, she did. For the most part, he was kind and loving. She tried to be a good daughter, to abide by his wishes.

To keep the peace.

But moments such as this, she wanted to scream.

"I had a chance to marry the man I loved eight years ago. It was you and Mother who determined he wasn't good enough for me. You said he only wanted me for my dowry and status. 'To elevate himself in society where he doesn't belong' were your words, if I recall. You told me if he had truly cared for me, he wouldn't have accepted payment to secure a position in the military. That to him, I wasn't worth more than a cadet's commission in the cavalry. You need not worry about Mr. Merrick pursuing me. I broke his heart along with mine when *you* persuaded me to give him up. He will never forgive me."

He stared at her wide-eyed. Her mother grew so pale, Honoria worried she might swoon on the spot.

Lessons carefully drilled into her through years of tutelage were forgotten.

Shame and power pulled her in opposite directions as she stared at her parents' shocked faces. She needed air.

Without another word, she turned on her heel and hurried from the room. Small knots of people moved out of her way, their gazes trained on her. Tears pooled in her eyes, and she willed them back.

Momentarily disoriented, she raced up the hallway. The sanctuary of her bedroom called to her, but tears blurred her vision. Where was the staircase? Worried she wouldn't make it to her room without being seen before losing her composure, she searched for a vacant room.

⚜

THINGS WENT AS WELL AS EXPECTED WITH AUNT KITTY. AS DRAKE explained his and Simon's plan—well, his plan—she sat and listened intently, only interrupting to ask questions to clarify.

"Do you mean to tell me you're doing all this for a woman?" Aunt Kitty looked positively flabbergasted.

"Not *a* woman," Drake insisted. "But to find a bride whose only concern isn't marrying a title."

"Pfft." Aunt Kitty batted an invisible fly out of the way. "There is no woman on earth who isn't swayed by a title."

Drake ran a hand through his hair, certain he was undoing his valet's meticulous styling. "I'm not saying this correctly. What I mean is someone who cares for me as a person first. Keeping a title out of the mix to muddle things seemed like a good idea."

Aunt Kitty appeared dubious. "Then why not marry some country girl? Not that your grandfather would have approved. Why bring the best of English society together for a house party in order to find your bride?"

During Drake's woefully inadequate explanation, Simon remained exceptionally—and uncharacteristically—quiet. Hairs on the back of Drake's neck rose when Simon opened his mouth.

"Aunt Kitty." Simon delivered the rakish grin that made many a woman swoon and follow him to his bed. "May I call you Aunt Kitty? What Drake is refusing to admit, even to himself, is there is one woman in particular he wishes to put to his test."

"Here? Among the other hopeful ninnyhammers?"

"Indeed she is," Simon said.

Drake glared at Simon. "She's not a ninnyhammer."

One of Aunt Kitty's wiry gray eyebrows quirked. "Ah ha! Sir Galahad defends his lady fair. What's her name? Do I know her?"

Did she?

If they were to continue with their ruse, they needed Aunt Kitty to cooperate, especially around Honoria. "Lady Honoria Bell."

Unfazed, Aunt Kitty continued, "The Marquess of Stratford's daughter?" Her gnarled fingers worked at her chin. "Let me think. There was a scandal some years back about her ruination when she became enamored with a comm—" The old woman's gaze snapped to Drake's. "You!" She clutched her cane, her sharp blue eyes studying him. "Don't deny it. I can see it in your face."

"Yes. My stepfather was Stratford's steward, and I was a groom on his estate in Somerset."

"Did you toy with her affections, young man?" Warning rang in the old woman's voice.

Drake was growing tired of Aunt Kitty's interrogation. "No! I loved her."

With a tilt of her head, she reminded Drake of a crow. "Loved? But no longer?"

Air stilled in the room as if it, too, waited for his answer. "It doesn't matter what I feel. She would not consider me. Her parents turned her against me before and no doubt would again."

"As the former groom on his estate, or even as Burwood's man of business, that may be true. Stratford isn't a bad sort, as men in the aristocracy go. Better than the monster I was married to."

Drake's head jerked toward her. He knew so little about anyone in his family.

"Like your grandfather, Stratford holds to a particular set of rules." She held up a hand, silencing Drake's unspoken argument. "There's a place for rules, whether you like them or not. But when you put rules above the happiness of those you love, they need to break." She grinned at him. "Or at least bend a little."

He shook his head. "Stratford would never bend. I need to consider another lady."

She studied him, her eyes clear and sharp. "Is it so important to you to maintain this ruse when revealing the truth would easily solve your problem and win the lady of your heart?"

Simon snorted a laugh.

"If a woman accepts me as a duke, how could I be sure it wasn't just the title that won her? It may seem petty to some"—he glared at Simon—"but I need to know I'm worthy in my wife's eyes as a simple man."

She nodded. "Very well."

"Then you won't give us away?" Drake motioned toward Simon, who again had lapsed into uncharacteristic silence.

"I'll do more than that. I'll help you. Allow me to speak with the lady of your interest to gauge her feelings."

He blinked, overcome by her offer to become an ally. "You would do that for me?"

"I will on one condition."

Drake pulled in a deep breath, preparing himself for the old woman's demand. "Which is?"

"Once the lady in question—whomever she might be"—Aunt Kitty's eyes sparkled with mischief—"accepts your proposal, you will not only end this farce forthwith, but you will never reveal I was party to it." She straightened her hunched shoulders. "I have a reputation to uphold."

Something about her last words made Drake laugh. He liked his newly found aunt—very much. "You strike a hard bargain, madam, but I agree." He held out his hand.

She batted it away. "None of that. Give your aunt a proper kiss."

She offered her cheek, and he gave her a chaste peck. "Thank you, Aunt Kitty."

She swatted at the air again. "No more of that if we're to be believable. You will call me Countess, or Lady Gryffin." She pulled a handkerchief from her reticule and dabbed at her eyes. "Have you had the servants dust recently? A particle must have floated in my eye."

Drake exchanged a smile with Simon. "You've been awfully quiet. Especially for you."

He placed a hand over his heart in dramatic flair. "I'm too choked up with emotion from this beautiful reunion."

Sharp as a razor, Aunt Kitty saw right through him. "Bah! Let's just hope my nephew's scheme doesn't blow up in his face and you end up with the woman he loves. If I know Stratford, he's already prepared the marriage contract with the Burwood name on it." She glanced Drake's way, no doubt assessing his reaction.

Which was not one of pleasure at the thought. He wanted to change the subject away from Honoria. "Aunt. Forgive me, Countess. You said you were my father's—Henry's—favorite aunt. What was he like?"

Her gaze took on a faraway, dreamy look. "Ah, he was my favorite, too. The best of the bunch. Level-headed. Kind. I was sorry to hear he'd died so young." She dabbed at her eyes again. "Please have your servants dust, or I will be forced to leave, and I have a feeling you're in need of me."

Drake glanced at Simon. "Burwood will see to it immediately, won't you, *Your Grace?*"

Taking the cue, Simon excused himself, leaving them alone.

"Forgive me, Aunt, but I don't even know if you're my grandfather's or grandmother's sister." Her comment about her husband had chilled him to the marrow. "Tell me about you and then more about my father."

"Your dear grandmother was my eldest sister. Oh, she was beautiful, a diamond of the first water. Burwood had yet to inherit, but he recognized a prize when he saw one. Snapped her up her first Season. I was but a girl then, but my parents—a baron and baroness—seized on the fact that Burwood could advance me in society as well."

She took a deep breath, and unlike the dreamy expression she bore earlier, her countenance appeared stormy and troubled. "At the age of ten-and-five, I was promised in marriage to the Earl of Gryffin. Two years later, I married him. It was a loveless and violent marriage. He needed my dowry and an heir"—oddly, she grinned at him—"which I refused to give him."

Drake stared in wonder. "The dowry or the heir?"

"The heir, foolish boy. I had no control over the dowry, which he well knew. But it gave me great pleasure that my body refused to provide the heir he needed." No doubt reading his questioning gaze, she clarified. "It wasn't for lack of trying on his part, if I may be indelicate. I simply could not bear a child. It infuriated him. And as much as I wanted a child to love, having Gryffin as a father would have sentenced the poor babe to a life of unhappiness. At least I kept that to myself."

She patted his hand. "But I found great joy in my nephews. Much like Stratford, Burwood placed great emphasis on titles and power, but he was at heart a good man and—as far as I knew—a good husband to my sister."

"How can you say that? He disowned my father. For falling in love, no less."

The pitying look on her face shamed him. "As I said, he placed great emphasis on the peerage. I don't know if he loved my sister or she him, but she seemed content. She died in childbirth." Aunt Kitty dabbed at her eyes again. "The child—the little girl she'd always wanted—" At this, Aunt Kitty choked up and wept openly.

On instinct, Drake wrapped an arm around her. "Do I have another living aunt?"

She shook her head, still trying to regain her composure. "The child came too early and didn't survive." She wiped her face, her lips trembling as she forced a smile. "Those servants need to dust!"

He wished he had not sent Simon away. Surely, he could ease her sadness. "Tell me more about my father and his brothers."

"Henry loved books. Your grandfather added to his collection mainly to please the boy, but he continued the practice long after they parted ways. I often thought it was in hopes that he would return."

Drake grinned at her. "It is extensive. I wondered about it." He sighed. "It would seem I take after my father in that regard." His mind momentarily drifted toward Honoria and their meeting in the library.

"Your uncles would tease Henry mercilessly. Especially Peregrine, the eldest. What a scapegrace that man was. Died in a carriage accident, no doubt driving like the reckless fool he was. Snapped his neck, they said. Perry would have run the dukedom into shambles. He liked expensive things and threw money around as if he had a never-ending supply. Forbes, the second oldest, would have been much better suited for the title, but he died at the Battle of Trafalgar. Heroically, I might add." She shook her head. "Such a loss. You would have liked him. I believe there is a son somewhere, born on the wrong side of the blanket."

"My cousin."

She nodded. "If you choose to claim him. But Forbes never married to produce legitimate progeny. After Forbes' death, your grandfather placed all his hopes on Gyles, the next in line. Unfortunately—or fortunately for you—he had no interest in marrying—try as your grandfather might to coerce him. If you care to know more about him, Gyles had a rather close friend, Reginald Ford. Reggie and Gyles were inseparable. Reggie was like an unanchored ship when Gyles died."

From Aunt Kitty's last comments, Drake had a suspicion why Gyles had never married. And although he suspected Aunt Kitty also surmised the reason, he kept his suspicions to himself. Such knowledge in the wrong hands could lead to devastating consequences.

"I should like to speak with Mr. Ford if you know where to find him, as well as my cousin."

"I have Reggie's information. But as for your cousin, I only have a name. Miles Grey. I'm afraid even that won't be much help in locating him. There must be an abundance of Greys in England."

When he'd received the letter from Aunt Kitty, dread had seized him, but gazing at the old woman, Drake was indebted to her. "You've helped more than you imagine, Aunt Kitty. As much as my fa—Francis

Merrick loved and cared for me, I always felt a little lost, like I didn't quite fit. I blamed myself for being an ungrateful son."

"Perhaps you can repay the favor and tell me about the man who reared you? Are he and your mother in attendance?"

Drake shook his head, a sadness overtaking him. "My mother is in Dorchester awaiting word from me. But she is well and spent a month here with me when I returned to England. My stepfather died three years ago when I was in India. He was a good man. Hard-working, honest . . . except for withholding the truth about my parentage." A dull ache squeezed Drake's chest. "According to my mother, they both sought to protect me from the pain of knowing the cruelty of my grandfather." His eyes darted to his aunt's. "Forgive me."

"Bah! Although I agree it was wrong of Burwood, I believe he meant it as an idle threat. He never imagined your father would choose love over his place in the family. Both were stubborn and not eager to admit fault in the dissolution of the relationship."

"Do you think my father was wrong?"

She shrugged. "Not wrong, but impetuous. If he had waited and done his best to convince your grandfather to accept your mother, there would be no need for this secrecy. And you"—she poked a bony finger in his chest—"would already have your lady love."

"And do you think my grandfather would have? Accepted my mother?"

She emitted a heavy sigh. "We'll never know. We can't undo the past; we can only move forward and take charge of our destiny that lies ahead." She sent him another watery smile. "I met your mother once."

Drake straightened in his seat. "You did?"

"Lovely girl. Well-mannered, especially for a Cit. Henry met her when he was in London for the Season."

Drake smiled, remembering Grandfather Abernathy, a London tailor. "Did they meet at my grandfather's shop?"

Aunt Kitty grinned. "Yes. Did you know your maternal grandfather?"

"I did, although we were unable to see him often. My father—Mr. Merrick, that is—found little time away from Somerset first as an apprentice steward to Lord Harcourt and later managing Stratford's estate. But once, my mother took me to London, and my grandfather provided me with new clothing for my twentieth birthday." He sighed, remembering how he'd hoped to wear them if he married Honoria.

"And those you have on now?"

Drake ran a hand down the fashionable dove gray coat. "Also expertly made by my grandfather. He apologized for keeping the truth from me, but said he was under strict orders from my mother."

Her sharp blue eyes studied Drake again. "I can't quite get over how much you look like him."

"My father?"

"Yes. I brought something with me. A portrait of your father, done right after he met your mother. Out of anger, Burwood was going to destroy it, but I talked a servant into removing it before he had a chance. Your butler said he would put it in my room."

"I should like to see it."

"Shall we go now?"

The moment he opened the door, and before he could step aside and allow Aunt Kitty to exit, Honoria fell into his arms.

CHAPTER 13

"Oof!" Honoria stared up into Drake's surprised face.

His arms wrapped around her, steadying her. "Honoria, what's wrong?" The gentleness of his voice and the safety of his arms only made her weep more openly.

Someone thrust a handkerchief between them, and Honoria peeked around Drake's broad shoulder to see a wizened woman gazing at them with great interest.

She pulled from Drake's arms as if he were on fire. In truth, it was she who was on fire—for him. Yet, having a witness to being in his arms would only lead to devastating consequences. The last thing she wanted was to trap Drake into an unwanted marriage. "Forgive me. I didn't mean to—"

"Shush, girl," the woman said, her voice firm, but not unkind. "No one is blaming you for anything, real or imagined."

"Countess," Drake said. "May I introduce Lady Honoria Bell, the daughter of the Marquess of Stratford? Lady Honoria, the Countess Gryffin, Burwood's great aunt."

"Call me Aunt Kitty." The woman's face cracked into a smile and a hundred tiny lines.

Honoria swiped the handkerchief under her eyes as she forced an answering smile. "Pleased to meet you, Countess—I mean Aunt Kitty."

"You didn't answer my question," Drake said, bringing her back to the argument with her father.

"It's nothing," she lied. "However, I seem to have become disoriented. Where is the staircase leading to the bedchambers?"

Aunt Kitty patted Drake on the arm. Odd that she would use such a gesture of familiarity with him. "I'll give you two a moment, and then perhaps we can all proceed upstairs together." She ambled off to the side, the cane in her grip shaking with each step she took.

An urge to rush to the woman's side and assist her replaced Honoria's concerns about her own troubles. "Will she be all right? She appears rather unsteady."

Drake, too, watched the woman, affection shining in his eyes, and Honoria's heart swelled even more for the man before her. "She'll be fine." He turned his attention toward Honoria. "What has you so upset? And don't tell me it's nothing. I know you, remember?" He took the handkerchief from her hands and held it to her nose. "Blow."

Gracious! She *should* be mortified, but somehow, she felt safe from judgement and did as he instructed.

His lopsided grin set wings battering her stomach. "There. Much better." He waded up the handkerchief and tucked it in his pocket. "Now, tell me."

"It's no—"

A sandy eyebrow quirked. "Honoria."

She had to laugh at his censorious tone. "My father and I had a bit of a tiff. I said something—disrespectful."

Both eyebrows shot up at her admission. "No! You? What were you arguing about?"

She cast her gaze to the floor. "You."

"Ah." He said nothing further, and when she peeked up at him, he seemed neither disturbed nor amused.

"You're not going to ask me to elaborate?"

"I don't have to. I imagine it was similar to the conversation I had with him." He touched the tip of her nose with his fingertip. "The one you rescued me from, if you recall. I assured your father I was not pursuing you and there was no reason to be concerned."

"Oh." Although she considered, even feared, Drake had put the past behind him, hearing him say it punched the air from her lungs. Hope that they could rekindle what they'd shared—as fragile as spun candy floss—shattered into a million tiny pieces.

"Now, let's not keep the countess waiting. She's had a long journey."

As Drake escorted them upstairs, Honoria tried to match Drake's words to his actions. His comforting touch on her face and the soft look in his eyes when he said she rescued him didn't agree with his insistence he was not pursuing her.

And the incongruity troubled her.

DRAKE DID HIS BEST TO MAINTAIN HIS COMPOSURE UNTIL HONORIA left him and Aunt Kitty at the top of the staircase, assuring him she could find her room from there.

"It's all over her face, you know," Aunt Kitty said. "She still loves you."

"No disrespect, Aunt, but perhaps your eyesight isn't what it used to be."

"Bah! Perhaps it is you who is blind. Now, where is my room?"

After asking a footman where Frampton had placed Aunt Kitty's belongings, Drake followed her into her room where a maid busied herself emptying his aunt's trunks. A large framed painting leaned against a wall, the back facing outward.

"You can finish that later," Drake said to the maid.

When the maid curtsied and scurried away, Aunt Kitty nodded toward the painting. "Does your staff know of this deception of yours? It seems odd the portrait should be left in this manner."

Drake nodded, wondering the same about the portrait.

"Turn it around," she said.

When he did, he understood exactly why Frampton had instructed the image to be hidden.

It was as if Drake were staring in a mirror at a slightly younger version of himself in clothing of an earlier era. "It's uncanny."

Aunt Kitty came beside him. "Now do you understand why I wouldn't believe your farce? You can't deny he's your father." She turned toward him, meeting his eyes. "Nor should you. He was a man you would be proud to call Father."

Something caught in Drake's throat, hard and unmovable. He'd missed out on so much, and as much as he had loved Francis, he wished he could have known the man in the portrait before him. "You said this was painted right after he met my mother. How old was he?"

"One-and-twenty. It was painted in celebration of coming into his majority, I believe. A handsome young man." She sighed. "As are you."

Drake stared again at the light brown eyes and sandy hair, the lopsided smile that caught—what he hoped was—a similar personality trait he'd inherited from his father. A Springer Spaniel sat at his father's feet, gazing adoringly at his master.

"His name was Flash," Aunt Kitty said, pointing to the dog. "Your grandfather forbid Henry to take the dog with him when he left. Flash died six months later, and to this day, I think it was due to a broken heart."

Drake knew about feelings of despondency and losing the will to live. It's what Simon had saved him from when they met not long after his arrival in India. He touched the face of the man he didn't remember.

Aunt Kitty patted his arm, pulling him from his maudlin thoughts. "It's yours if you want it."

He nodded, unable to speak. The lump in his throat seemed to have grown even larger. Gathering his courage, he forced it down. "Thank you. I'll have it moved to my room. I don't expect anyone to wander in and see it there. Only my valet and the maids." He patted his aunt's hand, even more grateful for her impromptu visit. "I'm glad you're here, Aunt Kitty."

She swatted his arm. "Lady Gryffin, my boy. We must keep up the deception."

He kissed her on the cheek and left her, then gave instructions to the hall footman to have the portrait moved discreetly to his chambers.

No one must see it until the charade was over.

⚜

IN THE SAFETY OF HER ROOM, HONORIA SAT AT THE ESCRITOIRE AND stared out the window. Dusk settled, casting the horizon in streaks of blue and pink. She'd always loved that combination of colors. It was as if the sky offered both a message of hope and regret all at once.

Exactly how she felt.

A soft knock sounded at her door. She brushed away the wetness still coating her cheeks. "Enter."

Doing her best to smile when her mother entered, Honoria rose from the desk to greet her. "Are you and Papa very angry?"

With the gentleness Honoria always loved, her mother took her hands in her own and led her to the settee. "We're both more surprised than angry. I've never heard you speak in such a manner."

Heat bloomed on Honoria's cheeks, and she fixed her gaze on their joined hands. "I'm sorry, and I should apologize to Papa."

"No."

Not only the word, but the vitriol in her mother's voice had Honoria jerking her head up.

"We needed to hear what you said." Her mother's countenance softened. "Although I cannot speak for your father, I believe we both did what we thought was best for you—and for Drake. I still believe it. You have only to look what he has made of himself. Do you think he would have done as well had you run off and married him?"

Honoria couldn't deny the truth in her mother's words.

"However, I am sorry it has caused you so much pain. Perhaps you could find it in your heart to forgive us."

Could she forgive them? More importantly, could she forgive herself?

"To be honest, Mother, the only forgiveness I desire is Mr. Merrick's."

CHAPTER 14

After her mother's encouragement, Honoria rose early the next morning. The breakfast room bustled with activity and chatter from all the guests. As Honoria placed a slice each of toast and sweet cake on her plate, Burwood approached her.

"You must eat a heartier breakfast than that." He placed several pieces of bacon on her plate, along with two other types of cake. "I understand fox hunting can be most taxing, chasing the poor unsuspecting animal around until everyone—including the fox—is exhausted."

She'd never thought of it quite that way. "And where did you receive such information?"

"Why Merrick, of course. Said it's what the finest people do. He says your father, in particular, enjoys the sport." He shrugged. "I hoped it would be a way of garnering his favor."

The man was a puzzlement. "And why would you wish to garner my father's fa . ." *Oh.*

He grinned at her. "Indeed. Merrick also said you sit a horse exceedingly well. Might I implore you to ride with me on the hunt?" He leaned in and whispered, "Perhaps you can keep me from falling off."

The idea made her laugh. "Surely you jest, sir."

He winked. "Stay by my side and find out."

Goodness, he was a horrible flirt.

Was he sincere in his flattery? And even if he was, did it matter? Although a union with him would please her parents, living in the same house with Drake, yet married to another man, seemed unfathomable.

As if confirming such a future, Drake called out, "Burwood, a word."

After making his apologies, Burwood left her to her breakfast. Out of respect, she nibbled on the bacon, but she discovered the cakes were delicious, and she ate every bite.

As everyone made their way outside, the fond memories of her rides with Drake spurred her forward. Even in his groom's uniform, or plain cotton trousers and shirt, he had always looked magnificent on horseback.

Saddled and ready, horses lined the path in front of the house. Drake had already claimed his mount, a beautiful white gelding, and Honoria's breath hitched at the sight of him. Dressed in a well-tailored red coat, tight buckskin breeches, and polished tan-top boots, he stood tall and proud next to the beautiful animal. Titled or not, he blended in with every other gentleman there.

Other men claimed their mounts. Honoria chuckled to herself as Dr. Marbry and Mr. Pratt argued over an enormous black beauty.

Priscilla Marbry appeared at Honoria's side. "Men." She clucked her tongue. "When will they ever learn?"

Honoria took in the delicate day gown her friend wore. "You're not going to join in the hunt?"

Priscilla shook her head, and uncharacteristic sadness came over her typically bright face. "Not today. I haven't been feeling well."

Concern for her friend had Honoria considering whether she should sit out the hunt as well. "Oh, no." She gathered Priscilla's hands in hers. "What is it?"

"Nothing serious. We thought perhaps I was . . . but . . ." She shook her head.

Honoria's heart squeezed for her friend. Priscilla and Timothy had been hoping for a child, but had yet to be blessed.

"It is a beautiful horse," Honoria said, hoping to lighten Priscilla's spirits.

"Mmm. But too much for my brother. I'm wondering if there's a particular lady who has captured his eye, and he's trying to impress her."

"As Lord Nash did for you?"

Priscilla shook her head. "He wasn't trying to impress me; he was goading my future husband. Nash confided as much to me later." A wistful expression crossed Priscilla's face. "Did I ever tell you how Timothy and I met?"

Honoria shook her head. "I don't believe so."

She laughed. "He fell off his horse and injured his ankle. So perhaps my brother *should* be the one to ride that black beast."

When all was said and done, Mr. Pratt did indeed win the argument, and Dr. Marbry chose an imposing dappled gray.

"Now, go choose your horse before the men take all the good ones." Priscilla gave her a little push forward.

Honoria moved toward a lovely golden gelding that reminded her of Buttercup.

While Honoria was only ten paces away, Anne raced up to the mounting block. "Oh, he's beautiful."

"Miss Weatherby. I would caution you."

Honoria spun to find Drake, his brow creased as he approached with long strides. "That horse has only recently been broken and requires an experienced rider." He darted a glance toward Honoria.

"Nonsense, Mr. Merrick," Anne said, giving a little shake to the red curls peeking from under her pale-blue bonnet. "I'm an excellent rider."

"Anne." Mr. Weatherby nudged his horse up to his sister. "You overestimate your abilities. Listen to Mr. Merrick and choose another horse."

Her mouth in a little pout, Anne shook her head again. "I like this one. You worry too much, Andrew. I've even been practicing my jumps." She jutted her chin and squared her shoulders, reminding Honoria of her seven-year-old niece Cassandra.

"Anne," Honoria said, trying to reason with her friend. "Mr.

Merrick is an excellent judge of horses. If he feels the horse is not the best choice for you, you should listen."

"Not you, too, Honny? I mean Honoria. You just watch me!"

Mr. Weatherby gave his head a resigned shake. No doubt he was even more accustomed to Anne's stubbornness than Honoria was.

Honoria exchanged a commiserating sigh with Drake. She stepped closer. "Is it truly unsafe for her, Drake? Perhaps Burwood could demand she dismount?"

"It's true Buttercup is newly broken and would benefit from a level-headed rider, but"—he gave her a weak smile—"the truth of the matter is, I selected him for you."

Oh. Her heart squeezed a bit, then *thumped* hard against her rib cage. "His name is Buttercup?"

Drake ran a hand across the back of his neck. "Well, um. Yes. I thought it fit him."

"I thought so, too." She gazed longingly at the horse, remembering his namesake, wet forget-me-nots, and declarations of love.

"Let's find you another." Drake motioned for a groom. "Saddle Mercy and bring her here as quickly as possible." He turned toward Honoria. "You'll like Mercy. She's a spirited chestnut mare who delivered a foal a fortnight ago. We've not been riding her, but she should suit you."

With the other riders mounted and ready to go, Honoria felt all eyes upon her as she waited for a mount.

Her father tugged on his riding gloves. "Did Burwood underestimate the number of riders, or was that your mistake, Merrick?"

Drake ignored him and mounted his white steed, looking very much like a knight to her.

When she thought she would dissolve in embarrassment, a groom rushed over with a little chestnut mare and helped her into the saddle.

Burwood trotted over on his black steed. "Let us begin."

Honoria patted Mercy on the neck and adjusted in the saddle, wishing she were out on a simple ride with only Drake by her side.

As they made their way toward the woods, Drake quickly steered his horse next to Anne, and Honoria recalled his words from the day before. *I assured your father I was not pursuing you.*

Had she misinterpreted his intentions? Was Buttercup's name a gesture of past friendship rather than a tribute to their love? And had he chosen a new path forward?

With Anne?

DRAKE CLUTCHED MAJOR'S REINS TIGHTER THAN HE SHOULD, THE tension in his head flowing throughout his whole body. He stayed close to Miss Weatherby, praying that she had not exaggerated her horsemanship prowess. Buttercup could be stubborn unless given a gentle hand—as Drake knew Honoria would.

The groom at his estate had balked when Drake insisted on breaking Buttercup himself. "Begging your pardon, Your Grace, but this one is spirited. He'll need a firm hand."

After being thrown twice, Drake doubted Micah's assessment. "He reminds me of a horse I broke for the Marquess of Stratford."

Micah's eyebrows rose, and Drake explained his former occupation, earning respect from the groom, who had already owned Drake's.

"A light touch is what he needs. Much like you and I, Micah, he craves respect from those around him, and if it's given, he will return it tenfold." Sure enough, with gentle prodding and a soothing voice, Drake quickly had the horse in hand. "I think I'll call him Buttercup."

Micah removed his cap and scratched his head. "Buttercup, Your Grace? You are aware he's a gelding?"

Drake patted the horse's neck tenderly. "I am. And he should be proud to bear the same name of such a fine mare."

Micah only shook his head and laughed. "He's your horse, Your Grace. I expect you can call him Twinkle Toes if you so desire."

But at the current moment, Drake wanted to call him something much more derogatory. As Miss Weatherby tugged roughly on the reins, Buttercup shook his head. He nudged Major next to her side. "Buttercup prefers a light touch, Miss Weatherby. Let the reins lie easily in your hands and trust him to do the rest. Like this." He demonstrated with Major's reins.

Miss Weatherby's blue eyes widened as she cast her gaze at him. "Mr. Merrick! You startled me. This horse doesn't seem to understand. I don't want to go to the left. I want to go that way." She pointed past him toward Simon on the right.

Ah. "You wish to be near the duke?"

Expecting to witness embarrassment for her transparency, Drake was surprised at her guileless answer.

"Well, of course."

Drake laughed to himself and shook his head. Perhaps she wasn't immune to the lure of a title. Although he knew he and Miss Weatherby weren't suited, he did like her honesty. "May I tell you something about the duke?"

"Oh yes, please!" The eagerness in her face set Drake's nerves on edge.

"He likes a challenge."

She blinked. "I beg your pardon?"

"Regarding women. He prefers to pursue those who rebuff his advances."

"Well . . . that's silly."

"I don't disagree. But if you are wondering how to win his heart, I would advise you to feign indifference or even dislike."

She gave a little pout that reminded Drake of a petulant child.

"But if you wish, keep Buttercup's reins loose in your grip and follow me." He gave Major a gentle nudge with his boot, gave a verbal command to Buttercup, and moved diagonally toward Simon.

Much to Drake's dismay, Simon trotted his horse next to Honoria.

"He seems to like Honoria," Anne said. "And she's not one to feign anything."

No, she isn't. The two chatted amiably, with Honoria favoring Simon with spirited laughter. Jealousy twisted in Drake's stomach like a pit of vipers. What was Simon playing at? He struggled to reconcile what he knew about his two favorite people with the scene before him and, possibly, even provide Miss Weatherby with a ray of hope.

"Ah, but that proves my point. Don't you think? If Lady Honoria has expressed her disinterest in the duke, he, no doubt, has taken up the gauntlet to win her over."

Anne's brow furrowed. "I don't think so."

"Take heart, Miss Weatherby. Perhaps as we grow near, their conversation shall shed light upon the matter."

Thankfully, Buttercup followed Major as Drake led Anne toward Simon and Honoria.

The proximity did nothing to alleviate Drake's unease.

"You look especially fetching today, Lady Honoria," Simon said. The honey in his voice so sickeningly sweet, Drake wanted to cast up his accounts on Simon's polished boots. "That shade of green matches your eyes exactly."

Drake ground his teeth. *Damn it, Simon.* However, every word was true. She did look lovely. Her little hat perched atop her red curls tilted at a perfect angle, and the seafoam-green color complemented her fair skin, the pink blush on her cheeks only accentuating her natural beauty.

Two could play at that game. "Miss Weatherby," he said, hoping his voice carried enough. "You have a wonderful seat."

Simon snorted a laugh.

What had he said that was so funny? He darted a glance toward Anne, who appeared mortified. "On the horse." It was a slight prevarication. She sat the horse adequately, but nothing like Honoria, who appeared regal in the saddle.

"Oh." Anne tittered a laugh. "Thank you, Mr. Merrick. When I was a child, I was thrown from a horse. I suppose that's why my brother was so concerned about Buttercup. But I haven't let that stop me."

"So you don't give up at the first sign of difficulty?"

"Oh, no, sir. I am unwavering in my determination."

"Would that determination also apply to matters of the heart, Miss Weatherby? Say, for example, you favored a man your family disapproved of. Someone not titled, perhaps. Would you be persuaded to give him up to please your family?"

"No, sir. I would be steadfast and true in my affection."

"I admire a woman who knows her own mind. She's the one I would choose as my wife."

Drake's attention had been solely on Honoria, watching for any little reaction to the conversation. He wished he could see her face. Strange satisfaction swept through him when her shoulders slumped a fraction.

However, when he turned back toward Anne, his stomach tumbled to his boots at her lovesick expression—focused squarely back on him.

What had he done?

CHAPTER 15

Drake's words sliced through Honoria's heart, condemning her. Did he realize she could overhear his words to Anne? How much they wounded—true though they were?

Surely not. He may have been careless with his conversation, but he would never be cruel.

Not *her* Drake.

And yet—he *wasn't* hers.

"You appear deep in thought." Burwood's words jolted her from her maudlin musing. Concern shone in his blue eyes, the seriousness of his expression replacing his lively teasing and easily given compliments. "Although I'm not the best of listeners, I do have two ears awaiting you. Should you care to avail yourself, that is."

"It's nothing," she lied.

From the look he delivered, as usual, she had mucked up the attempt at prevarication.

She offered something more truthful, even if less than an accurate account of her true thoughts. "I hope the fox gets away."

His echoing laugh cracked like thunder. Behind them, one of the horses whinnied. "You do realize this is a fox *hunt*, my lady? The purpose being to *catch* the animal."

No condescension colored his voice, and amusement painted his face.

"I do, sir. However, from what I understand, men prefer the chase more than the capture itself. The excitement, the uncertainty of the outcome, makes it all the more appealing. Once the victory has been won, they quickly lose interest."

"You speak of more than the pursuit of foxes."

She forced herself not to look back at Drake. "Perhaps."

Burwood shook his head. "You have little faith in us, I fear. You are a lover of books. Don't the great poets speak of woman's inconstancy? Of their fickle hearts in the face of obstacles?"

"But were those poets not men who have no knowledge of the pain in a woman's heart? Consider that which men perceive as inconstancy is merely a matter of survival when living with a heart irretrievably broken from a poor choice. For women are instructed not to express their true feelings, but to withhold them. We are not allowed to convey what is in our hearts until the man has done so first." She chanced a glance back at Drake. "You speak of poets, but I think Miss Austen had the right of it."

"You believe women are more stalwart in love than men?"

"Perhaps not more stalwart, but rather holding on to love with tenacious claws when hope no longer exists."

Burwood appeared uncharacteristically pensive for a moment. "So no killing the fox if captured?" He grinned, breaking through the cloud of sadness and regret that hovered over her.

As they neared the woods, the hounds bayed furiously. A white-tipped russet tail flicked near the underbrush.

"Tally ho!" the master of hounds called, and everyone sprang into action.

"Stay near, Lady Honoria." Burwood kicked his horse into action. "You may be the only hope in saving our furry friend."

As she suspected, his assertion regarding his lack of prowess on horseback proved to be an exaggeration, for he maneuvered the horse admirably through the thick brush.

"There! Straight ahead!" Victor Pratt called.

Over a fallen tree, the fox jumped—the hounds in fast pursuit.

Drake raced his horse past her, bent forward in the saddle, his face a blur of concentration.

"Wait for me, Mr. Merrick!" Anne's horse darted past Honoria to follow Drake.

Riders cleared the obstacle with ease and wove their way farther into the woods. In one fluid motion, Drake jumped his horse over the debris, landing with grace on the other side. Honoria held her breath as Anne followed, releasing it only when Anne completed the jump safely.

It wasn't prudent to take chances when riding sidesaddle.

Burwood pulled back on his mount and turned toward her. "Can you make the jump?"

Honoria normally didn't fall prey to competitiveness, but something about Burwood's words and Anne's actions spurred her forward. "Of course!" She prepared herself for the jump, pleased when her horse didn't balk and landed on the other side as sure-footed as she could have hoped for.

Burwood followed, giving her a nod of appreciation. "Well, done!"

She'd learned most of her riding techniques from Drake, and although she smiled at the compliment, she would have preferred Drake had delivered it. She wanted to make him proud.

But Drake's focus was on Anne as they hurried through the woods after the fox. He remained close to her side rather than riding ahead, as he surely could have.

Much like Burwood was doing. "If you wish to ride ahead, Your Grace, please don't let me keep you."

He shook his head. "This was Merrick's idea. I tend to be more of your persuasion, my lady. The poor fox is only minding his business."

"You wouldn't say that if the fox began attacking your chickens."

The two of them were well behind the pack of riders, and Burwood reined his horse in. "You should tell him."

"Who?"

"Drake."

"Tell him what? To watch the chickens?"

Burwood raised a dark brow. "What's in your heart. Don't let society's expectations and demands rob you of what you so deserve."

Startled at the duke's exhortation, she blinked. Had he been trying to make Drake jealous with his flirting? He obviously knew she still cared for Drake. But what purpose would it serve to bare her heart only to have him tell her she was eight years too late, and he had put the past behind him?

Shouts sounded ahead, and Burwood turned his attention toward the commotion. "But at the moment, perhaps we should try to save the fox."

As Burwood kicked his horse back into action, Honoria followed him, vowing to give his entreaty serious consideration. Some things were worth the risk.

DRAKE DID HIS LEVEL BEST TO STAY CLOSE TO ANNE. BUTTERCUP fought against her direction more than once as she ignored Drake's warning and tugged the reins a bit too firmly.

The hounds closed in on the fox. At the moment, the little beastie sat upon a group of fallen trees as if to taunt both hounds and riders. Stacked on each other precariously, the trees formed a flattened and splayed X, and the fox perched at the summit of one. The hounds clawed at the fallen oaks, trying to climb their way to their prey, their baying increasingly frenetic. With an agile flip of its tail, the fox jumped off and raced away on the other side.

Chaos erupted. The hounds scratched and clawed their way up and over the fallen trees through the dip at the juncture. Some of the more skillful riders risked the leap over the trees, their horses skidding on wet leaves when landing on the other side. Stratford and other riders took a longer, more circuitous route around the debris.

"Go around, Miss Weatherby." Drake nodded in the direction the more prudent riders had taken.

Before Drake could gain her agreement and lead her, Victor Pratt's horse lost its footing and stumbled on the leap over, tumbling Victor from the saddle. Victor held up a hand to signal he was uninjured. However, as he scrambled to rise, his limp said otherwise. Someone needed to see to him.

Drake repeated his order. "Go around, Miss Weatherby. I shall meet you on the other side."

He dropped back a good distance. Victor and his horse still blocked the lowest clearing. Drake would need to work up speed for the jump. If any horse were capable of clearing the greater height, it was Major. With a determination he hadn't felt in years, he kicked his mount into action.

He cleared the stacked trees with only an inch to spare, and although Major slid on the wet leaves, he quickly regained his footing. Drake jumped off, pulled Major to the side, and hurried toward Victor. "Mr. Pratt, allow me to assist—"

"I'm coming across, Mr. Merrick!"

A chill slid down Drake's spine at Anne's call. As if his body refused to move faster, he seemed to pivot in slow motion, then held his hands up to stop her. "No, Miss Weatherby!"

But she was already racing toward them, trying to leap at the same spot he'd only barely cleared.

⁂

UPON HEARING THE COMMOTION AHEAD—THE FURIOUS BARKING OF the dogs and unintelligible shouts—Honoria and Burwood hastened their approach, only to arrive in time to witness the nightmarish events.

Utter horror locked the words in Honoria's throat at the scene. However, if she were a less genteel woman, she would have cursed. Burwood said the words for her, his profanity forgivable under the circumstances.

"What the blazes is she thinking?" Burwood said, after sending her an apologetic look for his previous expletive.

Drake and Victor Pratt watched dumbstruck from the other side of several large downed trees as Anne foolishly raced forward in an attempt to clear the debris.

Honoria's gaze snapped to Drake's, the terror in his eyes matching that compressing her chest.

Burwood stated the obvious, "She'll never make it."

They all shouted for Anne to stop, but she ignored them. Fighting the urge to close her eyes and pray, Honoria willed Buttercup to either veer off or soar across. It didn't matter, as long as Anne remained safe.

Buttercup did neither. Several feet before the debris, the horse balked, throwing his head down, coming to a complete and sudden stop and pitching Anne forward from the saddle across the fallen trees to the other side.

Burwood leaped from the saddle, then quickly assisted Honoria down. They rushed toward the fallen trees. With a grace matching his title, Burwood vaulted across the dip at the lowest point.

Honoria struggled to get a foothold and climb over, the leather gloves protecting her hands from the sharp bark.

"Allow me." Burwood held out his hands, and she gave a short nod. He lifted her by the waist and hauled her across.

Drake had not budged from where he knelt by Anne's side. Across from Drake, Victor Pratt also bent down over Anne's still form.

Honoria's heart pounded fiercely against her ribcage as she lowered herself to Anne's side next to Drake. "Is she . . ." Unable to finish the sentence, she met Drake's eyes again.

"She's breathing."

At his words, a rush of air escaped Honoria's lungs, as if she had withheld her own breath in solidarity with Anne.

Drake patted Anne's cheeks. "Miss Weatherby, wake up. Can you hear me?"

Tears formed in Honoria's eyes, but she willed them back. She must remain calm in order to assist. At Anne's feet, Burwood had crouched beside her, and she turned toward him. "Retrieve her brother, and Dr. Marbry if you can locate him."

Burwood nodded and rose.

Victor stood and grabbed Burwood's arm. "I'll go with you. We can split up if necessary in order to find them."

Drake continued to stare at Anne, stroking her face with a gentleness that broke Honoria's heart. Momentarily glancing up at Burwood, he said, "Take Major. It will be quicker if you don't have to go around. And hurry." His voice cracked on the last words.

Once Burwood and Victor raced off to search for help, Drake wiped a hand down his face. "It's all my fault."

"No!"

He shook his head. "It is. I should have forbidden her to ride Buttercup. He's stubborn and needs a gentle, trusting hand. He doesn't like to be forced."

"Just like Anne."

Drake's gaze snapped to hers.

"It's true," Honoria said, the admission breaking her heart, especially considering the recent consequences. "If you tell her not to do something, that's exactly what she winds up doing. She's headstrong and impetuous."

"I told her to go around. Mr. Pratt injured himself on the jump over, and I wanted to assist him. I told her to meet me on the other side." He shook his head again. "Even for Major, the jump was risky."

She touched his arm in an effort to reassure him. "And yet you did so without regard to yourself. You couldn't have known Anne would get it in her head to emulate you. You're such an excellent horseman, you probably made it look effortless."

He gave her a wobbly smile. "Always seeing the best in people." He stared back at Anne. "But I should have insisted you ride Buttercup."

"And what weight would your order have carried? Perhaps if Burwood had given the command. But Drake, be realistic. Does anyone in the *ton* listen to someone not of the peerage?"

"Say what you will, Honoria. I take full responsibility for this."

Anne's bonnet had flown off with the fall, and Drake brushed a lock of red hair from Anne's face, then turned toward Honoria, pain radiating in his eyes. "If she would only wake up."

Time passed slowly as they watched Anne's face for any sign she would wake.

"What's keeping them?" The strain in Drake's voice matched the tension coiling in Honoria's chest.

At last, the sound of horses' hooves grew closer. Honoria cupped Drake's face. "Take heart. Help is on the way."

Victor Pratt led the way, with Mr. Weatherby right behind. Mr. Weatherby practically jumped from his horse before it came to a full stop. "What happened?" His gaze shot frantically from Anne, to Drake, to Honoria.

Drake opened his mouth, and Honoria placed a hand on his arm again, giving it a squeeze and hoping he would take heed and remain quiet. He shouldn't take the blame for something that was a horrible accident. "Anne's horse balked and threw her when she tried to jump the trees. Mr. Merrick warned her, telling her to go around."

"It's true, Weatherby," Victor said. "We both told her to stop, as did Lady Honoria and Burwood."

"Where is Burwood?" Andrew Weatherby said as he crumpled to the ground beside Anne and picked up her hand.

Before anyone could answer, Burwood approached with Dr. Marbry close behind.

Drake finally spoke. "Thank God."

"Oh, Anne," Andrew said, stroking her hand again. "What am I to do with you?" He glanced up at Drake. "We both warned her not to ride that horse, yet she wouldn't listen. She never listens." He wiped a coat sleeve against his face.

Dr. Marbry raced up, gently moving Andrew and Drake aside. "Give me some room, please."

Honoria wished more than anything she could pull Drake into her arms and comfort him. She knew him well enough to understand the guilt he was laying upon himself.

As Dr. Marbry examined Anne, lifting each eyelid and carefully palpating her head, a collective hush fell over the small crowd gathered around her tiny form. More riders approached, abandoning the chase and giving the fox an unexpected reprieve. Murmured questions rose among the recently joined members.

Dr. Marbry looked up, his face a mask of solemnity. "We need to get her back to the house. Pockets, Oliver's son, experienced a fall from a velocipede some years back, and Ashton helped treat him. Perhaps he will have some advice."

Drake rose. Sheer determination colored his voice. "I'll take her."

Dr. Marbry looked toward Andrew and raised a questioning brow.

"Oh, for goodness' sakes." Honoria's patience had worn thin. "Now is not the time to worry about propriety. Mr. Merrick is the best horseman here. If anyone can get Anne safely back to Hartridge House without further injury, it is he."

"Not only that," Burwood added, "there is no man here I would trust more with a woman's virtue than Mr. Merrick. I personally vouch for him."

Honoria glanced over at her father who stood next to Lord Harcourt. He opened his mouth as if to protest Burwood's accolades, but under the circumstances must have thought better of it and remained silent.

"Very well," Mr. Weatherby said.

Drake climbed over the fallen trees to the other side while Mr. Weatherby gathered Anne in his arms. After much back and forth transferring poor Anne's body, which still did not rouse her, Drake mounted Simon's horse and had Anne settled on his lap. Anne's head rested against his chest while he supported her, one arm wrapped around her waist.

As Honoria watched him ride off, she was certain of one thing. Drake's sense of honor and responsibility would steer his course—away from her. And if Anne didn't survive—well, he would shut himself off emotionally to everyone. Whatever the outcome—good or bad— Anne's fall had changed everything.

CHAPTER 16

Drake stood in the corner of Anne's bedroom as Ashton examined her. Andrew paced the floor around the bed. Alice Weatherby tried to comfort her husband. Drake wanted to meld into the wall and disappear, but he refused to leave Anne's side.

All my fault.

Had his careless words led Anne to believe he had genuine interest in her?

He'd recognized the look of infatuation in Anne's eyes as they rode toward the hunt. Had she tried to impress him? To win him over by exhibiting her prowess on horseback?

Or was bravado more of a masculine thing? Drake was too unschooled in the ways of women to know.

When he had cradled her against his chest on the ride back—trying desperately not to jostle her too badly—he stared into her face. With her eyes closed, if he focused on her hair alone, he could almost imagine she was Honoria.

If only she would wake up!

The duke straightened and turned toward Andrew. "There's nothing to do but wait. Her breathing seems normal, and her pulse is strong and steady." He put a hand on Andrew's shoulder. "Good signs,

Andrew. Her brain is more than likely repairing itself from the trauma, and to do so, it shuts down." Ashton placed his stethoscope back into his medical bag. "I recommend someone stay with her at all times to alert either me or Dr. Marbry when she wakes. We shall know more then."

"When? Not if?" Andrew asked, his voice conveying the hope they all felt.

Ashton nodded. "When. Let us remain positive for Anne's sake."

Weariness lined Andrew's face, the slump of his shoulders supporting the effect.

"We must trust Harry, Andrew. Go rest, I'll sit with her," Alice said. She, too, looked as if a slight breeze might blow her over.

Drake stepped away from the wall. "I'll stay with her. You should both get some rest."

Ashton canted his head, understanding shining in his eyes. "It might be best for a woman to sit with her."

Drake's ears burned. "Of course. For propriety. I wasn't thinking. I just want to do *something*."

"My mother should be notified. In case . . ." Andrew didn't need to finish the statement. "I live in Kent, but my mother is visiting a friend in Lyme for the summer. If someone could fetch her . . ."

Alice wrapped an arm around her husband's waist.

"I'll go," Drake said. At least he would have a mission, something to occupy his mind. "As for someone to sit with Miss Weatherby, I trust no one more than Lady Honoria. She has a level head and a calm manner."

"She does indeed," Ashton said. "An excellent suggestion."

Andrew wrote a brief message to his mother and gave it to Drake with her location and friend's name.

Grateful he saw no blame in Andrew's eyes, Drake assured him he would make haste. "Let me fetch Lady Honoria so you may rest. Then I'll be on my way immediately."

Drake didn't have to go far to find Honoria. She had gathered several doors away with Lady Charlotte and Lady Miranda. With solemn faces, they turned toward him.

"How is she?" Honoria asked.

Drake shook his head. "Still unconscious. But Ashton is optimistic she will awaken. Her mother is visiting a friend in Lyme. I'm going to fetch her." When he saw Lady Miranda's face blanch, he added, "A precaution only. It may help to hear her mother's voice."

He darted a glance toward Honoria and knew immediately she saw through his reassurance. It would seem time had not dulled their ability to read each other's emotions. "Lady Honoria, would you sit with her so Mr. and Mrs. Weatherby may rest?"

"Of course."

"We can as well," Lady Miranda said. "We'll take turns."

"Honoria, don't overdo. Call us when you need us," Lady Charlotte said.

Honoria nodded, and Drake led her to Anne's room. "You have good friends."

"I do indeed." She glanced over her shoulder, then leaned in. "Tell me the truth. How is she really? Worry shows on your face."

"I spoke the truth that the duke is optimistic. However . . ." Unable to finish, he shook his head. "It's all my fault, Honoria."

She grasped his arms. "Listen to me. It is *not* your fault. Please be careful retrieving Mrs. Weatherby. I couldn't stand it if anything happened to you, too."

Why did those words make him happy? He didn't deserve happiness. Not while Anne lay unconscious.

How had he survived the past eight years without Honoria's calm head to steady him? Unable to say what he must if he witnessed the pain in her eyes, he jerked his gaze away and stared toward the room where Anne—and possibly his future—lay. "I swear with all that is in me, I will do what I must to make it up to her."

And like the coward he was, he turned and walked away from all that he loved.

A PALL HAD FALLEN OVER EVERYONE AND EVERYTHING. BRIGHT sunshine peeking through the slit in the curtains of Anne's room belied the gloom cloaking the house like a funeral shroud.

At regular intervals, soft knocks drew Honoria's attention away from her book as she sat reading by Anne's beside. Either the duke or Dr. Marbry appeared every fifteen minutes to check Anne's pulse and lift her eyelids. Each time they left, their expressions darkened further.

Occasionally, Honoria would wipe Anne's forehead with a cool, wet cloth, whispering words of encouragement. "Please, Anne, you have played the sleeping beauty long enough. We miss your joyful laugh and playful spirit. If you wake, you may even call me Honny."

Interspersed with the doctors' appearances, Charlotte and Miranda enquired if they could relieve her for a few moments. Each time, she would refuse—even when her eyelids drooped as she read—stating she was fine and she would call on them when necessary. Drake had specifically asked her to watch after Anne, and she would not disappoint him—again.

Even Andrew and Alice Weatherby—reappearing and looking no more rested—could not convince her to abandon her post, and she remained as a silent witness to their torturous vigil. When Andrew could bear it no longer, Alice led him from the room.

The stream of light from the slit in the curtain dimmed, and her mother appeared. "Honoria, you must eat something. You've been in here for hours. At least allow me to request a tray be sent up."

At the mention of food, Honoria's stomach rumbled. "That would be wonderful. Not much, just a small bite."

Her mother nodded and left.

The chime from a clock announced the time as eight fifteen when Burwood entered carrying a tray of food. "I didn't want a footman to bring it in case you sent him away. You can hardly refuse to eat for me." Even the duke's rakish grin seemed to have waned. He set the tray on a table, and Honoria noticed the additional plate.

Lifting the domed coverings, he said, "I thought I would join you."

"But your guests?"

He shrugged. "As you can imagine, no one is in the mood for a large supper gathering." He glanced toward Anne. "Still no change at all?"

Honoria shook her head, wishing she had better news, and joined him at the small table. "You're taking a risk, Your Grace, being in here with me alone."

A ghost of a smile crossed his lips as he poured them both some wine. "We're not alone. Miss Weatherby is here." He pointed to the entrance with his fork. "And I've left the door open. If someone comes in, I will say I popped in for a moment to check Miss Weatherby's status."

Oddly, she found herself smiling. "And how would you explain the additional plate of food?"

"Simple. The events of the day left you famished."

At that, she laughed outright. Anyone who knew her would see that for the lie it was. Which made her wonder. "Your Grace, may I ask something?"

"Of course." He speared a piece of beef.

"You said you are my ally. How much has Mr. Merrick told you of our past . . . acquaintance?"

"There is no need to mince words with me. If you're worried about the unsavory gossip, don't. Middlebury tried to bring it up with me, but I informed him it was utterly false, and if I heard him trying to spread it among my guests, he would be summarily escorted out."

Heat rose in her cheeks. "Did Mr. Merrick tell you . . ."

He shook his head. "Merrick would never take advantage of a woman. However, I do know you were both desperately in love." Sliding the meat into his mouth, he studied her. Finished chewing, he dabbed the serviette to his lips. "You don't dispute it. From your face, I see your feelings haven't changed.

"Do you always speak so frankly, sir? Among polite society, some find such forwardness rude."

His dark eyebrows quirked.

She began to see why Charlotte found him vexing. "My feelings are of little consequence. It was I who broke our attachment. By rights, he should despise me, and I believe any residual feelings Mr. Merrick may have had for me have been replaced." She glanced toward Anne, still in silent repose.

"You can't really believe he's fallen for Miss Weatherby?"

Under other circumstances, Honoria would have laughed at Burwood's incredulous tone, but Drake's parting words were clear enough. He bore guilt for Anne's accident, and if she so desired him as a husband, he would marry her to atone for his perceived sins. "Perhaps not love, but responsibility. And unless his years in India have changed him drastically, I believe he feels his course has been set."

Burwood mumbled something that sounded vaguely like the curse he uttered right before Anne's accident.

And she knew from his demeanor she had the right of it.

DRAKE PUSHED MAJOR HARD AS HE MADE HIS WAY TO LYME, ALL THE while his mind bouncing between Honoria and Anne Weatherby. He'd been a fool. A damn fool.

Honoria—calm, controlled, someone he could depend on. Someone who would help him navigate the rough waters of English society. But more importantly, someone who still loved him. It wasn't her love that was inconstant. No. That had been as unwavering as his own stubborn and wounded pride.

Anne—young, vibrant, and reckless. More in love with the idea of love than in love with him. How could she be when she didn't really know him?

If—no—*when* she woke up, he would tell her everything about himself. Well, not *quite* everything. Knowledge that he was actually Burwood would color her decision. No, that would come after—and *if* —she still wanted him. Could she accept a man who was more interested in quiet nights sitting by a fire and reading than one who would escort her to soirées and balls? One who was still uncomfortable in the ways of the *ton*?

Oh, he would learn to manage. He accepted that. He couldn't isolate her from everything, not if he wanted to make a difference in Parliament. As remote a possibility as that seemed, he would have to mingle among the elite in order for his voice to be heard. And a diplomatic and charming wife was necessary. Not to mention his need for an heir if he wanted the Pendrake line to continue.

The last thought generated another set of concerns. Would he be able to be the type of husband she deserved, or would he think of another redhead each time he took her in his arms? Would he imagine Honoria's lips as he kissed and made love to Anne?

He would be trading one guilt for another more insidious secret shame. Would Anne see through his attempts and grow to resent him? Would he grow to resent her for simply not being Honoria?

Gah!

He would go mad if he continued to dwell on it.

Cool breezes blew the scent of sea air toward him as he crested a hill. Lyme's silhouette emerged beneath him, casting long shadows in the late afternoon sun, and he began his descent. After locating the home of Mrs. Thompson, Mrs. Weatherby's friend, he was informed the ladies had decided to escape the heat of the house for a walk along the Cobb.

He left his horse in the care of Mr. Thompson's groom and set out on foot toward the seawall. Waves crashed against the stones and dotted his face with the salty sea spray. Gulls squawked above him. He scanned the groups of people walking along and stopped a few, asking if they knew a Mrs. Thompson and Mrs. Weatherby.

"I passed Mrs. Thompson and her friend not moments before," a portly gentleman said, pointing in the direction Drake was heading.

Drake tipped his hat and hurried to catch them. "Mrs. Weatherby," he called to two women strolling arm-in-arm.

When the woman turned and they came face-to-face, he knew immediately she was Anne's mother. A lock of her red hair had escaped from her bonnet and fluttered against her cheek, her blue eyes inquisitively searching his. It was like glimpsing Anne thirty years into the future.

Her lips curved in a tentative smile. "Do I know you, sir?"

He removed his hat. "No, madam. My name is Drake Merrick, the Duke of Burwood's man of business. I come from Hartridge House with a message from your son." Coward that he was, he didn't have the heart to break the news to her himself, but handed her Andrew's note.

Yet something in his eyes must have given him away. Her hand trembled when she took the missive from him. "Before I open this, sir, please tell me no one has died."

He answered truthfully, at least to the best of his knowledge, "No one has died." The word *yet* burned on his tongue, and he prayed it would remain there forever.

Her friend, Mrs. Thompson, watched in silence, her hand supporting Mrs. Weatherby's arm.

"It's Anne," she told her friend. "She's had a fall." She turned toward Drake. "How did it happen?"

"She was thrown from a horse."

Mrs. Weatherby swayed, and Drake reached out to steady her. "I must go to her."

As they hurried back to Mrs. Thompson's, Drake offered his arm, filling them in on some of the details. "I came on horseback in order to travel more expeditiously, but I will hire a carriage for you, madam."

"There is no need, sir," Mrs. Thompson said. "You may borrow mine and my driver."

Once the carriage was readied and Mrs. Weatherby made her goodbyes to her friend, Drake tied Major to the back and helped Anne's mother inside. He'd debated riding Major back, but she appeared to want the company.

"Tell me the truth about what happened, Mr. Merrick. I suspect you are omitting some information."

Drake's throat tightened as he prepared his confession. "Fallen trees blocked the way, and although I begged Miss Weatherby to go around, she insisted on trying to jump." He turned away to avoid seeing the anger in Mrs. Weatherby's eyes. "It's my fault."

"How could this be your fault, sir? I know my daughter, and the moment you tell her *not* to do something, that is precisely what she *will* do. Please cease from condemning yourself."

If only he could. He'd replayed the horrendous events over and over in his mind. He should never have left Anne's side to attend to Victor. He should have never said those careless words, encouraging her to act so recklessly to impress him.

Unable to do anything at the moment for Anne, Drake sought to distract her mother during the three-hour journey. "Tell me more about Anne. What was she like as a girl?"

As Mrs. Weatherby recounted tales of Anne's youth, Drake allowed himself to drift into a state of acceptance. One thing was certain, it would appear life with Anne would not be boring. He wasn't certain his nerves would survive.

But if Anne's heart was set on marrying a title, and she believed his ruse, he might yet wiggle out of it.

Although the Weatherbys weren't titled, it didn't mean Anne didn't hold aspirations. "May I ask a question?" When she nodded, he proceeded. "Do you place great store on Miss Weatherby making a titled match?"

"The only thing I wish for my children is their happiness. My late husband Ambrose and I longed for a daughter. There are fifteen years between Andrew and Anne, yet only two between Andrew and Arthur, my second eldest. We had almost given up hope. I fear we may have overindulged Anne."

Drake stopped her. "Forgive me, but everyone's name starts with A?"

Even in the dire circumstances, she gave a tiny laugh. "Yes. In fact, when Andrew met Alice, he took it as a sign. That and his heart left him the moment he laid eyes on her. Alice's parents are merchants."

"So she's told me. I planned to purchase some spices from them."

She nodded. "But she's also the great-niece of the Dowager Countess Brakefield. Neither mattered to Andrew or to his father and me."

"Is Arthur married?"

"He is. His wife's name is Lavinia. Her father is a baronet."

"Ah. No A?"

"No, but my grandson is Austin. However, Andrew and Alice have broken the pattern. Their twin girls are Indira and Eleanor. They said they didn't want them to be forced to find husbands named Alphonse or Aloysius. And I suspect Anne cares little about marrying a title or the letter his name begins with." Mrs. Weatherby studied him. "You seem to have a special interest in my daughter, sir. Might I presume that your concern stems from more than a sense of duty?"

How could he answer truthfully yet not arouse suspicion of his motives if he proposed to Anne? "Miss Weatherby's recovery and happiness are paramount to me, madam."

Let her deduce what she would from that statement, but it seemed to appease her.

"My daughter is indeed fortunate to have such a gallant champion."

Perhaps a future as part of the Weatherby family would not be so terrible.

At least they liked him.

CHAPTER 17

After finishing their meal, Burwood left Honoria to resume her vigil by Anne's beside, entreating her to allow either Lady Miranda or Lady Charlotte to take her place, at least for a while.

She promised she would do so soon, hoping by then Drake would have returned with Mrs. Weatherby. Night had fallen, and she stood and stretched her stiff limbs.

Hushed voices echoed from the hall, growing louder as they approached until Mrs. Weatherby rushed into the room. "Oh, my poor child. What am I to do with you?"

Drake followed, along with Andrew and Alice Weatherby.

Honoria quickly stepped away from Anne's bedside. Bone-weary, she turned to leave.

"Lady Honoria," Mrs. Weatherby called. "Thank you for your vigilance. His Grace told me how you refused to leave Anne's side. I'm so grateful Mr. Merrick's wisdom assigned you the task."

Honoria's gaze darted toward Drake.

Pink tinged his ears. "I merely told Mrs. Weatherby that your calm and reassuring demeanor made you the best equipped for the undertaking, and I had no doubt that you would give your all for Miss Weatherby."

Honoria mumbled something—she wasn't quite sure what—before scurrying from the room and praying the Weatherbys didn't see the desperate love on her face.

In the safety of her room, she rang for Susan, thinking she'd ready herself for bed and perhaps do a little more reading. Although she'd been sitting the majority of the day, her body stiff from inactivity, she collapsed in a chair and breathed a deep sigh of relief.

At the soft knock, she called, "Enter," surprised when Drake, not Susan, opened the door and peered inside.

Remaining outside, he shifted on his feet. "You look exhausted. Is there anything I can do for you? Have you eaten?"

She nodded. "Burwood saw to it. I'm just worried about Anne."

His head turned toward Anne's room. "Still no signs of her waking?"

"There was a moment, briefly, when I thought she stirred. But I worry my eyes were playing tricks."

"As I said, you're exhausted."

"I could say the same for you. The journey to Lyme and back, although not terribly far, no doubt has taken a toll. Have *you* eaten?"

He shook his head. "Not yet. Time was of the essence to retrieve Mrs. Weatherby."

"Then go. Eat and rest. It will do Anne no good if you're falling over on your feet."

He nodded and flashed her a grim smile, the distress on his face painful to see.

It took all her strength, which admittedly had waned, not to rush to him and pull him into her arms.

He left without another word, closing the door with a soft *click*.

After Susan came and prepared her for bed, Honoria searched for the book she was reading, then realized in her haste to leave she left it in Anne's room. Wrapped in her dressing gown, she padded down the hall and poked her head in. Mrs. Weatherby sat by Anne's side and looked up when Honoria knocked.

"Forgive me, I came to retrieve a book I was reading." Her gaze traveled to the small table by the bed, but the book was gone.

"Mr. Merrick took it when he left for the night." Mrs. Weatherby held Anne's hand, stroking her fingers as mothers do. "Such a kind man. He must care for Anne a great deal to have taken it upon himself to fetch me. Andrew told me he insisted."

"He is the best of men, Mrs. Weatherby. Not only kind, but honorable."

Turning her gaze from her daughter, Mrs. Weatherby said, "Do you know him well?"

"Very well. Eight years ago, he was the groom on my father's estate."

Flickering candlelight played tricks on Honoria's eyes as Mrs. Weatherby turned toward her. For a moment, Honoria thought the woman's eyes widened, a spark of recognition crossing her features. But she remained silent and turned back toward Anne.

"I shall leave you," Honoria said, feeling like an intruder. "If you have need of me, I'm but three doors down on the left. I would be happy to sit with Anne again."

As she turned to leave, she heard Mrs. Weatherby whisper, "And you are the best of women, my dear."

Only as she walked back to her room, did she wonder why Drake would have taken her book.

⁂

EARLY THE NEXT MORNING, HONORIA ROSE, DRESSED, AND returned to Anne's room. Mrs. Weatherby slumped in the chair by Anne's bed, no doubt having spent the entire night there.

Honoria touched the weary woman on the arm. "Mrs. Weatherby?"

Bed linens rustled behind her, and a soft moan followed.

Honoria spun around, and Mrs. Weatherby sprang from her chair as if she were a woman half her age.

"Anne!" they said in unison.

Color had returned to Anne's face, and she stared groggy-eyed at them. "Mother? What are you doing here? And why does my head hurt?"

"You've had an accident. Mr. Merrick brought me to you from Lyme."

Anne's brow furrowed. "An accident?"

Honoria rushed over to the bell pull, giving it a sound tug. When a footman appeared, she directed him to locate either Ashton or Dr. Marbry posthaste.

Returning to Anne's side, Honoria said, "Don't you remember? The fox hunt? You tried to jump over debris in the path."

Anne's brow furrowed. "Oh. I suppose I didn't make it then."

Honoria couldn't help but smile. "You made it, but without the horse."

Anne's mother also expressed her delight at seeing Anne awake and lucid. "It would seem the horse had more sense than you, my dear."

From the familiar pout on Anne's face, Honoria grew confident she would make a full recovery.

Quick, heavy footsteps sounded, growing near, and both Ashton and Dr. Marbry raced into the room. Dr. Marbry stood by, allowing the duke to take the lead in the examination.

After taking her pulse, looking at her eyes, and asking her a few questions—which Anne complained were ridiculous—they proclaimed her out of danger.

"Why are all of you fussing? It was simply a little fall."

Everyone exchanged a glance, and Mrs. Weatherby made the pronouncement. "It would seem my daughter is no worse for wear."

"Even so," Ashton said, "I recommend she remain in bed a few more days as a precaution."

Anne crossed her arms over her chest and pouted. "And miss all the fun?"

Dr. Marbry, no doubt used to such stubbornness from Priscilla, offered a compromise. "At least refrain from any strenuous activity." He grinned. "Such as jumping recalcitrant horses."

After Anne agreed—albeit reluctantly—the doctors left. "Is there anything I can do for you, Anne?" Honoria asked.

"Where is Mr. Merrick? I should like to speak with him and thank him."

All the elation Honoria experienced when Anne awoke seeped out as if a slow, unstoppable leak had pierced her heart. "I shall bring him to you."

She searched the library, the drawing room, and the breakfast room. No one had seen him. When she came across Burwood, he stopped her, his face unusually serious.

"You appear distraught. Please don't tell me Miss Weatherby has taken a turn for the worse."

Honoria shook her head. "She's awake and asking for Drake."

"Ah." The compassion in Burwood's eyes did nothing to ease the ache in her heart. "He said he needed some solitude to think. I believe he's out on the terrace."

"Thank you, Your Grace." She turned to leave.

"And Lady Honoria. Tell him to be honest with himself before he makes any rash decisions."

Without turning around, she nodded, knowing full well Drake's mind was already made up.

As Burwood suggested, she found Drake sitting on the terrace bench, back to her and head bowed.

"Drake?" At first she wasn't certain he heard her, so she moved closer and saw him hastily slip something into his pocket. A book lay open on his lap. "I didn't mean to interrupt, but I came to tell you about Anne."

His gaze snapped to hers, his face a mask of terror. "She's dead." His hand drifted to his pocket, and he murmured something that sounded like *my unfaithfulness did this,* but she couldn't be sure.

Quickly, she sat beside him, wishing she could pull him into her arms for comfort. "No. No. She's awake and both Ashton and Dr. Marbry believe she will make a full recovery."

His eyes shuttered. "Thank God."

"She's asking for you." The words stuck to her tongue like glue, the taste bitter. Her gaze dipped to the book. "Is that the book I left in Anne's room?"

"Yes." He looked like he wanted to say something else, but changed his mind. "Come with me?"

No need to ask where. She simply nodded and followed him to Anne's room. When they arrived, people crowded the room. Andrew and Alice had joined Mrs. Weatherby with Andrew sending Anne a brotherly glare. Miranda and Charlotte stood on the side of the bed opposite Anne's family. Near the door, Burwood leaned against the wall, his long legs crossed at the ankles. His gaze was trained on either Miranda or Charlotte, but from the frown on his face, Honoria thought it was likely Charlotte.

He straightened when Drake stepped into the room. "Shall we throw a party and invite the other guests?"

Clearly, Anne didn't realize he jested, because she sat upright in bed. "I love parties."

Burwood's dark eyebrow quirked, and he turned toward Drake. "She's all yours. If any of you have need of me, ring for Frampton." When he passed, he leaned toward Honoria and whispered, "Did you tell him?"

"Tell me what?" Drake asked, his gaze sliding from Burwood to Honoria.

"Apparently not. When you want something done." Burwood huffed a sigh. "I told her to tell you to be honest with yourself before you make any rash decisions. You know, the kind that have lifelong consequences?"

With that, he stepped from the room.

Brows furrowed, Drake stared at Burwood's retreating back.

Anne straightened in bed. "Mr. Merrick. You came."

Charlotte and Miranda moved aside as Drake tentatively stepped up to the bed. "Miss Weatherby. Relief doesn't nearly express my emotions at seeing you awake. You gave us all such a fright."

"My mother told me you rode all the way to Lyme to bring her here."

Honoria's heart broke a little more at the adoring look in Anne's eyes as she stretched out her hands toward Drake and he took them in his own.

"Could everyone give Mr. Merrick and me a few moments?" Anne's gaze never left Drake's face.

Andrew Weatherby shook his head. "That wouldn't be proper, Poppet."

"Honoria can stay as a chaperone," Anne said. "Everyone trusts her."

Numbness inched its way through Honoria's body. Drake's gaze turned toward her, his face apologetic and strained. "Perhaps someone else, Miss Weatherby? Lady Charlotte or Lady Miranda? Your mother? Lady Honoria has been tirelessly by your bedside. She deserves a rest."

Anne shook her head. "But that's why I want her. She truly cares. You will, won't you, Honoria?"

"Of course." Honoria eked out the words and forced a smile.

"Very well." Anne's mother addressed Honoria. "Will you call for me when they're finished?"

Honoria could only nod.

Charlotte and Miranda both brushed her arm as they left, and Charlotte whispered, "Stop this nonsense, Honoria. Tell Anne the truth."

But the *truth*, as Charlotte called it, was only Honoria's truth, not Drake's, and she could only give her friends a weak smile.

Everyone filed out, and Honoria longed to slow them down to avoid the inevitable. Alas, she, Drake, and Anne were quickly alone.

Honoria wanted to hold her hands over her ears as Anne poured out her heart to Drake.

"Andrew told me how gallant you were after my fall. He said you brought me back to the house yourself, carrying me in your arms like a knight in shining armor."

"It was the least I could do. It was my fault."

The sigh Anne emitted was similar to the one Honoria remembered escaping from her years ago when Drake held up water-logged forget-me-nots.

Drake continued to blame himself. "I should have insisted you not ride Buttercup. If there is anything I can do to make it up to you, only say the word."

Honoria's gaze locked on Anne's adoring face. *Oh, dear.* Drake had opened the door and Anne was more than willing to step through. Well, leap through was perhaps more in line with Anne's response.

"Mr. Merrick, from our first meeting, I sensed a connection between us." Anne fluttered her eyelashes as she gazed down at their clasped hands. "I should very much like to explore that further."

"Miss Weatherby." Drake's voice held a note of caution. "Are you not hoping to make a more advantageous match than with a simple man of business?"

Something about the way Drake phrased his question pricked at Honoria's mind. He was typically so straightforward.

"But you are the *duke's* man of business, and he includes you in his social gatherings." Anne cast him a flirtatious grin. "Wouldn't your wife also be included as well? Invitations to balls, garden parties, and soirées?"

"That would be up to the duke. But Miss Weatherby, I'm a quiet man. I don't care much for large crowds. I much preferring sitting in silence and reading."

Honoria thought back to her conversation with Burwood the first night, when she admired his library and asked if he enjoyed reading. He and Drake were so opposite, much like she and Anne.

Anne brushed it off. "Oh, I would change your mind. We would have so much fun, Mr. Merrick. And you do like me, don't you?"

"Of course, Miss Weatherby, I like you very much." Drake paused, as if gathering his thoughts.

Honoria held her breath, anticipating what was to come.

"So, you accept me for who I am, Miss Weatherby?"

"What you are is wonderful, Mr. Merrick." She smiled prettily. "Does this mean we have formed an attachment?"

Drake didn't answer immediately, and Honoria prayed she had misread the direction of the conversation.

His next words shattered the fragility of her hope. "I suppose it does." He patted her hands. "Now, I should leave and let you rest. I shall check on you later." He strode from the room, not bothering to even look Honoria's way.

As Honoria's world collapsed around her, she struggled to breathe.

"Oh, Honoria! Isn't it wonderful? I'm so happy." Joy radiated on Anne's face.

Honoria could only nod. "I'll go find your mother. If you'll excuse me, I don't feel well."

Anne's soft answer barely registered as Honoria exited the room, moving as quickly as possible yet remaining polite. Charlotte waited a few doors down. "Honoria, what happened?"

If she talked about it, she would break down in front of Charlotte. "Could you please find Mrs. Weatherby? I'm not feeling very well." At Charlotte's nod, Honoria made it to her room and let the tears flow.

CHAPTER 18

Guilt prevented Drake from meeting Honoria's gaze as he left Anne's room. Unsure if he would see pain or indifference, he only knew either would wound him, and his pain already approached unbearable.

If only Honoria had given the slightest indication that her father no longer held sway over her, perhaps he wouldn't be in this predicament. He dismissed the notion as quickly as it came. He couldn't blame Honoria.

No, the weight of things rested squarely upon his own shoulders. He had flirted with Anne—as well as Miss Whyte and Lady Miranda—in a vain attempt to test Honoria's feelings.

It had been impulsive, and now he paid the price for his foolishness. At least it was only an *attachment*. Whatever that truly meant in society's definition. They weren't actually betrothed—yet, although he had no doubt Anne expected a proposal to be forthcoming.

As he strode down the hall, his destination the library, he passed Lady Charlotte. With all the seriousness of Honoria, she possessed none of Honoria's softness to temper it—as if life had stripped away any joy from her. He found it sad.

She studied him with those dark brown eyes. "You appear distraught, Mr. Merrick."

"Would you please see to Lady Honoria? She may be in need of a friend." He said no more, but hurried away to avoid any further questioning.

At last in the library's sanctuary, he closed the doors behind him, only to jump at Simon's voice.

"There you are. I suspected you would make your way here after seeing Miss Weatherby. What happened?"

An odd sight, Simon in a library. With him, seated on the chair Honoria had occupied the first night of their reunion, Aunt Kitty didn't mince words. "Did you do something foolish, boy? Didn't propose to the chit, did you?" She shook her head. "Attempting a difficult jump on a stubborn horse—and sidesaddle no less. What is wrong with youth these days? Reminds me of my husband's great nephew Charlie Dickens. The boy thinks he can make a living writing novels. And as much as I enjoy reading them, those who write them are typically penniless and starving. Such foolishness. Can you even imagine?"

Drake and Simon exchanged a glance.

"That's fascinating, Aunt Kitty," Simon said, "but perhaps we should get back to the matter at hand." He turned toward Drake. "Did you propose?"

"Not exactly."

Aunt Kitty huffed. "Either you did or didn't. It's like being with child. You either are or aren't."

"She asked if we were forming an attachment, and I told her I supposed we were." He ran a hand across the back of his neck. "What was I to say? It's my fault what happened to her, and I vowed to do whatever I could to make it up to her, if she would only recover. I promised God."

Aunt Kitty shook her head. "Never a good idea. The fellow seems to have a strange sense of humor."

"Anne accepts me as a simple man of business with no title, no vast wealth, no connections to society"—he shot his gaze toward Simon—

"except you. She seems to believe we would be included in most events because of you."

Simon lifted his eyebrows. "That doesn't seem to indicate she's totally immune to the lure of a title. Are you completely certain she's looking at this whole thing clearly?"

"No," he admitted. "I don't think she has true feelings for me. She seems to have romanticized the whole incident with the fall." He plopped into the empty chair, his body numb. "What am I to do?"

"Someone needs to talk some sense into that girl," Aunt Kitty said. The old woman began to rise, her hand shaking as she bore her weight on her cane.

"Wait," Simon said. "I have an idea."

As they listened, Drake had to admit Simon's idea was a good one, but he worried his friend might be throwing himself on his sword to no avail.

CRUMPLED ON HER BED, HONORIA CRIED UNTIL EVERY DROP OF liquid seemed drained from her body. Then she cried some more. Finally exhausting her supply of tears, she rose from the bed, washed her face, and fixed her hair. She needed to make an appearance downstairs before someone came looking for her.

Eyes still red, she cast her gaze away from the mirror to the small box on the dressing table. Her father had given it to her on her sixteenth birthday, and she took it everywhere with her. Inlaid with mother-of-pearl, the polished mahogany case held her most treasured possessions. She removed the top contents, exposing the thin paper on the bottom. Carefully, she lifted it from its container and peeled back the edges. Encased inside sat the pressed and dried forget-me-nots Drake had given her over eight years ago. She ran a finger across one faded blue flower.

Fragile from age, it crumbled under her touch.

Just like her hopes and dreams.

She stared at them a few minutes longer then, with painstaking care, rewrapped them and laid them back inside the box. It was time to move forward with her life.

Downstairs, she made her way to the library in search of another book. The older woman Drake had introduced as Burwood's Aunt Kitty sat in one of the chairs by the hearth.

Honoria tipped her head toward the woman. "Countess. I hope I'm not disturbing you."

"Not at all, my dear. My nephew and his man of business just left, and I was hoping for more company." Her lined faced cracked into a smile. "At least someone who enjoys a good book as you do."

Honoria's thoughts immediately turned to Drake, who not only loved books but had taken hers, resulting in her decision to come to the library—where she apparently had missed seeing him again by mere moments. Yet, something about the countess's comment perplexed her. "How did you know I enjoy books?"

As if batting at a pesky fly, the old woman waved the question away. "I just know. I can tell a lot about a person from the way they speak and how they conduct themselves. It's an inner eye so to speak."

Honoria stared, dumfounded. "In truth?"

Lady Gryffin's countering cackle had Honoria's face heating. "My nephew told me you like to read. He sets great store by you." She shook a bony finger at Honoria. "But there is some truth in what I said. I can't explain it, but I get a feeling about people." Her gaze turned serious. "And I'm rarely wrong."

Honoria took a seat in the opposite chair, completely forgetting about her search for another book. Lady Gryffin fascinated her. "And Burwood—your nephew? I gather this is the first you've met him. How do you find him?"

"I would say he is a rare sort in the aristocracy. Serious, loyal, honorable. Perhaps the last to a fault. Even going against what is in his best interest for the sake of duty."

Burwood? Although Honoria liked the duke very much, he had an air of whimsy about him that had led her to believe he rarely took anything too seriously. And she never would have imagined he would sacrifice his own happiness for duty. Perhaps she had misjudged him.

Or cataracts blinded Lady Gryffin's *inner eye.*

"He fancies you, you know." The countess's words pulled her back. "And in my opinion, you would make a fine duchess. Much better than some ninnyhammer who tries to jump a stubborn horse."

That settled it. The old woman was definitely confused. "It is Mr. Merrick who has formed an attachment with Miss Weatherby, Countess. Not Burwood."

The old woman simply smiled. "I understand the doctors expect her to make a full recovery. Perhaps when her mind isn't scrambled, she will see the folly of such a match."

Oddly, Honoria felt the urge to defend both Drake and Anne. "Any woman should be overjoyed to make a match with Mr. Merrick. Anne is wise to see his worth."

"Ah, I see I have besmirched your friend's good name in your eyes, and for that, I apologize. As an old woman, I have grown accustomed to speaking my mind." Her lined faced split into a smile again. "But that doesn't mean I'm wrong. They are not suited for one another."

On that, Honoria agreed. But it was neither her nor the countess's place to make that determination.

"As much as I enjoy chatting with you, if you would help me up, it is time for my morning constitutional."

Honoria rose, then grasped the old woman's upper arm, finding she didn't need to exert much effort to lift the countess from her seat. Honoria suspected she would have managed fine on her own.

After straightening her gown, Lady Gryffin said, "If you came looking for a book, I believe this is the one you were missing." She tapped a book on the table.

By the time Honoria had picked up the book, which was in fact the copy of *Persuasion*, Lady Gryffin had quit the room.

What a strange old woman.

Honoria rather liked her.

When she sat to read, the pages of the book fell open, revealing a small blue flower pressed between the pages. Her gaze darted down to the words Captain Wentworth had written to Anne Elliot.

I am half agony, half hope.

With tenacious claws, she clung to the words like a lifeline.

THE DREARY MOOD IN THE HOUSE LIFTED WHEN WORD SPREAD about Anne's recovery. Everyone's spirit seemed buoyed—except Drake's. The next day, when Anne came down to the drawing room where everyone had gathered, all fresh-faced and bubbly, Drake forced a smile and strode to her side.

"Are you certain you should be up, Miss Weatherby?"

The touch of her hand on his sleeve didn't evoke the same sensations as Honoria's had. "Call me Anne. I think it's safe to dispense with formalities. At least when we're out of earshot of others, don't you?"

His cheeks hurt from maintaining the smile. "As you wish. You may call me Drake." He escorted her to a chair and made sure she was comfortable.

"I thought I would go mad if I stayed in that bed one moment longer. How people can be invalids is beyond me."

Drake blinked at her statement, finding it a mite uncaring. "I doubt, given a choice, they would choose such a state, Anne."

Her blue eyes widened. "Oh! I didn't mean it that way. I'm always saying things I shouldn't. Of course they can't help it. I only meant it must be horrible for them."

Relieved—a little—Drake nodded. Honoria would never say anything so unfeeling. But perhaps it was Anne's youth—which led him to ask, "Forgive my impertinent question. But might I enquire as to your age?"

"Two-and-twenty, sir. But I'm told I appear much younger."

She did indeed, not to mention acted much younger. Only three years younger than Honoria, yet Honoria seemed ages ahead in maturity.

"Andrew was pleased as Punch to hear of our attachment. He thinks you're quite the gentleman." She batted those eyelashes at him again—a behavior he found a trifle annoying. "He says he will welcome the day when you offer for me."

Had his valet tied his neckcloth too tightly? He suddenly found it difficult to breathe. His cheeks throbbed again as he forced another smile. "That might be a bit premature. We have only begun to get to know each other. I wouldn't want you to make any hasty decisions."

Time. He needed time, especially considering Simon's proposed plan.

However, the dejected expression on Anne's face tugged at his heart, and the image of her lying unconscious on the ground poked at him, reminding him of his promise. *If she survives...*

Speaking of Simon, his friend tapped a spoon against a crystal glass, drawing everyone's attention to where he stood. "Ladies and gentleman. Allow me to speak for everyone here regarding our relief that Miss Weatherby appears to be no worse for wear after her horrendous fall. It's time for our festivities to recommence. Tomorrow I've planned something more sedate, to make sure Miss Weatherby doesn't overdo." Simon sent a wink in Anne's direction.

She laughed, her cheeks pinkening a little.

"Then in two days," Simon continued, "will be the ball, followed by fireworks. I have spared no expense for your entertainment."

Drake chortled to himself. Easy for Simon to say, as the money was not his to spend. However, Drake especially looked forward to the ball. Dressed in his finest evening wear rather than the rough clothes of a groom, he would dance with Honoria to music from a real orchestra, twirling her around on a real dance floor instead of in a field of flowers and humming a tune that was out of fashion. And Honoria would look gorgeous in her gown—

"Oh, a ball and fireworks," Anne said, shattering his daydream. "How romantic." From the dreamy expression on her face, Drake could only guess she would expect a proposal that very night.

He prayed Simon's plan would work.

CHAPTER 19

"Such a ridiculous game." Charlotte glared at Burwood, her dark brows drawn low over her eyes.

Honoria, on the other hand, found charades rather amusing. "Come now, Charlotte. Admit that you find it entertaining. Watching Lord Middlebury try to act out Julius Caesar was priceless. When he clutched at his chest and fell to the floor, I almost believed his heart had given out."

"Odious man," Charlotte mumbled, not quite low enough to avoid others in the vicinity from hearing.

Next to Charlotte, Viscount Montgomery gave a soft laugh—his wife less subtle.

"We should all be so lucky," Lady Montgomery said.

Her husband chastised her. "Bea." But there was no heat to his words, and the ghost of a smile breached his face.

At the moment, Anne was growing frustrated acting out her assigned task, as were the onlookers.

"A squirrel on a camel," Burwood shouted.

Anne's shoulders slumped. "No!"

"No talking, Anne," Miranda shouted.

Only two days since Anne had awakened from her fall, the poor dear would be back in bed if someone didn't guess soon.

Once more, Anne's arms moved in an arch formation.

"The Arch of Constantine," Drake called out.

Anne opened her mouth, snapped it shut, then shook her head. Stopping for a moment, she placed a finger on her chin. Her eyes brightened as if a brilliant idea occurred to her. She started making poking motions, jabbing something in thin air, then she made additional motions, jerking up and backward.

"A war," Honoria called out.

Anne touched the tip of her nose.

"Waterloo," Victor Pratt called.

Anne made the arching motion again, then a swimming motion.

Weren't most wars fought overseas? England was, in fact, on an island. Suddenly, Anne pointed at Ashton, who appeared nonplussed to be singled out.

Everyone's attention turned toward the duke, but he shook his head, clearly not understanding the connection. "The Peninsular War?" he asked, his own voice indicating his doubt.

"No. She said it wasn't Waterloo," Victor said.

A small heated discussion arose that Waterloo was a later battle and not part of the Peninsular War. For a moment, everyone forgot Anne—except Honoria.

Anne began mimicking drinking tea, then acted as if she were throwing heavy objects. Then she flailed her arms up and outward.

A splash?

Honoria's mind started clicking the pieces together. War. Tea. Something heavy being thrown into the water. Ashton. The last piece didn't seem to fit until she remembered Ashton had spent time in America. "The war with America!" she called.

Anne jumped up and down and pointed to Honoria. "Yes!"

"Well done, Lady Honoria!" Burwood called out. "Miss Weatherby, choose the next victim . . . err . . . participant."

Charlotte leaned in. "I owe you for saving us all from enduring another tortuous moment of this buffoonery."

For one of the few times that day, Honoria laughed. "You're being dramatic. Perhaps you should go next?"

Charlotte's eyes widened, no doubt horrified at the suggestion, but Anne saved her from her perceived humiliation.

"I choose Drake . . . I mean, Mr. Merrick to be next."

Drake selected a piece of paper from the bowl Burwood held aloft. When he glanced at it, he winced.

What on earth could he have selected?

For a moment, he stood perfectly still.

"We're waiting, Merrick," Burwood goaded.

Drake flashed him a disdainful glance, and Honoria worried he might jeopardize his position with the duke.

His gaze snapped to Honoria, his face apologetic. Then, moving toward Anne, he dropped before her on one knee and stretched out his arms as if in supplication.

A hard lump lodged in Honoria's throat.

Beside Honoria, Miranda muttered, "Oh, no. I believe he selected mine."

Anne, on the other hand, seemed to have forgotten they were playing a game, for she, too, seemed overcome by emotion. "Oh, yes, Mr. Merrick! Yes! I accept."

Gasps sounded around the room.

Eyes widened, face paper white, Drake shook his head frantically. Ignoring the murmurs of speculation around him, he continued the game, jumping up and pantomiming fencing an opponent. Then he pretended to drink something and fall to the floor.

Anne fell to his side. "Mr. Merrick! Drake! My love!"

Honoria's legs grew weak, and her head was spinning.

Miranda grasped her arm. "I should end this travesty. Romeo and Juliet!"

Drake bounded to his feet—almost knocking Anne aside—tapped his nose and pointed to Miranda. "Yes!" Relief painted his face.

But the damage was done.

Anne's besotted expression told a tale almost as tragic as Shakespeare's star-crossed lovers.

Unable to witness the display any longer, Honoria fled from the room.

THE FATES WERE AGAINST HIM. IT WAS THE ONLY EXPLANATION Drake could manage as Anne stared adoringly at him. When he'd read what was written on the slip of paper he was doomed to act out, he wanted to go to Honoria and play out the scene with her.

But how would that have looked to Anne? Not to mention Stratford. In his haste, he had chosen poorly.

Lord Middlebury waddled up. "Is there something you wish to announce to all present, Merrick? We've all heard about your gallantry to Miss Weatherby."

"He was my knight, Lord Middlebury." Anne threaded her arm through Drake's and gazed at him with lovesick eyes.

Drake wanted to run from the room. "Thank you for assisting me in the charade, Miss Weatherby. How astute of you to discern my task was *Romeo and Juliet.* You played your part well." He hoped she understood that's all it was—playacting.

She batted her eyelashes. "It is easy to play what one truly feels, is it not?"

Oh, dear God.

Middlebury studied them, setting Drake's nerves on edge.

"Choose the next participant," Simon called, his tone not as jovial as it had been with Anne.

When Drake caught his gaze, Simon glowered at him.

Who remained who hadn't played? Drake scanned the room, deliberately looking for Honoria. She'd been standing by Lady Miranda and Lady Charlotte, both of whom had their heads together discussing something. But Honoria was nowhere to be seen.

Where was she? When he'd chanced a glance at her during his ill-fated performance, she looked mortified—and hurt. "Lady Charlotte, you have yet to participate."

Apparently, it was Drake's day for mortifying gently bred ladies.

Lady Charlotte shook her head. Drake supposed much like he had when Anne presumed he was proposing.

Glee broke across Simon's face as he held the bowl high, shaking it and rustling the slips of paper within. "Yes. Yes. Lady Charlotte."

Miranda gave Charlotte a little nudge forward.

The scowl Charlotte directed toward Simon could have frozen the hottest spot in hell. As she attempted to make her choice, Simon jerked the bowl away and out of her reach, causing her to stumble against him.

Oh, there is definitely something *there.*

"That's not very gentlemanly, Burwood," Victor Pratt called out. "Allow the lady to make her choice."

Simon lowered the bowl, and Charlotte snatched a slip, sending Simon one final frosty look. "Thank you, Mr. Pratt. At least someone here knows how to treat a lady."

As Charlotte reluctantly began her pantomime, Drake had no idea what she was acting out; his mind slipped away to Honoria. "Miss Weatherby . . . Anne, if you would excuse me for a moment?"

"Only a moment. But I shall miss you, nevertheless."

Slipping her a quick smile, he hurried away. Moments after he made it out of the room, someone called his name.

He turned to find Lady Miranda. At first eager to brush her off and continue his search, he realized she might speed the progress of his quest. "Forgive me, but do you know where Lady Honoria went?"

"To her room, I believe. She suddenly felt ill." When he tried to step away, she stopped him. "Mr. Merrick, is your affection toward Anne genuine?"

"I beg your pardon?"

"Please don't play coy with me, sir. Both Honoria and Anne are my friends, and I don't wish to see either of them hurt. Do you have genuine affection for Anne, or is this some form of martyrdom on your part from a sense of guilt?"

Certain his mouth fell slack, he could only stare.

"Don't look so surprised. Anne tells us everything, even if Honoria remains tight-lipped. Anne is under the impression that your intentions are to offer for her. Her judgment may be somewhat, shall we say, clouded. So my question is quite straightforward. Do you hold genuine affection for her?"

She held up her hand when he opened his mouth. "And by that I mean, do you love her as she deserves? As a husband should love his wife? Answer me truthfully. I promise I will not think less of you if your answer is no."

"I hardly know her. Love can grow within a marriage."

"True. My brother and Bea are a good example, although we discovered Bea had loved Laurence for years prior to their marriage. But they're alike." Her lips curved in a tiny smile. "A little odd, both of them, but together, they're perfect. However, others aren't as fortunate —especially if they have little in common. They drift apart, resentment grows, and each is miserable. I've seen enough matches like that to know I wouldn't wish it upon my worst enemy, much less a dear friend. Which is why I must ask you again, perhaps more bluntly. Do you love Anne?"

"No. But I could learn to." He forced out the lie, or at the best, the hopeful goal.

Miranda shook her head. "Not good enough. I want my friends to marry someone who loves them completely. Who doesn't think of someone else each time they look at them."

Drake's ears burned from the direct hit. "You have lofty ideals, my lady. I thought people in the aristocracy married for position, wealth, or power." It was a low blow, he admitted.

Miranda didn't flinch. Apparently, she was made of sterner stuff. "Most do. But I've discovered there is more to life. I urge you, Mr. Merrick, to put an end to this farce as soon as possible. The longer you delay, the greater the injury to all involved." With that, she turned on her heel and left him.

Free from Miranda's interrogation, he proceeded toward the staircase to check on Honoria. He only made it ten paces when a slightly deeper, more imposing voice stopped him.

"Merrick." Stratford barked Drake's name as if it were an obscenity.

Drake returned the volley. "Stratford."

"*Lord* Stratford to you, sir. Where are you going in such a hurry?"

"That, *sir*, is none of your concern. I live here, and I can go where I please."

"You live here by the grace of Burwood. You would be wise not to forget it."

The irony of Stratford's words was not lost on Drake. He felt his mouth creep into a smile. "I couldn't if I wanted to. Now, if you would excuse me."

Stratford would not be deterred. "It might surprise you to know I've come to congratulate you."

Well, that *was* a surprise. "For?"

"Your attachment to Miss Weatherby. It seems you have lowered your standards—although they're still exceedingly high for someone like you."

"Someone like me?" The man hadn't changed at all, it seemed. Still an arrogant, snobbish—

"A nobody. Less than a nobody. A servant."

Drake clenched his fists, keeping them tight at his side lest he do something he would regret. "Is that what you think of *your* servants, my lord? Oh, wait. Of course it is. It's how you treated my father, mother, and me. And to be clear, Francis Merrick was not a servant. True, you employed him, but as steward, his status was higher than others in your household."

Stratford sneered. "Such as a groom?"

Drake had walked right into the jab, and he blamed himself for allowing his emotions to take control. Memories assaulted him. Standing in front of Stratford's desk. His cap clutched in his nervous fingers. Asking for Honoria's hand in marriage. Laughed at. Threatened. Turning down the offer to pay for a commission in the cavalry, only to accept it two days later when Honoria rejected him.

He fought back the bile rising in his throat.

"I'm no longer a groom nor in your employ. You saw to that eight years ago when you bribed me to go away. Now, please take your insincere congratulations and leave."

"Oh, but they are most sincere. Anything that keeps you away from my daughter is most welcome. Perhaps now she will free herself from the notion of rekindling her association with you and be open to a more advantageous union. Burwood perhaps."

Drake had had enough of the man's taunts. "Don't count on it." As Stratford continued to rant behind him, Drake bounded up the stairs. But by the time he reached the landing, Stratford's last words niggled at his brain.

Free herself from the notion of rekindling her association with you.

Had Honoria expressed such a desire to her father, or was it speculation on Stratford's part?

As he strode toward Honoria's room, he considered both, along with Lady Miranda's plea.

He stood for long moments, his hand poised to knock on her door, debating the best course of action.

HOW MANY TIMES WOULD SHE RUN AWAY FROM THE PAIN? HONORIA paced the floor of her room, trying valiantly to push the image of Drake and Anne from her mind and failing miserably.

She had debated a marriage to Burwood, but as difficult as it would be to live in the same house as Drake, it would be exponentially more difficult if he were married to Anne. Seeing them together, day after day, would crush her.

No. A marriage to Burwood was out of the question.

Three sharp raps sounded at her door. Expecting to see Miranda, or perhaps Charlotte, she prepared a—hopefully—believable reason for disappearing.

However, she did not expect to see her father waiting on the other side.

"Honoria. May I come in?" He peered behind her, then scanned the room.

It wasn't until she widened the door to allow him entrance that he met her gaze. His brows drew together. "Your eyes are red. Have you been . . . weeping?"

The strangled sound of the last word almost made her laugh.

Almost.

But not quite.

Her father had always been uncomfortable around strong emotions; he believed them a sign of weakness.

"Nothing with which to concern yourself, Father. Why did you wish to see me?" She could count on one hand the number of times he appeared in her room, typically leaving the task to her mother, or at least her maid.

"You left abruptly." He looked around the room again.

What did he expect to see?

"The hours spent at Anne's bedside have taken their toll. I merely came up to rest."

"Alone?"

She jerked back at his implication. "Of course alone. Who did you expect to be with me?"

It was a day for rare occurrences, for he pulled his gaze away. His lips tightened in a grimace, the expression on his face like a small boy caught doing something naughty. "Well . . . I saw Merrick heading upstairs shortly after you left and—"

"You thought I had made an assignation with him?!" She had never wished to strike her father, but at the moment, she envisioned delivering a sound slap. It remained an unexecuted action. But words, those were a different matter. "How dare you!"

"Honoria." He held out his hands in supplication, and her mind immediately went to Drake's pantomime with Anne. "We can't let that ugly bit of gossip resurface. It could ruin any chances you have with Burwood. You must understand."

"Oh, I understand. You don't trust me." She kept to herself that if circumstances were different, she might very well have suggested a liaison with Drake.

"It isn't you I don't trust. It's Merrick. I've seen how you have been mooning over him. Say what you will about him; the man isn't blind. Men will take what isn't theirs if they think it's freely offered—intentions honorable or not."

"Drake isn't like that."

"No?" He waved it aside, no doubt realizing he fought a losing battle. "Nevertheless, perhaps now that he's attached himself to the Weatherby girl, you will see the futility of any future with him."

"On that, you can rest easy, sir. I understand the implications of his attachment to Anne all too well."

More than you realize.

His expression softened, and at that moment, he looked more like the father who had bounced her on his knee as a child. Devoted. Loving. Protective. "I only wish for your happiness, my dear. Burwood, although not the most couth of men, has shown great interest, and with your gentle touch, he could become a duke you would be proud to call husband."

"My happiness?" She did laugh then. "If you had cared for my happiness, I would be married to Drake this very moment. Perhaps with children you could dote upon."

"Honoria," he pleaded. "You were a child. Incapable of making good decisions. What father would allow his well-bred daughter to marry a groom?"

"One who loves his daughter."

The door to her room remained open and a servant passing stopped and peered into the room, her eyes widening.

Honoria recognized the maid from when she came in to tidy her room earlier. "It's fine, Cora. My father and I are just having a disagreement."

The maid hurried past, and her father's brows shot up. "You don't need to explain *anything* to servants. They are paid to keep their mouths shut."

He turned in a circle, pacing in place. "I do love you." His hand rubbed at the back of his neck. "I know I'm not demonstrative, but I've only wanted what's best for you."

"And, in your estimation, would that now be Burwood?" She shouldn't goad him, but she needed to make him understand.

He waved a hand in front of him as if he were presenting an argument before Lords. "You women are always going on about a man's appearance. Burwood's certainly not old or hideous, and he seems in good health. He has a sense of humor." He mumbled something that sounded like *although crass.* "I believe he would give you the affection you seem to crave."

Did he truly believe that was all it took? "What you say is all true. I'll not deny it. But you forget one very important detail."

"Which is?" Her father appeared genuinely interested in what she would say.

"As Burwood's man of business, Mr. Merrick resides here. It would break my heart to see him constantly, especially if he were married to my friend. Rather than bringing my happiness, it would be a living hell."

"Honoria, watch your language!"

"No! I'm tired of watching my language and tired of sacrificing to please you."

He blinked repeatedly, his mouth hanging open. "I . . . you . . . still love him that much after all these years?"

Angry tears flooded forth. "Yes. I've always loved him. Why do you think I've discouraged every suitor who came after him? Perfectly lovely gentlemen—whose own hearts belonged to another. How could I do that to both them and myself?"

"I had no idea your feelings were so strong." He stepped closer.

Although it was her first instinct, she didn't back away, but allowed him to wrap stiff arms around her and pat her back awkwardly.

"Please leave, Father."

He nodded, shuffling to the door as if he had aged twenty years in the last few minutes. With one final, imploring look, he closed the door behind him with a soft *snick.*

CHAPTER 20

Bent over in a chair in his room, Drake held his head in his hands. "What am I to do?" he asked absolutely no one. His audience was perfect, because he truly didn't want to hear the answer.

He knew what he wanted to do. Tell Miss Weatherby that, although she was a perfectly lovely young lady, his heart belonged to Lady Honoria and always would.

Could he break his promise to God? Would he break Anne's heart? He rather thought the answer to the latter was no, but it didn't relieve him of his obligation to the former.

Aunt Kitty had tried to reason with him, telling him God was bigger than Drake presumed and would certainly understand a promise made in desperation. And wouldn't it be better to cause the young lady a little pain now rather than be in a loveless marriage?

Argh! He ran his hands through his hair.

Knock, knock. "Drake," a familiar feminine voice called from out in the hall.

He bounded from the chair and raced over to the door, throwing it open. "Mother! Juliana! What are you doing here? You were supposed to wait in Dorchester until you received word from me." As much as he wished to chastise them for ignoring his instruction, he couldn't help but be grateful they had.

His mother bustled past in a swish of lilac and silk. His sister, half-sister to be exact, followed her. "Simon implored me to return. Something about hurrying back before you do something you shouldn't. He was rather cryptic, but he mentioned a young lady. Have you selected a bride?"

"It's more like she selected me."

Juliana's blue eyes sparkled. "Can women now propose to men?"

"Hush, Juliana," his mother said, then turned toward him. "Why don't you look happy about this? Or is there another matter that's upset you?" She touched his face as mothers did, tenderly and with concern.

He cupped it against his cheek—her touch soothing—and sighed. "It's a rather long story. Have you just arrived? I'll send for refreshments, and then I'll tell you everything."

After ringing for a servant, he settled them in chairs, and—pacing the room—recounted the tale of the fox hunt, Anne's fall, his vow to God, Aunt Kitty's arrival, and most importantly, his unchanging feelings for Honoria.

Both sat silent during his narration, his only pause when Frampton brought in a tray with tea and sandwiches.

Juliana nibbled on a cucumber sandwich, her blue eyes luminescent. "Oh, Drake. What a pickle you have found yourself in."

His sister's soft heart had always leaned toward the romantic, but in this case, she had the right of it.

Placing her teacup delicately on her saucer, his mother studied him. "I haven't seen Lady Honoria since Francis died and we moved away. The last I heard, the Marquess of Edgerton's brother courted her. But I don't follow the scandal sheets like Juliana."

"Mother says not to believe a word that's written in them. But I find them so deliciously wicked."

Drake raised an eyebrow at his sister. She was a mere girl when he left, still with plaited hair and scraped knees, but at twenty, she was now a woman fully grown. "No talk of wickedness, please. I have enough to worry about at the moment. But once I'm married, I shall have to secure a suitable match for you."

She straightened her shoulders. "You just said Miss Weatherby selected you as husband. Why can't I do the same?"

He ran a hand across the back of his neck. "It wasn't exactly as if she proposed to me. She sort of assumed my concern was more than it was."

"And Honoria?" his mother asked, returning to the crux of the matter. "What of her feelings?"

"Stratford implied Honoria's feelings remain unchanged as well."

"Of course he's here," his mother muttered, then took another sip of tea. "And he spoke to you directly?"

"He did, reminding me I still wasn't good enough for his daughter."

Juliana shook her head. "But you're a duke! How isn't that good enough?"

"Ah, but remember, they don't know that yet. You must keep silent until I'm ready to reveal that. It's why I was reluctant to have you present." He turned toward his mother. "Not you, Mother. But Juliana has never been able to keep a secret."

"I'm no longer twelve, Drake. I've kept plenty of secrets from Mama."

His mother lifted a delicate blond brow. "Such as?"

Juliana ignored her. "I promise I won't say anything. After all, you'll always just be Drake to me."

"Good. Remember that and I'll consider allowing you to attend the ball."

In the middle of chewing another bite of her sandwich, Juliana asked, "Will there be other eligible men—beside Simon, that is? He's too much like a brother."

Drake had to laugh, happy his mother and sister had arrived. Juliana always had a way of lifting his spirits. "There will be, but I doubt if any will take you seriously if you speak to them with your mouth full."

In typical Juliana fashion, his sister switched to a complete non sequitur. "I can't wait to see Honoria again. She was always so kind to me."

Once again, Drake's mind latched onto the one word that mattered. Honoria. And she *was* kind—to everyone, no matter their station.

It was one thing he loved most about her.

If he hadn't been such a stupid fool, he might be announcing his and Honoria's engagement at the ball.

But there was still time.

If Simon's plan worked.

When Honoria returned downstairs for supper, guests had gathered in the drawing room. At the side of the room, a semicircle of people formed around Burwood. Drake stood next to the duke, his head of sandy brown hair rising above the group around them. He looked up, his gaze locking on her.

Honoria's stomach gave a familiar flip and then tumbled to her toes when she saw Anne next to Drake, her smile directed Honoria's way. Anne held out her hands in invitation. Honoria could hardly ignore her friend.

When she drew closer, two familiar faces came into view. Drake's mother and sister had arrived.

But why?

Then it dawned on her that perhaps an announcement was forthcoming, and Drake wished for them to be present.

Juliana's face split into a smile. "Honoria!"

Mrs. Merrick admonished her daughter. "*Lady* Honoria, Juliana."

Anne glanced quizzically from Drake to Juliana, and finally to Honoria. "Do you know Miss Merrick?"

"I do. Hello, Juliana. Mrs. Merrick." Honoria smiled and nodded to the two women who, at one time, she hoped would be mother-in-law and sister-in-law.

"My husband served as steward for Lord Stratford," Mrs. Merrick said, her gaze trained on Honoria before turning to Anne. "Didn't Drake tell you? My son served as a groom."

Anne blinked. "Oh. I thought you were in the military before you became Burwood's man of business."

"That is true, Miss Weatherby," Drake said. "But I had a life before the military."

Burwood slapped a hand on Drake's shoulder. "Of course, Merrick's life really started when he met me. Which is undoubtedly what the lovely Miss Weatherby had in mind." The man winked at Anne, and she blushed.

Once, during one of their rides, Honoria had casually mentioned that her father suggested a match for her with the heir to a viscountcy. When she said, although she'd only met him once, she found the young man handsome, Drake had grown sullen, muttering something unintelligible.

However, Drake ignored Burwood's obvious flirtation with Anne and instead smiled.

Odd.

"You're delusional, Your Grace," Drake said.

Juliana moved from her mother's side and slipped her arm through Honoria's. "*Lady* Honoria and I played together. Although she's older than I, she has always treated me as a friend."

"Because you were a friend. *Are* still a friend, I hope." Honoria took Juliana's hands, holding her out so she could look her over. "Has it really only been three years since I've seen you?"

Dressed in a fashionable gown of creamy ivory, the fabric a finely weaved muslin, Juliana glowed. It spoke well of Drake that he saw to his mother's and sister's needs since his father had died. *Burwood must pay him exceedingly well.*

"Drake tells me there is to be a ball. It will be my first."

"Then we must make it especially memorable," Burwood added, sending another wink Anne's way.

What was the man up to?

"I have something very special planned regarding the dancing. I do hope to have one with Miss Weatherby." He winked again. "Maybe two."

Something most definitely was afoot.

Her fan whipping furiously, Anne blushed. "Of course, Your Grace. Who can refuse a duke?"

A roguish grin broke across Burwood's face. "It's what I tell Merrick all the time."

Still, Drake did not object to Burwood's obvious advances toward Anne. Did he refuse to do so for fear of losing his position? Yet, how did that bode for Anne if she married Drake and lived under the duke's roof?

As if reading her mind, Anne asked, "Could I have a word in private, Honny?"

Honoria nodded, and as she and Anne moved toward an unoccupied corner of the room, she could hear the surprised voice of Mrs. Merrick behind her. "Honny?"

"I really dislike that name, Anne."

Anne pursed her lips in a little pout. "Drake has asked me to stop calling you that as well."

Honoria's heart twinged upon hearing Anne speak Drake's Christian name. Apparently, their relationship had grown to allow such familiarity. Another reason to support her argument against marrying Burwood. However, Burwood's attentions seemed to have shifted to Anne. She intended to approach the topic delicately, but she gave Anne preference. "What did you wish to speak with me about?"

Anne darted a glance over her shoulder toward the group they'd just left. "Burwood." She sighed. "Perhaps it's my imagination—goodness knows Andrew says it's vivid—but he seems to be *flirting* with me."

Ah, so their topics were one and the same. It made things so much easier that Anne had brought up the matter. "He does appear to enjoy the pastime. Is it making you uncomfortable?"

Anne's cheeks darkened. "Not exactly." She flashed Honoria a guilty grin. "I rather like it."

Why didn't that surprise her? "You're not returning his advances, are you?"

"No. But . . ."

"But what, Anne? Are you having second thoughts about Mr.

Merrick?" Honoria tried to hold back the creature inside that wished for her friend to say *yes*.

Anne slanted a glance toward her, her words tumbling out. "He's a duke, Honoria. A *duke*! I could be a duchess." A dreamy expression replaced the guilt on her face.

The creature clawed its way free and took control, but Honoria convinced herself she had everyone's best interest at heart. "Anne. If you are considering a match with Burwood, is it fair to Mr. Merrick to lead him on?"

Anne's bottom lip puffed out, reminding Honoria how much like a child Anne was. "But what if the duke isn't serious? You know Mr. Merrick. Wouldn't he be jealous? If I break the attachment with Mr. Merrick, then I shall have nothing. What should I do?"

"Oh, Anne." Honoria took Anne's hands in hers. "I can't speak for Mr. Merrick. But if I had one wish for you, it would be that you would marry the man who makes your heart sing each time you see him. Who looks at you as if you light up his world. In other words, I wish you to marry for love." Unbidden, her gaze traveled to the small group. Even across the room's expanse, Drake's eyes locked with hers. *To feel like this.*

"But what if that never happens? I want to be married. And I *do* feel that way . . . at least when I first meet them."

"Them?"

"Eligible men."

"No one in particular? Not Mr. Merrick?"

"He is handsome." Anne's gaze shifted to the small group. "But so is Burwood." Her shoulders slumped.

"Handsome is all well and good. One should be attracted to one's spouse, I would think. But what about character, or similar interests? Can you imagine yourself thirty years from now with either of these gentlemen?"

Tears formed in Anne's eyes. "I don't know. I'm confused."

Honoria patted Anne's hands. "You're still recovering from your fall. Give yourself some time."

Anne nodded. "Thank you, Honoria." Her face brightened. "Perhaps everything will become clear during the ball."

Honoria forced a smile. "Perhaps."

With a quick peek over her shoulder, Anne sighed. "I should get back. Thank you for listening, Honoria."

As Anne made her way back to Drake, Honoria couldn't help but wonder if the ball would solve everyone's problems, or create new ones.

"Have you told her?" Charlotte's voice jolted Honoria from her musings.

Honoria sighed and faced her friend. "No." Any attempt to feign ignorance of which Charlotte referred was futile. "I can't tell her about what happened between Mr. Merrick and me. My father is already worried about the scandal resurfacing. And although she wouldn't intend to, Anne says things without thinking."

"I see your point." Charlotte threaded her arm through Honoria's. "He asked me to look after you, you know. Your Mr. Merrick."

"He's not mine, Charlotte." *Not any longer.* "But I'm fine, really."

"Liar. And a poor one at that."

They both watched Anne rejoin the group of people surrounding Burwood.

"That man is up to something." Charlotte's brow knit together.

"Burwood?"

"Hmm." Charlotte nodded. "Don't misunderstand, I still think he's obnoxious, but if he's trying to draw Anne's attention away from Mr. Merrick, I may change my opinion"—Charlotte's grin was nothing less than lethal—"slightly. Perhaps from loathsome to merely exceptionally disagreeable."

Amused by her friend's distaste for the duke, Honoria snickered. "He's not that bad. Anne thinks he's handsome."

"Anne thinks any man is handsome." Charlotte tilted her head. "I suppose if he kept his mouth shut, he would be tolerable." She turned her attention toward Honoria. "But the man is as fickle as the wind. Wasn't he fawning over you recently?"

"Not fawning, merely being sociable." She thought back on their conversation while they dined by Anne's bedside.

"You're not interested in him, are you? If so, I would say it's fortuitous the leopard is showing his spots now rather than after you marry him."

Honoria shook her head. "I'm not going to marry Burwood." She held up her hand. "He hasn't asked, if you're wondering. But even if he would, I couldn't bear it. Not if Drake and Anne—"

"Say no more. Then let's hope whatever the duke is playing at changes Anne's mind."

CHAPTER 21

With Anne across the drawing room, Drake leaned in toward Simon and whispered, "Do you have a tic? Your eye keeps twitching."

Withholding a laugh, his mother's lips pressed together. Juliana had no such restraint.

"Too much?" Simon asked, a grin breaking across his face.

"It's becoming annoying," Drake said.

Simon shrugged. "It's working. Did you see her blush?"

Drake narrowed his eyes. "Any woman would blush with such overt advances. Perhaps try something more subtle."

"Ho. Like you? Failing to tell the woman you love of your feelings? Besides, my wink has led to many amorous encounters."

"You are to flirt, not seduce, Simon. That is, unless you *want* to find yourself married to Miss Weatherby? Her brother would no doubt demand it if you compromise her."

Simon's eyes widened in horror. "God forbid! First, I'm not ready to settle down, and even if I were, my tastes lean more to the mature woman."

"How old is she? She seems so young," Drake's mother whispered.

Before Drake could respond, Anne, the object of his mother's

176

assessment and Simon's flirtation, finished her conversation with Honoria and approached.

"Is all well?" Drake asked.

"Hmm?" Anne jerked her gaze away from Simon, who continued to grin at her like a dolt.

"Your conversation with Lady Honoria? You both looked so serious," Drake said.

"Oh, yes. Um." Anne shifted her eyes up and to the left. "We were discussing *The Muckraker*."

"That gossip rag?" Aunt Kitty's voice sounded from behind him, and he turned to face her.

"Not that I've been a subject of it, but that spurious venom has injured more than a few good names." Aunt Kitty gave a sharp jerk of her head as if to drive home the point. "Might you have been one of them, young lady?"

"Well, um." Pink blossomed on Anne's cheeks. "Perhaps. But not as much as Honoria."

Simon's eyebrows hitched, and Drake's mother and sister exchanged glances at Anne's bad form.

Aunt Kitty minced no words. "It is uncharitable to cast another in a bad light in order to remove it from yourself."

Once pink from embarrassment, Anne's face drained of color.

"I'm certain Miss Weatherby meant no disrespect to Lady Honoria, Countess," his mother said, then turned toward Anne. "You two are friends, I understand."

"Oh, we are, Mrs. Merrick. And I would never disparage Honoria. I love her as if she were the sister I never had. Sometimes my words don't come out as intended."

Aunt Kitty grunted a *hmph* at the same time Frampton appeared announcing supper.

"Never mind, Miss Weatherby." Simon moved to Anne's side and placed her hand on his arm. "You shall sit by me at supper. You, too, Aunt Kitty. Perhaps you two should get to know each other better." He held out his arm to Aunt Kitty and led the way into supper.

During the meal, Drake's attention was divided between Simon flirting with Anne, and Honoria seated across from him. His mother and sister flanked him. The arrangement—another of Simon's ideas—drew glares from Lord Stratford, seated several places away.

Odd, though. Stratford's scrutiny appeared less hostile and more curious. He glanced between his daughter and Drake as if he searched for an answer to an unsolvable puzzle.

Drake's tongue became glued to the roof of his mouth each time he looked across at Honoria.

Every lift of her fork, graceful, each bite of food, so delicately chewed, her conversation, pleasant and inoffensive, her laugh, light as air, she was the epitome of a woman bred to be a duchess. No wonder her father had objected to her lowering herself to marry a groom.

Lord, she was perfect.

Candlelight illuminated her face, calling attention to the freckles dotting the bridge of her nose and otherwise marring her ivory complexion. She'd been out in the sun too long. Oh, and that nose. Upturned just enough to make him want to kiss the tip. Her chin short, her forehead perhaps a bit too high.

And her lips? He couldn't stop staring at them each time she slid a piece of food past them, and he thought of the night in the library when she'd licked chocolate from her fingers.

Someone groaned.

"Drake?"

He tore his gaze from Honoria.

His mother's brows knit together. "Are you unwell?"

Realizing he had been the *someone*, he said, "I'm fine, Mother."

"Then why are you moaning like a cow?" Juliana said.

Heat rushed up his neck, reaching the tips of his ears. He peeked over at Honoria.

A tiny smile graced her lips as she cast her gaze down toward her roast duck. "Perhaps he prefers beef. Otherwise he might have quacked."

"Honoria!" Juliana giggled. "I don't think I've ever heard you make a funnier joke."

Neither had Drake. He couldn't restrain the smile tugging at his lips. "And at my expense. For shame, Lady Honoria. For shame."

"I blame Juliana. She always did bring out the worst in me."

Or the best. Drake loved the playful side she kept hidden but shared with him during their rides on her father's estate.

Laughter erupted at the head of the table, and Drake darted a glance toward Simon. His head thrown back, Simon's hand pounded the table in glee. Anne held a serviette to her lips, but her eyes gave her own laughter away.

Aunt Kitty, on the other hand, appeared appalled.

What bawdy story has he told this time?

Everyone at the table turned toward the spectacle. Stratford's glare turned deadly, but for once Drake had not precipitated it.

As usual, Drake's mother had the good sense to divert the attention of at least those in her proximity. "Have you known Miss Weatherby long, Lady Honoria?"

"Not terribly long. We met at a fête several years ago. People kept commenting how much we looked alike. In fact, at Ashton's masquerade ball this year, Victor Pratt mistook Anne for me. And before you ask how I knew it was him"—she turned her attention to where Victor was chatting with Lady Miranda—"that should be obvious. That long blond hair of his tied back in a queue is quite unmistakable. A bit out of fashion, but also dashing, don't you think, Juliana?"

Drake chuckled at the dumbstruck expression on his sister's face as she gazed at Pratt and nodded woodenly.

When his attention returned to Honoria, jealousy churned his stomach. Perhaps he should grow out his short cropped hair. As he mused about what attracted Honoria to a man, she continued her story.

"I had promised him the next set, but when the time came for the dance, he approached Anne instead. We were both wearing the same shade of green." She waved a delicate hand. "Even for an artist such as Mr. Pratt, it was an easy mistake."

Drake's attention returned fully on Honoria. "But you have green eyes and Miss Weatherby has blue eyes. Surely he should have noticed that?" Drake was certain *he* would. He had memorized Honoria's eyes. Still, a small portion of him envied the fact that Pratt had been promised a dance.

But tomorrow . . .

Juliana swatted him on the arm. "Quit butting in and let her finish the story."

Honoria nodded and smiled, informing him she hadn't minded his interruption in the least. "I suspect Mr. Pratt's offer was more courtesy than actual interest. But, of course, Anne viewed it as a forthcoming proposal." She emitted another musical laugh. "I exaggerate, of course. However, Anne gave more weight to what she viewed as an impetuous request. Later that evening, Mr. Pratt approached me, acting rather uncomfortable. He hemmed and hawed a bit before apologizing for any misperceived overtures seeking an attachment."

Tension in Drake's chest eased that the man Honoria found *dashing* had not pursued her.

"It was at that time he studied me more closely, noticing not only the difference in eye color, as you pointed out, Mr. Merrick, but also the slight difference in our gowns. I explained he had mistaken the other lady for me."

Juliana had stopped eating and leaned closer, as if she didn't want to miss a word. "What did he say? Was he upset?"

Honoria laughed. "Not in the least. Mr. Pratt is a most agreeable man. However, he was concerned the young lady might expect something from him he was not prepared to give. I promised I would explain things on his behalf. Anne was disappointed, but she is resilient, so no real harm was done. We both agreed had he spent a little more time with us he would have discerned the difference, as we are nothing alike in reality."

Truer words. Drake glanced back toward the head of the table. Aunt Kitty had wisely decided to focus on her meal, but Simon continued to flirt and regale Anne with his "charm."

Anne seemed enthralled.

Perhaps Simon's plan was working.

BITTERSWEET. THE ONLY WORD THAT CAME TO MIND AS HONORIA tried to focus on something other than Drake's handsome face. It helped to have Juliana's bubbly personality to distract her.

Somewhat.

Yet each time Drake's eyes locked with hers, her heart rate increased and her stomach performed little flips.

And each time, she reminded herself that he had formed an attachment with Anne. Who, at the moment, seemed entranced by Burwood.

Honoria glanced at Anne, then tilted her head toward Drake in question, but he only smiled, setting her heart fluttering again.

Didn't he mind? Even Anne questioned it. How to bring it up casually?

Ah, yes.

"It's certainly wonderful to see Anne back to her ebullient self, is it not, Mr. Merrick?"

Drake glanced toward Anne and . . . smiled? "It is indeed. She seems to be enjoying herself tremendously."

"Drake told us about Miss Weatherby's fall," Mrs. Merrick said. "Is she typically headstrong?"

"A bit, although I like to think of her as more enthusiastic than willful. When Anne decides on something, she gives her all." Honoria gave Drake a watery smile.

"You mean how she's decided my brother is her rescuing knight?" Juliana waved the bit of duck on her fork. "Oh, she told me all about how he carried her back to the house."

"I was on horseback," Drake said, looking down at his own duck with something akin to dislike. "Someone had to get her back for medical care."

"And you were the best horseman there," Honoria added.

Drake's gaze lifted to her, pride shining in his eyes.

"It's true. Even if it weren't, Mr. Pratt was injured himself, Mr. Weatherby was distraught with worry, and Burwood said he wasn't the best rider, although I suspect he was being modest."

"Modest?" Incredulity rang in Drake's words.

"Does that surprise you, sir?"

Drake nodded. "He's typically a bit of a braggart around women. He must respect you too much to deliver his usual blather."

"You have one of those faces people trust, Lady Honoria," Mrs. Merrick said. "Approachable. Understanding. Kind."

Honoria's cheeks heated, and she stared at her plate, uncomfortable with the compliment.

"It's true," Drake said. "And in this case, it reflects the person within."

Unable to bear Drake's praise any longer, Honoria placed her serviette next to her plate. "If you will excuse me." She made no explanation, but rose as quickly yet politely as possible.

Outside the dining hall, she pulled in several deep breaths, her lungs burning from the influx of air. Pain, dull and throbbing, assaulted her heart.

A soft, comforting feminine voice sounded behind her. "My lady?"

Quickly wiping away the building tears, Honoria spun around. "Mrs. Merrick."

Compassion shone on Mrs. Merrick's face. Even as a girl of thirteen, Honoria would run to the Merrick cottage when she had a scraped hand or knee. Mrs. Merrick never lectured about the proper comportment of young ladies.

"My son is a fool."

Blink.

"I beg your pardon?"

"Oh, he believes he's doing the right thing. The honorable thing, but he's wrong. He does Miss Weatherby, himself—and you—a disservice by pursuing a woman he doesn't love all because of a perceived duty."

"She is correct, Honoria."

Honoria spun toward her mother's voice. When had she joined them?

Mrs. Merrick curtsied. "Lady Stratford."

"Mrs. Merrick." Her expression inscrutable, her mother nodded toward the other woman, then turned her full attention on Honoria. "Unless overcome by illness, one typically remains at the dining table until the host rises. Naturally, your father and I grew alarmed at your sudden departure." No censure tinged her mother's words, only genuine concern. "But it would appear it is not illness of the physical variety that precipitated your withdrawal. Perhaps Mr. Merrick has something to do with your distress. Especially given Mrs. Merrick's statement when I appeared."

Mrs. Merrick remained stoic, yet she defended her son as any mother would. "My son would never intentionally do anything to cause Lady Honoria pain, my lady. In fact, he wished to attend to her himself, but I dissuaded him, explaining it wasn't proper."

The movement so minimal, one would easily miss it, but her mother's brows lifted a fraction. "Indeed? Then we are of like mind, Mrs. Merrick. It would not do for either my daughter or your son to be caught in a compromising position."

"Drake would never!" The words flew from Honoria's mouth before she could call them back, and this time, her mother's brows did rise.

"Let us hope not. Nevertheless, I agree with Mrs. Merrick that a union with Miss Weatherby would be unwise if he only does so out of a sense of duty."

Was this the same woman who had stated it was Honoria's duty to marry well? Who had convinced her to give Drake up?

"Mother, I don't think I've ever heard you say something so . . ."

"Plebeian?" her mother asked, a slow smile spreading across her face. "Perhaps I'm learning something from all you young people with your ideals of marriage being based on love. I've only to observe Ashton and the duchess, Lord and Lady Montgomery, and yes, even that rake who left you for an American, to see the power that love can wield."

Honoria was speechless. A small spark of hope flickered to life to have the two women she loved dearly as champions.

"Now, if you must take your leave, go now. Mrs. Merrick and I shall make your apology to Burwood and the other guests."

"What of Father?"

"Leave your father to me, but regarding the conversation between the three of us, perhaps we should keep him in the dark."

Her mother took Mrs. Merrick's arm, a tiny smile gracing her face.

"Come, Mrs. Merrick, let us repair to the dining room as if nothing has happened."

And as the two women walked away, Honoria glimpsed her mother as she must have been as a young girl, full of mischief and the love of secrets.

She wished she would have known her mother as she was then, and her heart squeezed.

CHAPTER 22

D rake's appetite vanished the moment Honoria left the table. He had to muster all of his strength not to rush after her. Only his mother's staying hand had kept him in his seat before she followed Honoria.

He pushed his roasted vegetables aimlessly around his plate with his fork.

"Are you going to eat those or just play with them?" Juliana asked, a smile tipping her lips.

"Why do you think she left in such a rush?"

"Mother?"

Drake barely refrained from rolling his eyes. "No, brat. Honoria."

"Probably because she grew tired of staring at your ugly face."

Drake fought the impending smirk. "Simon should have requested you stay in Dorchester."

"Then who would be here to pound some sense into you? Simon?" She snorted a laugh, drawing a disparaging glance from Lord Middlebury several seats away. "He understands women about as much as this duck on my plate."

"The duck is deceased, Juliana. The poor thing can hardly defend itself against your judgment."

"My point exactly."

Before he could ask his sister to enlighten him, his mother and Lady Stratford reentered the dining room. Honoria was not with them.

As his mother reseated herself next to him, he kept his attention focused on Lady Stratford, who leaned in and said something to Lord Stratford.

"How is Honoria? Did her mother upset her?"

"Her mother was most understanding. You might be surprised, Drake, but I think you may have an advocate in her."

Surprised didn't nearly describe his reaction. Astonished came closer.

"Now if you would only end this foolishness with Miss Weatherby," Juliana said, poking the duck she had compared to Simon.

Drake ignored her and instead signaled to a footman. "Have a maid take dessert up to Lady Honoria's room. It's one of her favorites."

The footman nodded. As he turned, Drake stopped him. "Oh, and if there are any left, have the cook add a few pieces of chocolate-covered marzipan to the tray."

When supper was over and Simon rose, Drake breathed a sigh of relief. The ladies left to gather in the drawing room, and Drake joined the men in the billiards room.

Simon handed him a brandy snifter, which Drake accepted. He needed a drink.

"My plan's working," Simon said, keeping his voice low. "Anne has asked me nonstop questions about my plans as duke, dropping not-so-subtle hints about how she could provide direction when planning parties."

"So she's forgotten me already?" The thought shouldn't gall, but it wounded his pride nonetheless. After all, Anne was supposed to be enamored with him. "It's taken little to turn her head."

Simon shrugged. "Well, when she offered her assistance, she hurried to clarify it would be because she would be easily available, living here as your wife." He clapped Drake on the shoulder. "But we're almost there. A slight nudge is all she needs. I suspect Aunt Kitty has some ideas."

Drake tossed back the brandy. "Should I worry about that? Aunt

Kitty did not appear *pleased* with your raucous behavior. She can hardly encourage Anne to consider you if, as your aunt, she disapproves."

"Why don't you make this easy on everyone and just tell the girl of your feelings for Honoria?"

"I won't be the one to break my promise. I know what that feels like. If Miss Weatherby changes her mind, that's another matter altogether."

"Then we must see to it that she does."

Once the men finished their drinks and cigars, they joined the ladies in the drawing room. Anne's face brightened upon seeing him, and he dutifully moved to her side. "Miss Weatherby, I trust you enjoyed Burwood's company during supper?"

"I did, sir. But have you forgotten we are using our Christian names?"

He motioned around them. "I thought perhaps since others are near . . ."

She dismissed his objection as if it were a trifle. "But everyone knows we have an attachment." She slid her hand around his arm. "There is no need to be so formal, is there?"

He swallowed an uncomfortable lump. "For propriety? Your reputation?"

"Listen to Mr. Merrick, child." As stealthy as a cat, Aunt Kitty appeared next to him as if she had taken form from the air. "Now, take Lady Honoria Bell for example. A finer example of how a young woman should comport herself cannot be found." The countess's gaze slid toward him. "Speaking of the young lady, what happened during supper? Is she unwell?"

Anne blinked, then looked around the room. "Honoria? I don't see her."

Aunt Kitty gave an exasperated *hmph*. "That's what I'm trying to find out, girl. She left rather suddenly during supper."

"She did?" Anne blinked, her head tilting. "I hadn't noticed."

Drake was quite certain if one of Honoria's friends had left abruptly during a meal, she not only would have noticed, she would have made it her business to find out what had transpired.

"Of course not. You were busy laughing at Burwood's ridiculous stories."

At his aunt's disparaging comment, Drake felt a bit of compassion for poor Anne.

However, the insult floated over Anne's head. "It was the most wonderfully humorous tale, wasn't it? I could listen to him all day." She exhaled a dreamy sigh.

Aunt Kitty's wiry eyebrows hitched, then she turned all her attention on him. "Back to Lady Honoria. Did she take ill?"

"I'm not entirely sure, Countess. Both my mother and Lady Stratford attended to her."

"Did I hear you talking about me, son?" Like Aunt Kitty, his mother materialized from behind him. She curtsied to Aunt Kitty. "Lady Gryffin."

Aunt Kitty nodded in greeting. "Mrs. Merrick. I was enquiring about Lady Honoria. Your son says you attended to her."

His mother answered, "All is well. She is perhaps still exhausted from her vigil by Miss Weatherby's bedside."

"A true friend puts another's needs before one's own," Aunt Kitty said, her gaze sliding toward Anne. "You, on the other hand, appear to be fully recovered. Perhaps next time you go riding, it would behoove you to listen to a more experienced rider." Without another word, Aunt Kitty departed their little grouping and joined Lord and Lady Stratford.

"What a disagreeable woman," Anne said. "Do you think she holds any sway over Burwood?"

"Would that be of importance to you?" Drake asked.

Anne shifted on her feet, her cheeks pinkening. "Well, only because we would live here with him—if we should marry, that is."

Drake wasn't especially adept at sensing when people lied, but he believed there was more to Anne's answer. Still, he answered truthfully. "Although the countess has only recently entered Burwood's life, he gives great weight to his family's approval."

The wisp of a smile brightened his mother's face. "On that, I can agree." Her attention turned toward the room's entrance. "She must be recovered."

Drake followed his mother's gaze to find Honoria had entered. And as it did every time, his breath caught in his throat.

"Mr. Merrick. Mr. Merrick? Drake?" Anne's voice finally registered in his addled brain.

But when he turned toward her, she studied him for a moment, shifted her gaze toward Honoria, then back to him.

From Anne's narrowed brow, he worried—or hoped—he had been found out.

⚜

WHEN A MAID HAD BROUGHT A TRAY WITH DESSERT TO HER ROOM, Honoria wondered who had been so thoughtful. But as she unwrapped the three pieces of chocolate-covered marzipan, she recognized Drake's hand in the gesture.

Would Anne appreciate his thoughtfulness and attention to her every need once they were married?

Honoria sighed as she picked up a piece of the confection and placed it in her mouth, her mind returning to her meeting with Drake in the library the first night.

Coward. The voice inside accused her. How many times had she run away or kept her feelings to herself to avoid conflict? *Too many*, the voice answered. She had taken a small step when she'd confronted her father earlier. But she needed to face the fact that, unless something drastic changed, Drake and Anne *would* marry.

She had no desire to cause her friend heartbreak, but she vowed she would take one final chance of discerning Anne's and Drake's true feelings for each other—no matter how painful the discovery might be.

And if true affection had grown between them, she would have to confront her own feelings and learn to live with the realization that she would always be second best.

Entering the drawing room, she searched for Miranda or Charlotte. Instead, her eyes locked with Drake's. By his side, Anne was saying something to him, her expression troubled.

Drake finally broke the spell when he turned back to Anne, and Honoria pulled much needed air into her lungs. Before she could make her way toward Miranda and Charlotte, the Countess of Gryffin approached.

"Lady Honoria. I hope your arrival means all is well. I noticed your abrupt departure at supper."

"Thank you, Countess. But there is no cause for concern. Simply exhaustion from recent events."

"It appears Miss Weatherby's fall has done more damage to others than to Miss Weatherby." The countess turned her attention toward Anne and Drake—the exact place Honoria hoped to avoid.

Given the circumstances, Honoria struggled for a response. "She is most resilient."

The countess pointed her cane toward Drake. "What is your impression of Mr. Merrick?"

"He's a fine gentleman. Honest, kind, intelligent." She forced a smile. "You can always count on him to do the right thing."

"Hmph. I seriously doubt marrying Miss Weatherby is the *right* thing. As I said before, they don't seem well matched."

Uncomfortable talking about Drake and Anne, Honoria changed the subject. "I understand this is the first time you've met your nephew. I'm sure he is most grateful for your support and will look to your wisdom in navigating society as he assumes his duties as duke."

"He needs a wife for that." The old woman tilted her head, eyeing Honoria as if measuring her for a new gown. "I'm not sure that Weatherby girl is the best choice."

Honoria stared at the countess. *The poor thing must be confused again.* "Oh, but her attachment is with Mr. Merrick, not Burwood."

"Is it? The way she flirted with our host at the dining table would lead anyone to believe she has set her cap for him."

Although Honoria had been taught to respect her elders, friendship demanded she defend Anne. "Miss Weatherby has always been exceedingly friendly. I don't think she's ever met someone she didn't like."

"Any man she didn't like, you mean. I've read some rumors about her in that scandal sheet, *The Muckraker.*"

"With respect, Countess, I fear you do her an injustice. Please do not set store by anything that despicable paper says."

"You don't like gossip?"

"I detest anything that aims to harm another."

Lady Gryffin's sharp blue eyes narrowed. "You, my dear, would make a perfect duchess." With that, she turned and ambled off.

Honoria could only stare at the woman's back. What in the world had all that been about?

Once again, her plans to join Miranda and Charlotte were halted when Drake strode across the room. His gaze trained on her, rooting her in place.

"Lady Honoria. Feeling better?"

"I'm much improved thanks to the thoughtful person who sent my favorite confection to my room."

A lopsided grin spread across his face. "I thought you might enjoy them."

Coward, the voice whispered. *Tell him how you feel.* She wanted to shush the voice into submission. However, she had vowed to discern Drake's true feelings for Anne, so she compromised with her inner creature. "Drake."

"Yes?"

Her stomach did several flips at his continued grin. She needed to keep this formal. "Mr. Merrick. About Miss Weatherby."

The grin vanished, and Drake slid his gaze away. "What about her?"

Now that she had broached the subject, she wasn't quite sure how to proceed. She couldn't exactly ask him if he loved Anne. Could she? How to couch it delicately?

"You're aware that Anne and I are friends?"

His gaze snapped back to hers. "Of course. How could I forget? Your unwavering support by her bedside spoke for itself. Although, knowing you as I do, you would have done the same for anyone. Even me."

Oh! Especially you. "Then you must be aware I'm concerned for her happiness."

"You don't believe I would make her happy?"

The voice grew insistent. *Ask him!* "May I be frank?"

His lips tightened, and he gave a soft huff of annoyance. "I wish you would instead of beating about the bush."

"Do you love her, Drake?"

"No. But I made a promise."

"To whom? To Anne?"

"To myself. To God." He ran a hand across the back of his neck. "Hell, I don't know. I prayed that if she recovered, I would make it up to her."

"For what? For her own recklessness? You tried to stop her, Drake. She didn't listen."

His voice escalated. "I shouldn't have let her ride the damn horse."

Lord Middlebury, standing nearby, turned and glared at them both.

With caution, she touched his arm. "Calm yourself. People are staring."

"Do you think I care?"

"You *should* care."

His brows lifted. "So, I embarrass you?"

"No." She kept her voice low but emphatic. She was making a muck of this. "What I meant is, as Burwood's man of business, if you are to be at his side in society, your own behavior reflects on him."

"So it's the duke you're concerned about, not me?"

"I care about both of you. It will be difficult for him in some circles. At supper the first night, he spoke of wishing to make some much needed changes. In order to be effective, people must respect him. Do you want him to succeed?"

"Of course."

"Then, as his right-hand man, you too must be beyond reproach. I know it doesn't seem fair, but it is the way of things in polite society."

He stared at the ceiling as if looking for an answer. "I suppose you're right."

They'd completely veered from the subject. She kept her voice low. "Is your sense of responsibility and duty fair to Anne? Doesn't she deserve to marry a man who loves her?"

"Are you asking me to end our attachment—if that's what"—he flicked a hand in Anne's direction—"this is between us?"

Say yes. The word gathered on the tip of her tongue but refused to release.

He waited, studying her with those golden eyes. Finally, he said,

"She accepts me for who I am. She doesn't care about titles, position, power, or wealth. Now, if you will excuse me, I should return to her."

He turned on his heel and strode through the crowd as purposefully as he had when approaching.

And as Honoria watched Anne laughing and brushing Burwood's arm with her fan, knowing Anne as she did, she questioned if Drake's assessment of Anne was true.

CHAPTER 23

The house was mercifully quiet the next day as Drake strode through its halls. The night before, Simon had announced he had nothing planned before the upcoming ball, and people could choose whatever recreation they wished at their leisure.

Many ventured outside to explore the grounds and gardens. Others decided to spend the day writing letters or reading in one of the many rooms. A few gathered in parlors for whist or other card games.

Most stayed away from the ballroom as servants worked to prepare it, setting up a dais for the orchestra, chairs for people who wished to rest, and tables for refreshments.

Drake wandered outside, seeking the solitude of the orangery. He loved the smell inside, especially when the trees blossomed, the citrusy scent reminding him of Honoria. Lush plants and the leaves from the trees provided shelter from the vast glass windows and domed roof magnifying the sunlight that allowed the trees to flourish.

After plucking a ripe orange from a branch, he settled on a bench and, using his thumb, poked a hole into the fruit. The sweet fragrance drifted up, enticing him, and he lifted the orange to his lips and sucked out the delicious nectar. A bit of juice dribbled down his chin, and he wiped it away with his fingers.

He chuckled to himself. Not an appropriate behavior for a duke. But for Drake Merrick, groom to Lord Stratford, it had been perfect. He remembered the orangery Stratford had on his estate, although he'd not been allowed inside.

Until, one day in April after a ride, Honoria had pulled him by the hand. "Come with me. I want to show you something." Her eyes were full of mischief. Not something he saw often but admitted he liked.

"What are you up to, my lady?"

She turned her pretty smile on him, and his knees buckled. "You'll see."

As she tugged him along, he glanced around, expecting someone to stop them at any moment. Excitement bubbled in his veins as she approached the orangery.

He stared like a dolt, his mouth surely hanging open when they stepped inside and the fragrance surrounded him. The trees were in blossom and he had never seen nor smelled anything quite like it.

"What do you think?" she asked. Complete seriousness had replaced the playfulness on her countenance, as if her world hinged upon his approval.

"It's . . . magnificent. I heard my father talking about it, but I had no idea it was so wonderful." He inhaled a deep breath of the intoxicating aroma.

She turned in a circle. "It is, isn't it? It's one of my favorite places." She grabbed his hand again, pulling him farther into the building. "And look." She plucked a ripe orange from the tree and handed it to him.

"There are oranges and blossoms at the same time?" It was miraculous.

"Yes. The oranges take a long time to ripen, so the blossoms are for new ones. Try one." She gave him a little push on his arm.

He pulled the knife from his pocket, but she shook her head.

"Wait. Let me show you how I do it." She plucked another orange and poked it with her thumb. A spritz of juice sprayed out, and she laughed. "Father would frown upon this way of getting at the juice, but I love it." She placed the orange to her mouth and sucked.

His heart stopped.

"Go on then." She nudged him again.

Suddenly, an echo of voices in the vast room popped the memory, and it dissipated like mist.

"In here," a feminine voice said.

He rose and peeked through the branches. Lady Charlotte and Anne Weatherby stood beneath one of the large trees.

"What is it?" Anne asked. From the tone of her voice, he expected her to stamp her foot like a child.

"Someone has to talk sense into you. I've elected myself."

Anne snorted. "You would."

Drake wished there was another door he could exit without being seen. Instead, he remained rooted, trying not to listen.

"Honoria may put up with your disrespect, but at the moment, it's only you and I here."

Honoria's name had him taking a step forward, landing on a dried leaf.

Crunch.

"What was that?" Anne spun around, her line of sight directed right toward him.

He slinked back into the shadows of the trees and held his breath.

"It was nothing. Probably an orange dropping from a tree. They do that sometimes. I know I'm not a man, but focus on me, Anne."

Drake stifled a chuckle. What was Simon's problem with the lady? She had a delightful wit.

Anne huffed. "You don't have to be rude."

"Do you care about Honoria?"

"Of course I care about her. She's certainly nicer to me than you are."

"Good grief, Anne. Everyone's nicer to you than I am. That's not the point. I need to talk to you about Mr. Merrick."

"What do you mean?"

"Are you serious about him?"

"Well, he did save me, and he's been so sweet since my fall. But . . ."

"But, what?"

Drake heard Anne's sigh even from his position several yards away.

"Well, the duke has also been most attentive. I'm so confused. I could be a duchess, Charlotte. A duchess! But how can I break Mr. Merrick's poor heart?"

"I don't think you have to worry about that."

"Well, of course I do. I'm not a monster, Charlotte. Unlike you, I care about men's feelings."

To her credit, Lady Charlotte didn't even flinch at the slight. "What I mean is, I think Mr. Merrick's heart belongs to another."

"Noooo." The incredulity in Anne's voice was almost comical. "Who? It's Lydia, isn't it? That scheming—"

"It's not Lydia. I want you to do something, Anne. I want you to pay very close attention to Mr. Merrick when he's around Honoria. Watch their faces."

"Honoria? Does Honoria have feelings for Mr. Merrick? Is he in love with Honoria? What did she tell you?" The questions poured from Anne's mouth faster than a galloping stallion.

"I promised I wouldn't say anything. Just watch them. I think you'll have your answer. And don't you dare tell Honoria or Miranda we had this talk."

Anne propped her hands on her hips. "Or you'll what?"

"You don't want to find out." With that, Charlotte trounced from the orangery.

Anne stood motionless for a moment, then shook her head. "Honoria and Mr. Merrick. It's unthinkable."

For a moment, he worried she might venture farther inside toward him, but the door opened and Simon popped his head around it. "There you are. We need another for whist. Would you care to join me, Miss Weatherby?"

"Oh, yes, Your Grace. I'd be delighted."

Tightness in Drake's chest eased as he was once again alone in the solitude he'd sought, the orange still clutched in his hand. Hope fluttered in his chest. Did Honoria truly still have feelings for him? It wasn't just Stratford's overactive imagination? He would wait a few more moments and then step outside. Possibly go for a ride to ponder the scene he witnessed.

It would appear, although at odds with each other, Simon and Lady Charlotte were his and Honoria's greatest advocates. He would tell

Simon later that they made a great pair—no doubt causing a string of curses to fly from Simon's lips.

While he waited a few more minutes before taking his leave, muted voices once again echoed from outside the building.

The door opened, and this time, Honoria stepped inside.

HONORIA HAD BEEN STROLLING THROUGH THE GARDENS WHEN Miranda stopped her.

"I've received some news about *The Muckraker* from my contact in London. I saw Charlotte and Anne go inside the orangery a while ago. It will be a quiet place for an impromptu meeting. If you hurry, you should catch them, and I'll join you shortly. I have to attend to something first."

Before Honoria could ask any questions, Miranda hurried off toward the house.

As she stepped through the door, the familiar fragrance greeted her, and memories of her father's orangery bubbled up. She scanned the lush foliage dotted with orange globes.

Where are they?

"Charlotte? Anne?"

Crunch. Crunch.

Footsteps sounded.

She turned in their direction.

There. Drake emerged from the green foliage and raised his hand in greeting.

"I'm looking for Lady Charlotte and Anne. Have you seen them?"

His gaze darted to the left, then returned to her. "I . . . I haven't spoken to them this morning, no."

Had Miranda sent her to the orangery knowing Drake was inside? Perhaps that's why she chose not to join her. "I should go."

Drake reached out an arm. In his hand, he clutched an orange. "Don't!"

She stopped short at his pleading expression. Besides, she could never refuse him anything. "Very well, but how would it appear should someone happen upon us? Especially Anne? I was told to meet her and Charlotte here."

"We shall keep a respectable distance." And yet he took several steps closer. "Besides, you can't leave until you've tried an orange."

She looked down at the one in his hand, a smile tugging her lips. "It appears you've already enjoyed that one."

He plucked another from a tree and, coming even closer, handed it to her. "Go on, then."

Oh, she shouldn't. They weren't sixteen and nineteen any longer. It wasn't dignified. Yet she saw the puncture in the orange he held.

"Very well." She broke through the rind with her thumb. Juice squirted out, and she couldn't help but laugh.

"Remember?" He whispered the question, a note of hope in the word.

"How could I forget?" The words sounded wistful to her own ears.

He took another step closer. What happened to keeping their distance? She found she didn't care.

"Go on." He prodded her, his eyes never leaving her face.

She lifted the orange to her mouth and, as daintily as she could, sucked the juice. A drop lingered on her bottom lip.

Before it could trickle down her chin, he brushed it away with his thumb, his touch caressingly tender. Then he placed his thumb in his mouth. "Sweet." He closed the distance with another step, standing but a breath away from her.

His gaze dipped to her lips.

Her knees grew weak. Had the temperature risen? Was it the room or him?

"Honoria," he whispered. "I want to kiss you."

No. She should say no. She swallowed. Her heart pounded against her sternum in a furious tattoo. "Yes."

As he lowered his head, the citrusy scent of his breath made her head spin. Light at first, as if he were testing, the kiss skimmed the surface of her mouth. His lips were soft, softer than she remembered, and sweet from the orange. Or was that him? She couldn't think.

When he increased the pressure, she sagged against him, her body pliable and boneless. Different from the tender kisses of their youth;

this kiss seduced with subtlety. She wrapped her arm around his neck and played with the soft hair brushing the collar of his coat.

Something plopped onto the ground by their feet, and he slipped a supporting arm around her waist to keep her upright.

Time whispered away as if they'd never been apart.

"Ahem."

Drake's lips were still pressed to hers. Who had spoken?

"My, this is a lovely orangery," Miranda's voice broke through Honoria's haze, and Drake bolted away from her as if she had burned him.

When Honoria turned, Miranda was staring at a tree, her body in profile to them. Honoria turned back to Drake, who had moved at least twelve feet away, his face crimson.

She lifted her hands to her own burning face, and he had the audacity to grin at her. "Miranda, what took you so long?"

"Perhaps too long? Or not long enough, depending on who you are. Should I announce I have witnessed a compromise?"

Both Honoria and Drake shouted, "No!"

Although Honoria didn't want to trap Drake into an unwanted marriage, her heart plummeted to her toes at his categoric opposition.

Perhaps she had misunderstood. Pain—or was it apology—shone in his eyes as he jerked his gaze toward her.

Honoria struggled to salvage the situation. "I was enquiring about Charlotte's and Anne's whereabouts from Mr. Merrick. They are not here."

Miranda's lips quirked. "Obviously."

"Perhaps they're in the house?" Drake's suggestion sounded exceptionally confident.

"Yes. The house." Honoria's face heated at her muttered nonsense.

Miranda motioned toward the door. "Shall we withdraw to find them, then?"

Honoria nodded and stepped forward.

"Lady Honoria," Drake said.

Honoria halted her steps and drew in a breath.

"Might I have a word before you leave?"

"I shall wait here." Miranda turned her back to them and hummed lightly to herself.

Honoria forced herself to face Drake.

He stepped closer, but kept a respectable distance and his voice low. "I'm not sorry, if that's what you think."

"For what?"

The lopsided grin spread across his dear face. "The kiss." Just as quickly, the grin vanished. "But I don't want you to be forced into something against your will."

"And there is Anne to consider."

His face fell even further. "Of course."

She wanted to reach out. To touch him again. "I should go."

His hand stretched toward her. "Before you do, promise me a dance at the ball?"

She sent him a tremulous smile. "As you wish."

Grateful that Miranda remained silent when she joined her, Honoria's mind remained on the press of Drake's lips to hers.

CHAPTER 24

Drake stared at the orange at his feet, his mind reeling back to the kiss.

Fool.

With one word, Honoria could have been his. Miranda had witnessed them together. All he had to do was confess to his inappropriate behavior and offer for her.

But hadn't her reputation been sullied enough? And just as he wanted her to choose him for him, he would never want her to question that he had chosen her out of love rather than obligation.

He kicked at the orange with the toe of his boot, taking his frustration out on the poor piece of fruit. After substantial grumbling to himself, he peeked around the door of the orangery, and strode back to the house. Perhaps in his own room he would have some undisturbed peace before the ball that evening.

Light laughter caught his attention as he passed one of the parlors. He stopped and peered in. Guests gathered around tables, playing cards, one of them Anne.

"I did warn you, Your Grace," she said. "My brother is quite competitive."

Indeed, Andrew Weatherby grinned as he announced, "That's

another trick for Alice and me. Tally things up, Alice. I believe that's two games in a row for us."

"Mr. Merrick," Mrs. Weatherby called, catching sight of Drake. "Would you care to play? I believe we've just frightened Anne and the duke away."

"Not frightened, Mrs. Weatherby. Simply partnerless," Simon said. "And although Miss Weatherby is deserting me for her meeting with Lady Honoria and Lady Miranda, Merrick isn't pretty enough for me."

Simon rose from his seat, then pulled out Anne's chair.

Anne breezed past Drake, sending him a curious glance.

Before he could take his leave, Simon stopped him. "Merrick, a word, please." He turned back to the table. "Mr. and Mrs. Weatherby, I shall do my utmost to find more players for your table." He chuckled. "Preferably ones with deep pockets."

"Don't send Montgomery." Andrew chuckled. "Or at least send him to another table."

With a nod, Simon left the room, grabbing Drake by the arm as he exited. "Andrew Weatherby will be a good friend to have if you join one of the London clubs. Although to hear him talk, Montgomery is an even better card player."

"I doubt he will be so keen to befriend me if he believes I trifled with his sister's feelings."

"Balderdash!" Simon's response was rather sedate, considering his usual choice of words. "The girl isn't in love with you, if that's what you're concerned about. Besides, my plan is working." Simon stopped, placed his hands on his hips, and studied Drake. "In fact, she asked me point-blank if you had an interest in Honoria."

"I might know what prompted that question."

"You do?"

"Yes. But first, what did you say?"

"Only that often when people have romantic feelings for each other, it shows clearly on their faces and perhaps she should observe and conclude for herself."

Drake couldn't help but grin. "That's what Lady Charlotte told her."

As if someone had planted him a facer, Simon jerked back. "She did?" His eyes narrowed. "And how do you know this?"

Drake relayed the conversation he overhead while in the orangery, leaving out the part where he kissed Honoria.

Simon grinned. "Perhaps you should have taken up the request to spy for the Crown. But I'll admit I'm surprised that shrew was so clever to suggest that to Anne."

"It appears the two of you are of like mind in that regard."

An inelegant snort escaped from Simon. "That harpy and I have nothing in common."

Drake kept the Shakespeare quote about protesting too much to himself, thinking it wasn't only relevant to women.

Simon's brow furrowed. "What are you grinning about?"

"Nothing." Drake pressed his lips together and raised his eyes. "Now, you were saying something about Miss Weatherby and your *plan*."

"Only that she's hanging on my every word. I've done my best to monopolize her time. However, she has yet to mention anything about how my attentions might look to you. You do your part and gaze adoringly at Honoria this evening, which should be no hardship for you, and Miss Weatherby should end this ridiculous infatuation."

Drake straightened. "Why is it ridiculous?"

"Well, clearly she should have been enamored with me from the start." Running a hand down his bespoke coat, Simon struck a haughty pose. "I am the more handsome of the two of us."

"You're delusional."

Simon planted his hands on his hips. "Do you want to rid yourself of the lady's ardor or not?"

"I do. But you may find yourself married before I am."

"There's yet a woman alive who's able to drag me before the parson. Once you're happily betrothed to Honoria, we can end this charade, and I will let Miss Weatherby down gently."

"From your lips . . ."

"God has nothing to do with this."

"That's what I'm afraid of."

GATHERED IN A PARLOR TUCKED AWAY AT THE BACK OF THE HOUSE, Honoria, Miranda, and Charlotte waited for Anne.

Honoria glanced toward the slightly ajar door. "Are you certain no one will disturb us here?"

"Burwood assured me its location made it unlikely anyone would seek it out intentionally." Charlotte ran a white-gloved finger across a table, then inspected it. "At least the servants keep it clean."

She held up a key. "Plus, he gave me this. Once Anne arrives, we shall lock the door. The cad even suggested that when we're finished, I remain confined in here for the duration of the house party." Her face scrunched in distaste, then morphed into truculence. "As if I would give him the satisfaction. I intend to plague him tonight at the ball."

"Plague who?" Anne rushed into the room, breathless. "I had a devil of a time finding where you were. I had to ask a footman." With an unladylike *plop*, she fell onto the settee next to Honoria.

Charlotte rose and locked the door.

Anne straightened from her relaxed position. "What are you doing?"

"What does it look like?" Charlotte rolled her eyes.

"Who?" Anne asked.

Everyone turned toward her with the same quizzical expression.

"Who what?" Honoria asked.

"Who is Charlotte going to plague at the ball?"

"Burwood, the cad." Charlotte's expression was worrisome indeed. The slight upward curve of her lips that didn't narrow her eyes reminded Honoria of Charlotte's brother, Lord Nash.

"You leave Burwood alone," Anne protested.

Their impromptu meeting was getting out of control. Honoria did her best to return to the matter at hand. "Let us worry about His Grace later. Miranda, you said you have news of *The Muckraker*."

Miranda nodded. "Not so much news as the lack thereof. My source in London wrote to me saying the rag has been ominously silent for days, even though Lord Felix Davies caused a disturbance in a gaming hell."

"That sort of thing is often hushed up," Honoria offered.

"True," Miranda said. "But in this instance, the gaming hell owner called a constable."

Anne's eyes grew large. "They arrested Davies?"

Miranda shook her head. "Only removed him from the premises in order to cool his head."

Charlotte's scowl deepened. "Davies probably paid them a tidy sum to keep it quiet."

"Didn't he court you?" Honoria asked Charlotte.

"Briefly. Before I discovered what a worm he truly is."

Miranda pursed her lips. "Even if Davies paid to keep the incident from the scandal sheets, my source says Dr. Somersby was called to the gaming hell and tended to a man injured in the brawl."

"I hope the injured party was Davies," Charlotte muttered. "But regardless, I doubt Dr. Somersby would say anything. He's not the type to spread gossip."

Miranda sank into her chair in a defeated slump. "I suppose you're right, even if it rebuts my supposition."

"Which is?" Honoria asked, although she had a good idea where Miranda's logic had led her.

"That the instigator is out of London. Perhaps even right here."

Anne vibrated with excitement. "One of the guests?"

Charlotte rolled her eyes. "No, ninny. One of the servants. Of course, one of the guests."

Honoria felt the need to interject. "Wait. Let's not rule anything out. It could very well be one of the servants. Think about it. Servants are unobtrusive. They're able to mingle among us and overhear things without anyone noticing."

"True," Miranda said. "But it would be unlikely for one servant of a household to be privy to what happens everywhere, as the perpetrator seems to be."

"Also, true," Honoria said. "Which makes Anne's deduction that it might be a guest logical."

Anne blinked. "You think I'm logical?"

Charlotte waved it away. "Honoria is being Honoria. Which is to say, generous and kind. Something you should consider if you recall our conversation."

Anne glanced at Honoria, her mouth opening then snapping shut.

What conversation?

At Miranda's dejected expression, Honoria said, "And it doesn't rule out Miranda's supposition. Surely, someone who witnessed the brawl would have said something. Davies isn't well-liked. But whether the perpetrator is still in London, here, or elsewhere, we must be vigilant. Perhaps the next publication will provide a clue."

"I've asked my contact in London to forward any copies to me at once," Miranda said.

Charlotte raised a dark eyebrow. "Are you ever going to tell us who this mysterious contact of yours is? Is it a man or a woman?"

Miranda's enigmatic expression gave nothing away. "I reserve the right to protect my sources." Her eyes shifted toward Honoria, and she delivered a sly smile. "I'm good at keeping secrets."

Honoria's cheeks burned at the memory of Drake's kiss.

"Why are you blushing, Honoria?" Anne's gaze locked on her, then a strange awareness covered her face, and she jerked her head toward Charlotte.

Giving an almost imperceptible nod, Charlotte rose. "Now, perhaps we should all retire to our rooms and rest before the ball this evening. I expect to do my share of dancing since Edgerton isn't here to approve my partners. I'm feeling generous enough that I may even dance with that irascible duke."

As Charlotte unlocked the door, Anne protested, "Burwood isn't irascible. He's wonderful."

Charlotte gave an unladylike snort and exited with Anne close on her heels, still arguing the point.

Honoria touched Miranda's arm, stopping her. "You won't say anything, will you?" She swallowed. "About what you saw in the orangery?"

Her face as placid as a summer pool, Miranda stared at her. "But I find oranges such an interesting topic of conversation." She smiled, patting Honoria's hand. "Don't fret. But I expect you to someday return the favor should I need it. In the meantime, if you require it, I could ask for the key to this room and lock both you and Mr. Merrick inside until you've both come to your senses."

With that, she left in a swish of lily-of-the-valley.

Honoria sank to the settee again, pondering everything that was said in the locked room. Could *The Muckraker's* culprit be among them? What did that silent exchange between Charlotte and Anne mean? Would Miranda remain mum about the compromising situation she'd witnessed?

But most importantly, did Honoria want her to?

DRAKE RAN A HAND DOWN THE SILVER WAISTCOAT AS HE GAUGED HIS appearance in the dressing table's mirror. It contrasted nicely with the jet black evening clothes he had custom tailored by his Grandfather Abernathy.

His valet gave a nod of approval. "Very befitting, Your Grace. Abernathy does excellent work. Should you announce your true identity this evening, you shall look every bit the duke."

"I'm not sure I'm ready for that, Dawson. But thank you." Drake tugged a little at the elaborately fashioned neckcloth.

Dawson's brow knit, and he reached toward Drake's neckcloth. "Is it too tight, sir?"

Drake shook his head. "I'm sorry. Nerves."

"Your Grace, as duke, if you choose to muss your cravat or even discard it entirely, no one would dare say a word."

"No. I need to do everything correctly." *Especially if I'm to win Honoria.*

"I have faith in you, sir. Will there be anything else?"

Drake shook his head. "Leave the door open if you would. I'm in need of some air."

Alone, he stood at the window, staring down at the darkened terrace.

"Oh, Drake. You look so handsome."

He spun around at his mother's voice. Framed within the doorway, she looked lovely. The deep shade of sapphire complemented her skin and blond hair.

"I pale compared to you. We should have your portrait done. To go with Father's." He pointed next to the painting of his father Aunt Kitty had brought.

"Oh." The tiny whisper escaped her lips as she floated forward, her hand clutched to her throat. Tears formed in her eyes.

"I'm sorry. I didn't mean to upset you."

She shook her head, and her lips trembled in a wobbly smile. "Just memories." She touched his arm reassuringly. "Beautiful ones. You look so much like him, but still seeing this . . ." She stopped, her voice choked with emotion. "Do you see the decoration on his waistcoat?"

Drake leaned in, examining the portrait closer. "Are those pink flowers?"

His mother nodded, wiping her eyes. "Yes. Rosebuds. I embroidered them—in error. His father was furious. But Henry . . . Henry said he loved them and would be proud to wear them in his portrait. It was the beginning of our romance."

Drake wrapped an arm around her waist, and they stood admiring the portrait together. "Tell me more about him. Aunt Kitty provided some information, but you knew him best."

"Do you see how his mouth curves upward in one corner?" She pointed to the lopsided smile his father wore in perpetuity. "You do that, you know. He always said it was his secret weapon. But his smile and the sparkle in his eyes belied the seriousness he held within. Although he was the youngest son and was expected to live a life without care, he had a strong commitment to doing what was right. It was imperative to him we pass that on to you."

"Is that what you meant when you arrived?"

She nodded, her eyes never leaving the image of his father's face. "He never gave up hope that his father would open his arms and welcome him —us—back. But when Henry wrote to him, informing him of your birth" —she shook her head, sadness overtaking her—"he never received a reply. But your father still held to the belief that we rear you as a gentleman. With his last breath, he made me promise to educate you, to teach you to respect women, and to act with honor." She gave a tiny laugh. "It wasn't difficult. Even at an early age, you devoured any books I provided, and it isn't in your nature to act any other way than with integrity."

Tilting her head, she studied him. "Although this nonsense with Miss Weatherby is unlike you."

"Actually, it is most like me. I feel responsible for her."

"And that's what I mean by nonsense. From everything I've heard about the young lady, no one could have dissuaded her from acting so recklessly."

He didn't want to talk about Anne. Hopefully, by the end of the evening, she would understand the folly of a match with him. "Did my stepfather agree with my father's wishes? Did he know of my heritage?"

She nodded. "I told him everything. It was his idea that we call you Drake, both to protect you and as a tribute to your father."

His jaw tightened. "He lied to me. You both did." Although he'd forgiven them, it still hurt.

"He loved you as if you were his own. Francis was a good man."

"Did you love him?" Drake held his breath.

She sighed. "I did, but not like I loved your father. Your father sacrificed so much for our love."

He took her hands in his. "Did he ever regret it?"

"Only he could answer that, but I don't believe so. At least he never made me feel like he resented me."

"If only Honoria would do that for me."

Sad understanding covered his mother's face. "This pretense of yours. Is it to test her? To see if she's willing to make the choice that she couldn't eight years ago?"

He turned away, not willing to meet her knowing gaze, and raked a hand through his hair, mussing Dawson's handiwork. "Wouldn't make, you mean. She chose her life as a marquess's daughter over me."

"Drake. Be realistic. She was only ten-and-seven."

"Old enough to realize I wasn't worthy of her. In her eyes, I'm still not worthy."

"I don't believe that, and I don't think you do either. Not the way she looks at you."

He sent her a rueful smile and traced a hand down his body. "A groom in duke's clothing."

"No! A duke in duke's clothing. You are what you were born to be. And even if you were still a groom, you would be good enough. It's what's inside that makes a man. Trust her, Drake. Don't let happiness pass you by again."

She straightened his mussed hair, then kissed him lightly on the cheek. Patting his chest, she said, "You'll do the right thing. It's who you are."

And as she closed the door behind her, Drake wondered who exactly he would be to Honoria.

A groom?

Or a duke.

CHAPTER 25

"Hold still, my lady." Susan's reflection in the mirror captured her frustration.

Honoria watched her maid with fascination as she worked Honoria's hair into a fashionable coiffure.

"There." Susan gave an approving nod, her frown morphing into a smile as she finished pulling several strands of Honoria's hair loose to dangle along her neck.

Honoria raised her hand to the wandering locks, but she didn't dare try to thread them back into place. Susan wouldn't be pleased. "I don't understand the purpose of spending so much time to pin hair up only to then pull it loose."

"The men folk like it, my lady." Susan wiggled her eyebrows. "But it must appear natural, like they fell loose all on their own."

Honoria shook her head, but admitted, "It does look whimsical. Like I've come inside from a vigorous ride."

Susan giggled, saying nothing. She curtsied and closed the door behind her.

After the meeting with the League, Honoria had retired to her room to rest before the ball, but the kiss she shared with Drake had made her efforts futile.

An aching tenderness swelled in her chest, and she touched her fingertips to her lips. Grateful she was alone, she stared in the mirror at the blush covering her cheeks. If just thinking about him stirred such a reaction, what would happen when she saw him again?

Had her feelings always been so obvious?

The clock on the mantle chimed fifteen past the hour. She did her best to school her features into a sedate and dignified expression, then rose and made her way down to the ballroom.

Burwood stood at the entrance greeting everyone, his gregarious smile on full display.

Until Charlotte approached. Then it vanished in an instant.

Honoria worked her way closer, curious to hear their exchange.

Burwood bowed over Charlotte's extended hand, taking her fingers as if some horrible disease covered them. "Lady Charlotte. I hope your corset is loose enough for you to enjoy the festivities."

Standing next to him, Drake surreptitiously elbowed the duke, who gave a soft *oof.*

"You look radiant, my lady," Drake said.

"Thank you, Mr. Merrick. At least someone has manners. But perhaps the duke's small clothes are too tight."

Honoria lifted a hand to stifle her laugh, her gaze locking with Drake's, whose own eyes danced with amusement.

Although Honoria couldn't see Charlotte's face, she could imagine her disdainful expression as she turned ever so slightly toward Burwood and snatched a dance card from his fingers.

The scowl on Burwood's face, on the other hand, was clear to all in proximity. Like the changing winds, his face brightened once again. "Ah, Lady Honoria!"

Drake's gaze swung to her. Resplendent in his perfectly tailored black evening clothes—the contrasting silver waistcoat giving light to his face—he smiled his lopsided smile, and fireflies skimmed her stomach.

Although, in truth, he could be wearing the rough clothes of a groom and Honoria would have still found him dashing.

Burwood snapped his fingers. "Frampton, Lady Honoria's dance card."

Cards were spread in a fan-shape across a mahogany table, except for one that sat to the side. Frampton plucked the isolated card from the table and handed it to the duke.

"A special card for you, my lady."

Unease quelled the fluttering in her stomach, the fireflies dropping like pebbles, especially from the mischievous grin on Burwood's face as he handed her the card. She glanced down and frowned. "But this has already been filled out, Your Grace."

"Yes, isn't it delightful?"

Drake leaned forward, trying to catch a glimpse of the card. His eyes lifted to hers.

Four of the sets had Drake's name written next to them, one of which was a waltz. Effervescent bubbles trickled through her veins. And yet . . . the completed card was most inappropriate. "And are the gentlemen aware of this?"

"They will be when I make the announcement." Giddy, Burwood grinned like a naughty schoolboy.

Honoria lowered her voice. "Your Grace, not to be indelicate, but this simply isn't done. Gentlemen request dances with the ladies of their choice. And never with the same lady more than twice."

Burwood swatted her protest away. "Bollocks!"

A feminine voice behind Honoria gasped.

"Forgive me," Burwood said, peering around Honoria and appearing not in the least apologetic. "But I thought it was about time to mix things up a bit. Have some fun. It's a ball, after all. No one will be a wallflower at my party!"

Her mind reeled with the unorthodox methods of the new duke, but she moved toward Drake.

He took her hand in his. "Lady Honoria, might I hope my name is on your card?"

"Four times," she whispered. What would her father think? Or Anne? "However, if you wish to change—"

"There will be no changes to the assignments," Burwood said. "Duke's orders."

She gaped at him, then glanced toward Drake. "Assignments? Do you mean these were intentional?"

"Not everyone's. That's what makes yours special. Everyone else's cards were distributed randomly. Making sure there were no overlaps on the cards took me two whole days of planning." Burwood gave a sharp nod, as if he expected congratulations for his efforts.

"I . . . don't know what to say." She truly didn't.

Burwood winked. "Thank you?"

Honoria mumbled something—she wasn't sure what—and entered the ballroom.

Soft candlelight from crystal chandeliers illuminated the enormous room. Tables heavily laden with epicurean delicacies lined the wall on the right. On a dais at the front, an orchestra began tuning their instruments. Along the wall on the left, chairs waited for dancers to rest their tired feet. People congregated in small groups, eager for the ball to commence.

Nothing was out of order, save for one small detail. Women gasped as they opened their dance cards, their eyes darting to the men before them who, no doubt, had requested the first dance. Confusion reigned supreme. If the perpetrator of *The Muckraker* was in attendance, the duke's method of securing dance partners would surely garner a prominent place in the scandal sheet.

Miranda hurried forward. "Look at your card!" Her muffled exclamation was loud enough to cause a stir from those around them.

"I've already seen it." She held out her card for Miranda's inspection.

"At least yours is agreeable. Look at mine." She held up the card, pointing to one name in particular.

"Lord Middlebury? Oh, Miranda, I'm so sorry. Perhaps you could discreetly disappear?"

Miranda's mouth puckered. "I would, except the set right after is with Mr. Pratt, and at least he's a marvelous dancer."

"A magical reappearance? Or simply not claim him?" Honoria pressed her lips together in a sly smile.

"Perhaps. I shall have to weigh the pros and cons of dancing with Middlebury."

"There are *pros?*"

Miranda tapped Honoria on the arm with her dance card. "Not *those* kind, but yes. Possibly."

"Are you going to tell me?"

"No." Miranda grinned.

Charlotte rushed over. "This is outrageous!" She waved her own dance card in front of them. "I refuse to dance with that man!"

"Middlebury?" both Honoria and Miranda asked in unison.

"No, although that would be equally disturbing. Burwood. Ugh. Just the thought makes me nauseous."

"Maybe we can trade?" Miranda asked. "I don't find him disagreeable at all."

"Burwood said there can be no changes to the assignments," Honoria said.

Both Miranda's and Charlotte's dark brows lifted.

"*He* did this? On purpose?" Charlotte glared in Burwood's direction as he entered the room. "That settles it. I'll dance with him and trod on his boorish boots every chance I get." A wicked grin spread across her face.

Anne appeared next to Honoria. "What are you grinning about?" she asked Charlotte.

"She's going to stomp on Burwood's toes," Miranda said.

Anne's eyes grew wide. "Don't do that. I'm supposed to dance with him this evening."

"Did you look at your dance card?" Honoria asked, worried that Anne might be disappointed if Burwood's name wasn't listed.

"No." Anne tilted her head, eyes narrowing? "Why?" Then, ever so slowly, she opened the card and peered down at it. Immediately, her head jerked up. "What's going on?"

As if answering Anne's question, Burwood drew the room to order. "Lords, ladies, and gentlemen, may I have your attention."

Chatter reduced to a hushed murmur as everyone turned toward the duke.

Honoria muttered to Miranda. "I hope he knows what he's doing."

DRAKE SHOOK HIS HEAD. "I HOPE YOU KNOW WHAT YOU'RE DOING."

"Don't worry," Simon whispered, then raised his voice for the masses. "As most of you have already noticed—at least the ladies have —we have something new and exciting this evening. The ladies have all received dance cards already populated with the names of partners."

Murmurs escalated to a dull roar as ladies who had not looked at their cards opened them and more than a few men groaned.

Burwood raised his hands to silence the protests. "Now, now, it's all in good fun. I want no lady to be without a partner. So gentlemen, I would ask you to accept gallantly when your partner approaches you. Ladies, do not be shy. At the end of the evening, we'll gather on the front lawn for a display of fireworks that will rival those of Vauxhall Gardens! Enjoy!"

Horrified expressions remained fixed on Simon, and standing next to him, Drake felt guilt by association. From the corner of his mouth, he muttered, "You've broken them. Do something."

"Come now!" Simon said, sounding a little less enthusiastic. "Ladies, find your partners for the first dance."

No one moved.

Simon's *idea* was a disaster.

Then Honoria broke free from the small cluster of ladies and headed their way, her head high and her back straight and proud.

God love her.

Drake tugged gently on the ends of his coat, his heart pounding like cannon fire against his ribcage. Four sets. Was this to be their first?

He felt his lips curve involuntarily as she came closer.

Then they fell when she stopped in front of Simon.

"I believe we have the first set, Your Grace." She held the card out as proof, as if the cad didn't already know.

Simon feigned innocence, placing a hand over his heart, the lout. "Why, we do, don't we? How delightful." He held out his arm to Honoria while sending a particularly odious smirk toward Drake—who wanted to plant his friend a facer in front of the whole assembly.

As Simon and Honoria took their position on the dance floor, no one else moved.

"Mr. Merrick?" a feminine voice called from his right.

"Lady Montgomery?" He stared at the petite redhead. Where had she come from?

"I believe this set is ours."

He glanced at the proffered card. "So it is. Shall we?" He held out his arm, and they joined Simon and Honoria.

"I apologize in advance," Lady Montgomery said.

"What for?"

"For trodding on your feet. I'm not the most graceful of dancers, but I've improved over the years, especially if I refrain from looking at my husband."

Drake tilted his head in question.

"He discombobulates me."

"I understand completely." Drake chuckled, sliding a glance toward Honoria.

Lady Montgomery announced—perhaps a little too loudly, "Lady Honoria, it seems redheads are the only ones present tonight with backbone."

Simon's notorious grin spread across his face.

Murmurs rose again, and one-by-one, women broke from their paralysis and approached their partners. Soon, two full lines with eight pairs each waited for the music to begin. Simon nodded to the orchestra.

Anne had paired with Victor Pratt, and for a moment, Drake wondered if Simon had done that intentionally. Then he saw Lady Miranda dancing with her brother, Lord Montgomery. Both of them appeared ready to break into fits of laughter.

"I fear the duke's idea may have some unforeseen consequences. Ladies don't dance with their brothers." Lady Montgomery nodded toward her husband and sister-in-law. She grinned at Drake. "I shall have to recheck my card to see if my brother, Timothy, is listed. If so, I shall take great joy in stepping on his toes."

Honoria glanced over, her bright laugh ringing like crystal bells.

Lady Montgomery was such a pleasant distraction, Drake barely remembered to send warning glares in Simon's direction as he flirted mercilessly with Honoria.

Barely.

But not entirely. As they made one final pass in the country line dance, he whispered. "Stop being charming."

Simon had the audacity to whisper back. "Can't help it. It's in my bones, old man."

The next set had Honoria paired with Ashton. The set after that, while Drake tried to navigate the dance with Lady Miranda, Honoria was paired with Lord Montgomery. Drake began to see a pattern.

Between sets, he stood by the refreshment table and leaned over to Simon. "Did you pair Honoria with any eligible gentlemen, or should I actually thank you?"

Simon peered over his glass of lemonade, his eyebrows wiggling. "What are you talking about? She danced with me, and as a duke, I'm the most eligible man here." He sipped his drink, no doubt waiting for Drake's retort. "Besides, I believe the next set is with you."

Drake's heart picked up its pace, and he turned toward the crowd, waiting for Honoria to approach and claim her dance.

Instead, Lady Charlotte strode toward them like a soldier on the first line of battle. She shoved her dance card in Simon's face. "Here."

Simon spat out the lemonade. "Good Lord, that must be a mistake."

"It says *Burwood*. Or can't you read?"

Drake bowed to Lady Charlotte. "If you would both excuse me."

The word *coward* rose behind him, and he chuckled.

His amusement vanished, and his breath caught as Honoria walked toward him. God, she looked beautiful. He should have said something earlier. He made a promise to remedy that as quickly as possible if the dance pattern allowed.

Loose strands of her hair draped seductively down her neck, and his fingers ached to play with them and test their softness. The décolletage of her dress was just low enough to make his mind whir in inappropriate directions as the creamy swell of her breasts caught his attention.

He decided he liked the design of the new gowns with their tapered waistlines and fuller skirts. Or maybe it was because they showed off Honoria's figure to perfection. Of course, anything would rise to the task when perfection was the starting point.

"Mr. Merrick." She gave him a shy smile.

Shy? After what they had shared earlier in the day? She had met his kiss with equal fervor. Did she regret it?

"You are to be my next partner," she said, holding up the card.

"Ah, a quadrille. I believe I've mastered the steps of that one, although it's not my favorite."

Before he could hold out his arm, Simon and Lady Charlotte walked past—or more accurately, tromped—leaving a trail of grumbled words in their wake.

Not everyone was as pleased with their partner as Drake.

They took a position opposite Simon and Charlotte and waited for others to complete the square. Drake had a suspicion Simon might appreciate a friendly face.

Honoria leaned in close, her citrusy scent teasing his senses and reviving the memory of their kiss in the orangery. "And what is your favorite, Mr. Merrick?"

"Favorite?" She muddled his mind to distraction.

"Dance. You said the quadrille is not your favorite."

"Ah. The waltz is my favorite."

Pink bloomed on her cheeks, and he fought a congratulatory smile.

"I believe we shall share that one as well," she said, keeping her eyes straight ahead.

Perfect.

CHAPTER 26

Heat rushed up Honoria's neck and face at the mere thought of Drake holding her in his arms for the waltz. She slid a peek at him and caught his lips tipping at the corners.

"What's so amusing?" Anne asked as she and Dr. Marbry joined them. She darted a questioning glance between Drake and Honoria, finally landing on Charlotte, who returned an enigmatic smile.

Burwood winked at Anne. "I believe Merrick and Lady Honoria were discussing their upcoming waltz."

"Oh." Anne's response sounded tiny, so unlike her usual bigger-than-life personality. She jerked her gaze toward Charlotte again.

What was going on between those two?

Before Honoria could suss it out further, another couple joined their group to complete the formation.

Other couples lined up on the dance floor in additional squares, and the orchestra began playing. Honoria found herself anticipating each touch of Drake's hand as they made their passes, and when he wrapped his arm around her waist to guide her in the turn, her knees melted.

But nothing compared to the longing on his face that matched the ache in her heart. She averted her gaze, knowing full well if she continued to stare at him, she would forget the steps completely.

She needed to concentrate on the dance, but the duke's actions weren't helping. Partnered with Charlotte, Burwood's eyes shifted toward Anne, then he gave several slight jerks of his head in Drake and Honoria's direction.

Anne's brow furrowed as her gaze darted between Drake and Honoria.

"Whatever is the matter with your neck?" Charlotte asked Burwood, loud enough for all in the formation to hear.

"I have a pain named Charlotte," the duke retorted, no less subtly.

Anne snorted a laugh, drawing a censorious glance from Charlotte.

Moments later, the duke bellowed, "Ow! That was my foot!"

"I'm trying to redirect your pain," Charlotte said.

Without warning, Burwood grasped Charlotte by the elbow and led her several feet away. Everyone remaining in the formation looked at each other in confusion.

"Keep dancing," Honoria said, motioning for Drake to follow her. They went through the steps without their opposing pair, but Honoria's attention remained fixed on Charlotte and Burwood.

Burwood leaned in, whispering something to Charlotte, who appeared ready for battle. Right before Drake wrapped an arm around her to lead her in the other direction, Honoria caught Charlotte's eyes widen, her gaze snapping to the incomplete grouping of dancers.

Charlotte and Burwood rejoined the formation as the other couples performed the steps for their respective sides. Anne stared at Honoria, then transferred her focus to Drake. The concentration on her face unnerved Honoria.

What was she looking for?

It was the most unusual set Honoria had ever participated in, and although she had enjoyed dancing with Drake, she was relieved when it finally ended.

She curtsied to Drake, his eyes imploring her with some unnamed request.

"Until our next dance, Lady Honoria," he said. "Let us hope it's less dramatic." He tilted his head toward Burwood and Charlotte, who miraculously had not killed each other.

"What do you suppose that was all about?"

Before Drake could answer, Burwood approached and tugged his arm. "A word, Merrick."

Drake craned his head, peering over his shoulder at Honoria as Burwood dragged him away.

The rich alto of Charlotte's voice snapped Honoria's attention away from Drake. "Do you have another dance with Mr. Merrick?"

"Yes. Three more, to be exact."

Anne sidled up to them. "Three more dances!" She looked down at her own card, her mouth forming a pout. "I only have one with him. I don't think I like this method of determining partners."

"No one asked you," Charlotte snapped. "Although since it was Burwood's idea, I'm inclined to agree with you. Except . . ."

"Except what?" Anne asked.

The hair on the back of Honoria's neck prickled, and it had nothing to do with the strands that Susan had so carefully crafted in Honoria's coiffure. No. All credit belonged to Charlotte's devious expression.

"Except," Charlotte said, giving a pregnant pause. "Honoria's card appears perfect."

Anne huffed. Honoria almost expected her to stamp her foot. "But she has four dances with Mr. Merrick! Surely, there must be a mistake." Anne's eyes widened. "Perhaps that was supposed to be my card."

As Anne reached for Honoria's card, Honoria pulled it away. "No! Burwood himself told me it was specifically meant for me."

Both Charlotte and Anne blinked.

Honoria felt the tiniest remorse at being so abrupt with her friend. But only for a moment. For once, or perhaps the second time in her life, she intended to stand up for herself, even if it meant a less than peaceful resolution. "I'm sorry, Anne. But it's true," she said, trying at least to smooth things over a little.

"Bravo, Honoria, and don't apologize to her," Charlotte said. "Anne, you cannot go snatching other people's dance cards because you think theirs is better than yours." The grin on her face reminded Honoria of

Charlotte's brother Lord Nash. "Although I'm tempted to let you have mine. I have the waltz with that boor, Burwood."

"And Honoria has the waltz with Mr. Merrick." Anne's disappointment tugged at Honoria's heartstrings. "I have it with"—she peered at her own card, her expression changing to horror—"Lord Middlebury."

Guilt twisted like a dagger at Honoria's conscience. For a moment, she considered—

"Where *is* Middlebury?" Charlotte asked, her brow furrowed as she turned and scanned the room.

The man was nowhere to be seen. And he, admittedly, was hard to miss. "He's gone," Honoria said.

"Good. Maybe he'll stay gone the rest of the night," Anne said, the desperation clear in her voice.

"He's probably offended and stalked off in a huff after his dance with Miranda," Charlotte said.

Unlike Anne, Honoria practically bubbled with anticipation for her waltz with Drake.

❧

"WHAT THE BLOODY HELL WAS THAT ALL ABOUT?" DRAKE SHOT—what he hoped was—a scathing glare at Simon.

The man had the gall to appear affronted. He held a hand over his heart, adopting an expression of innocent ignorance. Neither of which ever applied to Simon. "I don't know what you're talking about."

"That business with Lady Charlotte. I'm surprised she didn't slap you across your arrogant face."

"That harpy doesn't need any encouragement to inflict pain. My toes may never recover. But if you *must* know, I simply reminded her that, surprising as it may seem, we were both after the same result."

Drake resisted the urge to grab Simon by his cravat and give him a good shake. "Which is?"

"To get Miss Weatherby to realize you and Lady Honoria are meant to be together."

Drake blinked and shook his head. "You're working together?" Inconceivable.

"You did say you overheard her telling Anne to watch your interactions with Lady Honoria, didn't you? When you were spying in the orangery?"

Drake tugged on his coat sleeve, keeping his voice calm. "I wasn't spying. I was enjoying an orange." *And later, a kiss, which was decidedly more enjoyable.*

Simon batted away Drake's objection. "Technicalities. Surely, you haven't forgotten our conversation from this afternoon already?" He tugged the cuffs down on his superfine evening coat. "Nevertheless, I simply informed the ice queen that when it came to you and Lady Honoria, she and I were in full agreement. I suggested she cease drawing attention to us with her childish behavior, thereby allowing Miss Weatherby to witness the affection you and Lady Honoria clearly have for each other."

He poked Drake in the chest. "Which *you* need to be demonstrating. You and Honoria have the supper dance, so even if Anne can't observe you two together then, she surely will when Honoria is at your side during supper. I'll try to arrange the seating so Anne's nearby with a good view."

"How will you do that if you don't know who her partner is before supper?"

Simon gaped at Drake as if he'd lost his mind. "Because I'm the duke, and I can usurp any other gentleman's claim to a lady."

"Need I remind you that in reality, you are *not* the duke and such behavior reflects poorly on me who is?"

"But that's the beauty of it, don't you see? They will be so relieved to find the well-behaved Mr. Merrick is the actual duke they'll forget you were raised as a commoner."

Drake barked a laugh.

"Nevertheless, Anne shall sit by me, and you and Honoria will be nearby. It will be perfect." Simon glared. "As long as you do your part. I want love to be clear on your face. Think about what it would be like to kiss her."

Heat burned Drake's ears. That would be an easy task. He'd only have to think back on their encounter in the orangery earlier that day.

"Good grief, man. I said kissing, not undressing her. Show us love, not lust."

"I *was* thinking about kissing."

Shaking his head, Simon leaned in and whispered, "Are you telling me you still haven't bedded a woman?"

"That's none of your concern. Now, Lady Miranda is approaching. She's either going to claim you or me as a dance partner, so look nonchalant."

After Miranda claimed Simon as partner for the next set, Drake wandered to the refreshment table, grateful no one had claimed him as partner. As he sipped the overly sweet ratafia—truly, why did the *ton* insist on serving such a drink at these gatherings—he watched the couples on the dance floor.

Simon flirted with Lady Miranda, no doubt pleased his toes had been spared from Lady Charlotte's wrath. Honoria partnered with Andrew Weatherby, which eased Drake's nerves.

He thought back to Simon's accusation, and heat rushed to his face again. Fully admitting he was a rarity among men, Drake had firmly believed it was unfair for a woman to remain untouched until marriage while men could gallivant about at will.

No, when he married, he could assure his wife that she was the only one with whom he shared himself. It certainly had nothing to do with the fact that no other woman was Honoria.

Or so he tried to convince himself.

"Deep in thought?" His mother's soft voice ended the debate. "You look flushed. Drink your ratafia."

He scrunched his nose. "This stuff is an abomination."

Her delicate brows lifted. "But you like sweet things."

Unbidden, his gaze traveled to Honoria. "Not too sweet."

As Drake's mind latched onto the sweetness of Honoria's lips, Lord Harcourt approached and sketched an elegant bow. "Mrs. Merrick. It's good to see you again. I haven't had an opportunity to speak with you since your arrival. My condolences regarding your husband. He was a fine man." Harcourt inclined his head toward Drake. "I must say, it was a pleasant surprise to discover your son was working for the new duke."

"It's good to have a familiar, friendly face among the duke's guests," Drake said.

"Ah, but I'm not the only one. There's Stratford and his family."

"Familiar, yes. Friendly is questionable," Drake muttered.

Apparently, the baron's hearing was unimpaired. He hitched a brown eyebrow.

How much did Harcourt know about what transpired eight years ago?

Drake had no time to question it when Harcourt said, "I couldn't help but notice, Mrs. Merrick, that you aren't dancing."

"Alas, I refused a dance card, leaving the merriment to those younger."

"Then, since this is a night to break with tradition, might I suggest we also do so? Would you do me the honor of the next set?"

There was a saying about the force of a feather. Drake reeled back on his heels as his mother gave a laugh that was uncomfortably like a giggle.

"I would be delighted, Lord Harcourt."

When the next set started and Harcourt led his mother to the dance floor, Drake wondered if he was the only man there who didn't have the nerve to go after what he wanted.

Determined to change that, he decided Simon's exhortation would serve dual purposes. He would make his love for Honoria clear to both her and Anne. By doing so, he prayed Anne would end things.

During the supper dance, he easily accomplished the first part of his task. Each brush of Honoria's fingers during the quadrille sparked a fire in him, and it was no hardship to gaze adoringly at her. The question remained: Would it be enough for Anne to understand the futility of their pairing and release him?

At supper, Drake never felt more at home than with Honoria by his side. Although Simon sat at the head of the able, Drake had no trouble imagining himself there with Honoria as his duchess. Easy conversation flowed between them, his mother, and Lord Harcourt, especially as Harcourt entertained them with stories of his grandchildren.

"Pockets?" Drake asked. He remembered Dr. Marbry using the strange name after Anne's accident.

Harcourt gave a chuckle, then wiped his mouth with the serviette. "Yes. Camilla tried to call him Philip, but Pockets just stuck to the boy. Perhaps it has something to do with his sticky fingers."

"Pockets, Ashton's ward Manny, and a young girl calling herself Fingers were all part of a pick-pocketing gang," Honoria explained.

He loved how she did so without making him feel stupid. "I see a pattern with their names, except for Manny."

When his mother placed a hand on Lord Harcourt's sleeve, Drake felt his eyebrows lift.

"What a lovely thing for your daughter to do, sir. Taking in an orphan and providing a loving, stable home is most admirable."

"I will admit"—a shadow passed across Lord Harcourt's face—"Pockets helped pull me from a dark place after my wife died."

His mother withdrew her hand, and an uneasy silence filled the gap in the conversation.

"I've met Manny, but haven't had the pleasure of meeting Master Pockets," Honoria said. "He's a fortunate child to be raised by your daughter and Dr. Somersby, Lord Harcourt."

Harcourt's mood brightened. "Yes. And they are fortunate to have him. Children have a way of brightening our lives. Camilla is expecting another child in a few weeks. It's one reason they were unable to attend. That, and Oliver volunteered to man the clinic in Ashton's and Marbry's absence. I couldn't ask for a better son-in-law, and I'm so grateful Camilla has a second chance at love."

Drake cast a glance at Honoria. Second chances at love. Exactly what he hoped for with Honoria. If it weren't for Anne . . . He peered at Anne next to Simon.

Her gaze bounced between him and Honoria, her brow furrowing as she settled on him.

Simon nodded discreetly, and Drake took his cue.

"Lady Honoria." If his face reflected the love flowing in his heart, Drake had no doubt his affection for Honoria would be clear to all, even Anne. "I'm looking forward to our waltz. I've been practicing nonstop with the dancing master."

His heart zinged when she rewarded him with a smile.

"Is that how you've become such an accomplished dancer?" She stirred her pea soup aimlessly, and her cheeks bloomed with color.

"Better than when we practiced in the meadow? I believe I stepped on your feet no less than twenty times."

"Twenty-seven to be exact. I thought my toes should never recover." The tiny smile crossing her lips belied her words. This was the Honoria he knew so well. The shy but clever girl who had won his heart so many years ago.

Someone cleared their throat, and Drake tore his attention from Honoria. The trace of a smile crossed Harcourt's lips, his spoon poised half-way to his mouth. "This soup is delicious. I must commend Burwood on his cook's ability." The sharp knowing that shone in his eyes indicated the soup wasn't the only thing to capture his attention.

When Drake turned toward Simon and Anne, Simon's smirk and Anne's pained expression confirmed it.

Mission accomplished—but at what cost?

CHAPTER 27

Supper was a blur. If Honoria had been asked what had been served, she would be hard pressed to answer. Sitting next to Drake and exchanging idle words—that couched much deeper meaning—had addled her brain.

The man could still send firefly sparks throughout her body from a simple look or word. His honeyed voice poured over her and soothed her soul. Oh, to experience the sensations every day. She turned her attention toward Anne, the creature within her growling with jealousy and searing her veins.

But the tight-lipped smile Anne returned sent Honoria's mind reeling. Anne jerked her gaze away and turned a bright smile on Burwood, her laugh sounding forced and perhaps a little too loud.

Oh, dear. Had she overstepped with Drake and offended her friend? She leaned in toward him, lowering her voice to a whisper. "I may owe Anne an apology."

Drake's brows bunched. "Whatever for?"

Was he really unaware of how their interaction may have looked to Anne? "She may have misinterpreted our exchange to be more than it is."

Keeping his own voice low, he leaned in. "Ah, but did she, or does she finally see clearly what everyone else does? You know it's true. I can no better hide my feelings for you than you can for me."

Oh. Her heart skittered. Hope rose from its slumber. A warm tingling spread throughout her body, exciting all her senses. Candles seemed brighter, the food aromas more mouthwatering, the tinkling of crystal and china more musical, the wine sweeter.

She yearned to ask if he planned to end things with Anne, but Anne wasn't the only one whose eyes were upon them. From Lord Harcourt's expression moments earlier, he no doubt had suspicions. And her father watched them with unbridled interest. Instead she resolved to ask him later, allowing herself to enjoy the moment.

Her body hummed electric, sending little sparks of excitement through her veins each time his knee accidentally brushed against her skirts under the table.

Although when his lips twitched with a ghost of a smile, she wondered how accidental it truly was. Especially when he said, "The fireworks display will be stupendous. Burwood has spared no expense."

Honoria rather thought she had a preview of said display, the butterflies in her stomach rioting, when Drake turned his brilliant smile on her and—leaning down—whispered, "When you were but sixteen, you told me you longed to go to Vauxhall to view them."

How would she survive the waltz when his mere breath against her cheek scattered her wits as quickly as a flash of lightning? She turned a quizzical gaze toward him. "Were the fireworks Burwood's idea or yours?"

"Both," he said, not meeting her eyes, but his lips quirked in their adorably lopsided way.

Thankfully, she got through the rest of supper without making a complete ninny of herself each time he smiled at her.

When the time arrived for the waltz, Honoria scanned the ballroom for Drake.

There. Across the room, standing next to Burwood.

In slow motion, he turned, his gaze locking with hers.

As she moved toward him, her heart snapped against her ribcage in time with her steps. The mere sight of him waiting for her caused her knees to weaken, raising concern she would be the one to step upon toes during their dance.

Then he moved forward, not waiting for her to fully approach him. Around him, the crowds melted away, parting as if he commanded to have a clear path to her. And unlike hers, his steps seemed sure and confident.

He appeared . . . regal.

A welcoming grin stretched across his face and crinkled the corners of his eyes as he held out his hand. "Are you ready for our dance, my lady?"

She squeaked out a timid, "Yes," and slid her hand into his. A frisson of electric crackled between them, raising gooseflesh on her arms.

His gaze slid to hers. "Did you feel that?"

His pupils had expanded so widely, his amber eyes looked almost black.

"Y-y-yes." Her shaky voice mimicked her insides as they tumbled about like riotous children.

As they took a position on the dance floor, Honoria gazed around the room. Other couples joined them, Burwood led Charlotte, neither of whom appeared pleased. With Lord Middlebury still missing, Anne partnered with Victor Pratt, her attention more focused on Honoria and Drake than on her partner. On the side of the room, Honoria's father stared at them, the expected scowl more like a mask of curiosity.

She tucked her hand into Drake's. When he wrapped his arm around her and pressed his fingers into her back, her knees buckled, but he steadied her, a tiny version of his lopsided grin inching across his face.

Her heart pounded a furious rhythm against her ribcage, in direct contrast to the smooth, easy rhythm of the waltz.

He'd held her around the waist many times before, assisting her in and out of the saddle. But this was different. This time, as she gazed into the depths of his eyes, adoration shone on his face for all to see.

In an instant, all her nervousness vanished. Nothing had ever felt as right as being in Drake's arms—where she was meant to be.

She had come home.

And at that moment, everyone else disappeared.

⚜

HEAT SEARED DRAKE'S FINGERTIPS AS HE PRESSED HIS HAND against the nip of Honoria's waist. Energy crackled and sparked between them like a lightning storm. He had no need to remember Simon's instruction. It came naturally as he stared into Honoria's green eyes.

"You're so beautiful this evening. I failed to tell you earlier, and I wish to remedy that immediately. You outshine every other woman here."

Pink rose to her cheeks, and she averted her gaze.

"No. Look at me." He smiled, hoping to soften his words, lest she think them a demand. "Please."

When she returned her attention to him, she was all seriousness. "You've never been one to exaggerate, Drake. Please don't begin now."

He shook his head. "I'm not. To me, you are the brightest star shining in the heavens. Your eyes are like jewels. Your lips like pomegranate. Your—"

She laughed. Not loudly, drawing attention as Anne might, but a soft vocalization of amusement.

He canted his head, unable to restrain his smile. "What?"

"Drake, you are many fine things. But a poet is not one of them." She shook her head. "Pomegranate? Really?" She uttered a soft laugh again. "But I am flattered by your attempt."

"My words may be clumsy, but the love in my heart is genuine." He paused, needing to give his next words the emphasis they deserved. "And it is yours and only yours."

Waiting, he searched her face. "I'd like to clarify something about when we were in the orangery today."

Her cheeks bloomed pink again. "About the kiss?"

"In a matter of speaking. Although I believe you enjoyed it as much as I did." He pressed his fingers against her back a little more firmly, not only to direct her in the dance, but to encourage her admission.

She peered over his shoulder as if afraid to meet his gaze directly. "You know I did."

"But what I want to make clear is why I objected to Lady Miranda calling a compromise."

"Oh." Her response came on an exhalation of breath so soft he barely heard her.

"It's not that I object to the idea of marrying you. On that my feelings have never deviated. I have wanted nothing else . . . no one else for these past eight years."

She remained silent. Fine luminescent lines of moisture rimmed her eyes at the bottom.

"But," he continued, "I didn't want to trap you into a marriage, which a compromise would surely do." He swallowed, hesitant to voice the alternative. "Or ruin you, should for whatever reason a marriage not take place."

"A reason such as my father's objection, you mean." No trace of anger laced her voice, only understanding.

He nodded. "Or your refusal." He held his breath, forcing himself to continue the steps of the dance. "You did also answer Lady Miranda in the negative."

"Because I didn't want to trap *you*."

He smiled at that, the joy of her answer lightening his heart and pressing him forward. "After all these years, we are still of like mind. Hearts in unison, as Miss Austen said." Wetness formed in his own eyes, and he blinked it away.

He pulled in a deep breath, preparing to pour out his heart. Simon would be proud. "But if we are to ever marry, I want it to be because you've chosen me of your own free will and that you want me for me. You will need to come to me."

Air stilled around her as Honoria fought to pull what was left into her lungs. What was he saying? That he wished to marry her, but she must do the asking? "But what of Anne? Do you intend to end your attachment?"

His mouth formed a tight line. "That is a problem. I fear I cannot be the one to end things."

"And yet you profess feelings for me. That is most unlike you, Drake, to lead two women on."

Shame filled his eyes, and he averted his gaze. "I know. But I'm honor bound by my promise, and I worry about damaging her reputation."

"Oh, Drake." The same reason she loved him now kept them apart. His unerring honor and loyalty. His desire to always do the right thing.

"So you see." It was a statement, because of course she saw, and he knew it. "She must be the one to end things."

Honoria wanted to tell him that Anne would understand if he were honest with her. But she knew her friend almost as well as she knew Drake. Once Anne had her heart set upon something, there was little one could do to dissuade her from her goal. Case in point—attempting to jump a stubborn horse. "Yes. I see your point. It must be her decision."

As quickly as hope had arisen in Honoria's heart, it drifted back to sleep. "But Drake, I cannot do what you ask until your attachment to Anne is dissolved. I *will* not. And it is unfair of you to even broach such a request with me."

He winced, her last words clearly landing a direct blow.

A hush surrounded them, and she realized that, although they continued to move in the three-four time of the waltz, the music had stopped.

How long had they been dancing sans accompaniment? Other dancers turned their attention on them, particularly Anne standing next to Mr. Pratt.

Drake escorted her off the dance floor and sketched an elegant bow. "Thank you for the dance, my lady. I will heed your words."

Pain clouded Drake's eyes, the stormy turbulence reflecting back and striking her squarely in the chest. As before, his pain became her own.

What a predicament. He wouldn't tell Anne. Honoria, in good conscience, couldn't say anything. Anne would surely accuse her of trying to steal her beau.

No. If Drake and she had any chance of happiness, Anne would have to release him of her own accord.

Then it would be up to Honoria to convince him that she wanted to marry him just as he was.

And face the fury of her father for marrying a commoner.

She glanced down at her dance card at Burwood's name for the next dance.

You have an ally in me.

His words rang in her memory.

Squaring her shoulders, she strode toward him as he leaned against the refreshment table.

"Your Grace. I believe we have the next set."

His mouth twisted in a distorted grimace, and he lifted his foot, swiveling it around at the ankle. "One moment while I recover from my set with Lady Charlotte."

"Ha! I like that one." Next to him, Aunt Kitty tilted her head toward Charlotte standing several feet away and looking very much like the cat who got into the cream.

Although Honoria agreed with the countess, she took pity on the duke. He appeared to require more than *one moment* to recover from Charlotte's *attentions*. "Perhaps if it is agreeable, we could forgo actually dancing. I should like to speak with you about something of importance."

He ceased his foot wiggling and glanced up, giving her a rueful smile. "You would be my savior, my lady. May I suggest the bench on the terrace if that's acceptable? Perhaps Aunt Kitty could accompany us."

"It sounds perfect."

As she threaded her hand through Burwood's proffered arm and he limped her out to the terrace, she caught sight of her father. He looked over from where he was speaking to Lord Cartwright, his face hopeful.

She would disappoint him once again.

But she didn't care.

CHAPTER 28

"Drake? Mr. Merrick?"

The feminine voice calling his name tore Drake's attention away from where Honoria and Simon had exited to the terrace.

He turned toward Anne. "Forgive me, Miss Weatherby. What were you saying?"

Uncharacteristic solemnity replaced Anne's usual exuberance, her clear blue eyes devoid of the playful sparkle he had typically witnessed in her presence. She held up her dance card. "We have the next set." *Sotto voce*, she added, "Finally."

He forced the smile to his lips. "Of course." Another quadrille. He groaned inwardly. Why couldn't it have been a country line dance where conversing with Anne would be relegated to short snippets as they passed briefly back and forth or promenaded down the center line? At least it wasn't the waltz where he would have to hold her in his arms. Unbidden, his thoughts raced back to Honoria. Had he squandered his precious time with her by discussing their impossible situation?

Nevertheless, Anne shouldn't pay the price; she deserved his full attention. At least he could give her that much. "Shall we?" He held out his hand, and she slid her gloved fingers over his.

Nothing.

No spark of attraction. No sizzling of energy running through his veins like wildfire and burning him from the inside out with passion.

They took their positions in a group with Ashton and his duchess, Lord and Lady Montgomery, and Dr. and Mrs. Marbry.

How had that happened?

Drake's skin crawled as he took in the happy, loving couples, knowing that he would never gaze at Anne the way each of the men looked at their wives.

A grin spread across Ashton's face. "Don't tell Burwood, but we broke the rules."

"It was Priscilla's idea." The duchess cast the petite blonde a conspiratorial smile. "And I whole-heartedly concurred."

"Well, we couldn't allow you to dance with Lord Middlebury, Maggie," Lady Montgomery chimed in, giving a little shudder.

"Cheers to my brilliant wife," Dr. Marbry said.

Mrs. Marbry blushed. "Well, it is the next-to-last dance of the evening, and I really wanted to dance with my dashing husband at least once."

"Ah, a group conspiracy," Drake said. "Your secret is safe with me. But I have the utmost confidence that Burwood would heartily approve—at least this once." He genuinely liked these people, and his opinion of the rigid *ton* softened—a little.

There was still Stratford. And although he was loath to admit it, he wanted to win over the man—for Honoria's sake.

The music started, and he waited patiently for his and Anne's turn in the formation.

Patiently, that is, until Anne addressed him. "Mr. Merrick. I'm curious as to your previous acquaintance with Honoria. Was it an . . . amiable acquaintance?"

His gaze snapped to hers.

Her face remained guileless. What was she implying?

Amiable? It was so much more than that, yet he chose his words cautiously. "As my mother said, I served as groom for Lady Honoria's *family*"—he refused to sour his mouth by speaking Stratford's name—

"and I accompanied her on her frequent rides around the estate. I grew quite fond of her."

"And she of you?"

Time had arrived for him and Anne to perform their steps, saving him from answering immediately. When they stopped their movements, he crafted his careful response. "I believed so, yes."

Anne spun toward him, but not to perform the dance steps. "Why are you evading my questions, sir? Did you—do you have a tendre for Lady Honoria and she for you?"

He kept his voice low, although they had already attracted the attention of those around them. "Miss Weatherby . . . Anne. Let us postpone this conversation until later." Honoria would never have made such a scene. Anne's bubbly effervescence and impetuousness suddenly seemed volatile and embarrassing.

"Once we've finished the dance, will you answer my questions?"

"To the best of my ability. You have my word." Oily shame twisted around his lungs, compressing them and restricting his breathing. Awareness of the pain he would inflict upon Anne when he admitted the truth bore down on him. Yet a small voice whispered the hope that the end to the farce might be near.

Mercifully, they finished the dance in silence. Yet, Anne's reserve and changed demeanor drew curious glances from Ashton and Dr. Marbry.

"Miss Weatherby," Ashton said. "Are you unwell? I'm worried you've not fully recovered from your fall."

"Perhaps some air would help?" Drake asked, hoping to remove her from the inquisitive eyes of the crowd.

"That's an excellent idea," Mrs. Marbry said. "If you wish, I could accompany you as a chaperone."

Lady Montgomery huffed a *ha*, and her husband delivered another chastising look.

"That would be most gracious of you." Drake held out his hand, motioning toward the terrace. "Shall we?"

Before they arrived at the terrace doors, Honoria entered the ballroom on Simon's arm. Aunt Kitty trailed behind.

Drake wished to wipe off the smug grin covering Simon's face. Aunt

Kitty's tight-lipped smile left him uneasy. Honoria glanced at him, then quickly averted her gaze, her cheeks blooming with color.

None of their expressions agreed in the least. What had they been discussing out on the terrace that entire time?

He turned, watching Honoria's retreating back with longing.

"Mr. Merrick?" Anne called. "Are you coming?"

He nodded and followed Anne and Mrs. Marby out to the terrace, in the completely opposite direction his heart called.

As Honoria and Burwood re-entered the ballroom from the terrace, she craned her neck to gaze back at Drake. What was going on?

Burwood patted her hand resting on his arm. "All will be well, my lady. I can feel it in my bones."

But as Drake moved toward the terrace with Anne, Honoria had her doubts.

"The last set was to be with Drake." She turned back to Burwood, disappointment drenching her words. "But he appears to be occupied with Anne."

"There will be a longer respite before the next set while I make an announcement, so perhaps whatever business he has with Miss Weatherby—and let us hope for the best—will be concluded before your final dance."

He patted her hand again. "Remember what we discussed. Now, if you would excuse me."

She nodded as the duke made his way to the dais for his announcement.

How *could* she forget what they discussed? She'd poured her heart out to Burwood, relaying the fraught conversation she and Drake had during their waltz.

"How can I even consider what he's asked of me while Anne still believes he has formed an attachment with her?" she'd asked.

Burwood had reassured her. "I believe she's questioning the wisdom of that attachment. She pressed me with some questions during our dance. What you must decide, my lady, is how to convince Drake of your devotion and commitment. My friend is a stubborn man. It might take something daring to make him believe you accept him as he is."

And that was when the idea popped into her head. Scandalous as it was, it would leave no doubt as to where her heart lay. But first, Anne must end things with Drake.

Burwood tapped a crystal glass, attracting her attention and that of the other guests. "Lords, ladies, and gentlemen. I hope you enjoyed the ball and our unusual method of selecting partners."

Grumbling arose from more than a few men and some women, but Burwood only chuckled.

He held up his hands. "Very well. I shall not repeat that method of selecting dance partners. After the final dance, I would remind everyone to gather on the front lawn for the fireworks display. After that"—he winked, and Honoria felt it was directed only at her—"it's all up to you."

Subdued laughter and a few feminine gasps of shock followed. As ladies searched the ballroom for their final partners, Honoria turned toward the terrace, debating if she should seek Drake out.

Why had he gone out to the terrace with Anne?

Since Priscilla had accompanied them, perhaps Dr. Marbry would know why. She scanned the crowd. There, standing next to Lord Montgomery, he smiled, catching sight of her as she approached.

"Dr. Marbry, might I have a moment?" She glanced apologetically toward Lord Montgomery.

"Please take him." Montgomery grinned. "He doesn't seem the least bit interested in my latest experiment. What good is a best friend if he can't even feign interest in a man's triumphs?"

"That's because your *triumphs* are more likely due to my sister." Dr. Marbry smirked.

"True enough. In fact, I think I shall seek out my brilliant wife and show her my appreciation." Montgomery winked, then stepped aside.

Dr. Marbry shook his head, then gave his full attention to Honoria. "You appear troubled. How may I be of assistance?"

Honoria thought back to when Dr. Marbry had courted her.

Although he had found love with her friend, Priscilla, he and Honoria had formed a bond of sorts—more as siblings or dear friends. At the moment, she counted on that bond.

"I saw Priscilla leaving with Mr. Merrick and Miss Weatherby. Might you know the reason they stepped outside and when they're expected to return?"

"Ah." The single word spoke volumes, as if he had opened her skull and methodically examined her thoughts. "Mr. Merrick took her outside for some air. Ashton suspected she had not fully recovered from her fall. But I"—his head canted as he continued to study her—"believe her malady is not physical but emotional."

Honoria gave herself a little shake, trying to decipher his meaning. "I beg your pardon?"

"May I speak freely, my lady?"

She nodded. Perhaps he really could see inside her mind.

"Priscilla and I owe you a great debt for which we are forever grateful. Perhaps I can repay a small measure."

He paused, as if collecting his thoughts. "A man has a certain look about him when he is in love—especially if he believes that love is hopeless. I recognize it now, even though I refused to admit it in myself for far too long." His smile broadened. "Until you forced me to face it." He grew serious again. "Mr. Merrick has that look about him."

"Oh." The word seeped out from her like air escaping a tiny leak.

"But not for Miss Weatherby. And I believe Miss Weatherby finally came to acknowledge that fact."

"Oh." Honoria's spine straightened, the word coming out with more conviction.

"You see, I believe Mr. Merrick holds that love for you, Lady Honoria. And if I may be so bold, my darling wife has pointed out to me that, as her dear friend, she suspects you are in love with Mr. Merrick."

Heat raced up Honoria's neck, and her cheeks flamed.

"From the look on your face, I would say that, not for the first time, my wife is correct."

She remained silent. Words seemed superfluous, her acknowledgment was unmistakable.

"Allow me to return the favor. If Mr. Merrick is not already aware—which I suspect he is—tell him you return his ardor. Grasp happiness while you can, my lady. Don't let it slip through your fingers."

"But Miss Weatherby believes—"

He held up a silencing hand, apology in his eyes. "Forgive me, but if someone needs to speak with Miss Weatherby and explain, I volunteer my services. Or if you prefer, Priscilla could. She's never been at a loss for words."

Honoria's lips trembled in a wavering smile. No, Priscilla had not. "I don't wish to hurt Anne."

Dr. Marbry nodded. "I quite understand. But speaking as a physician, sometimes a little pain to excise a tumor is better than allowing that tumor to grow. Do you really wish your friend to have a loveless marriage?" His smile didn't reach his eyes. "I rather think not. You saved us both from such a fate when you rejected me and set me on the correct path to happiness."

The orchestra returned to their places, tuning their instruments in preparation for the final dance of the evening.

"Thank you, Dr. Marbry—Timothy. I have the final set with Mr. Merrick. But I will take your words to heart, and if I have need of you or Priscilla, I will let you know."

"I wish you all the happiness, my lady. If anyone deserves it, you do."

Couples strolled to the dance floor for the final country line dance, and Honoria scanned the faces once again. Drake and Anne were nowhere to be seen. She wove her way through the crowd and stepped outside.

Soft moonlight spilled onto the stone floor of the terrace. Dim shadows flickered as a cloud passed over the nearly full moon. Honoria squinted, blinded at first by the brazier torches lining the terrace perimeter, steps, and long walkway of the gardens.

Movement from the left drew Honoria's attention. Standing out of the light, their figures mere silhouettes, a couple embraced. Wind stirred and a subsequent blaze from a torch flared, shedding more light on the couple and illuminating a flash of the petite woman's red hair.

Unbidden, Honoria's hand rose to cover her mouth and stifle her gasp. She squinted again, the light from the torch retreating. The man with the woman was tall and broad shouldered. Try as she might, Honoria couldn't make out his features. Bent down for a kiss, his face was obscured by the back of the woman's head.

Frantically, she surveyed the area for Priscilla. There. Along the path to the garden, a woman strolled alone.

Honoria's gaze darted back to the couple. Nothing made sense. Her mind fought against the logic of what she witnessed. Drake wouldn't lie about his feelings.

Would he?

And if so, why?

Had something changed?

She turned from the embracing couple and hurried back inside the ballroom. Figures blurred as she blinked back the tears.

Burwood's voice stopped her. "Good Lord, what did he do?"

CHAPTER 29

Relief mingled with guilt as Drake studied Anne's face. With the back of her hand, she swiped at the tears flowing down her cheeks. "You must think me such a ninny, sir. To pin my hopes so vainly on an attachment."

He pulled a handkerchief from his coat and handed it to her. "Not at all. I take responsibility for encouraging your hopes. I wanted to make amends to you after your fall. It's no wonder you interpreted my actions as you did."

She sniffed, wiping her eyes and then her nose. Sending him a shaky smile, she shook her head. "I should have seen it sooner. The way you look at Honoria and she looks at you. But why didn't you say something?"

Her tone did not accuse, yet he felt ashamed as if it had. "It seemed hopeless at first. You asked about our prior relationship. I asked her to marry me eight years ago, and she refused me, no doubt because in her father's eyes, I don't measure up."

"You said, 'at first.' Has something changed?"

He shrugged, not certain of the answer himself. "It depends if Lady Honoria accepts me as I am." He squeezed her hand. "But thanks to you, I can hope for that now."

Her blue eyes widened. "Me?"

"For releasing me from our attachment. You must know she would never consider me if you and I . . ."

"No. She wouldn't. Not Honoria." She wiped her eyes again. "She's been a loyal and kind friend to me. It's time I return that kindness."

"Thank you, Anne. Now, at least Honoria and I have a chance." He turned, looking for their chaperone. "Shall we call Mrs. Marbry back and go inside?"

"In a moment. I have a request."

He almost said 'anything,' but thought the better of it. It was Anne after all. Once bitten, twice shy, as they said. "What is it?"

"I know everyone thinks I have loose morals. But I've never been kissed. Would you kiss me? I should like to experience it." She held up a hand. "Even though it won't mean anything."

"I shouldn't. What if someone sees us?" Pity banded his chest at her dejected expression. "Besides, wouldn't you want your first kiss to be with someone who lights up your world?"

She sighed. "I suppose you're right." A spark of her personality bubbled up from her sadness. "Have you kissed Honoria?"

He waggled a finger at her. "Ah. A gentleman never tells. But suffice it to say that when you do find that special man, it will be like the heavens have opened up and shined down upon you."

"So you *have* kissed her?!"

Unable to stop the smile pulling at the corners of his mouth, he rose from the bench beneath the terrace wall and held out his hand. "Let us fetch Mrs. Marbry and join the others before the fireworks commence."

With Mrs. Marbry collected, the three of them strolled across the terrace toward the doors to the ballroom. A soft laugh caught Drake's attention, and Lord and Lady Montgomery emerged from the shadows.

Lord Montgomery's hair appeared mussed.

Lady Montgomery exchanged a furtive glance with her husband. "Are you feeling better, Miss Weatherby?"

"A little. As His Grace suggested, I'm most likely suffering from residual effects of my fall. But I have every confidence I shall recover quickly." She cast a gentle smile at Drake, and his heart lightened.

Perhaps the tides truly had turned in his favor.

"May I suggest we rejoin the assembly?" Lord Montgomery tugged his wife to his side. "Bea and I are eager to see the fireworks display. It will remind us of our wedding trip to Scotland."

Drake suspected there was more to that story, but from the expression on Montgomery's face, Drake also suspected the details of such an explanation would be private. Plus, he was too impatient to tell Honoria his news.

Gesturing for them to lead the way, Drake focused ahead of him, ready to search for Honoria and—hopefully his future.

No sooner had he stepped inside the ballroom, Simon pulled him aside, not bothering to apologize to Anne.

Simon's nostrils flared. "What the devil did you do?!"

Drake recoiled involuntarily, as if Simon had physically struck him. "What are you talking about?"

"Honoria went looking for you on the terrace and when she returned, she was visibly upset."

Drake pivoted, his body twisting this way and that as he frantically scanned the ballroom for Honoria. Rows of couples assembled for a country line dance, but Honoria wasn't among them. "Where is she? And why do you think I'm responsible for upsetting her?"

Lord and Lady Montgomery doubled back, their gazes curious.

Simon shrugged. "I'm not certain. She didn't make a lot of sense, which is most unlike her. Something about being wrong and"—he darted a glance toward the Montgomerys and lowered his voice— "witnessing an embrace on the terrace. She said she needed a quiet place to think."

Lady Montgomery gave a tiny gasp.

Anne stared wide-eyed.

Drake frowned. *Embrace?* However, one thing was clear. "The library. I must go to her and find out what's going on."

Lady Montgomery laid a gloved hand on his arm. "Please, sir. Allow me. I may be able to resolve this."

"Thank you, Lady Montgomery. Will you tell her I need to speak with her?" Drake asked.

"Call me Bea. And, of course."

"Bring her out to the front lawn. We'll be gathering there as soon as the dance is finished," Simon said.

Lord Montgomery kissed his wife's hand. "I'll wait for you right outside, my darling."

After Bea left them, Drake continued to puzzle about what had caused Honoria's sudden departure from the ball before their last dance began. And what did Bea know?

At Drake's questioning glance, Montgomery jerked his chin, indicating they should step aside.

Montgomery peered around Drake to where Anne remained with Simon. "I'm afraid Lady Honoria might have witnessed my wife and me in . . . a . . . ahem, rather passionate moment. Since both Bea and Miss Weatherby have the same coloring, and you and I are approximately the same height . . . well . . ." He grinned at Drake sheepishly.

Oh? Ooooh. "She thinks I was kissing Anne Weatherby."

"Indeed. Not to worry, though. Bea will straighten everything out. She has a way about her that is straightforward but kind."

"Thank you, Lord Montgomery."

Montgomery slapped Drake good-naturedly on the arm. "To follow my wife's lead, as I've learned to do, call me Laurence. And I'm happy to help out a fellow victim of cupid's arrow. I wish you the best of luck, sir."

The list of people Drake felt he could trust continued to grow. But what would happen when he finally finished this farce?

One thing was certain. He could face it all if Honoria was by his side as his duchess.

ONCE ENSCONCED IN THE LIBRARY, HONORIA TOOK DEEP BREATHS and pondered what she had observed.

No matter which scenario she followed, what she saw didn't make sense. Drake wouldn't profess his love for her and then kiss Anne.

He simply wouldn't.

The tiny, wicked voice in her head taunted her.

He's not the boy you once knew.

Hadn't he, himself, admitted to being hardened by his time in the military?

No. She couldn't accept he'd changed that much. Sincerity shone in his eyes when he admitted he needed her to choose him of her own free will. He wouldn't say that if he only meant to use her.

But what of Anne? Was the kiss in keeping with what Anne might expect?

Gah!

"Forgive me for intruding."

Honoria spun toward the library's open door. "Lady Montgomery." She forced a smile and fought to find a valid reason for excusing herself. The answer was at her fingertips. She plucked a book from the shelves, not caring what it was. "I just came in to retrieve a book."

"Call me Bea, Honoria. I'd like to think of us as friends." Bea stepped forward, peering down at the book in Honoria's hands, a sly smile breaking across her lips. "Plato's *Symposium*. An excellent choice. Particularly the section by Aristophanes. But I find that Plato's objection to two split halves has merit."

What?

No doubt sensing Honoria's confusion, Bea clarified. "The theory of soulmates. Fascinating reading, and apropos, considering my reason for seeking you out."

"You came specifically for me?"

Bea nodded. "To explain. I believe you witnessed my husband and me on the terrace not long ago and may have mistaken us for Mr. Merrick and Miss Weatherby."

"How . . .?"

"Laurence and I were on the terrace when Mr. Merrick, Miss Weatherby, and my sister-in-law, Priscilla, came up the steps from the garden below. I'm afraid they, too, may have caught us stealing a kiss.

Laurence does get carried away at times." Bea's smile indicated she didn't mind her husband's lack of control in the least.

"But why have you sought me out?"

"When we rejoined the assembly, Burwood mentioned you were upset and said something about an embrace. Mr. Merrick was quite concerned and wished to speak with you. But I thought you would be more open to hearing the explanation from me."

"Oh." Tears welled in her eyes again, but this time, they were from happiness.

"Now," Bea said, "I think the fireworks are about to begin. Shall we join our gentlemen?"

Our gentlemen? Could Drake be hers soon? Stunned from Bea's revelation, Honoria simply nodded and stepped out of the room.

Bea wrapped her arm around Honoria's waist, giving it a squeeze. "Take heart, Honoria. From my own experience, I've learned that sometimes the darkest of times offer the greatest hope."

As they exited the house and joined the other guests already gathered on the front lawn, Lord Montgomery met them at the front door and pulled Bea aside.

Honoria turned to express her thanks, but Bea and Laurence were already deep in conversation. The brief gusts of wind earlier on the terrace had subsided, and the air stilled around her, settling as if in anticipation of what was to come.

Murmurs rose from the crowd clustered in small groups and interspersed along the front of the house and spilling onto the front lawn.

Miranda appeared beside her. "Where have you been? Your parents were almost apoplectic until they noticed Mr. Merrick conversing with my brother."

"My father, you mean." From her conversation with her mother, Honoria doubted she would be as distraught. "Where are they?"

"To your left."

When she caught her father's eye, she raised her hand and offered him a reasonable facsimile of a smile. In the dim light of the brazier torches, she hoped it appeared genuine enough to assuage his worry.

He gave a sharp nod, then bent toward her mother, pointing his chin in Honoria's direction.

A girlish giggle erupted to Honoria's right, and she expected to see Anne giggling with Drake, but instead found Lydia Whyte flirting shamelessly with Victor Pratt.

Where was Anne?

Where was Drake?

"I can see the wheels turning in your head," Miranda said. "Anne's with her mother, brother, and sister-in-law. At your two o'clock."

Squinting in the dim light, Honoria made out Anne's petite frame when Mr. Weatherby shifted to his right.

Before she could search further for Drake, Burwood took his place in the center of the gathered crowd. "Lords, ladies, and gentlemen. Now is the time you've been waiting for. In order to enjoy our display to its fullest, I'm going to have the footman extinguish the fires in the torches. Please remain where you are to avoid injury. And enjoy the show."

He gave the signal and in dramatic fashion, the fires went out two-by-two, starting from the outside of the half-circle to the innermost torches until Burwood himself was but a shadow in the faint moonlight.

Hushed voices quieted until only the sounds of frogs croaking in a nearby pond remained.

A whistle and sparks shooting into the sky garnered *oohs* and *aahs* from even the staunchest members of the *ton*. Someone brushed Honoria's hand, and she whispered over her shoulder, reluctant to take her eyes off the night sky, "It's beautiful. Isn't it, Miranda?"

"Not as beautiful as what's beside me," the deep baritone voice responded.

"Drake!" Where had he come from, and where had Miranda gone?

He placed a finger to his lips. "Come with me." He tugged gently on her hand.

"But the fireworks?" She craned her neck to continue viewing the colored explosions.

"You can still see them from over here." He led her along the front of the house, skirting the crowd too busy to notice them. Only the flashes from each colorful burst provided light enough to navigate their way, but Drake maneuvered them effortlessly. When they reached the side of the house, two large yews provided shelter from prying eyes, and he tucked her between them.

Her heart thudded against her ribcage. "I saw you leave the ballroom with Anne. I thought—"

He placed a fingertip against her lips. "Shush. You need not worry about Anne any longer. She's released me."

Another explosion lit the night sky, her heart bursting in colors just as beautiful. "Is she terribly hurt?"

His eyes didn't reflect his feeble smile. "How like you to worry about Anne. Rest assured, she will recover. She admits it is for the best." He stroked her cheek. "But with Anne and so many others aware of my feelings for you, I worry about what your father might do to come between us. Only my attachment with Anne has kept him at bay."

On that, like so many other things, they agreed completely. "I won't let anyone get in our way again."

She meant every word, and she was willing to prove it to Drake.

CHAPTER 30

No words could have been more beautiful to Drake's ears than Honoria's whispered commitment to him.

"Are you certain?" His own doubt clawed to the surface. "I meant what I said earlier. If there is to be a future for us, it must be your decision. Unencumbered and not influenced by others—including me. How—and indeed if—we proceed is entirely up to you."

"I promise you, Drake."

It would be so easy to be swept up by her enchanting green eyes, her lovely smile, her sweet voice. To fall under her spell again and leave his heart open and vulnerable. But experience had a way of making one wary of the fire once one had been burned.

He kept his voice as gentle as he could. "You promised me before, remember? Then you broke my heart when you refused me."

Oh, it was unfair to lay all the responsibility on Honoria's shoulders, to be sure. The pain swimming in her eyes told him as much.

"I thought it was for the best."

"So you said. But it wasn't best for me, Honoria."

"Wasn't it?" She traced a hand down his bespoke coat. "Would you have left for the military so quickly—"

He pressed a fingertip to her lips. "Hush. What's past is past and cannot be undone. It no longer matters." The crushing weight of her rejection eight years ago pressed upon him anew, ripping his heart open again. He had no desire to relive it. "Let's look to the future. What I ask is simple. Think long and hard about what you truly want. Consider all consequences. If your decision leads you to me, I will be waiting. But the choice must be completely yours. Are you willing to face the wrath of your father? To risk a divide with your family?"

When she opened her mouth, he raised a hand. "Don't answer hastily. I couldn't bear it if you said yes now but changed your mind later as you had before."

He wished he could tell her of his father's hasty decision that led to the separation from his family. Would his father have received better medical care and still be alive? Would he and Honoria have met at some *ton* fête and already be happily married, perhaps with the joyful sound of children scampering about the enormous mansion?

Fully admitting his stubbornness in not confessing his true identity, he convinced himself it was a matter of pride. He not only *wanted* her to choose him regardless of his station—he *needed* it. He needed to feel valued, accepted, and loved for himself as a man, not a title.

"Now"—he squeezed her hand—"let's enjoy the fireworks. I've waited eight long years for you, Honoria. I can wait as long as necessary." Banding his arms around her waist, he pulled her in front of him. With her back pressed against his chest, he rested his cheek against hers.

And he prayed he was doing the right thing.

WRAPPED IN DRAKE'S ARMS, HONORIA ALLOWED HERSELF TO SAVOR the moment. She would prove her devotion and commitment to him, and together they would face her father. But unlike eight years prior, if all went according to her plan, she would have a secret weapon in her arsenal to use if necessary.

For once in her life, she would stand up to her father, making it clear in no uncertain terms that she had chosen Drake, and no amount of persuasion would make her change her mind.

Peace settled around her, even amid the *bangs, sizzles*, and showers of sparks. She glanced over to where her parents watched the colorful display. Although she loved them both, even with their faults, Drake was her future, come what may.

"I should return you before your father notices," Drake whispered, his warm breath brushing against her cheek.

Carefully, he guided her across the front of the house, behind the crowd, back to where she had stood before. Miranda waited nearby, as if keeping watch and marking their destination.

Unable to keep her amusement to herself, she said, "Did you involve Miranda in your scheme to abduct me?"

His delicious chuckle vibrated across her skin. "Abduct? I merely escorted you to the most advantageous viewing spot. And yes, Lady Miranda may have agreed to point your position out to me. It is rather dark, you know."

"Hmm. I suppose you put Burwood up to extinguishing the braziers as well?"

"I admit to nothing. Except wishing we were alone. I very much want to kiss you goodnight. But even in the darkness, it wouldn't be prudent with all these people present . . ."

She laughed. "Then you are not as adept at planning as it would appear. For you had your chance while we were still hidden in the shrubbery."

He snapped his fingers. "Drat. You're right. I shall do better the next time I engage in stealthy behavior. But until then, goodnight, my lady." He lifted her hand and placed a kiss on her fingers, his eyes never leaving hers. "Sleep well."

With that, he disappeared into the darkness moments before footmen relit the torches.

As the crowd dispersed back inside, her parents wound their way toward her.

She smiled in greeting. "Mother. Father. Did you enjoy the fireworks?"

"Bah, a waste of money," her father groused, but there was a slight twinkle in his eyes.

"Don't let him fool you," her mother said. "He was as enthralled as everyone else. I believe I even heard a few oohs from him."

"We should have the physician check your hearing, woman." The twitch of his lips gave him away.

"Father, you *did* enjoy them."

"Very well. I did."

With his agreeable mood, Honoria plucked up her courage. She might not have a better time to present her case. "Father, might I have a word in private?"

He cocked his head, his brows drawing down. "Can't it wait until the morning? All this ball nonsense and fireworks has taken a toll."

Was it the dim light, or did he suddenly look older? An unwelcome foreboding tripped up her spine. "Are you unwell? Should I fetch Ashton or Dr. Marbry?"

He batted a hand. "Bah. Just old."

Her mother pulled her wrap up around her shoulders. "Can we discuss this inside?"

How could she be so selfish? With her mother cold and her father tired, her own needs seemed less urgent. She kissed her mother on the cheek. "Go." She waved them forward. "What I have to discuss can wait until tomorrow."

"Thank you, dear. Come, Stratford." Her mother threaded her arm through her father's.

As she watched her parents enter the house, her heart grew heavy. She prayed that she could persuade her father to understand. Could she enlist Colin's help? Although he'd been opposed to the match all those years ago, she wasn't a child any longer. Between her mother and brother, could they get her father to see reason? Or would she lose her family?

"All alone?" She practically jumped at Burwood's appearance.

His simple question gave voice to her fear.

FILLED WITH BOTH ELATION AND NERVOUS ENERGY, DRAKE PACED the floor of his room. Free! No longer bound by his hasty promise to Anne, he could finally breathe. Stopping by the open window, he pulled a great lungful in, then coughed, the air still smoky from gunpowder.

So racked with his coughing, he didn't hear the knock at his door—if there even was one.

"There you are." Simon entered, then closed the door behind him.

Even Simon's lack of respect for Drake's privacy couldn't sour his mood. Still, he had no qualms about needling his friend. "Who let you in here? Can't a man have a moment of peace to himself without you barging in uninvited? And what if I weren't alone?"

Simon snorted a laugh. "Shall I look under the bed for your hidden paramour? You're about as likely to have a woman in your room as I am to entertain the *pleasure* of Lady Charlotte." He snorted another laugh to prove his point. "And"—he pointed a finger at Drake—"the only woman who's not your relation you would want in your room would be Honoria. And we both know that's even more unlikely."

Drake propped his hands on his hips. "What's unlikely? That I would want her in my room, or she'd be here?"

Simon pursed his lips and rolled his eyes to the ceiling.

Drake wanted to hit the fool. "Well?"

"Can't you see I'm thinking?"

"Ha! Don't strain yourself."

"The point is, if you even have to ask me that, I worry seriously about your future with Honoria. I would *hope* you would want her in your room—maybe even dreamed about it. You *do* know what to do when the time comes, I hope?"

Drake bristled. "Of course I know what to do. In theory," he mumbled the last. "Remember, I was a groom on an estate."

Simon barked a laugh. "I hope you don't treat Honoria like some prized mare to be bred. Each woman is different, and you have to know what pleases her in particular. Some require tenderness and some prefer, shall we say, a more vigorous approach. You must attune to her needs."

Drake's face heated. "Why are we having this conversation?"

"Because with luck—and as long as you don't muck things up—you will find yourself married to Honoria, and I don't want you fumbling about on your wedding night like some green school boy. Not only is it my duty as your friend, but I like Honoria far too much to have you bungling things with her in the marriage bed. From your red face, it's clear you need my instruction."

"Go away, Simon."

Rather than graciously heeding Drake's request, Simon helped himself to the chair by the window, settling down like he expected to be there for quite some time. "Did Lady Montgomery straighten things out with Honoria? And what happened with Anne? You were gone for some time before the last set."

Knowing full well Simon wouldn't leave until he received a satisfactory answer, Drake took a seat on the bed. "It's over with Anne. She's released me."

A devilish grin spread across Simon's face. "I knew my plan would work."

Drake wanted to wipe off the smug look. "I don't think it was just your attention toward her. Anne admitted to being blinded by her own hopes. But when she took care to notice, it was clear to her how I feel about Honoria." He shook his head. "I hated hurting her, but I'm grateful for her understanding."

"And Honoria?"

Drake drew a hand down his face, exhaustion from the day finally manifesting. "She promises she won't let anything stand in our way again. I want to believe her. Really, I do." Simon had no idea how much. But the demons of doubt had a stranglehold on him.

"Then believe her. I spoke with her this evening before you left with Anne. She's ready to do what she must to prove she still loves you, even defy her father."

"I pray you're right. But I don't want Honoria to feel like she has to choose between me and her family. When I was young and foolish I did. But no longer. Family is important. My own parents' history taught me that lesson. I don't want Stratford to disown her like my grandfather did to my father."

"That's all very noble, but Stratford won't object when you tell him who you really are."

Drake bolted from the bed. "Don't you understand? It's not only Honoria's acceptance I want. It's Stratford's. You weren't there when I asked for Honoria's hand. He looked at me like I was muck from the stables he wanted to wipe from his boots. I want to be worthy of her in his eyes for who I am as a man—not because of a title. And this struggle is pulling me apart."

"I understand perfectly. Your pride stands in the way of your happiness. Perhaps it's not Honoria's or Stratford's acceptance of you that's the problem. Maybe *you* need to believe in your worth." Simon rose and placed a hand on Drake's shoulder. "Have faith in yourself. But don't let pride rob you of the happiness you deserve. Marry Honoria and, if it's still important to you, prove your worth to Stratford by showing him the man you truly are." After giving Drake's shoulder a squeeze, Simon left, closing the door behind him with a soft *click*.

Drake collapsed back onto the bed. Simon was right.

He not only needed to trust Honoria and put the past behind him. He needed to believe in his own worth.

CHAPTER 31

Honoria paced the floor of her bedchamber. The house had finally grown silent. Murmurs of voices had drifted away as people retired to their beds after the night's festivities.

Yet sleep was far from Honoria's mind. If Drake wanted proof of her devotion and commitment, she would give it to him—in the most drastic way she knew how.

Well, the truth was—she didn't know *how*. But she hoped he would guide her. Not only would her action prove her love, but her father would have no choice but to accept Drake's offer of marriage if she told him what she'd done.

She hoped it wouldn't come to that, but desperate times and all that.

And if her father still didn't accept Drake? Although she wanted his blessing, she didn't need his permission. She would marry Drake with or without it.

The time had come to put her plan into action.

Her heart pounded like timpani. Each bang against her ribcage shouted a warning. Her mouth was as arid as a desert. Still, she pressed forward, determined to be brave—even fearless.

She peeked out into the candlelit hallway, pleased it remained deserted. Downstairs a clock chimed three, its low sound reverberating in the still house. She stepped from her room and closed the door behind her with a *click*. Ten seconds later, when no one opened their own bedchamber door to investigate the noise—which to her sounded louder than a clap of thunder—she tiptoed toward her destination.

Eight doors down on the right from hers, the distance seemed to go on for miles. She counted carefully, ready with a quick excuse of sleepwalking should someone discover her.

Five, six, seven, eight. At last she stood before the door to either her humiliation or her ecstasy, praying Juliana had given her the correct location.

Perspiration drenched the palm she placed on the doorknob. She tried to twist, but nothing happened.

Was it locked?

After wiping her hand on her nightrail, she tried again. The knob moved, and the door creaked open, allowing her to peer inside. Streams of moonlight filtered in from the windows where the curtain had been pulled back, illuminating the sleeping figure on the bed.

When she pushed the door open more fully, it squeaked, freezing her in place. The figure in the bed shifted but then settled. She held her breath and counted to twenty before proceeding. Once inside, she closed the door, her muscles tensing as it squeaked again, then sealed with a soft *snick*.

As her eyes adjusted to the darkness, she squinted, trying to discern the features of the man who lay before her. Was his hair brown or darker? Everything appeared gray or slate-colored. She crept closer to the bed.

Her breath hitched at the sight of Drake.

Bare shoulders, arms, and chest peeked from the thin linens covering him from the waist down.

Her cheeks heated at his state of undress, yet she couldn't tear her eyes away. Rather than serene repose, his countenance appeared troubled—his brow furrowed, and his hand twitched restlessly.

The courage she had called forth upon leaving her room deserted her, and cold panic gripped her chest—squeezing.

What had she been thinking?

This is a horrible mistake.

When she backed up, ready to turn and flee to the safety of her room, she bumped into a table behind her, jarring something resting on top. The *b-ring, b-ring, b-ring* alerted her the *something* was about to fall.

She spun around and steadied the empty crystal glass and brandy decanter, stilling the accusatory sound.

Just as she was about to release the breath she held and make her escape, creaking from behind froze her once again.

"Uhh," Drake groaned.

Cautiously, she peeked over her shoulder, catching Drake sitting up and running a hand over his face. The linen sheets dropped lower on his body, exposing a bare hip.

Oh, dear Lord. Although her mouth was dry, she swallowed the air stuck in her throat.

She turned fully, ready to face him.

His head jerked in her direction. "Who's there?" A beat passed. "Honoria?" Incredulity rang in his voice, reminding her of the traitorous glass.

"Y-yes. It's me." Her voice sounded like the squeak of a mouse as she forced out her admission.

He began to rise from the bed, but apparently thought better of it and pulled the linens up higher around his waist. "Is something wrong?"

She shook her head, her bravado completely gone, leaving her stumbling and shy. As if reconsidering, the small voice in her head called from a distance. *Tell him.*

"I—I wanted to see you. To give you something."

"In the middle of the night? It couldn't wait until morning?"

"No." Words crowded on her tongue, refusing to leave their haven. As she coaxed them forward, she realized none of them were sufficient. So, rather than speak, she showed him.

With shaking hands, she tugged the ribbons on her nightrail and slipped it off one shoulder, then moved to the next.

"Stop!"

Heat flamed her cheeks at the one-word command, and she was

enormously grateful for the dim lighting. Tears welled in her eyes, and she jerked the nightrail back into place. "I'm sorry to have disturbed you. Please don't mention this to anyone."

She turned to leave, but a soft rustling from behind stopped her.

"Wait, Honoria. Don't go."

She felt the heat of his presence behind her and the brush of his breath against her neck.

His hand, gentle and warm, on her shoulder halted her. "You wanted to give me something. It must have been important. What is it?"

A fat tear dripped down her cheek. Knots in her stomach twisted. "It doesn't matter."

"It does. If it matters to you, it matters to me." He brushed a lock of hair from her neck, his fingers eliciting gooseflesh over her entire body. Even her nipples rose to attention, brushing against the cotton of her nightdress.

Heat emanated from him as he moved closer. "Something's troubling you. Won't you face me?"

The tenderness in his voice flowed through her. This was the Drake she remembered. The caring, gentle man she'd held in her heart and mind for eight long years.

And, oh, how she'd missed him. Turning slowly, anxious as to what she might see, she tried to keep her gaze elevated toward his face, but unbidden, it drifted to his lower body.

He'd wrapped the bed linens around his waist and held them in place with one hand. "Forgive my state of undress. I'm used to sleeping without a nightshirt from the Indian heat." The lopsided smile she loved so much spread across his face. "Besides, I didn't expect such lovely company."

Unwittingly, she licked her lips.

He groaned. "Oh, Honoria. You have no idea what you do to me, especially when you're standing there in your nightdress." He took her hand and led her to a chair on the far side of the room—away from the bed and her destination.

She tried to form the words she wanted to say, but he'd thoroughly scrambled her wits.

He lit a candle on the table by the chair, then studied her face. "You've been crying. Are you certain there is nothing wrong?" He brushed a thumb across her wet cheek. "If someone has hurt you, I will have harsh words with them."

As she gazed up into his face, even in the dim light, his affection was evident, and it gave her the courage she needed.

"I've come to tell you I love you. Still love you. To prove my love."

No words could be sweeter to Drake's ears. And although when he'd finally come to his senses he *knew* she loved him, to hear her speak them aloud was bliss. Oh, he'd heard them many times before in his dreams, and like those dreams, she stood before him in dishabille.

But unlike those dreams, he'd stopped her from going further—proof his groggy mind had awoken fully.

Silence stood between them like an unwelcome intruder as she waited for his response.

Struggling to make sense of the situation, he closed his eyes and breathed a heavy sigh. "Is that why you started removing your nightdress?"

She nodded. "I wanted to give you my body as a pledge. But I've offended you with my wanton behavior."

Is that what she thought? He'd hardly been offended in his dreams. But this was reality, and she was an innocent. He knotted the linens around his waist, then crouched before her. "Oh, Honoria. Nothing could be further from the truth. I want you more than you imagine. But I don't want you to do something you'll regret."

Her gaze snapped to his. "My only regret is I didn't offer myself to you eight years ago."

Brushing his fingertips over her cheek, he gave her a rueful smile. "That would have been more of a mistake than this is."

"Mistake? Why?"

"Because I wouldn't have been able to resist you then."

The pain in her eyes lanced at his heart.

"You said you wanted me, yet you're able to resist."

"I'm not a boy any longer. I've learned to control my appetites."

"Oh." The exclamation, no more than a whisper, gut punched him. "Is it because I'm . . . inexperienced and will disappoint you?"

"You could never disappoint me. But I might disappoint you." A weak smile tugged his lips. "I'm also inexperienced."

She blinked. "What? I presumed . . ."

"That because I'm a man, I've had sexual encounters?" He shook his head.

"Never?" she whispered.

"Oh, I've been tempted. I'm human, after all. But I never could bring myself to be with someone I didn't love. If complete fidelity is expected of a woman, why not from a man as well? It never seemed quite fair to me."

Slow realization bloomed on her face. "You only wish to be with your bride."

"Yes."

"Then let that be me."

"And if your father objects?"

"My whole life I've tried to please my parents. To be the daughter they expected me to be. Sacrificed my own happiness. As hard as it would be, for once I'm choosing what I want, even if that means I could lose my family."

Unbidden, his gaze darted to the untied ribbons of her nightrail. "And this has something to do with you coming to me in the middle of the night?"

Lifting her chin, she straightened her shoulders, her gaze direct. "Exactly. I'm here to prove my love to you in no uncertain terms. To give myself to you in pledge."

Lord, she was serious. "You realize that once done, what you're suggesting can't be undone."

"Well, of course. That's the point. You did say you wanted me to choose you. To come to you of my own free will."

"So you would compromise us both?" He wanted to laugh at the absurdity, but there was nothing humorous about what she proposed.

Those determined shoulders slumped. "I didn't think of it that way.

I only wanted to prove my love to you. To give you something I could only give once."

He gathered her hands in his. "Then marry me, Honoria. I promise I will do whatever I can to win your father over. I've come to learn how important family is, especially when it's too late to do anything about it."

She threw herself into his arms, peppering his face with kisses.

As wonderful as her show of affection felt, he needed to hear the words. "So you'll marry me? Regardless of who I am?"

"No."

His heart fell at the single word, his mind a confused mess. "But you said you wanted to be my bride."

She cast him a coy smile—the tease. Not something he expected of his proper Honoria.

"Not *regardless* of who you are, but I'll marry you *because of* who you are. The man I love, have always loved. The only man I'll ever love. You're honest and kind. I don't care who else you are."

The word *honest* seared him like a branding iron, but he pushed it aside.

"What if we have to live somewhere other than this magnificent house? If I lost everything I have?"

"I don't care about any of that. Yes, this house is wonderful. Grander than my father's, but if Burwood dismisses you, and we are forced to live in a hovel somewhere, if I have to darn your stockings and tend sheep, I don't care."

He laughed, returning her kisses. "Do you even know how to darn?"

"No, but if there is a book about it, I can learn."

He picked her up and spun her around. "I love you, woman."

When he set her back down, he trailed a finger down her cheek. "Now, hurry back to your room before someone discovers you in here."

Eyes filled with determination gazed back at him. "No." To further her point, she crossed her arms over her bosom, drawing his attention to the nightrail's gaping neckline.

"Your promise to marry me is sufficient, Honoria. I will not take your virtue before we are wed."

But, oh, how he wanted to. Every moment Honoria remained,

restraint ebbed from him. Try as he might to hold back the floodgates of his passion, Honoria's persistence chipped away at his resolve.

She wouldn't budge. "We should have been wed eight years ago. I'm tired of waiting. Let me prove this to you, Drake. It's because of your honor that I want to do this. I know you won't desert me—and I want to wipe any doubt from your mind that I will not be deterred from my promise. As you said yourself, once done, it cannot be undone. Give me this one night."

Perhaps he should have allowed Simon to provide some informative instruction. At least if he fumbled his way through his wedding night, Honoria would already be his. "And if I disappoint you?"

"You couldn't even if you tried. Besides, how would I know what is good or not?"

Overwhelmed by her trust in him, he pulled her into his arms. "Well, I would hope you would know because it makes you feel good. It *is* supposed to be enjoyable."

"Then let us learn together."

"You're absolutely certain? You can change your—"

She answered him with a kiss.

CHAPTER 32

If Drake continued his protests, Honoria would lose her nerve. She pulled him down and sealed her mouth to his, silencing him the only way she knew how.

Taking action sent a thrill through her. She had never felt so powerful and in charge.

And it was exhilarating.

She should have pushed past her fear years ago.

Warm and soft, the press of his lips on hers was heaven on Earth. He threaded a hand through her hair, pulling her closer to him, his mouth hungry and demanding.

So different from their kiss in the orangery, but no less wonderful.

When he pulled away, she chased his lips, wanting more, but he rested his forehead against hers. The soft panting of his breath brushed against her skin.

He kissed the tip of her nose. "I like this side of you." Those luscious lips curved in his lopsided smile. "So fierce. Like a tigress, ready to take on the most fearsome of enemies."

She laughed. "My father?"

"Yes, him. But also the *ton*. The world."

"For you, I would."

Closing his eyes, he grew serious. "I thought I knew what love was, but I was wrong."

"You were?" Her words came out like wispy tendrils of wonder.

His grin returned. "Um-hmm. I was a boy, heartsick over a lovely girl. But now"—his eyes grew hooded—"now, I see love is so much more. It's taking *and* giving. Of being the best you can be for the one you love and helping them be the best they can be. It's not just accepting, it's celebrating who the other person is."

"Oh, Drake. I take it back."

His warm brown eyes widened. "What? Not your promise to marry me?"

She shook her head. "You *are* a poet."

He scooped her up, and she squealed. "I'm a man in love who is about to make love to the woman of my dreams. There is no better inspiration."

As he carried her toward the big bed, the linens around his waist slipped loose, and his foot tangled in the folds, propelling him forward.

Unsure how in the world Drake performed the maneuver, Honoria found herself lying on top of him in the middle of the floor—several feet from the bed.

With a sigh, he banged his head against the floor and squeezed his eyes shut. His mouth tightened in a straight line. In a word, he appeared mortified.

"So much for my attempt at gallantry. I'm a bumbling dolt."

She giggled and gave him a peck on the lips. "No. You are my hero. All you need now is a handful of wet forget-me-nots."

"Lord, you remember that, do you? The difference being, then I could blame Buttercup, whereas now"—he motioned around him—"I have nothing to blame but my own clumsiness."

"Not true. The sheets are the culprit. Perhaps you should remove them."

"I don't have anything on underneath. I'd hoped to spare you the shock until—" His cheeks darkened.

"Oh." Heat flooded her own cheeks. My, but they were a pair. "Might I suggest you forgo trying to carry me and we walk to the bed?" She eased off him as gracefully as she was able.

Knock. Knock, knock.

Honoria froze at the sound, her gaze darting toward Drake.

"Quick, in the bed. Get under the covers," Drake said, his heart pounding harder than the knock at the door.

She pointed to the sheets wrapped around his body. "You have them on you."

"Oh, right. Um, hide behind the curtains. Whoever it is, I'll send them away quickly."

Once Honoria had concealed herself, Drake marched toward the door, ready to give whomever it was a firm dressing down. He yanked open the door.

Simon!

Drake glowered at his *friend*. "What the devil do you want?" he asked through gritted teeth. "It's the middle of the night. Shouldn't you be asleep?"

"I heard a noise. A rather large thump. You would think these walls would be sturdier. As any good friend would, I came to see if everything was—" His gaze jerked toward the window, and his eyebrows popped high on his forehead. "Ah, never mind."

Drake spun around, surveying Honoria's hiding place and wondering what gave her away. It wasn't the curtain moving ever so gently. The open window could explain that. No, the toes poking from underneath the fluttering curtains had betrayed them.

He spun back to Simon, who grinned like a fool.

Simon leaned in, lifting a finger and keeping his voice low. "A few words of advice. Kiss and touch her—"

"I don't know what you're talking about."

Simon narrowed his eyes. "I wasn't finished. Everywhere. Don't rush, although God knows you'll want to. Make it about her." He winked. "And do try to keep it down. Some of us are actually trying to sleep." With that, he strolled back to his room, a soft chuckle following in his wake.

Relieved to hear the soft click announcing that Simon was safely sequestered back in his room, Drake closed his own door. He resisted the urge to bang his head against it and instead leaned his forehead against the cool wood and sighed. Not quite how he envisioned his first time with Honoria.

His body warred with his conscience. What if it had been anyone other than Simon who had heard them? How could he do that to her?

"Drake?"

At the sound of Honoria's sweet voice, he reconsidered her wild idea. He steeled himself for a night of disappointment, preparing to tell her to return to her room.

Until he turned. The thought flew from his mind, and his heart stopped, rising up into his throat at the sight of her spread like a feast upon his bed. And truly, he was a starving man. When had she . . . ?

She propped herself on her elbows. "Burwood?"

What? He shook his head to clear it. "I'm sorry?"

"At the door. It sounded like Burwood." Her nightdress had slipped down one shoulder, exposing creamy skin. He'd seen her shoulders before. That very evening, in fact, thanks to her provocatively low-cut ballgown. But somehow, the sight of her on his bed was very different.

Drake's tongue clung to the roof of his mouth, and he could only nod. The weight of Simon's words slammed into him. *Don't rush.* And the man was right about one thing; Drake wanted to. Years of pent up longing and desire battered his willpower, like an enemy army laying siege to a fortress. The only thing that would stop him was Honoria.

But Simon's other words seeped through Drake's lust-fogged brain. *Kiss and touch her.* As if he didn't know that—want to do that already. *Everywhere.*

Careful not to trip and fall, making a fool of himself again, Drake bunched the linens in his hands. Lifting them from the floor, he stalked toward the bed.

Every muscle in his body tightened. Exhilaration? Fear? Both? A low growl formed in the back of his throat, and Honoria's eyes widened.

The last thing he wanted to do was scare her. He was terrified enough for the both of them.

Control yourself, man!

He eased onto the bed beside her, willing—what he hoped was—a reassuring smile to his lips.

He cleared his tight throat. "Now. I suggest we begin with kissing."

⚜

THE FURIOUS POUNDING OF HONORIA'S HEART AS SHE'D CREPT toward Drake's room earlier paled in comparison to the explosions occurring in her chest at that moment. She feared her heart would burst right out from her ribcage.

"Yes," she choked out. "Kissing sounds wonderful."

Gently stroking his knuckles against her cheek, he smiled. "We'll learn this together. But I need you to do something for me."

"W-what?"

"Relax. And tell me what you like or don't like."

"I like kissing."

His eyes grew hooded as he leaned over her. "Good. So do I." Moving his hand to the back of her head, he pressed his lips against hers.

She didn't know what to do with her hands, so she slipped them around his shoulders. His bare skin against her fingers intoxicated her. Muscles rippled and bunched under her hands as he shifted his arms and propped himself on his elbows above her.

A smattering of hair dusted his chest, and her fingers itched to see if it was soft or wiry.

"You can touch me anywhere you like," he whispered, his breath brushing against her lips.

Needing no more encouragement, she tested it.

Hmm. A little wiry, but not distastefully so.

He moaned into her mouth.

Emboldened, she flattened her hand on the hard muscles of his chest. His heart pounded against her palm. Apparently, she affected him as strongly as he did her, and she smiled. His nipples—small but firm—peaked when she ran a fingertip over one, and his chest muscle twitched.

"You're good at this." Trailing little kisses across her cheek, he paused at her earlobe and nibbled it.

"Oh!" Effervescent bubbles tingled from the top of her spine down to her toes.

"Like or don't like?"

"Like. Very much like."

His chuckle, deep and raspy, vibrated across her skin, igniting gooseflesh.

"Are you cold?"

"No." She was veritably on fire.

"What about this spot?" He moved down a bit to where her neck met her shoulder.

"Yes," she answered, her voice breathy. "Will you touch me, too?"

His gaze locked on hers. "I thought you'd never ask." One hand slid to her waist, the heat from it searing through the cotton of her nightrail and spreading through her like warm honey.

"I think more kissing," he whispered against her mouth before sealing it with his. More urgent than his previous kisses, his tongue traced along the seam of her lips, urging them to open.

When his tongue probed inside, she tentatively brushed hers against his, sending those tingles racing once more. A warm ache pooled low in her belly, and she squirmed against him, seeking relief.

She wanted him to touch her. But how to ask? The heat low inside her rose to her neck and face as she plucked up her courage. "I like when you touch me."

"Like this?" His hand moved from her waist. Up, up, up, resting on the underside of her breast.

She sucked in a breath. "Don't stop."

Complying, he gently cupped her breast, then slowly flicked her nipple with his thumb. "Yes or no?"

"Yes. Oh, yes, yes."

He toyed with the shoulder of her nightrail. "This is in the way. May I remove it?"

An odd utterance came from her mouth. It sounded like *yug*. He'd turned both her brain and speech into mush.

Drake's eyes sparkled, the corners crinkling. "I'm going to presume that's a yes." With the sheet still wrapped around his waist, he rose, resting on his knees before her, and held out his hand. "Let me help you sit up."

The erratic thudding of her heart beat against her sternum like a thousand racing horses. Yet, as she placed her shaking hand into his, it settled. Still rapid, but even and steady.

Inch-by-inch, he tugged the garment down her shoulders in agonizing slowness, his eyes never leaving hers. When it slipped down, pooling around her waist and exposing her breasts, his gaze dropped, and he sucked in a gasp.

Her racing heart slowed, freezing. "Am I not . . . do you not find me pleasing?"

"No . . . yes. I mean, you're more beautiful than I ever imagined." He reached out, his hand hovering a breath away from her skin as if he were afraid to touch her.

She placed her hand on his and completed the trajectory. "You imagined me? Specifically me?"

His shadowed face darkened slightly. "I said I was inexperienced. That doesn't mean I didn't fantasize. I'm not so perfect as that." He lifted his gaze back to hers. "And it was always only you."

He resumed his ministrations at her breast, caressing and stroking. Her nipple rose to attention, tingling and tightening in a pleasant torture when he ran his thumb over it. Carefully, he lowered her back on the bed and stretched out beside her. Waves of power flowed through her at the awe in his eyes.

In turn, she splayed a hand against his chest again, relishing the difference in their bodies. The hair on his chest continued down his abdomen, forming a little line that disappeared beneath the bed linens. She ran a fingertip down its length, and he drew in a shuddering breath.

She hooked a finger in the linens and tugged at them. "Perhaps you'd be more comfortable with these off."

He chuckled, deep and delicious. "Why, Honoria, in all my fantasies, I never imagined you so bold."

"Is that bad?"

"What do you think?" His widening grin answered for him.

It pleased her to no end. "In those fantasies, what did you do?" She trailed her finger in circles on his chest and abdomen. "And would you like to do that now?"

The gleam in his eyes grew devilish. "This, for one thing." He lowered his head, but instead of returning to her lips, he suckled at her breast, and she was the one who shuddered.

As he laved her breast with his tongue, her pleasure built.

She needed to reciprocate. Where did that line of hair go? Tugging at the linens wrapped around him, her hand lurched up suddenly, knocking him on the chin.

He broke his seal on her nipple. "Ow!"

She wanted to die.

CHAPTER 33

Oh, Lord! Did he bite her?

"I'm so sorry," they said in unison.

Drake rubbed his throbbing chin and darted a glance at Honoria's breast. The blow to his chin had landed hard enough to force his jaw shut. Thank goodness no teeth marks marred her skin. The slight metallic taste in his mouth gave testament to his tongue's sacrifice in shielding her.

"Did you want me to stop?" he asked, still rubbing his chin, although the throbbing had eased.

Honoria appeared absolutely horrified, her lovely eyes so wide as to be almost comical. "No. I didn't mean to hit you. Does it hurt very much?"

"Just a little. You pack a good punch." He grinned, hoping to ease her embarrassment. "A kiss would help."

Her lips curved in the shy smile he loved so much. "Very well." She leaned in and placed a chaste peck on the tip of his chin.

"And this hurts, too." He pointed to his cheek, which she kissed.

"And here." His index finger touched his lips.

She laughed at his feeble attempt to manipulate her. "Now, you're exaggerating. But as you wish."

As she brushed her lips against his, he flattened her on the bed. "Now, what were you trying to do other than plant me a facer?"

She laughed—a little too loudly—and he quieted her with a kiss.

The fire within him returned in full measure, the kiss more heated and insistent. How would he ever last for her? He broke away, panting, and placed his forehead against hers. "You were going to say?"

A coy smile tipped the corners of her lips and scattered his thoughts. "I was trying to remove the linens. I want to see where that trail of hair leads." Somehow she slipped her arm between their bodies, and her finger set him on fire as she traced it down his stomach.

"First, you. I don't want you to run off now that I have you in my bed." He kissed the tip of her nose, then gave her a more proper kiss on the lips.

He would never get enough of her. Not in a hundred lifetimes as either groom or duke. But he prayed he wouldn't bungle things for their first times. The pounding in his chest grew so furious, he thought he would have a heart seizure. Reluctantly breaking away again, he gathered the folds of her nightdress in his hands. "Lift your hips." When she did as he asked, he slipped the garment from her body, tossing it aside.

His breath hitched in his throat. Simon's words—which at the time were unwelcome—came back to him. *Kiss and touch her. Everywhere.*

Oh, how he wanted to.

Would she allow him?

Drier than the Great Indian Desert, his throat constricted as he tried to form the words he wanted to say. He could only gawk in wonder at the vision of her.

Slow, man. Go slow.

Her glorious hair, plaited in a long braid, draped across her shoulder.

"Undo your hair for me." Lord, but he sounded demanding. "Please."

Completely transfixed, he watched her nimble fingers unwind the plait. When she finished, he spread it around her head on the pillow like a halo. His angel.

"You are magnificent. I want to worship you with my body."

She held out her arms to him, beckoning him.

He needed no more encouragement.

Worship her he did, paying attention to her moans of pleasure when he touched or kissed a particular place.

When his hand drifted lower on her stomach, teasing the top of the curls between her legs, she squirmed. His fingers inched closer. "May I?"

Her nails scraped his back. "Yes. Oh, yes."

Thank you, Simon.

⚜

How could any one person withstand so much pleasure? The insistent need building low inside her grew almost unbearable. Unsure exactly what she needed, she hoped Drake would provide it.

Gripping his shoulders tighter, she held on as if her life depended on it.

His eyes locked with hers. "I love you more than you will ever know."

When he reached between her legs, her hips bucked off the bed.

Before he could ask, she answered the expected question. "Yes."

"Yes. You like it?" He teased her with his fingers, and his lopsided grin made an encore appearance. "Or yes, you want me to stop?"

Her breath came in short pants. "Like it. Don't. Stop."

His lips vibrated against hers as he chuckled, deep and delicious, sending another shock of gooseflesh flaring. Those amber eyes of his grew hooded as he lowered his head for another kiss.

No longer tentative, she met his tongue stroke for stroke, the play becoming more insistent and frantic. She tugged at the sheets around his waist. "I want to see you."

"My, aren't you the impatient one? Soon, my love. I want to make sure you're ready. Once there isn't anything between us, my fading restraint will all but vanish."

He kissed her until her head spun. When he broke the kiss, she wanted to cry out for him to come back. But then he moved lower, teasing her navel with his tongue. And lower still.

She lifted her heavy head off the pillow to peer down at him, kneeling between her legs, and then—

"Oh!" Waves of pleasure shot through her. Flashes of light exploded behind her eyes closed tight. She reached for purchase, trying to ground herself, and grabbed fistfuls of Drake's hair.

He continued the sweet torture until the spasms ebbed, then he rose and propped himself on one elbow by her side. "So?"

She wanted to laugh at the self-satisfied grin on his face. "Where did you learn about that?"

He shrugged and touched his fingertip against her nose. "I just wanted to kiss you. Everywhere. I don't have to ask if you liked it."

She ran a hand down his chest. "I feel so relaxed. Like a big pot of honey."

He laughed, deep and hard. "And just as sweet. Now, you were asking me to—"

Somehow, she managed enough strength to pull the linens from his body. Thankfully, without inflicting injury.

She stared like a ninnyhammer. Nothing like statues or paintings in museums, he was fully erect and ready for her.

For her.

She wanted to weep with joy.

"It's an odd-looking thing, I know."

She tore her gaze from his arousal to meet his eyes. "No. You're beautiful. Like a Greek god."

Closing his eyes, he hooked his arms behind his head and leaned back flat on the bed. A slow smile spread across his face. "A Greek god, eh? So more worshipping?"

Oh! Her gaze snapped back to his pelvis. She couldn't. Could she?

The trail of hair she'd been so curious about led a path straight to his groin.

She bit her lip and darted a glance back to his face, confirming his eyes were still closed. Then, starting from his chest, she traced that path of hair. Lower, lower, lower, she inched along. When she reached his abdomen, his muscles twitched under her touch, and his member bobbed in invitation.

As she touched the drop of moisture on the velvety tip, Drake's eyes popped open, and he sucked in a hiss.

She grasped him and stroked her fingers downward on the shaft, relishing the contrast of the soft tip and the hard length of him. Unable to keep the grin from her face, she asked, "Like or don't like?"

The heat in his gaze answered her.

DRAKE ROLLED TOWARD HER, SCOOPING HER INTO HIS ARMS, HER hand still wrapped around him. "Like, oh, very much like. But if you continue that, I won't finish what we started." Heat rushed up his neck. "Well, *I* will finish, but not as I planned."

Her confused expression was simply adorable. "Am I not touching you correctly?"

If she only knew. "Your touch is perfect. So excellent that I will spend all over your hand if you continue."

"Oh!"

A stronger man would send her back to her room and save her innocence.

Drake swallowed, accepting he was not that man. Her hands on him and her scent drove him to distraction. He could still taste her on his lips. Selfish, true. But he wanted—*needed*—to be inside her. He kissed her nose and stared into those incredible green eyes. "Now, shall we explore this uncharted territory together?"

She gave a tiny nod.

"I adore you." He kissed her again, tenderly. "I've heard there can be some pain the first time. I'll do my best to be gentle." His stomach knotted at the mere thought of hurting her.

Trust shone in her eyes, and he vowed he would do everything in his power to never break that trust. He kissed her again, deeper, her tongue tangling with his, urging him on.

He caressed her breast again, the nipple peaking under his fingers, then slid his hand down between her legs.

Still wet from his earlier efforts, she moaned as he did his best to prepare her.

Bracing on one elbow, he positioned himself. Lord help him if he spilled the moment he entered her. She deserved better. He took a deep breath, then guided himself forward.

"Relax," he whispered, unsure if it was to her or to himself.

With the softest of caresses, she stroked his face and kissed him. "I want this, Drake."

Oh, God. Nothing had ever felt so good—or so right. Every intention he had to ease slowly inside vanished, and he thrust forward, fully seating himself.

"Oh!" she cried.

He forced himself to still.

Tears gathered in the corner of her eyes. One leaked out, trickling down her cheek.

He kissed it away. "Forgive me. I'm so, so sorry. Does it hurt very much?" Tendrils of guilt snaked up his spine.

She gave her head a little shake. "No. I'm weeping with joy because I'm finally where I belong. I'm home."

His chest swelled at her beatific smile.

His angel.

His Honoria.

His.

Finally.

Satisfied her discomfort was minimal, he began to move.

Oh, God. He willed himself not to shake—the pleasure was so intense—and he cursed himself for being so inexperienced. *I will make it up to you, my love.*

Slow at first, his movements increased in intensity. The friction and heat from her grew unbearable. His thrusts became more urgent and erratic.

Her scent, her hands in his hair, her nails scraping down his back, her mew of pleasure seeped beneath his skin, stirring the inferno inside of him and burning away the self-control he fought to maintain.

Resisting the urge to squeeze his eyes shut, he met hers directly, needing to stare into their depths when he—

His shout echoed through the bedchamber as he spilled his seed into her.

❦

Honoria didn't lie when she told Drake she wept with joy. Like Drake, she, too, fantasized about being with him, although perhaps not quite in the same fashion he may have.

But being in Drake's arms, becoming completely his, was the nearest thing to heaven she could imagine.

He eased off of her, pulling her into his arms.

She snuggled into him and laid her head on his chest. "Is it really true? This was your first time as well?"

He smiled, his eyes crinkling at the corners. "You doubt it? My stumbling didn't give me away?"

"You were wonderful." She trailed a finger across his chest. "And I'm glad you waited—for me as I had for you."

He pulled her closer and grinned. "You did seem to enjoy it."

"I've never experienced anything like it."

"I should hope not." He chuckled.

She playfully swatted him on the arm. "That's not what I meant. The sensation was like fireworks exploding throughout my body."

His fingers trailed lazily up and down her arm. "It is, isn't it? Earlier this evening, Lord Montgomery mentioned he was looking forward to the display because it would remind him of his and Lady Montgomery's wedding trip to Scotland. It seemed curious at the time, but I wonder if that's what he meant."

They fell into a contented silence, sharing kisses and gentle caresses. She drifted into a peaceful slumber, never wanting to leave the bed—or his arms.

Unsure how long she slept, she woke to find Drake propped on one elbow, staring down at her.

She gazed at him in wonder, his face serene in the moonlight. "How long was I asleep?"

"I'm not sure. I dozed off, too." He played with a strand of her hair. "You're so beautiful with your hair down."

"Do you remember when I gave you a lock of it?"

"Remember?! One moment." He rose from the bed.

When he strode toward the dressing table, she couldn't help but smile, admiring his firm backside.

Contented warmth flowed through her body as he rummaged through drawers.

"Ah, here it is." He climbed back onto the bed, handing her the locket she'd given him over eight years ago.

Amazed, she stared at him. "You still have it."

"My talisman." He touched a finger to it. "Open it."

When she popped the latch, she found the strand of her hair still curled up inside. Love expanded in her chest to near bursting.

"I asked you to marry me that day. My proposal, my words were clumsy and unromantic. I fear I haven't done much better this time. Allow me to try again."

He rose again from the bed and fell to one knee before her. "Marry me, Honoria. Be my wife."

CHAPTER 34

As proposals went, Drake's current attempt wasn't much better than his previous one. Fitting, though, that he should be naked before her. Guilt jabbed like a hot poker that he still cloaked himself in deceit.

The time had arrived.

He should tell her.

Yet the voice that taunted him for eight long years grew louder.

She'd promised him before, then yielded to her father's iron will. He couldn't bear to go through that again.

Kneeling before her, exposed and vulnerable in more than his lack of clothing, he succumbed to his doubts.

He must be certain.

"Say the words, Honoria. Will you marry me no matter what?"

She grew serious. "Drake. I know I hurt you all those years ago. And for that, I'm so sorry. Earlier tonight, I wanted to tell you something. It wasn't the time or place, but I need you to know now before giving you my answer."

An icy dread seeped through him. "Very well."

"When you left for the military, I believed you took my words to heart and enlisted to make something of yourself. That the burden of a wife would hold you back from your dreams."

He opened his mouth to protest, but she held up a hand to stop him.

"And you *have* made something of yourself. And although I loved you as you were then, I don't know if *you* were proud of yourself."

Simon's words came back to haunt him. *You need to believe in your worth.*

"You've proven you belong in society. Not only to others, but—I hope—to yourself. You can be proud of who you are."

"I don't deserve you."

She shook her head. "None of that. We will strive to deserve each other every day of our married life."

He couldn't restrain his grin. "So?"

She scooted to the edge of the bed and threw her arms around his neck, practically toppling them both to the floor yet again. Her green eyes, so trusting, gazed at him. "I will marry you. No matter what."

Three heavy knocks sounded at the door.

"What now!" He rose and grabbed the linens, hastily wrapping them around his waist. "Hurry, hide again."

When she moved toward the window, he said, "Not there! Quick. In the dressing room."

Confident Honoria was out of sight, he strode to the door.

Ready to pummel—or dismiss—whoever had interrupted his confession, he threw the door open.

Simon practically fell on him from the open doorway. "Hurry, get her out of there. The servants have been up for hours completing their morning rounds."

Drake blinked and stepped out into the hall, partially closing the door behind him. He narrowed his eyes. "What time is it? And how do you know?"

"It's after eight in the morning, and I've been out here keeping watch."

"What?!"

"Keep your voice down. That's precisely why I felt it was my duty to keep a vigil by your door. There were some fairly loud noises coming from inside your room." He grinned. "Although I didn't expect to hear any cries of pain from *you*. What happened?"

Drake rubbed his chin. "Never mind." He glanced both ways down the hall. "I don't see anyone."

"I ordered the maids to start with the unoccupied rooms. But you don't have much time; your valet seemed anxious to lay out your clothing for the day. I gave him a pair of boots to shine. Now, go! I'll keep watch at the end of the hall and detain anyone if they start heading this way."

Once Simon raced down to the end of the hallway, Drake stepped back inside.

How could it be morning already? Sure enough, light spilled in through a slit in the curtains Honoria had hidden behind earlier.

He rushed to the dressing room and tugged Honoria gently by the hand.

"What's wrong?"

"The servants are coming. You need to get back to your room." Drake spun in a circle, searching for wherever he'd tossed her nightdress.

"Was that Burwood again?" Her soprano voice pitched higher.

"Yes. No. Yes. I'll explain later." He tugged open the curtains a breadth wider for more light to find her nightdress. He couldn't have her wandering the halls naked. And he couldn't have her discovered in his room.

The last thing he wanted was to force a marriage by compromise. He needed to ask her father for her hand like a gentleman. To prove to her as much as—

There!

Half under the bed, the garment lay taunting him. He snatched it up, then handed it to her. "Hurry. He's keeping the staff at bay down the hall."

"What?!" Her eyes grew huge. "He . . . knows?"

"He won't say anything. And he doesn't know for certain it's you in here."

Her hand froze mid-air while tying one of the ribbons of her nightdress. "Who else would it be? You said . . ."

He hated doing it, but he grabbed her by the shoulders. "All will be well, my love. Trust me. But you must get back to your room!"

Once she'd finished tying her nightdress, he opened the door and peeked out, confirming the hallway was still clear of servants. He turned and motioned her forward.

More light from the risen sun illuminated the room, and Honoria paused halfway to the door, her head turning toward the wall on the left.

Damnation! The portrait!

"Wh-who is that?" Her head jerked toward him, her eyes questioning.

"A relative of the duke's. Now hurry." He grasped her arm and tugged. "Hurry."

With her head still craned toward the portrait of his father, she followed.

At the door, he gave her one quick kiss. "I'll speak to your father first thing after breakfast."

He watched as she hurried down the hall, only releasing his breath when she slipped inside her room.

Moments later, Simon raced back down the hall toward him.

"Is she gone?"

Drake nodded, too exhausted to find the words to answer.

Simon grinned wickedly. "I hope congratulations are in order."

"Shut it." Drake turned to go back inside and get dressed.

Simon laughed. "I meant for your upcoming nuptials."

Drake slammed the door in his friend's face. He had no doubt that Honoria's father would give his blessing for their marriage. Once he learned the true identity of the Duke of Burwood, that was.

Honoria would be another matter.

And that was Drake's greater worry.

In her room, Honoria raced over to the bed, rumpling the smooth linens and counterpane.

Her hands flew to the hair swinging down and curtaining her face.

Where was her ribbon? In her haste, she must have left it in Drake's room where she'd unfastened her plait.

Think, Honoria. Think.

The clock on her mantle marked the quarter hour. Susan would arrive soon to lay out Honoria's clothing for the day.

Honoria scrambled to the dressing table and searched for another ribbon. If she could braid her hair quickly and get back into bed, Susan would be none the wiser.

With a creak, the door opened. "My lady. I didn't expect you up so early. Not after the ball last night." Susan breezed into the room and threw open the curtains. "Looks to be a sunny day," she said, as if the bright yellow streams of light didn't already give evidence to that fact.

Honoria fumbled in the dressing table drawer, latching upon a hairbrush. *Thank goodness.* She managed to get it through her hair as Susan turned and faced her.

"Oh, my lady. Let me do that." Susan snatched the brush from Honoria and began pulling it through her hair. "Was the ball wonderful? We could see the fireworks from the windows." She sighed.

"It was lovely, Susan."

Susan paused her brushing and met Honoria's gaze in the mirror. "You have a glow about you this morning. Especially for as little sleep as I expect you had."

If only she knew how little sleep Honoria actually did get. On second thought . . . Fire burned her cheeks at the memories.

Susan's eyes widened. "Oh, did a gentleman show particular interest? Perhaps the duke? The other maids say he's looking for a bride."

Susan prattled on about other gossip, but Honoria only caught snippets. Something about that portrait in Drake's room gave her pause. The man in it looked incredibly like Drake. But Drake said it was a relative of the duke's.

"What's wrong?" Susan asked.

Wrong? Sure enough, when Honoria peered at her reflection, a deep frown covered her face. "I'm sorry. Nothing. What were you saying?"

"I was telling you about Mr. Merrick. *The Muckraker* arrived, and it says he's to marry Miss Anne Weatherby."

Honoria shot from her seat, a strand of hair caught in the hairbrush and pulling against her scalp. "When did it arrive?"

"Just this morning. Came all the way from London. It talked about her fall from the horse and how gallant Mr. Merrick was. How do you expect it knew?"

Indeed. Perhaps Miranda's suspicions were correct and the instigator of that atrocious rag was among them there. "That is a very good question, Susan."

More importantly, whoever the source was didn't have the most current information. Not that that was a surprise.

"Is it true then?" Susan asked.

"Hmm?"

"About Mr. Merrick and Miss Weatherby?"

Honoria shook her head. "No. She broke off their attachment last night."

Susan visibly relaxed. "Oh, thank the stars. I've heard he fancies you, my lady." She blushed. "His valet said he didn't believe his master loved Miss Weatherby and that his heart was set on another."

Unbidden, a smile tugged at Honoria's lips.

"Oh, my lady! It *is* you, isn't it? Archie said he thought it might be."

"Who in the world is Archie?"

"Mr. Merrick's valet, Mr. Dawson. Although he said I could call him Archie. He's ever so nice." Susan broke into a wide grin.

"Why, Susan, have you developed a fondness for Mr. Merrick's valet?"

Susan's blush deepened. "I know it can't come to anything. But I was hoping if you and Mr. Merrick . . ."

Champagne bubbles, more glorious than anything she had ever drank, effervesced in her veins. Oh, how she wanted to tell someone of her news. But could she trust a gossipy servant?

"Let's not get ahead of ourselves," Honoria said, averting her eyes from Susan's interrogating gaze. "Please bring some hot water for a bath, and I think I'll wear the green sprigged muslin today."

Once she'd bathed, finished dressing, and her hair had been

fashioned—which took longer than expected thanks to Susan's chattering about Mr. Dawson's fine qualities—Honoria made her way down to the small dining room for breakfast.

Relieved to find it practically empty, she helped herself to a piece of toast and some tea.

"Good morning, Lady Honoria. I trust you slept well."

Honoria spun around.

Burwood leaned in the doorway, a shoulder resting lazily against the frame. He straightened and stretched his arms over his head, emitting a rather raucous yawn. "I, for one, did not."

Her insides chilled even though her face burned.

"Is a cow dying?" Charlotte gave Burwood the side-eye as she brushed past him into the room. She stopped short and jerked back, staring at Honoria. "Why is your face red?" She spun back toward Burwood. "What did you say to her, you oaf?"

"Never mind." Honoria tugged Charlotte toward the dining table. "My maid told me a copy of *The Muckraker* arrived this morning." She leaned in, lowering her voice. "With news of the house party."

Charlotte's dark brows lifted. "Really?" She motioned for a footman standing near the sideboard. "Fetch me a copy of that scandal sheet."

The footman nodded and raced off.

"Good of you to order my staff around like that. You could have at least said 'Please.'" Burwood took a seat sideways on the chair, stretching out his long legs, and glowered at Charlotte, who ignored him.

Charlotte narrowed her eyes at Honoria. "There's something different about you this morning."

"Ha!" Burwood chortled.

Honoria frosted the duke with an icy glare.

A grin appeared on Charlotte's face. "Well. That settles it. You're hiding something." Moments passed in silence as Charlotte clearly pondered the matter.

Then, her brows drew down into a pronounced V. Her gaze darted between Honoria and Burwood. "No!" The word flew from Charlotte in a rush of incredulity. "The two of you?"

"No!" both Honoria and Burwood answered.

"Not that she isn't—" Burwood sputtered.

"Although I like him very much," Honoria interjected.

Charlotte slumped back in her chair. And Charlotte *never* slumped. "Well, that's a relief."

Burwood straightened, lifting his chin and appearing every inch the affronted duke. "I beg your pardon?"

"I'm sure Lady Charlotte didn't mean any offense, Your Grace."

Charlotte rolled her eyes and snorted. As snorts went, it was actually quite dainty. "I'm relieved for my friend. She deserves better than the likes of you."

Burwood opened his mouth, no doubt to protest his worthiness, when the footman returned with the scandal sheet.

Charlotte's gaze darted across the paper. "Well, they are correct on one account." She cleared her throat dramatically. "It would appear that Lady Charlotte Talbot is not impressed with His Grace, the new Duke of Burwood. Our sources say they have exchanged heated words throughout the course of the house party."

Burwood snatched the paper from Charlotte's hands, and her eyes widened.

"How dare you!"

"I want to see that thing." Like Charlotte, he scanned the gossip rag, his normally congenial face growing cloudy. "How the hell do they know these things?"

Charlotte bristled. "Language, sir!"

Honoria stifled a chuckle. Knowing Charlotte's brother Lord Nash as Honoria did, she suspected Charlotte had heard much worse over the course of her lifetime. "We suspect the source of the material is in attendance here, Your Grace."

"We?" Regardless of Charlotte's opinion, Burwood was clearly sharp-witted.

Glancing toward Charlotte, Honoria tilted her head in silent question. With another eyeroll, Charlotte sighed. "Very well. Tell him."

"Lady Charlotte and I, along with several others, have formed a group dedicated to unmasking the perpetrator of these vicious attacks. We would appreciate your discretion in the matter. Although we operate under the guise of a charitable foundation, we prefer to remain incognito."

The appalling publication slipped from Burwood's fingers as he stared, first at her, then Charlotte. "Like spies?"

Charlotte stared back, her own glare challenging. "You find that inconceivable, sir? Perhaps because we are women?"

"I find it . . . marvelous." He leaned in. "How can I assist?"

Charlotte snapped up the gossip rag. "By staying out of it and keeping your mouth shut." She pushed away from the table, the chair screeching in protest, and stomped from the room.

Oh! Honoria jerked her gaze back to the duke, who seemed transfixed by Charlotte's hasty exit. *Ooooob.*

Honoria's father entered the room, his head craning back toward the hall. The frown on his face disappeared the moment he saw Honoria and Burwood at the table together. "Ah. Good morning, Burwood. Honoria. Fabulous fête last night, sir. A night to remember, surely."

Heat returned to Honoria's cheeks, and she ducked her head. Unfortunately, not quickly enough.

Her father swung his gaze between her and Burwood.

"Thank you, Stratford." Burwood saved her, his attention remaining exclusively on her father. "I was hoping to catch you early this morning. After you refresh yourself with some breakfast, I would like a word in private."

What?

Burwood's gaze remained fixed on her father—who suddenly stood taller, the wrinkles in his face smoothing out, making him appear a decade younger.

"No need to wait. I've just come back from a ride. I can break my fast later."

"As you wish. Follow me to the study." Burwood rose and sketched an elegant bow. "Lady Honoria, if you would excuse me."

Honoria squeaked out a feeble, "Of course."

As they left, Burwood stopped and whispered something to a footman, who nodded and raced off.

What in the world was going on?

CHAPTER 35

Drake nervously paced the length of his study, his empty stomach flipping around like a fish on dry land. Good thing he hadn't eaten anything, or he would have cast it into the chamber pot.

Still aglow from his wondrous night with Honoria, he'd washed and dressed quickly, but his euphoria quickly faded as he anticipated meeting with her father.

Simon promised to watch for Stratford in the breakfast room and bring him to the study posthaste.

Drake didn't want to delay any longer.

He believed Honoria would choose him regardless of her father's dissent.

And dissent he would. Drake was certain of it—as certain as he was that she would not cave to her father's objections.

She'd proven that to him mere hours before.

He ran the paper outlining the marriage contract between his fingers, the wording precise and careful, eager to see Stratford's reaction when he read the details.

What was keeping them? Had the old man changed his habit of rising shortly after dawn to go for a ride? Drake had cursed many a day when, with sleep still heavy in his eyes, he'd had to saddle a horse for his employer.

The door swung open and Simon stepped inside, Stratford following.

Drake restrained his laugh as Stratford jerked to a halt, his eyes widening. "What are you doing in here?"

Drake could practically taste the vitriol with which Stratford delivered his question, and although he desired nothing more than to deliver a cutting retort, he choked it down and focused on his purpose —to win the man over.

For Honoria.

"Please, Lord Stratford, have a seat." Although his insides were a jumbled mess, Drake kept his voice calm. He motioned to a high-back chair in front of the massive desk.

Stratford's gaze bounced between Drake and Simon, finally coming to rest on Simon. "Your Grace?"

Simon held out a hand toward the chair, and Stratford lumbered toward it and took a seat.

Standing across from Stratford at the desk, Drake placed his hands on the mahogany surface and leaned forward. "Lord Stratford, I wish to offer for Lady Honoria's hand in marriage."

Stratford's head swiveled back to Simon. "But I thought . . ."

Simon shook his head. "I'm afraid not. Although she's a lovely woman. I'm here for support." He moved to the corner of the room, lazed against the wall, and yawned.

Drake fortified himself for Stratford's outrage: the expected argument that he would not allow Honoria to marry beneath her and a barrage of insults against Drake's character.

The man merely hung his head and sighed. "Very well."

What?

Drake's legs threatened to buckle, but he forced himself to remain upright.

Even Simon straightened from his position in the corner, a whispered, "Bloody hell," drifting across the room.

Tired from lack of sleep, Drake shook his head. "Pardon? Could you repeat that?"

Stratford's ice-blue eyes met Drake directly. "I agree to the marriage. But, do not misunderstand. I don't like it. You may have elevated your status from groom to a duke's man of business, but you're still not good enough for her." He paused, his lined face showing his age. "But I love my daughter. I presume you've spoken with her?"

Drake allowed his body to fall into the chair. "Yes, sir. She has accepted my proposal."

Stratford narrowed his eyes. "What about the Weatherby chit?"

"Miss Weatherby released me last night. *Before* I asked for Lady Honoria's hand."

Stratford ran a hand through his thinning gray hair. "Although it pains me to admit, you've always been a man of honor. However, you should know I released Honoria's dowry to her a few months ago. It's a substantial sum. I expect you to do right by her on that account. Make sure she wants for nothing. And if you should need financial assistance, come to me."

"That won't be necessary, and Honoria can retain her money. I don't want it." He tapped the papers in front of him, pushing them toward Stratford. "Simon has laid it all out in the marriage contract."

"Simon?" Stratford frowned. "Who is Simon?"

A cough from the corner drew Stratford's attention, and Simon raised his hand.

"Why would a duke be drawing up a marriage contract? And why do you call him Simon? Such disrespect! I expected more from you, Merrick."

Drake barked a laugh. "From our recent encounters, I wasn't aware you expected anything from me, other than to be a fortune-hunting nobody. However, reading the contract should enlighten you."

Stratford continued to eye him as he picked up the papers. Then he began to read.

Ah! There.

The precise moment the truth became known, Stratford's head shot up. "What is this? A joke? If so, it isn't funny."

Drake rose, hands pressed against the desk, and leaned forward again, confidence flowing through him. "It's no joke, my lord. So tell me. Would a duke be good enough for your daughter?"

THE SLICE OF TOAST SAT BEFORE HONORIA, HALF-EATEN. WHY HAD Burwood asked to speak with her father?

Something was wrong. Where was Drake?

She pushed the plate aside and strode toward the door.

The footman blocked her way. "I'm sorry, my lady, but I'm under orders to keep you here."

"I will not be kept in here like a prisoner. Now, stand aside." Honoria had never before spoken harshly to a servant, and the man flinched at her raised voice.

Dread seeped under her skin, burrowing and taking root like black tar. Something was wrong.

Much taller and broader than she, the man refused to budge from the doorway. "I'm under orders."

"You've said that." She pushed at the man's arms, but he remained steadfast.

"Stand aside, sir, and allow my daughter to pass." Her mother's voice, firm but calm, broke through Honoria's anger.

The footman turned. "But my lady—"

"The duke himself has requested me to retrieve my daughter. If you value your position, you will stand aside."

As if her mother waved a magic wand, the footman removed himself from the doorway, and Honoria hurried past lest he change his mind. "Mother, I thought Burwood was with Father."

Her mother gestured her forward. "He is, dear. In his study. Come, come, don't delay. There is wonderful news!"

"What is it? Where is Drake?"

An enigmatic smile tugged at her mother's lips. "You will soon see. Now, no more questions. We must hurry. They're waiting."

Honoria stepped into what had to be Burwood's study and froze at the sight before her. She stopped so abruptly, her mother nearly collided into her from behind.

Her gaze darted between her father, Drake, and Burwood.

Her father grinned broadly. In fact, his face had stretched so widely, she thought it would break.

Burwood appeared half asleep, leaning against the wall and yawning.

But Drake? Drake seemed almost apologetic. What had he to be sorry for?

What had happened?

The words came out of her mouth before she could pull them back. "What is going on?"

"Wonderful news, daughter." Her father clapped his hands together. "Burwood has offered for you, and I have agreed."

What? What?!

The room tilted, making her nauseous.

Drake shifted his gaze away, looking very much like a schoolboy who had been caught cheating.

"No." She shook her head. "No. No. No." She gaped at Drake. "How could you stand by and allow this to happen? You were supposed to offer for me."

Drake held out his hands. "I did, Honoria. You don't understand."

Her father's head jerked toward Drake. "Good God, man. You mean she doesn't know?"

"Know what? None of you are making sense. Tell me what you're talking about!"

"I'm Burwood," Drake answered, his voice soft.

Icy cold snapped through her. She stumbled back, her joints stiff and uncooperative.

Drake moved from behind the desk and took a step forward. "You're trembling. Perhaps you should sit down."

"I don't want to sit down!"

Frozen moments before, her body turned liquid, and someone wrapped an arm around her waist.

She turned toward her mother, who struggled to keep her upright.

Drake rushed to her side. "Allow me."

Batting his hands away, she regained her strength. "No! Keep away from me."

He jerked back as if she'd slapped him.

Perhaps she should! "You lied to me. Lied to everyone here." She shook her head. To clear it? In answer to his deception? She wasn't sure. Nothing made sense.

"Was it all a lie?" She croaked out the words, terror clamping her chest and tightening her throat. "Last night?"

His eyes widened. "No!" He lowered his voice. "Now is not the time to discuss that."

Her father strode forward. "Discuss what?"

She held her arms out, holding them all at bay. "I can't breathe. I need to get out of here."

Shouts echoed behind her, but she ignored them and raced from the room.

AT FIRST STUNNED, ALL DRAKE COULD DO WAS STARE AS HONORIA hurried from the room.

Everyone called for her to return, one of the voices sounding suspiciously like his own, but he couldn't be certain. Everything distorted, his vision blurred; a buzzing in his ears muffled the sounds around him. The room closed in on him, squeezing him tight.

Someone shook his shoulder. "Don't just stand there. Go after her."

He expected Simon, but he saw Stratford—his jaw set, his eyes serious.

Gathering what remained of his wits, Drake chased after Honoria. People turned and gawked, scrambling out of his way. He bumped into Lord Middlebury and brushed past him, not bothering to apologize for the tea that splashed on the man's waistcoat.

Out of breath, Drake finally reached her as she stepped outside the front entrance. "Wait, Honoria. I can explain."

She spun on her heel, anger flashing in her eyes. "Explain what? You lied to me. To everyone here."

"I had to." He cringed at the pleading tone in his voice.

"You *had* to? Why?"

"To protect myself. How else could I be certain whomever I chose wanted me for me?"

She gaped at him. Why couldn't she understand? Then, in one fluid motion, she reeled back and slapped him hard across his face.

His eyes watered from the sting. "Honoria, please understand."

As she paced before him, he'd never seen her so angry. In fact, he couldn't ever remember seeing her angry at all.

"Understand? Oh, I understand. Everything is about *you*. Honoria should just understand and forgive, like she always does. Is that about the right of it?"

He blinked. "Yes. But why are you speaking about yourself in third person?"

"Because it's as if I'm never my own person. I must always bend to everyone else's wishes. Keep everyone else happy. Keep the peace. It doesn't matter what *I* want, what I need. You're as bad as he is."

"Who?"

"My father. You don't trust my feelings any more than he does."

"But, my love—"

She jabbed a finger in his chest. "Don't *my love* me, sir. Admit it. You didn't trust me with the truth. Did you really think it made a difference to me who you are? I loved the man inside." She jabbed him again, harder. "Or at least I thought I did."

The words hurt more than the slap or the jabs. "You *thought*?"

"I don't even know who you are anymore." She paused, glaring. "*Your Grace*."

"I'm the same man I've always been."

"No." She stamped her foot. "You are *not* the same man. The man I remember would never deliberately lie to me. That man trusted me."

"Honoria, think. What if you're . . ." He lowered his voice to a mere whisper, even though they were quite alone. "With my child?"

"Your child? *Your* child? Again, it's all about you. If I find myself as such, then I will have *my* child. Mine. And I will love it enough for both of us. Now, I plan to go for a ride to clear my head. Do *not* follow me." She turned and trounced off to the stables.

For several minutes, he stood speechless until she disappeared from his view. Someone grabbed his shoulder, and he spun around.

"I told you this was a bad idea," Simon said, although he didn't grin in the *I-told-you-so* way Drake expected. Which only made his words hurt more.

"Shut up."

"Give her time to cool down."

Drake ran a shaky hand through his hair. "I was going to tell her sooner. This morning. Until you"—he poked Simon in the chest—"interrupted me. I was so worried she would get caught in my room . . ." He shook his head. "I never expected she would be so angry."

"Come back inside. She loves you. She'll return more willing to listen to reason."

"She has to marry me, Simon. She just has to."

They turned toward the door, and Drake's footsteps stumbled.

In the open doorway, Lord Middlebury sipped his tea, his brows lifting.

CHAPTER 36

Honoria pushed Buttercup to his limit as she galloped across the expanse of Burwood's—Drake's—estate, her head pounding each time she thought about his deception. Her hair had blown free from the confines of the pins Susan had so carefully placed earlier that morning. Sun beat against her face and arms, sure to leave freckles on her unprotected skin.

She reined in the horse by a riverbed that cut a swath through the property and found a place where a log provided a perfect mounting block. Carefully maneuvering the horse over, she slid off the saddle onto the log, then lowered herself to the ground.

"Good boy." She patted the horse on the neck, then pulled out a carrot from a bag the groom had provided, and gave Buttercup his reward.

How Drake had managed to name the horse after her favorite mare back at Overton House slammed into her. Her fingers tangled in Buttercup's mane, and she leaned her head against his neck and wept.

All along, Drake had been the owner of the beautiful estate. Not a simple man of business as he claimed, but the duke himself.

Like scattered pieces of a puzzle assembled into a complete, recognizable image, comments from Aunt Kitty—which Honoria had attributed to the countess's aged mind, took on new meaning. Did the old woman know? Had she been trying to tell Honoria?

And that portrait in Drake's bedchamber. *A relative of the duke's* indeed!

She wiped her nose on her arm—her mother would be appalled—then to further the insult, she picked up a stone and flung it into the river. "Take that, Drake Merrick."

Goodness. Was it even his real name?

Buttercup whinnied and tossed his beautiful mane as if he shared Honoria's outrage.

More than a few stones later, she allowed her exhausted body to drop to the log which had assisted her as she dismounted. "Thank you, log." She wiped her nose on the skirt of her gown.

She didn't know how long she stared at the flowing river while Buttercup treated himself to the tender grass along the bank.

Birds twittered above her in the branches of the sturdy oak. How dare they be happy when her heart had been ripped from her chest? Sunlight poked through the leafy branches, dappling the ground and moving like ghosts from the gentle breeze ruffling the leaves.

A perfect day. Except when it had gone horribly wrong.

She picked up another stone and threw it into the river.

"Gah!"

A twig cracked behind her. She jumped up and spun around. "Father."

He walked toward her, leading his horse. "I was worried."

She turned away and wiped her face with the back of her hand. "Well, you can see I'm fine. Now, go away."

He came closer, and she prepared for a lecture about manners and decorum.

"Try this one." He tossed a stone into the air and caught it. "Heavy. It will make a good splash." He held it out as if it were a peace offering.

She snatched it from his hand. "You're as bad as he is."

Staring out at the river, he nodded. "True. But we have one other thing in common."

"Hmph." Although he wasn't looking at her, she crossed her arms over her bosom to make her point.

"We both love you more than ourselves."

"You have a strange way of showing it. Both of you." She turned on him. "And I thought you hated Drake. Why are you defending him?"

He shook his head, still staring at the infernal river. "I'm not. What he did was wrong." He turned, meeting her gaze fully. "But I was wrong, too. I've come to apologize."

She huffed her disbelief, and his gray brows rose. "Oh, I'm certain you're agreeable to the match now that you know he's a duke."

"When he offered for you, I agreed before I knew."

The heavy stone she was still clutching, slipped from her fingers, falling to the ground with a *thud*. "You did?"

He nodded, once. "And I never hated him. Not really, which made it all the harder to refuse his suit years ago. I knew him to be a good man, young though you both were. Hard-working. Loyal to a fault." He paused, and a ghost of a smile crossed his lips. "Much like myself."

Her hands fisted at her sides. "You called him a fortune-hunting upstart. As if he couldn't truly want me for *me*." The words snapped from her.

He winced. "I was trying to protect you. You deserved so much more than the prospect of living hand-to-mouth. He may have loved you, but how would he have provided for you? You were destined for greatness, Honoria, not as the wife of a groom."

She picked up the heavy stone and drew her arm back. With all her might, she threw it into the water. It made a glorious splash indeed. "I had a dowry, and you could have helped us."

"Which is precisely what a fortune hunter would expect." He chose a stone from the ground, considered its weight, then pitched it farther than hers. "You were young. I believed it was a young girl's infatuation, and you would soon forget him once he was out of your life."

Toe-to-toe with her father, she glared. "Did you know he would enlist?"

He had the gall to look sheepish. "I offered to purchase his commission."

"What?" She shook her muddled head.

"To protect your reputation, although it was too late for that. If it makes a difference, he turned it down initially, only accepting when you refused him."

Oh! And she believed he'd enlisted because he thought he was better off without her. No wonder he had tried to protest her explanation.

"That doesn't change what you did."

He met her eyes. "No. It does not. And I'm here to apologize. Not because of who *he* is or is not. But because of you. I love you, daughter, and I want you to be happy. And if marrying Drake Merrick makes you happy, then so be it. You have my blessing."

"I don't want to marry him now." She flung the words, heedless of her recalcitrant behavior.

He jerked back. "Because he's a duke?"

Oh, how she wanted to stamp her foot like a petulant child. What didn't these men understand? "Because he lied!"

Her father wisely remained silent, staring back at the moving current. He stooped, picked up another rock, but rather than throw it, he turned it over in his hand.

"Do you ever think about the power of water?"

What?

"It is gentle and yielding. You can put your hand in it, your whole body, and it doesn't hurt; it simply flows around any obstacle. But over time, water has the power to smooth the rough edges of an unyielding stone so it's smooth as glass. It's the persistence of water over time that makes big changes."

He tossed the stone into the river. "Give Drake a chance to explain. It will take time to win back your trust." His smile wavered. "And I will venture to win your trust as well." With another glance toward the river, he said, "Try not to remain out here too much longer. Your mother is beside herself with worry."

Without another word, he strode back to his horse, mounted, and rode off, his head and shoulders tall and proud as she always remembered him.

OUT OF SIGHT, AND AT SOME DISTANCE FROM HONORIA, DRAKE reined in Major under a copse of trees and waited. "Easy, boy." He could hardly blame the horse when he was just as restless. Strange how he'd rode alongside Stratford in relative silence, searching for Honoria but sharing an unusual camaraderie.

Even stranger when Stratford suggested—rather than demanded—he approach Honoria first.

"Better I gauge her anger and have it directed at me," he'd said.

But as Drake watched the exchange, doubt rose that the marquess had made any progress in quelling Honoria's fury as she pitched rock after rock into the river.

He cringed. Was she imagining his head?

Drake wished he could transform into a bird and perch on a tree branch to hear their words.

He straightened in the saddle when Stratford remounted his horse and trotted back toward him—without Honoria.

Not good. Not good at all.

Stratford's expression didn't help. Those gray brows drew into a pronounced V over his icy eyes.

"Will she forgive me?" Drake asked once Stratford reached him.

"Perhaps. Given time. At the moment, she says she no longer wishes to marry you. I thought it best to refrain from telling her I already signed the marriage contract."

A tight knot formed in Drake's stomach. "But she *must* marry me."

Stratford's brows made an abrupt about-face, arching high on his forehead. "What do you mean she *must?*"

"I . . . just . . ." Had the sun become hotter? His face was on fire. Was it as red as Stratford's at that moment? "Did you take advantage of her?!"

Drake gulped, forcing the increasingly large lump down his constricted throat. "Keep your voice down, sir."

"I have a mind to go right back and insist she marry you as soon as we can obtain a special license, or I will shoot you dead!"

"Allow me to talk to her. I'll get her to see reason." Lord, he certainly hoped so, or if he had to live without her, maybe it would be better if Stratford did kill him.

The short-lived truce between them vanished, and Stratford glared like the man Drake remembered. "Wait a while before you go to her. I've never seen her so angry. Worse than a wet cat. I'll give you until the end of this infernal house party to make things right, or I will demand satisfaction to defend her honor."

With a jerk on the reins—a mite too forcefully in Drake's opinion —Stratford turned his horse and galloped back toward the house, leaving Drake to plan a strategy.

What could he do? He pondered for a while, watching the flowing water.

A brilliant idea formed, and he turned Major—more gently than Stratford had with his horse—and raced back to the house and stables. He'd have to be quick if he hoped to catch Honoria still by the river.

HONORIA'S ACHING ARMS TREMBLED AS SHE BALANCED ON THE LOG and tried to pull herself into the saddle. Perhaps she had flung one rock too many. Her empty stomach grumbled and churned, complaining both for its lack of food and the dread pooling within.

She had to return to the house—and Drake—sooner or later. With all her strength, she pulled up and pushed off the log. The log tipped forward, and her half-boots slipped. Buttercup whinnied and shied away. Losing her grip on the saddle, Honoria windmilled her arms to maintain her balance.

The log continued its forward roll, pitching her backward. Leaves rustling and someone running barely registered in her panicked mind.

"I've got you," Drake's deep voice called as he caught her.

The force of her momentum sent them both flying backward, and she landed on him with an *oomph*.

She twisted around toward him, and he had the gall to grin up at her.

"We've done this before. Last night, in fact."

Pushing against his chest, she righted herself and scooted off of him. "I don't want to discuss last night."

"Honoria, let me explain."

"Help me up on the horse."

He folded his arms over his chest. "No. Not until you listen."

"Are you commanding me as a duke, Your Grace?"

He held out his arms. "Do I look like a duke?"

No, he did not. Threadbare trousers and a rough weaved cotton shirt replaced the deep-blue superfine coat and impeccably tailored black trousers he'd worn earlier when he broke her heart with his lies. Not secured by an expertly fashioned crisp white cravat, the dull-brown shirt hung open at his neck.

"Why are you dressed like that?"

Rather than answer, he held up a book and turned to a page he had marked with a pressed flower. "You pierce my soul. I am half agony, half hope. Tell me that I am not too late, that such precious feelings are gone forever. I offer myself to you again as a lowly groom with a heart even more your own than when you almost broke it eight years ago. Dare not say that man forgets sooner than woman, that his love has an earlier death. I have loved none but you. I have given myself to none but you. Although I've lied to protect myself, I am heartsick with sorrow for my deception. But please know, I have never been inconstant in my love."

Stunned, and admittedly touched, she stared at him. "I've memorized that passage. That's not exactly what it says."

As if he needed more ammunition to besiege her heart, he pulled out his secret weapon and leveled his lopsided grin at her. "I may have embellished a trifle to fit our situation. But Honoria, whether groom or duke, I'm just a man who loves you."

Every part of her wanted to throw herself into his arms, but she would not give in so readily. Still, she couldn't withhold her smile. "You didn't deface the book by writing those embellishments on the pages, did you?"

His hand flew to his heart. "I would never! I have visions of us curled up by the fire on a winter's night reading to each other in our old age."

"You do, do you?"

"Umm-hmm." He stepped closer.

"Stay back." She took several steps back and bumped into the treacherous log.

Grasping her around the waist, he righted her. His eyes grew hooded, his lips drew dangerously close to hers. "Please, Honoria, hear me out and allow me to explain. Then I'll help you back on Buttercup."

"Let go of me first. I can't think when we're this close."

Oh, she shouldn't have admitted that.

His lips curled upward, but he released her nonetheless. "First, let me say I was completely wrong to lie to you. I can't change what's done, but if I explain, I hope you will find the grace to forgive me."

Shuffling his feet, he cleared his throat, looking so much like the boy she remembered. Unsure and shy. "When you refused me eight years ago, I believed you decided I wasn't good enough for you."

She opened her mouth to protest, but he raised a hand and silenced her.

"Please allow me to finish before you rage at me. I wanted to be loved for me. Who I am, not *what* I am."

"I do—I did."

"I know that now. But, I was hurt, Honoria." He held up the book. "These words could be mine. I wanted to die rather than live with the belief you had rejected me. I did stupid, reckless things. They earned me medals for valor, but they were stupid nonetheless. Simon saved my life."

Unbidden, she pulled in a gasp.

"He tried to talk me out of this scheme, so do not think less of him for agreeing to it. He did so unwillingly." The ghost of a smile reappeared. "Although he enjoyed lording it over me at times, pretending to be a duke."

When he moved forward, she worried he would try to embrace her again, but he stepped around her and headed toward the riverbank. Stooping, he picked a bouquet of forget-me-nots. "I had these planted specifically for you." He held them out.

Suspicious wetness formed in her eyes, and she blinked it back. "I still have the ones you gave me that day. The day I knew I loved you."

"Forgive me, and I will spend the rest of my life making it up to you. I stand before you as a humble groom. If that's the man you want, I'll give all this up." He swept his arms out.

Of course, she knew it wasn't that simple. One couldn't refuse a title or entailed property. Still, her wall began to crumble.

But sometime during the house party, she had changed. She would no longer give in to keep the peace. And she needed time to allow her heart to heal. "I shall consider it. It's the best I can offer."

His smile wavered, and he nodded as if his head weighed several stone. "It's all I can ask for. Now, shall I assist you onto Buttercup so we can return to the house? Your mother and friends are worried."

"Just one more thing before we go."

"Anything. You only have to name it."

"Pick me more flowers, closer to the water's edge."

As he stooped again, she nudged Buttercup forward, and as if the beast understood, he lowered his muzzle and pushed Drake into the water.

CHAPTER 37

S oaked through, Drake's spirits were anything but dampened as he
and Honoria rode back to the house in silence. Her anger had
cooled. The tiny smile gracing her very kissable lips gave her away.

She would forgive him—if she hadn't already.

But he would be true to his word and give her time to decide on
her own.

Just as he had needed her to accept him for who he was, she
needed to make her own choices about her future.

As they approached the house, Honoria broke their silence. "I'm
not the only one you need to apologize to for your deception. You
need to tell your guests. I would suggest you do so without delay."

"As soon as I change, I will have Frampton gather everyone in the
ballroom." Taking a chance, he added, "Will you stand next to me?"

She shook her head. "You need to do this alone."

A short distance from the house, he helped her down from
Buttercup, then after watching her go inside, took the horses back to
the stable.

Micah, the groom, glanced up from where he was brushing the
black beast Mr. Pratt had ridden during the hunt. "Did you catch her,

Your Grace?" His smile broadened. "Or did you decide to take a dip in the river?"

"Both." Drake dismounted and handed him Major's and Buttercup's reins.

"I trust Lady Honoria had no trouble with our friend Buttercup."

"None at all. She was born to ride him." Drake stroked the horse's neck.

"Might I expect to be saddling him for her in the future?"

"That remains to be seen. But I certainly hope so. Thank you for the loan of the clothes. I'll have them washed and returned."

Micah shook his head. "I don't think I'll ever understand you, Your Grace, but I'll say one thing. Working for you won't be dull. As for the clothes, don't bother yourself. I only wear them for mucking out the stable."

No longer able to put off the inevitable, Drake strode back to the big house, garnering several odd looks from a few of the guests—primarily Lord Middlebury and Lydia Whyte.

Ignoring them, he called on Frampton, instructing him to tell the guests the duke had an important announcement in the ballroom, then raced up to his room to change.

He skidded to a halt inside his room. "Honoria!" Memories of the night before flooded back.

She stood peering up at the portrait of his father. "Even in the dim light of morning, I knew there was something familiar about this man. You said he was a relative of the duke's."

"My father. Not Francis Merrick. Henry Pendrake. My real name is Pierce Henry Quincy Pendrake."

Still not looking at him, she said, "Will you tell me how this all came about?"

"Of course. Any time you're ready. I was just going to change and then make my confession to the guests."

She turned, giving him a tremulous smile. "Then I shall leave you." She looked up at the portrait again. "I think I would have liked him. He had a nice smile."

As she quit the room, his heart had the audacity to hope her request to know his history meant she had forgiven him—or at the very least, had begun to.

Once presentable for his announcement—thanks to Dawson's fastidious eye—Drake strode toward the ballroom, hoping the quaking of his knees didn't show through his trousers.

Simon waited for him in the hallway. "Did you fix things with Honoria?"

"I'm trying. At least she listened to my poor explanation."

"The fact you admit it was poor gives me hope. I suggest you take that approach with your guests."

Drake nodded. "Remain by my side?"

Simon patted him on the shoulder. "Of course. Although I draw the line at defending you when they go for your throat. I'll be busy fending them off for my own part in your duplicity."

Pleasant chatter greeted them as they walked into the ballroom. Drake cringed, expecting things to change quickly.

He scanned the faces before him. Who would forgive and who would give him the cut direct? From the corner, Stratford scowled a warning, and Lady Stratford wrung her hands.

Next to his mother and sister, Aunt Kitty fanned herself, her sharp eyes studying him. His mother smiled encouragingly.

His chest tightened.

Where was Honoria?

Even if she wasn't by his side, seeing her face would give him courage.

Simon nudged him. "Merrick. They're waiting."

Right.

He cleared his throat. "Honored guests. I have a confession." Words stuck in his throat as everyone stared.

Aunt Kitty's fan stilled.

Lord Middlebury paused, a glass of sherry half-way to his quirked lips.

Where was Honoria?

"I am not who I've purported to be."

As if one unified body, the assembled guests leaned forward.

Honoria moved from behind Victor Pratt, her lovely green eyes sliding over him like a caress. He could almost hear her say, *You can do this.*

"I've perpetrated a deception on you all. I offer no excuses." *Say it. Just say it.*

"Spit it out, man," Middlebury said, as if waiting for the tastiest of morsels.

"I am the Duke of Burwood."

Several moments of tense silence passed.

Mouths hung agape.

Heads turned toward each other, sending questioning glances.

Murmurs of *Did you know?* drifted through the room.

Anne Weatherby, front and center, squeaked, her hand going to her throat.

Priscilla Marbry pointed at Simon. "Then who is he?"

"Priscilla," her husband admonished, darting Drake an apologetic glance.

"Simon Beckham is my man of business. He has presented himself as the duke at my request. Do not hold this deception against him."

"This was not well played, Burwood," the Duke of Ashton said, although he appeared sympathetic.

"I'm sure he has his reasons, Harry," the duchess said.

"But the new duke is a Pendrake," Lord Harcourt said. "Your surname is Merrick."

"We can explain that, my lord," his mother answered. "Francis agreed to rear Drake as his own, but he was not Drake's father."

Chaos erupted as people shouted more questions.

He raised his hands. "Please. Please. I promise I will explain everything."

Honoria wove her way to the front. Her voice was loud and clear and sounded exactly like an angel's. "His Grace may not wish to make an excuse for his deception, but I believe I understand his reasons. May I demonstrate?"

Demonstrate?

"With your permission, Your Grace. If everyone would follow me to the music room."

Like a lovesick pup—which in truth he was—he, along with the crowd, followed Honoria through the house to the music room.

Once there, she took a seat at the pianoforte.

What was she doing?

The telltale sign of trembling hands gave her away. Even a wisp of hair hanging seductively at her nape fluttered from the pulse at her neck. She took several deep breaths, then placed her fingers on the keyboard. "Your Grace, would you be so kind and assist me?"

Unsure what she had planned, he took tentative steps toward her. He leaned down and whispered, "What are we doing?"

"*William and Mary*. A duet as before."

In her humility, she underestimated her skill at the keyboard, and she played the opening measures perfectly.

Too stunned by her request, he was unable to force the first notes and words out. But her tremulous voice and panicked eyes brought him to his senses, and he joined her in song.

Treacherous tears clouded his vision, and he blinked them back. And although her voice grew strong and sure, his quaked and broke from the emotion flowing through him.

At the last stanza, he dropped to his knees before her and sang.

Forgive me, dear maid, then William he said,
Your love it was only I tried.
To church let's away, for ere the sun sets,
I'll make little Mary my bride.

Grateful his back was to the crowd—the gathering tears dripping down his cheeks—he whispered, "Do you forgive me?"

"A little louder, please." Her smile lit up his world.

"Do you forgive me? And will you marry me?"

HONORIA'S HEART BEAT A RAPID TATTOO THROUGHOUT THE WHOLE song. The fear of playing and singing in front of others, especially at such a large gathering of members of the *ton,* was nearly paralyzing.

But Drake's bravery in admitting his deception had given her courage.

He swiped at his face, and her tears mirrored his.

"Say yes!" Burwood—eh, Mr. Beckham cheered, drawing titters of laughter.

Unable to speak the word, she nodded.

"What's that? We can't hear you," Mr. Beckham taunted.

She cleared her clogged throat and gazed into Drake's hopeful eyes. "Yes. I'll marry you, but it will take me a little more time to forgive you completely."

"Not too long, I hope." His gaze dipped to her abdomen. Rising, he gathered her hands in his and tugged her upright. "You are all my witnesses. She can't cry off now."

Sighs from several of the ladies accompanied chuckles from the men.

"You're brilliant," Drake whispered, his breath tickling her ear.

She patted his chest. "Careful, we're not married yet."

"Pity, as I very much want to kiss you. Thank you for helping me mend the trust I've broken with these good people."

"Isn't that what a duchess does? Help her husband navigate society?"

"You will be the perfect duchess—in general and for me."

Her heart, near bursting, swelled further as her parents joined them. Her mother's face beamed with happiness, and her father's eyes seemed suspiciously wet.

"Well, I see there will be no need for pistols at dawn," he said, causing a little squeak from her mother.

"Bertram, really!"

Mr. Beckham strolled up. Goodness, how would she ever think of him as anything other than Burwood? "Good news for you, Lord Stratford. Your future son-in-law is a crack shot."

Her father glared. "You, sir, should have ended this farce long ago. My daughter may have forgiven the true Duke of Burwood, but you, sir, should be ashamed for posing as nobility."

"Trust me, sir." Mr. Beckham tugged at the cuffs of his sleeves and darted a glance toward Charlotte. "It was more hardship than you imagine."

Honoria threaded her arm through Drake's. "Mr. Beckham, I'm

most relieved I won't have to fret about you donating all the books in the library to charity."

"Please, call me Simon, my lady. And I shall leave all the books to you and your husband."

Husband. Honoria locked eyes with Drake, the love reflected there warming her throughout. Was she dreaming?

People gathered around them, waiting to offer their felicitations, she supposed. Miranda grinned at her. Charlotte nodded her approval, her lips curling in an uncharacteristic smile.

But Anne. Oh, Anne appeared devastated.

Honoria turned to Drake. "Please excuse me, Your Grace."

The moment Anne saw Honoria approaching, she dashed from the room. Honoria rushed after her, making apologies and thanking people for their well wishes.

"Anne. Anne. Please wait."

Anne paused halfway up the staircase. "I wish you joy, Honoria." Sniffles belied her words. "Mr. Merrick—I mean the duke—is a good man."

Pain lanced through Honoria for her friend. "Anne, I'm sorry."

Anne's shoulders drooped, and she shook her bowed head. "You have nothing to be sorry for. He loves you. I was such a fool. I should have seen it sooner."

An odd doubt crept up Honoria's spine. "You did release him from your attachment?" Surely Drake wouldn't have lied about that as well?

Anne turned toward her. "Yes. But I didn't know he was a *duke!*"

"Oh, Anne." Honoria hurried toward her, then wrapped her arms around her friend. "If it's not too painful, would you be my attendant at the wedding?"

"What about Charlotte or Miranda?"

"Oh, them, too. But I want you to be the primary one, with a place of honor."

Anne smiled through teary eyes. "I should like that."

Hugging her, Honoria said, "Somewhere waiting, there is a man who will love you more than life itself. I feel it, here." She pressed a fist to her heart. "Would you really rather have a man marry you out of obligation?"

"No. I suppose not." She wiped her nose with the back of her hand and gave a little sputtered laugh. "But he's a *duke*."

Honoria fought a smile. She didn't care about that at all. She loved Drake for who he was. A man who loved her in return.

For her.

EPILOGUE

TWO WEEKS LATER . . .

"Hold still, Honoria." Charlotte's chastisement did little to accomplish her request.

Honoria craned her head around the doors separating the narthex from the church's nave. "Has anyone checked to make sure he's here?"

Miranda snorted a laugh. "As if he'd even consider leaving you at the altar. He's only now regaining trust within society for his deception. Besides, the man is besotted with love for you." She tucked a final forget-me-not into Honoria's hair, then gave a nod of approval. "There. Finished. Squirm all you wish."

Anne rushed in from the nave. "He's here! He's here!"

Unlike six weeks prior, when Anne had rushed into their meeting, Honoria had no need to ask who *he* was.

"I'll put away my pistol then," her father said, chuckling. "Now, my dear, are you ready to become a duchess?"

"No."

Her father froze, his eyes widening with horror. He'd gone to great lengths to obtain a special license, the archbishop arguing he saw no need to rush the ceremony.

Until Drake interceded and explained he had waited long enough—eight years to be precise—to know his mind. With pressure from both a marquess and a duke, the archbishop had little choice. However, Honoria suspected the archbishop acquiesced more because Drake also promised a generous donation.

She slid her hand onto her father's arm. "But I am ready to become a wife."

Her father visibly relaxed, his exhale audible. "Then let us get you married."

She could have sworn he muttered *at last*.

Everyone did agree on the location for the ceremony, deciding to forgo the pomp at St. George's in Hanover Square. Garlands with late summer blooms decorated the church on her father's Somerset estate, the fragrant blossoms scenting the air. But none were so cherished as the simple flowers in her hair. That was to be a surprise for Drake.

People spilled from the church out to the grounds around it, as all tenants were invited to attend. Although Honoria requested a quiet, private ceremony, it had been an argument she had lost with her father.

But Honoria had learned much about herself during Drake's house party. So, as a compromise, she made her father promise to provide a sumptuous feast at the estate's assembly hall for all his tenants in celebration.

As she stepped into the church on her father's arm, she saw the wisdom of his decision. Friendly faces she had known her entire life smiled at her as they rose in deference. But nothing compared to the sight awaiting her at the front of the nave near the transept.

Drake stood tall and proud, as handsome as ever in his royal-blue superfine tailcoat and silver waistcoat. When she reached his side, her breath hitched in her throat. As if he'd read her mind, embroidered forget-me-nots adorned the points of his waistcoat.

Simon grinned next to him, poking Drake with his elbow. Honoria expected an endless source of amusement from Drake's man of business.

As her father placed her hand into Drake's, nothing else mattered. Similar to when they sang the duet, she concentrated only on him, so much so that she nearly forgot to repeat her vows, the name Pierce Henry Quincy Pendrake sounding strange to her ears.

But as she stared into his amber eyes, she remembered to say the most important words, "I do."

ALL THROUGH THE CEREMONY, DRAKE COULDN'T KEEP HIS MIND focused on anything but Honoria. His gaze kept drifting to the forget-me-nots dotting her glorious hair. She'd chosen a pale-blue gown, also embroidered with the tiny flowers along the neckline and edging of the sleeves and hem. He smiled to himself, wondering if his mother had a hand in the embellishments for both of them.

As lovely as the gown was, he couldn't wait to get her out of it and see her hair spilling across the pillows on their bed.

His face heated at the image.

Simon poked him again. "Say 'I do.'"

Loud and clear, Drake's confident 'I do' rang throughout the church for all to hear, but his hand shook slightly as he slipped the ring on her finger.

After the ceremony and signing the church's register, they returned to Overton House for a lavish wedding breakfast.

As people swarmed around Honoria, Simon pulled him aside. "Lady Miranda didn't want to upset Honoria, but this arrived from London this morning." He held out a copy of *The Muckraker*.

Drake met Simon's gaze, understanding that whatever *news* the gossip rag held, it wasn't good.

Simon pointed to one item in particular.

Lady Honoria Bell is to exchange wedding vows at last with the newly minted Duke of Burwood. As before, scandal continues to follow that young lady wherever she goes. Not only did the duke perpetrate an unforgiveable deception upon society at his house party this summer, but sources say that he may expect a "premature" heir less than nine months from the wedding. It would appear that the two are a perfect match.

Drake gave a humorless laugh. "Well, they have the last part correct. We *are* a perfect match."

"I trust Honoria told you about her club to bring this scoundrel down?"

Drake nodded. "Of course. There are no secrets between us. Not anymore."

"Good. Let me know what I can do to help. In the meantime, I would postpone showing this to her until tomorrow, if possible." Simon grinned. "I would hate to have it ruin your wedding night."

"Unless you plan on traveling to Hartridge House and knocking on my door at all hours of the night, I don't think anything can ruin it." He folded the scandal sheet and tucked it inside his coat. He would share it with Honoria later.

When he rejoined his beautiful bride, he took her hand and kissed it, wishing it were her lips. "Miss me?"

"Always."

"But?"

"I was thinking about Colin."

"I'm sorry he couldn't make the wedding. Any word on Margery?"

Honoria poked at a small piece of plum cake that had broken off from the whole, her face growing solemn. "We received a letter with his regrets this morning. She's taken a turn for the worse. Colin says she's become despondent. As much as they adore Cassandra and Elinor, Margery blames herself for not giving him an heir. And now she believes it's too late."

She toyed with the broken piece of cake, pushing it around with her fork. "Drake?" She shook her head. "Goodness, should I call you Pierce?"

"If you wish, but I'm more likely to answer to Drake." He grinned.

When she didn't return his smile, he brushed a red tendril of hair from her neck. "What is it? Something more than Margery?"

"What if I can't give you an heir?"

Inwardly, he cursed the people around him. He needed to kiss her, pull her into his arms, and reassure her.

"Do you truly believe I care about that? If I were still a groom, would it matter to me if I had a son to inherit my legacy?" He shook his head, still struggling with the odd notions of the aristocracy. "If we have children, they will—no doubt—enrich our lives. Sons. Daughters. It doesn't matter to me. If we don't, well"—he gave her hand another squeeze—"we shall have a grand time trying."

A blush bloomed on her cheeks.

He leaned in. "And speaking of, I'm eager to whisk you away. It's a long journey to Hartridge House, and if we are to arrive before nightfall, we should make our goodbyes." In truth, he had received more verbal instruction from Simon that he was impatient to try. He vowed he would perform much better on his wedding night than his first fumbling attempt when Honoria had impetuously given herself to him.

Amid joyful tears and well wishes, they raced from the house and into his carriage.

Thankfully, the journey was free from difficulty, and he spent a goodly portion of the ride enjoying Honoria's sweet lips, leaving him more than ready to fulfill his husbandly duties.

He chuckled softly to himself. *Duties*. How anyone could call such a pleasant pastime a duty was beyond his ken.

As soon as the carriage pulled to a stop, he jumped out, not waiting for the footman, and held his hand out to Honoria. Only Frampton's upticked brow curtailed Drake's urge to swoop Honoria into his arms and race up to the bedroom.

"I trust you had a pleasant journey, Your Graces. May I offer a light supper?"

Drake cringed inwardly at his inconsideration. *What a cad.* He turned toward Honoria. "Are you hungry?"

"Not very. Perhaps something light that can be assembled quickly, Frampton."

"Have a tray brought to Her Grace's room," Drake added.

"Very good, Your Grace." Frampton bowed, his lips twitching slightly.

Once upstairs, as he waited for Honoria to finish her light supper, he paced the floor of his dressing room, stopping only to allow Dawson to assist him in undressing.

Dawson shook the banyan he held out. "Sir?" The tight-lipped smile on his valet's face belied the man's serious tone.

Drake paced for another eight minutes, repeatedly glancing at the clock on the wall. He jumped at the soft knock on the connecting door, then raced over to answer it.

Susan, Honoria's lady's maid, curtsied. "Her Grace is ready, Your Grace."

All this Grace business was going to drive him mad. "Thank you, Susan, or do we need to call you by your surname now?"

She giggled. "Susan is fine, sir. But my surname is Price."

Transfixed by the sight of Honoria brushing her hair at her dressing table, he nodded stupidly. Once the soft snick of Susan closing the door behind her registered in his brain, his feet developed a mind of their own, and he traversed the length of the room as if by magic.

He touched the silkiness of her hair. "You kept it unbraided."

Her smile wavered. "I remember you liked it down."

Drake leaned in, nibbled at her neck, and whispered, "Are you nervous? You seem so solemn. I promise I'll do my best not to bungle things."

Her seafoam-green eyes widened and her lips tipped up. "Not about *that*. It's just . . ."

Kneeling before her, he took her hands in his. "Then what? Remember, you can tell me anything. No more secrets between us —ever."

"I want to be a good duchess."

He suspected his face mirrored hers as it had appeared moments before. "How can you even wonder about that? It's what you were meant to be."

"Well, yes. You and I were meant to be together—"

He shook his head. "Not just that, although it's true. I meant you were reared to be a grand lady. Don't tell him, but I finally understand your father's objections years ago. Marrying me then, a poor groom with no prospects, would have limited what you could do. As my duchess, you will be able to do great things. I can feel it, in here." He pressed a fist to his heart.

She sent him a coquettish smile and threw her arms around his neck. "Like catch who is responsible for *The Muckraker*?"

"Even that. But for the time being, I have a very important and pressing assignment for you."

"What is that?"

He picked her up and carried her to the bed. "To be my wife in every way."

Would you like a peek three years into Honoria and Drake's future? Scan the QR code below and sign up to my newsletter to receive an exclusive bonus epilogue, news about my upcoming books, contests, cute cat pictures, and lots of fun! You may unsubscribe at any time. No hard feelings.

WHEN AN IRRESISTIBLE FORCE MEETS AN UNMOVABLE OBJECT, explosive consequences follow.

Find out what happens with Simon and Charlotte in *Every Rake Has a Silver Lining.* Coming soon!

If you enjoyed *A Duke In the Rough,* consider leaving a short review on Amazon. Reviews help other readers find books they'll love.

AUTHOR NOTES

One thing I love about writing historical romance is researching the history. There never seems to be a lack of things I need to look up when an idea pops into my head. Putting fictional characters in historical settings can be both fun and challenging. You find yourself looking up the strangest things—and often going down rabbit holes.

This novel was no different. But unlike my previous novels that centered around The Hope Clinic, instead of medical practices of the 19th century (although there was one thing that will come into play in the next book—did you catch it?) I found myself learning about various activities offered during an English house party.

Games were part of the entertainment when people got together just as they are today. And some of those games are still with us— although now they're typically played by children. If you thought there was a typo for blind man's buff, I don't blame you at all. I remember it being called blind man's bluff (and that name is more commonly used today for the children's game). The *buff* part comes from the fact that the blindfolded person ("it") was pushed or "buffed." The game originated in ancient Greece and was quite popular in the Regency era.

Along with games, I researched popular songs of the times. I found a marvelous website called *The Contemplator* that had a wealth of songs organized by themes and time period. I spent an entire day (maybe more) listening to songs and reading lyrics until I found—what I believed to be—the perfect one.

The song Honoria and Drake sing, *William and Mary,* was an actual song of that time period. It is in the public domain, allowing me to share some of the lyrics in the novel. This lovely website not only has the songs with the lyrics, but it also has small MIDI files with the melodies—so you can listen and follow along with the words. I wished I could thank the person who put this website together, but alas, I couldn't find a way to correspond with him. If you'd love to hear the song and read all the lyrics, you can do so here (https://www.trishamessmer.com/english-folk-songs/) on a secret page on my website.

Another "oddity" I stumbled upon was the phrase *pleased as Punch*. One of my critique partners gently suggested I had capitalized in error. However, the origin of that term harkens back to Punch and Judy. Puppet shows featuring the married couple were quite popular during this time period. Mr. Punch is "pleased" as he beats up his enemies with a stick/club (often killing them!) even his wife! So there is a dark, sinister side to what we typically think of as a humorous puppet show. Whew!

Needless to say, when Anne makes the comment that Andrew would be pleased as Punch if Drake offered for her, that has a strange connotation, but keeping the language within the time period, the phrase Anne uses would have capitalized the *p* in Punch.

Fashion also plays a big part in historical descriptions, and gowns had changed from the high empire of the true Regency to the lower waistlines and fuller skirts which ushered in the Victorian era. And those narrower waistlines meant a move from stays to corsets.

My notes wouldn't be complete without full acknowledgement of the inspiration for this story. *Persuasion* has always been my favorite Austen novel. *Pride and Prejudice* lovers, do not throw stones at me—I love Lizzie and Darcy as much as the next person. But I always loved the maturity of Austen's Anne Elliot—not to mention the long-standing (and unwavering) love between Anne and Wentworth.

And of course, there's the letter from Wentworth that Drake paraphrases to beg Honoria's forgiveness. *Sigh*

So when I prepared to write Honoria's story, it was a no-brainer. Initially, Honoria was just a blip on my radar (sorry Honoria). The first time she's even mentioned was in *Healing the Viscount's Heart*. Laurence is trying to discover the identity of the woman with red hair and green eyes he encountered in Harry's library during a masquerade ball. (If you haven't read that one, it's probably my most humorous book). Miranda mentions Lady Honoria Bell, but states there was some scandal involving a commoner.

Folks, that was one of those times where my fingers knew Honoria's story before I did. It's one of those joys of being an intuitive writer.

Then in *Saving Miss Pratt*, Honoria makes a list of possible suitors for Priscilla and mentions the new Duke of Burwood who has been out of the country in India. That's when things clicked for me and I knew what her story would be.

No spoilers, but I had one of those *Aha!* moments in this book for one of the ladies of the League's future hero.

I attribute moments like these to my ability (I truly cherish it as a gift) to make connections and see how everything intertwines for a reason. Which speaking of, if you've ever read anything by Charles Dickens (and I would presume you have), you will notice this in his works. I expect Dickens would have scored super high in Connectedness on the CliftonStrengths© assessment. I hope you enjoyed my little nod to him in the book.

It was a joy to write this book and give our long-suffering Honoria her own happily-ever-after ending. I hope you enjoyed it.

ALSO BY TRISHA MESSMER

The Hope Clinic Series

No Ordinary Love (Prequel Novella)

The Reluctant Duke's Dilemma

A Doctor For Lady Denby

Healing The Viscount's Heart

Saving Miss Pratt

Redeeming Lord Nash

The London Ladies' League

A Duke In The Rough

Every Rake Has A Silver Lining (coming soon)

Contemporary Romance

Different World Series

The Bottom Line

The Eyre Liszt

Look With Your Heart

ABOUT THE AUTHOR

❧

Trisha Messmer had a million stories rattling around in her brain. (Well, maybe a million is an exaggeration but there were a lot). Always loving the written word, she enjoyed any chance she had to compose something, whether it be for a college paper or just a plain old email. One day as she was speaking with her daughter about the latest adventure going on in her mind, her daughter said, "Mom, why don't you write them down." And so it began. Several stories later, she finally allowed someone, other than her daughter, to read them.

After that brave (and very scary) step, she decided not to keep them to herself any longer, so here we are.

She hopes you enjoy her musings as much as she enjoyed writing them. If they make you smile, sigh, hope, and chuckle or even cry at times, it was worth it.

Born in St. Louis, Missouri, Trisha graduated from the University of Missouri – St. Louis with a degree in Psychology. Trisha's day job as a product instructor for a software company allowed her to travel all over the country meeting interesting people and seeing interesting places, some of which inspired ideas for her stories. A hopeless (or hopeful) romantic, Trisha currently resides in the great Northwest.

f

Printed in Great Britain
by Amazon

37330439R00192